SHADOWS

Blake froze momentarily, gaping at the vision which stared back at him from the water.

It was his reflection but the features were contorted into a mask of sheer terror. The mouth open in a soundless scream, eyes bulging wide in the sockets.

The reflection disappeared and, as the water slowly regained its stillness, Blake found that his image had also returned to normal. For long moments he looked down, as if expecting that terror-stricken visage to appear once more, but it didn't. A particularly cold breeze ruffled his hair and he shivered slightly, deciding that it was time he returned to the house.

Whistling through the branches of the nearby tree, the wind sounded like soft, malevolent laughter.

Also by Shaun Hutson
and available in Sphere Books:

SLUGS

SPAWN

EREBUS

BREEDING GROUND

RELICS

DEATHDAY

VICTIMS

ASSASSIN

SHAUN HUTSON

Shadows

SPHERE BOOKS LIMITED

For Niki
with thanks
I'll slow down after the next one
maybe . . .

A SPHERE Book

First published in Great Britain in 1985 by
Star Books, A Division of
W. H. Allen & Co plc
This edition published in 1990 by Sphere Books Ltd

ISBN 0 7474 0785 1

Reproduced, printed and bound in Great Britain by
BPCC Hazell Books
Aylesbury, Bucks, England
Member of BPCC Ltd.

Sphere Books Ltd
A Division of
Macdonald & Co (Publishers) Ltd
Orbit House
1 New Fetter Lane
London EC4A 1AR
A member of Maxwell Macmillan Pergamon Publishing Corporation

Acknowledgements

I would particularly like to thank Miss Eleanor O'Keefe of the Society for Psychical Research, whose help and kindness were invaluable during the research for this book. I am greatly indebted to her. Also, thanks, as ever, to everyone at W. H. Allen. Special thanks to Mike Bailey ('If there had been an Institute in Germany, the director's name would have been Beckenbauer'). To Bob Tanner ('Blood, guts and Rock and Roll, what a combination'). To Ray, Peter and Tony ('Enjoy your breakfast'). Indirect thanks to Iron Maiden, Liverpool F.C., John Carpenter, Tobe Hooper and Sam Peckinpah. And, finally, thankyou to my Mum and Dad, for everything. And to Belinda who really saw this one through from beginning to end. For listening to me blow up buildings, murder babies and slaughter people, this one is for you, with love.

Shaun Hutson

'Hence, horrible shadow.
Unreal mockery, hence.'
— *Macbeth, Act III, Scene IV*

PART ONE

'Dreams are true while they last, and do
we not live in dreams?'
— *Alfred Lord Tennyson*

'We're running with the Shadows of
the night. . .'
— *Pat Benatar*

1

She had never seen eyes like his before.

She shuddered slightly as the piercing orbs bore into her like lasers. As if they were staring at her soul, searching for something elusive.

His eyes sparkled like chips of sapphire, the whites surrounding them unblemished but for the tiniest red veins which dared to intrude from his eye corners.

His gaze was unbroken even by the movement of his eyelids and, as he extended a hand to guide her backwards, she felt as if she were drowning in those eyes. As she lay on the couch she finally closed her own eyes, aware now only of his presence beside her.

The room was dark.

There was little sound.

An occasional cough, muted and self-conscious. And there was his breathing. It became more laboured as he stood over her and he spoke something softly to her.

Without opening her eyes, she raised her hands and began unbuttoning her dress, exposing her stomach. As she touched the flesh of her abdomen she winced and sucked in a painful breath. She almost screamed aloud as she felt his hands touch her flesh. His fingers stroked and probed the area around her navel, pausing every so often over one particular place.

Lucy West lay perfectly still, aware only of the hands which roamed her lower body with swift urgent movements but conscious of the three large intestinal growths which nestled like bloated parasites within her.

The first doctor had suspected ulcers. Nothing more. Tests had shown them to be steadily growing abscesses but a second opinion had revealed what she herself had always suspected.

The growths were tumours. Malignant and deadly.

She had been told that they were too far advanced for surgery to make any difference. At the most she might gain a six month reprieve. But of that there was no guarantee.

She felt the hands on her stomach, moving gently.

This man was her last hope.

Jonathan Mathias looked down at the woman on the couch, his brow furrowed. She was, he guessed, forty-five — five years older than himself but the ravages of pain and her disease had carved lines into her face which had no right to be there. She looked twice her age.

Mathias wore a dark shirt, the sleeves of which were rolled up displaying thick, hairy forearms. As he continued to play his fingers over the woman's abdomen, the muscles of his arms began to bulge, as if he were holding some great weight. His eyes rolled upward slightly so that she was only in the periphery of his vision. He began to breathe more deeply, less regularly. A bead of perspiration popped onto his forehead and trickled slowly past his left eye.

He sucked in a long breath and held it, raising his hands over the woman.

For what seemed like an eternity, neither moved nor made a sound.

Mathias' eyes twisted in the sockets, then he suddenly plunged his hands down, as if to drive them through Lucy West's body.

He grunted loudly, his palms pressed flat to her stomach. His fingers were splayed, quivering wildly. Then, with infinite slowness, he raised his hands an inch or two.

Beneath his palms, the flesh of her abdomen began to undulate in small, almost imperceptible, movements at first but then stronger, more urgent motions.

A bulge appeared just below her navel, the skin stretching to accommodate the pressure from within.

Mathias was shaking now, his hands still positioned mere inches from the woman's stomach. Perspiration sheathed his forehead and face, glistening in clear droplets on the light hair of his arms.

There was another movement, another undulation, this time an inch or two above her pubic mound.

Lucy West made no sound. No movement.

9

Mathias grunted something unintelligible, his fingers curling inward slightly as the third bulge began to stretch the flesh until it was shiny. And finally, his eyes swivelled in the sockets until they were glaring down at his own hands.

At the movement beneath those hands.

His entire body jerked spasmodically, as if someone were pumping thousands of volts of electricity through him. His eyes narrowed to steely slits, his teeth clenched together until his jaw began to ache.

The skin just below Lucy West's navel began to split open.

Like tearing fabric, it began as a tiny hole then gradually lengthened into a rent about five inches long.

Mathias began to breathe rapidly, his cheeks puffing with each sharp exhalation. He noticed a pungent odour as a second tear began to form beneath the first.

There was no blood. Only the smell. A rancid stench of pus which rose like an invisible cloud to envelop him.

He watched as the third razor-thin cut began to open.

Still Lucy West did not move.

Mathias drew in a deep, almost agonised breath and held it, his face contorted unnaturally for interminable seconds. The sensation of heat which he felt in his fingertips began to spread until it seemed to fill his entire body. He felt as if he were on fire. More sweat dripped in salty beads from his face. He glared down at his hands.

At her stomach.

At the three long thin splits in her flesh.

'Yes,' he grunted, his fingers twisting inward like hooked claws.

Something began to move in the cut above her pelvis. Something thick and solid. It was ovoid in shape, a reeking egg-shaped lump which nudged through the cleft of flesh as if coaxed by Mathias. His eyes bulged madly in their sockets as he saw the growth and his body began to shake with increased intensity.

From the cut below her navel another bloodied clot of dark brown matter began to rise.

The three narrow tears drew back like obscene lips, expelling their foul contents, and Mathias reached feverishly for the three rotting growths, scooping them into his hands like so many putrescent eggs.

His fingers closed around the lumps and a single droplet of pus dribbled through and ran down his arm as he raised both hands into the air above the unmoving body of Lucy West.

Mathias kept his eyes fastened on the trio of wounds, now slightly reddened at the edges. He closed his eyes tightly, body still shaking, the growths held aloft like grisly trophies. A vile stench surrounded him, almost palpable in its intensity, yet he seemed not to notice it. As he snapped his eyes open once more he looked down to see that the three rents had closed. The skin looked as smooth and unblemished as before he had begun.

For a moment he stood sentinel over her motionless form.

Another man, younger than Mathias, came forward carrying a shallow stainless steel bowl. He held it before Mathias who slowly lowered his arms, opening his hands to allow the growths to tumble into the bowl with a liquid plop. The man handed Mathias a towel, then retreated back into the shadows.

'Sit up,' Mathias said to the woman, his voice a low whisper.

Lucy West struggled upright, aided by Mathias' outstretched hand, and once more she found herself gazing into those hypnotic twin orbs of blazing blue.

'It is done,' he told her.

Lucy coloured slightly, aware that her dress was still open. With shaking fingers she began to button it once more. Mathias noticed her slight hesitation as she reached her stomach, the flicker of anxiety behind her eyes as she reached her navel.

He beckoned to his assistant and the younger man returned, carrying the bowl. Mathias took it from him and held it before Lucy.

She looked in at the growths. They reminded her of rotten plums but for their pale colour. The dark tinge which they'd had earlier seemed to have drained from them, creating the small amount of blood which was puddled in the bottom of the bowl.

She touched her stomach tentatively, both relieved and surprised to find that there was no pain. She pressed harder.

No pain.

It was at that point she broke down.

11

Tears flooded down her cheeks and she gripped Mathias' hand, as if threatening to wrench it off. He smiled thinly at her, those brilliant blue eyes twinkling with an almost blinding iridescence.

Another man, also dressed in a dark suit, approached from the other side and placed his hands on Lucy's shoulders, guiding her away from Mathias who walked forward towards the swelling cacophony of shouts and applause which filled the hall. As the lights inside the building were flicked on once more he gazed out at the dozens of people who stood watching him. Dozens? Hundreds? He wasn't sure how many. Some could nöt stand because they were in wheelchairs. Some could not clap because they had withered limbs. Some could not see him because they were blind.

He raised his arms once more, a gesture designed to encompass them all.

The applause and shouting did not diminish for some time, not in fact, until Mathias turned and walked off the stage, the cries still ringing in his ears.

And some of them were cries of pain.

2

Mathias entered his dressing room and slammed the door behind him, as if eager to be away from any more prying eyes. He leant against the door, wiping the sweat from his face with one blood-smeared hand.

He crossed to the washbasin on the far side of the small room and turned the cold tap, splashing his face with water. As he straightened up he gazed at his own reflection in the mirror above.

Jonathan Mathias was a powerfully built man, his jaw square and heavy. Clean shaven and carefully groomed, he looked younger than his forty years, particularly when his eyes sparkled as they did now. Nevertheless, his forehead was heavily lined and his thick eyebrows, which strained to meet above the bridge of his nose, gave him a perpetual frown. He dried his face and sat down at his dressing table. Even now he could hear the persistent applause generated by those who had yet to leave the hall.

It was like this every time. At every meeting.

He held three a week. The one today had been conducted in a large red-brick building on New York's West Side. Next time it might be in Manhattan, Queens or the Bronx. Or maybe somewhere in one of the city's more affluent areas. Over the years he had found that the rich needed his attentions as badly as anyone else.

Those he didn't reach in person could see him twice a week on CBS, his hour-long television show attracting an audience in excess of 58,000,000. He was known throughout the country and most of Europe for his abilities as a psychic but, of the man himself, little had ever been revealed. He spoke with a New York accent but the harder edges had been smoothed off and he came across as a cultured man, though he was respected and ridiculed in roughly equal proportions. There were those who still branded him a fraud and a charlatan. With an annual income of 20,000,000 dollars, the barbs seemed to cut less deeply than they might otherwise have done.

He smiled at his own reflection and began wiping his face with a paper cloth.

There was a light rap on the door and Mathias turned in his seat as if he were expecting to see through the partition.

'Who is it?' he asked.

'Blake,' a distinctively English voice told him.

'Come in,' he called, his smile broadening.

As David Blake entered the room, Mathias studied the newcomer warmly.

He was twenty-eight, about five-ten, dressed in a pair of faded jeans and a sweatshirt which, despite the folds of material, could not disguise the powerful frame beneath it. A packet of cigarettes bulged from one of his pockets and, as the young man sat down, he took one out and lit it up.

'Very impressive,' he said, re-adjusting the tinted glasses on his nose.

'It isn't intended to create an impression, David,' said the psychic. 'You know that.'

13

'Well,' Blake told him, smiling, 'That's exactly what it does. Like it or not. I should know, I was in that audience tonight. It's remarkable.' He drew hard on his cigarette. 'I've seen scores of faith-healers, most are just elaborate con men. But not you. There's something more.'

'Thanks for the compliment.'

'I saw you cure a terminally ill woman tonight, without even touching her, without using any tools or implements.'

'Is it really that important to you, David?' the psychic asked. 'Must you discover how I perform my ...'

'Miracles?' Blake interrupted.

Mathias smiled.

'I was going to say "work".'

'Yes, it is important. I don't like mysteries,' the Englishman admitted. 'Besides, if I do find out, there's a lot of potential there.'

'For a new book you mean?'

Blake was almost reluctant to admit it.

'Yes,' he said, shrugging his shoulders. He took a last puff on his cigarette and ground out the butt in an empty matchbox.

'Have you ever heard of a man called José Arrigo?' the psychic asked.

Blake nodded.

'He was killed in a car crash in Brazil in 1971. He was a psychic too. They called him the Phantom Surgeon. He performed nearly half a million operations between 1950 and 1960, all done with scissors and penknives and without anaesthetic. He removed a vaginal tumour the size of a grapefruit from a woman using only a kitchen knife. He was locked up a couple of times for practising medicine unlawfully.

'But people always went back to him. They went to him for the same reasons they come to me. Desperation and fear. When conventional methods won't work, people seek help elsewhere.'

'Arrigo claimed his powers came from Christ,' Blake protested. 'I've never heard you mention religion. You're a faith healer without any faith.'

'Power,' said Mathias, flatly. 'A strange choice of word, David.'

14

'Why? The abilities which you possess are a power of some description,' Blake said. 'I'd like to know where that power comes from.'

'It comes from here,' said Mathias, jabbing his own chest. 'From inside *me*.'

The two men regarded one another in silence for a while. Blake rubbed his chin thoughtfully. In the past five years he had written five world-wide best-sellers, all concerned with different aspects of the paranormal (supernatural was a word he disliked for it implied something which defied logical or reasoned explanation and Blake was concerned only with facts). But, in that time, he had never encountered anyone like Mathias. The man was an enigma, exuding a mixture of menace and benevolence.

Then there was his power.

Blake had seen it at close quarters during the five days he had been with the psychic and so far had collected reams and reams of questions but no answers — a wealth of research material with no discernible potential. He felt frustrated, almost angry with himself and he harboured the nagging conviction that the key to Mathias' power was something simple, so simple it could be easily overlooked. Mass hypnosis? Thought projection? He wondered if such tricks of the mind could work on the massive scale required for Mathias to retain credibility. Was it possible for someone to hypnotise an audience of 58,000,000 viewers so that they believed everything they saw? Blake doubted it.

He took a paper tissue from his pocket and began cleaning his glasses.

'Inside all of us there is another person,' Mathias continued, quietly. 'An inner being. Some psychics and probably you yourself know it as the Astral body. Jung called it "the other within". In ancient times it was thought to be the soul.'

Blake listened intently as the other man continued.

'To someone with the knowledge, the power, the Astral body can be projected and manipulated.'

'But lots of people are able to project themselves astrally,' Blake insisted. 'The sensation of leaving your

15

own body is a skill which can be learned.'

'I agree.'

'Then I don't see what this has to do with your *powers*.'

'I can control other people's Astral bodies.'

Blake frowned, taken aback by the psychic's words.

Mathias returned his gaze, unblinking. There was a twinkle in his blue eyes which Blake mistrusted. He studied the American as if he were an exhibit in a museum, trying to muster his own thoughts.

'It's impossible,' he said, softly.

'Nothing is impossible, David,' the psychic told him.

Blake shook his head.

'Look, I know plenty about Out of the Body experiences,' he countered. 'I've met dozens of people who've had them but the idea of being able to manipulate someone else's Astral body ...' The sentence trailed off as he felt his body stiffen. It was as if every muscle in his body had suddenly contracted and the sensation forced a gasp from him.

Overwhelming, numbing cold enveloped him until he felt as if his blood were freezing in his veins. He shuddered, the flesh on his forearms rising into goose-pimples. He caught sight of his own reflection in Mathias' dressing room mirror and his skin was white. As if the colour had been sucked from him.

Mathias sat unmoved, his eyes never leaving the writer who was quivering violently.

He felt light-headed, a curiously unpleasant sensation of vagueness which made him grip the chair as if anxious to assure himself he were not going to faint.

Mathias lowered his gaze and Blake felt the feeling subside as quickly as it had come. He sucked in a deep breath, the warmth returning to his body. He shook his head and blinked hard.

'Are you OK?' Mathias asked.

The writer nodded.

'Very clever, Jonathan,' he said, rubbing his arms briskly.

'*Now* do you believe me?' the psychic wanted to know. 'Can you deny what you felt?'

'If you have this ability, how does it tie-in with the faith-healing?'

'I can reach inside people. Inside their minds. Their bodies.'

'Then it would have to be a form of hypnosis, to make the subject believe you could cure them.'

'I can't give you all the answers, David,' Mathias answered. 'It doesn't matter. You can't alter the facts, you can't deny what you saw on that stage tonight or what you yourself felt here in this room.'

Blake chewed his bottom lip contemplatively.

'Think about what I've said,' the psychic added.

Blake got to his feet and announced that he had to get back to his hotel. The two men shook hands and the writer left the building via a side entrance. The sun outside was hot and the pavement felt warm beneath his shoes in a marked contrast to the coolness of Mathias' dressing room.

He spotted a cab and sprinted across the street, clambering into the vehicle. As the cab pulled away, Blake glanced over his shoulder at the red brick building, watching as it gradually disappeared from view.

Jonathan Mathias sat before the mirror in his dressing room contemplating his own features. He rubbed his cheeks and blinked hard. His eyes felt as if they had grit in them but, as he sat there, he allowed his hands to drop to his thighs, one hand curling into a loose fist. He inhaled and looked down, his fist opening as he did so.

Cradled there, now shrunken and withered like rotten, foul smelling prunes, were the three growths he'd taken from the body of Lucy West.

3

As the yellow cab threaded its way through the tapestry of traffic which clogged the streets Blake looked abstractedly out of the side window. On all sides of him buildings poked upward at the sky like accusatory fingers, probing towards the occasional banks of white cloud which passed overhead. Apart from the odd smattering of cloud and the vapour trails of aircraft, the sky was a deep blue and the sun continued to bathe the city in its warm rays. But, for David Blake, there was nothing pleasant about the warmth because with it came humidity. He could feel the perspiration on his back and face despite the fact that the air conditioning was on. The driver was a fat negro who looked as if he'd been wedged behind the steering column. As he drove his chubby fingers tapped out an accompaniment on the wheel to the music which screamed from the radio. It partially covered the insistent roar of engines, the blare of hooters and the shouts and curses of other motorists.

Blake allowed his head to loll back onto the seat. He could feel the beginnings of a headache gnawing at the base of his skull. A condition which wasn't helped when the driver slammed on his brakes to avoid colliding with a bus which had stopped abruptly in front of him.

'Motherfucker,' growled the driver and swung the cab out and around the bus, giving the other driver the finger as he drove by.

Up ahead, Blake saw his hotel and he fumbled in his pocket for his wallet, pulling out a ten dollar bill. The taxi came to a halt and Blake got out.

'How much?' he asked.

'Call it an even five,' said the driver, pushing down the arm on the meter.

'I haven't got anything smaller,' Blake said, offering the ten. 'Keep it.'

The hotel doorman nodded politely as he passed but Blake didn't return the gesture. He walked across to the reception desk and got his key.

He rode the lift to the thirty-second floor, casting a cursory glance at his fellow passenger — a porter who was cleaning his ears out with the corner of a tissue.

On reaching his room he closed the door and locked it, glad to be away from things for a few hours. The room was large, comfortable without being extravagant. The writer crossed to the window and stood gazing out for a moment or two, looking over the vast expanse of greenery which was Central Park. It looked particularly inviting amidst the grey concrete and glass of the city.

He turned and walked into the bathroom where he turned both taps. As the water splattered noisily against the enamel he undressed and lay on the bed, eyes closed. He lay there for a moment or two, massaging the back of his neck in an effort to dispel some of the tightness there, then he got to his feet and wandered back into the bathroom where he switched off the taps. Steam swirled around the room like hot fog and Blake retreated, deciding to allow the water to cool off slowly. He remembered that he hadn't eaten since breakfast so he called room service.

As he sat waiting for the snack to arrive he thought back to the incident with Mathias earlier on. Had the psychic actually managed to summon Blake's own Astral body? Was it some form of mind control? He pulled a pad towards him and scribbled:

1. Hypnosis
2. Mind control
3. Astral Body

Beside the last of the three he drew a large question mark and underlined it. Mathias obviously had more weapons in his psychological arsenal than Blake had first thought. But, manipulation of someone else's Astral body? He shook his head, his thoughts interrupted by a rap on the door. Blake got to his feet and was about to open it when he realized he was still naked. He grabbed a towel and hurriedly wrapped it around his lower body. The maid swept in, deposited the order on the table near the window then swept out again.

Blake devoured two of the sandwiches then headed

towards the bathroom once more.

The steam still swirled around and Blake almost slipped over on the tiles. He lifted the toilet seat and urinated noisily; then, discarding the towel, he turned towards the bath.

There was a body floating in the water.

Blake took a step back, nearly overbalancing, his eyes glued to the naked body before him. The entire corpse was bloated, the skin tinged a vivid blue, mottled from what appeared to be a long time in the water. The mouth was open, lips wrinkled and cracked. A swollen tongue protruded from one corner.

Blake shook his head, studying the face more closely.

He may as well have been looking in a mirror.

The corpse in the bath was identical, in every detail, to himself. He felt as if he were staring at his own dead body.

The writer clamped his eyes shut, screwing up the lids until white stars danced in the blackness. He raised both hands to his head and sucked in a deep breath.

'No,' he rasped.

When he opened his eyes again the corpse was gone. Nothing remained in the bath but the water. No bloated body. No deceased look-alike. Just water.

Blake swallowed hard and reached out a hand tentatively towards the surface of the water, staring intently at it as if he expected the apparition to appear again.

He heard soft chuckling and snapped his head around.

It was coming from the bedroom.

The writer felt peculiarly vulnerable and he found his breath coming in low, irregular gasps. He edged towards the bathroom door gripped by a hand of fear which tightened its hold as he drew closer.

Again he heard chuckling.

By this time, his fear had gradually become anger and he stepped into the room without hesitation.

It was empty.

He walked across to the bed. Checked the wardrobes. Passed through into the other part of the room which served as a sitting room.

Empty.

Blake looked around him, wiping perspiration from his

face. He was alone in the apartment. He headed back towards the bathroom but, as he reached the door he slowed his pace, his eyes scanning the bath anxiously.

There was no corpse floating there.

The writer licked his lips, finding that his mouth was dry and chalky. He crossed to the sink and spun the tap swallowing large gulps of cold water, then he turned towards the steaming tub once more.

The water looked inviting enough but it was a long time before he would step into it.

4

Oxford

'There was so much blood. It was everywhere. All over the floor and the bed. There was even some on the wall. It wasn't at all like you see on films or the television. When I shot her in the face her head just seemed to cave in and then the blood started spurting everywhere. I suppose that's how it got on the wall over the bed, it was like a fountain, especially from her neck. I suppose that's where the pellets hit her jugular vein. That is the big vein isn't it? The jugular? You see when you fire a shotgun at someone from close range there isn't time for the shot to spread. A shotgun cartridge is full of thousands of little lead pellets but, when you fire from close range, well, it all comes out in one lump. And I was standing very close to her. I had the barrel about an inch from her face.

'There was some thick, sticky looking stuff on the pillow. It was sort of greyish pink. I think it must have been her brain. I'd seen sheeps' brains in butchers' shops and it looked a bit like that so I suppose it must have been her brain. Anyway, when I went to move the body this sticky stuff got on my hands. It felt like ... like porridge. I left her on the bed in the end.

'The baby had woken up, I suppose it was the noise of the

21

gun. It was crying, not loudly, just the way it does when it wants feeding. I went into the nursery and picked him up but he wouldn't stop crying. Perhaps he was frightened of the blood and the smell. That's another thing they never tell you on the TV. Blood smells. It smells like copper. When there's lots of it.

'Well, I just dropped the baby on its head. It didn't move after that so I thought it was dead. I picked it up again and took it back to the bedroom and put it on the bed beside my wife.

'I'd left the hacksaw under the bed earlier so I ... I only had to decide which one to start with. I cut up the baby first. The left arm to start with. I cut it off just below the shoulder but as I started cutting it screamed. I think the bang on the head only stunned it. The arm was almost off when it started to scream but it didn't move again after that. I cut off its right leg at the hip. It was easy, I suppose it's because the bones are still soft with babies. It wasn't even a year old you see. There was more blood, more than I'd expected. Especially when I cut the head off. It's funny isn't it? You wouldn't think a body that small could hold that much blood.

'I left the pieces on the bed then I started on my wife. It was harder cutting her leg off, sawing through the bone was like cutting wood but the noise was different, a kind of squeaking and all this brown stuff dribbled out of the bone. Was that the marrow? I suppose it was. Well, it took me nearly an hour to cut them both up and I was sweating when I'd finished. Butchers must be really fit, I mean, they cut up meat every day don't they? I was tired when I'd finished and I noticed that there was some ... mess ... well excrement. You know ... faeces on the bed. I didn't know that happened when someone died. That they sh— that they messed themselves.

'I cut one of my wife's breasts off. I don't know why. Just to see what it was like I suppose. I expected it to puncture like a balloon, you would wouldn't you? But it didn't. I just cut most of it away and left it with the other pieces. So much blood though. So much blood. Funny really.'

Kelly Hunt reached forward and switched off the tape recorder.

She had heard that particular tape half a dozen times in the last week. This had been the first time she'd managed to sit through it without feeling sick. She pressed the 'rewind' button and the recorder squealed as the spools spun in reverse. She stopped it, pressed 'play'.

'... So much blood. Funny really.'

She heard her own voice.

'And the dream is always the same?'

'Always. It never varies. Every detail's the same.'

She switched it off again and ran a hand through her shoulder length brown hair.

Beside the tape recorder on the desk in front of her there was a manilla file and Kelly flicked it open. It contained details of the voice which she'd been hearing on the recording, facts and figures which made that voice a human being. To be precise, Maurice Grant, aged thirty-two. An unemployed lathe operator by trade. Married for ten years to a woman four years younger than himself named Julie. They had a ten-month-old baby, Mark.

Kelly had been working with Grant, or rather studying him, for the last seven days. The recording was one of many which she and her colleagues had made.

She scanned the rest of the file which contained further personal details about Grant.

He'd been unemployed for the last six months and, during that time, relations both with Julie and their baby had become somewhat strained. Kelly tapped the file with the end of her pencil. And now the dreams. Grant always described them as dreams — never nightmares — though God alone knew that what he experienced during sleep was the stuff of nightmares. His detached attitude was unnerving. The tape recordings were made while Grant slept. By a combination of drugs, he could be unconscious and yet able to speak and to relay what he saw in his dreams. Dreams had been studied and monitored in the past, Kelly was well aware of that, but never before had the subject actually been able to speak whilst in that dream state, to describe the events as dispassionately as if he had been a mere observer.

In order to achieve this state, Grant was given a shot of Tubarine, a muscle relaxant usually used in medicine with a general anaesthetic, which would induce sleep. Prior to that, he would receive 45mg of methylphenidate orally. The drug was a derivative of amphetamine, designed to stimulate the brain. By this combination, Grant could be *forced* to dream. His observations would then be recorded as *he* saw them in his mind's eye.

Kelly knew, from what she had read in the file, that Grant and his wife had rowed constantly during the months leading up to his arrival at the Institute. Their marriage was virtually in ruins and Grant sometimes spoke of her with ill-disguised anger. An attitude mirrored, subconsciously, in his dreams.

Kelly looked at the tape recorder once more, wondering whether to run the tape again. Instead she got to her feet and crossed to one of the filing cabinets propped against the far wall. Above it was a photograph of her and several of her colleagues. It had been taken just after she joined the Institute fifteen months ago, two weeks after her twenty-fourth birthday.

The Institute of Psychical Study was a Victorian building set in six acres of its own grounds. The weather-beaten walls were the colour of dried blood, crumbling in places. The entire structure, covered by a clinging network of ivy, looked as though it would collapse but for the tangled tendrils which snaked over it like so much flexible scaffolding. Repair work had been done to the west wing of the building, the renovated brickwork and the large plate glass windows looking strangely innocuous set against the latticed panes which dotted the remainder of the structure. The building was being dragged, albeit reluctantly, into the twentieth century. Telephone wires ran from the pole on the roof, suspended above what had once been belching chimney stacks but were now sealed holes. The gravel driveway snaked away through the grounds until it joined the main road which led into Oxford itself. Cedars and poplars lined the drive like sentinels.

However, if the outside of the building belonged to a more sedate age then the interior was modern, almost futuristic.

The old rooms had, over the years, been converted into fully equipped offices and laboratories, the latter providing every means possible for Kelly and her companions to pursue their very specialized work.

Since its inception in 1861, the Institute had devoted itself to the investigation and recording of all manner of psychic phenomena ranging from hauntings to telekinesis. Within the vast library beneath the building was housed the accumulated knowledge of over a century. But, during that time, progress had intervened and investigators now used word processors in place of quill pens and electronic surveillance equipment instead of eye-witness accounts and hear-say.

Kelly had plenty of eye-witness information about Maurice Grant including the file which she now slid from the drawer and glanced at.

It held an EEG read-out, one of the many taken from Grant while he slept. She studied it and shook her head. The puzzle was there before her.

The reading comprised five lines, four of which were flat, each representing an area of the brain.

It was the fifth line which interested her.

The tracer had drawn huge, irregular strokes across the read-out, indicating an incredible amount of activity in one particular part of the brain.

Kelly was convinced that it was the portion which controlled the dream response.

And yet she knew that there should have been movement shown on *all* the lines.

But for that one area of activity, the reading may as well have been taken from a corpse.

The office door opened.

'Excuse me barging in, Kelly,' the familiar voice apologised. The man smiled curtly, almost as an afterthought. 'I wanted to speak to you.'

Dr Stephen Vernon smiled again; a twitchy, perfunctory smile which never touched his eyes. He was what people euphemistically call portly. In other words he was fat. The buttons of his grey suit strained against his belly as if threatening to fly off at any moment. He kept his jacket fastened but, like his trousers, it was immaculately pressed. His trousers bore creases sharp enough to cut your hand on, even if the legs of the garment were two inches too short. For a man of fifty-five, Vernon had thick, almost lustrous hair which glistened beneath the fluorescent lights. His moustache, by comparison, resembled the type sprayed on advertising posters by paint-happy kids. He had narrow, hawkish features and eyes the colour of slate nestled between his puffy eyelids. Grey suit. Grey hair. Grey eyes. Vernon resembled an overcast day. But, there was a darting energy in those eyes and in that overweight frame. Vernon was as thirsty for knowledge now as he had been when he'd first joined the Institute nearly twenty-five years ago. He'd spent the last twelve years as its President. He was respected by all his investigators, both for his knowledge and also for his dedication. He would sit, most nights, in his office on the second floor, reading reports. Staying there until the small hours sometimes, when he would wander the empty corridors and deserted labs, enjoying the silence. He felt secure within the confines of the Institute walls.

He lived eight or nine miles away but it was almost with reluctance that he returned home at the end of the day.

Home.

Could he still call it a home when he was afraid to return there?

As Kelly passed him she caught the familiar smell which seemed to follow Vernon everywhere. It surrounded him like an invisible cloud. The scent of menthol. He was forever sucking cough sweets although Kelly had never known him to have so much as a cold. He carried a packet in his breast pocket as if it were a pen. As she sat down he popped another one into his mouth.

'Have you made any progress with this fellow Grant?' Vernon asked her.

Kelly told him about the tape recordings, the recurring nightmares.

'Yes, yes, I know about those,' he said, tersely. 'I heard something about an EEG.'

Kelly's green eyes met his slate grey ones and they held each other's stare for a moment.

'May I see it?' he asked.

Kelly handed the read-out to Vernon who shifted the menthol sweet to the other side of his mouth and ran an expert eye over the series of lines.

'His brain was stimulated?' Vernon asked.

'Yes,' Kelly told him. 'We're still using amphetamines.'

Vernon nodded slowly. As a qualified doctor he realized that the read-out should show much more activity. He was one of four physicians at the Institute. At least one had to be present to administer the drugs to subjects and to check that there were no adverse effects on them.

'Then why is only one area of the brain affected?' he mused aloud.

'It certainly looks as if it's the area which controls unconscious thought,' said Kelly. 'The reading taken when Grant was awake showed only minimal movement in that region.' She pointed to the jagged line.

The older man sucked hard on his sweet then folded the read-out and laid it on her desk.

'Run another EEG while he's awake,' Vernon instructed. 'Then another while he's asleep — but not a drug induced sleep. I want to see the normal readings.'

Kelly nodded.

Vernon crossed to the window and peered out at the rapidly falling rain.

'This is very important to me, Kelly,' he said, clasping his hands behind his back. He reminded her of a headmaster about to admonish an unruly pupil.

'The reading from the EEG would certainly seem to indicate that the subconscious mind is capable of functioning independently,' he said. 'We have to find a way to unlock that hidden area.'

She detected a note of something akin to desperation in his voice. It seemed only a matter of time before they discovered what they sought but time was one thing Vernon didn't seem to have. Not a day passed without him visiting Kelly in the lab or her office, and it had been that way ever since the research began. There was an urgency about his interest which eclipsed his usual involvement. He was becoming obsessive. And Kelly couldn't help but wonder why.

She studied his broad back as he stood by the window, his fingers knotted together like fleshy hemp.

'I'll see about running the EEG now,' she said.

Vernon turned, nodded and swept towards the door.

'I'll be in my office,' he told her. 'Let me know as soon as you have the results.'

She smelt the menthol as he passed her, closing the door behind him. Kelly heard his footsteps echo away down the corridor.

27

She slipped the file back into its drawer, then she herself left the room, walking briskly towards the stairs which would take her down to the laboratories.

Stephen Vernon slumped into the leather chair behind his oak desk and closed his eyes, massaging the bridge of his nose between thumb and forefinger. In the outer office he could hear the clacking of his secretary's typewriter. An accompaniment to the tattoo which the rain was beating on his window.

His office was large, as befitted a man of his seniority. It was one of the few rooms in the building which acknowledged a debt to the past. The wood panelling of the wall smelt as if it had been newly waxed, as did his desk. Opposite him, above the empty fireplace, was a very passable copy of Gericault's *'Brigadier Gerard'*. Vernon regarded the painting blankly, his mind occupied with other thoughts.

Could the EEG of Grant's brain truly have exposed an area of the mind previously hidden? The key to the subconscious. After all these years, could he dare to hope for a breakthrough?

He sat forward in his chair and glanced at the phone.

The call might come in five minutes. Five hours. Five weeks.

But he knew it would come and he had been waiting a long time for it.

5

Paris

'Keep your eye on the watch.'

Jean Décard focused on the gently twisting gold object, watching as it spun gently around. His breathing had slowed to low rasping inhalations punctuated by small gasps as the air escaped his lungs once more. His right arm was propped up on the arm of the chair, his left lay across his lap.

'Clear your mind of all other thoughts,' the voice told him. 'See nothing but the watch. Think about nothing other than what I tell you.'

The voice seemed to be coming from a hundred miles away.

It was, in fact, coming from Alain Joubert who was kneeling less than a foot or two from him. It was he who was holding the watch, allowing it to turn gently back and forth at the end of its chain.

Beside him, Michel Lasalle watched the proceedings with a pen gripped firmly in his hand, prepared to write down whatever might happen. At thirty-eight, Lasalle was two years older than Joubert but his full features and ruddied complex-ion did not testify to that fact. They had worked together for the past two years and, during that time, had become close friends. Now Lasalle watched intently as Joubert leaned closer to Décard whose eyelids were begin-ning to sag.

'You are asleep but you will still hear my voice, you will still answer my questions,' said Joubert. 'Do you under-stand?'

Décard nodded slowly.

'Do you understand? Say so.'

'Yes.'

'What is your name?'

'Jean Décard.'

'Where do you live?'

'Sixteen Rue St Germain.'

'How old are you?'

'Forty-one.'

Lasalle scribbled something on his pad then watched as Joubert pulled a pen light from his breast pocket and shone it into Décard's eyes.

'He's well under,' Joubert said, noting the vastly dilated pupils of his subject. 'But, let's just make sure.' He reached back to the table nearby and retrieved two long, thick needles each one about six inches in length. Then, he pinched the skin together on the back of Décard's right hand and, slowly, pushed the first needle through.

There was no reaction from the subject.

'Can you feel any pain, Jean?' asked Joubert.

'No.'

He took the second needle and, opening the loose fist which Décard had made, Joubert pushed the second needle under the nail of the man's index finger until only the eye showed. There was no blood.

'Do you feel anything?'

'No.'

Joubert nodded to his companion then hastily tugged the wicked points free.

Lasalle pulled a pack of playing cards from his pocket and handed them to Joubert, standing behind his friend so that he himself could see the slim plastic sheets. The first one was the seven of spades.

'Which card am I holding, Jean?' Joubert wanted to know.

Décard told him.

'And this one?'

'Queen of Diamonds.'

Correct.

'Next?'

'Ten of Clubs.'

Correct.

They went through thirty cards and Décard was accurate every time.

'Amazing,' said Lasalle. 'Are you going to bring him out of it now?'

'In a moment,' Joubert assured him. Then to Décard;

'Jean, I am going to think of some words, I want you to tell me what they are. Do you understand?'

'Yes.'

Joubert scribbled them down on a piece of paper and showed it to his companion. Décard recited the words almost rhythmically.

Joubert smiled. Lasalle could only shake his head in amazement.

'There will be a bus crash in the Rue De Bologne.'

The words came from Décard with the same monosyllabic drone as before. Both Joubert and Lasalle looked at him aghast.

'Repeat what you said,' Joubert urged.

Décard obliged.

'When? How do you know?'

30

'I can see the ... the dead.' He was staring blankly ahead as if looking beyond the walls to something which neither of the other men could see.

'When is this crash going to happen?' Joubert asked.

'At 3.49 today.'

Lasalle shot an anxious glance at his watch.

'It's 3.46,' he told Joubert.

'How do you know this is going to happen?' demanded Joubert.

'I can see it now.'

'How many will die?'

'Four.'

'Is it possible?' Lasalle said, his brow furrowed. 'Can he really be seeing it?'

Joubert didn't answer, he merely looked at his own watch and saw that it was 3.48.

Jean Décard was silent for a moment then his mouth opened wide in a soundless scream, his face contorted into an attitude of fear and pain so profound that Lasalle took a step back. Then, with a low grunt, Décard blacked out.

It took the two men ten minutes to revive him and, when he finally regained consciousness, he still seemed to be in a trance. He tried to rise but fell, knocking a table over in his wake. After another thirty minutes he was coherent. His face was ashen with dark smudges beneath his eyes.

Joubert gripped his arm.

'Jean, can you remember anything of what you said earlier?'

Décard shook his head.

'I feel sick,' was all he could say.

Lasalle fetched him a glass of water.

As the three men sat in the room there was a loud knock on the door and, a moment later, a thick-set man in the uniform of a gendarme entered.

'Which one of you is Jean Décard?' the uniformed man asked.

'I am,' Décard told him.

'And you two?' the gendarme wanted to know.

'We both work here at the Metapsychic Centre,' said Lasalle.

'Step outside, please,' the gendarme said.

31

'No,' said Décard. 'It's all right, what have I done wrong?'

'Nothing, Monsieur,' said the gendarme almost apologetically. 'I must tell you that I have some bad news.'

Lasalle and Joubert exchanged glances then directed their gaze back at the uniformed man. He had lowered his voice slightly, an air of expectant solemnity having fallen over the room.

At approximately 3.49 that afternoon, Jean Décard's twelve-year-old daughter had been killed when a lorry smashed into the bus which was carrying her and her schoolfriends home. There had been three other deaths besides hers.

'Where did it happen?' Décard wanted to know, tears filling his eyes.

The gendarme cleared his throat.

'The Rue De Bologne.'

6

Michel Lasalle scooped some cool water into his hand and then swallowed it. He felt the tranquilizer stick in his throat for a moment so he swallowed more water, finally wiping his hands on the towel beneath the sink. He exhaled deeply and replaced the bottle of pills in his trouser pocket. He probably didn't need them any longer but, over the past eighteen months since the death of his wife, the pills had become more than a mere psychological crutch for him. Lasalle was dependent on them, not daring to see what life was like without the temporary relief which they brought him. He did not look like a man who had suffered a nervous breakdown, but then again his wife had not looked like the kind of woman who would die suddenly of heart failure aged thirty-five. Lasalle had retreated within himself after her death. Like a snail inside its shell he refused to be coaxed out again by work or friends. He became hermit-like in his existence.

He and his wife had been childless. She had been infertile

— her Fallopian tubes blocked. Lasalle's parents had been dead for five years so he had no one to turn to for help. His breakdown had begun slowly, gradually building up like some festering growth within his mind until, finally, his sense of reason seemed to collapse in on itself like a crumbling house.

He turned away from the sink and looked across the room at Joubert who was sitting with his eyes closed, a cigarette held delicately between his fingers. The ash looked as if it were about to drop off and Lasalle watched as smoke rose lazily from the butt. When Joubert finally moved his hand, the ash dropped on to the carpet. Lasalle quickly trod it in.

Lasalle had worked at the Metapsychic Centre for the past twelve years. The building itself stood on the outskirts of Paris, a large modern looking edifice constructed in the shape of a gigantic 'E'. Its smooth unbroken lines gave it the appearance of having been hewn from one single lump of rock instead of constructed piece by piece. Lasalle lived less than a mile from the building, near the church yard where his wife was buried.

As he stood looking absently around the room he tried to drive thoughts of her from his mind but every time he heard of more death, as he had with Jean Décard's daughter, the memories came flooding back.

His companion, Joubert, had no such ties. He was single once more after the break-up of his marriage but then again he had always found the attractions of work infinitely more exciting than those of domesticity. Despite being two years younger than Lasalle, he was possibly better informed on the subject of the paranormal, having worked at the Laboratory of Parapsychology in Utrecht for six years where he completed his Ph.D in Human Science. He had then moved on to the University of Frieburg in West Germany prior to joining the Centre in Paris.

Joubert was every bit as different psychologically from his colleague as he was physically. There was a certain detached coldness about Joubert. He saw everyone and everything as potential sources of information and study. The human volunteers with whom he worked might as well have been laboratory rats. He showed as much feeling towards them. To Joubert, work was everything and knowledge was the pinnacle. He would never rest until he had solved a problem. And, at the moment, he and Lasalle had a problem.

'Precognition.'

Lasalle looked at his companion.

'The business with Décard,' he continued. 'The telepathy and then seeing the accident. It had to be precognition.'

'Do you think he was able to see the vision because it involved his own daughter?' Lasalle asked.

'Décard didn't know that his daughter was going to be one of the victoms, only that there was going to be a crash and that four people would die. The fact that he was close to one of the victims isn't necessarily relevant.'

'What are you getting at, Michel?'

'We've tested three people, the same way we tested Décard. The results were the same in each case. Each one showed varying forms of telepathy while hypnotised but, with the other subjects, we brought them out of their trances earlier, quicker. If they had been under longer then they too may have been able to predict future events.'

Joubert got to his feet, crossed to the pot of coffee on the table nearby and poured himself a cup. He took a sip, wincing slightly as it burned the end of his tongue.

'Depending upon the susceptibility of the subject,' he continued, 'there's no limit to what future events we can learn of.' A brief smile flickered across his face. Not only could disasters be averted but foreknowledge of events could have its more lucrative side as well. Could a subject foresee the outcome when a roulette wheel was spun? Joubert took another sip of his coffee, this time ignoring the fact that it was so hot.

'But Décard was only able to foresee the future while in a hypnotic trance,' Lasalle interjected.

'Which points to the fact that there is an area of the mind which *only* responds when the subject is unconscious. An area previously unexplored, with the capacity for prophecy.'

There was a long silence finally broken by Lasalle.

'I'd better phone the Institute in England,' he said. 'They should know about this.'

'No,' said Joubert. 'I'll do it.'

He stepped in front of his colleague and closed the door behind him, leaving Lasalle somewhat bemused. Joubert went to his office and sat down behind his desk, pulling the phone towards him. He lifted the receiver but hesitated before dialling.

'An area of the brain previously unexplored,' he thought. His features hardened slightly. The discovery, once announced, would undoubtedly bring fame to himself.

It was not a secret he wanted to share.

He tapped agitatedly on the desk top, cradling the receiver in his hand a moment longer before finally dialling.

Kelly picked up the phone and pressed it to her ear.

'Kelly Hunt speaking,' she said.

'Miss Hunt, this is the Metapsychic Centre.'

She did not recognise the voice.

'Lasalle?' she asked.

'No. My name is Joubert. Alain Joubert. We have not spoken before.'

Kelly disliked the coldness in his voice. She was, however, relieved that he spoke excellent English, just as Lasalle did. Her French was no more than passable.

'Did you receive the copy of the tape recording I sent?' Kelly asked.

'We did,' he told her.

'Have you made any progress with your subjects?'

There was a hiss of static. A moment's hesitation.

'None,' Joubert said, flatly. 'That is why I am phoning. I feel that it is unproductive for our two Institutes to continue exchanging information on this subject.'

Kelly frowned.

'But it was agreed from the beginning that the research would be undertaken jointly,' she protested. 'You would use hypnosis, we would use drugs.'

There was a long silence.

'The subject we tested today was unreceptive,' the Frenchman lied.

Kelly sensed the hostility in the man's voice and it puzzled her.

'Lasalle told me that your use of hypnosis seemed to be showing results,' she said, irritably. 'He was very happy with the way the research was going.'

'My colleague has a tendency to exaggerate,' Joubert said,

35

stiffly.

'Where is Lasalle? May I speak to him?'

'He is working. I don't want to interrupt him.'

'So you have nothing at all for me?'

'No.' The answer came back rapidly. A little too rapidly. Kelly moved the receiver an inch or two from her ear, looking at it as if she expected to see Joubert magically appear from the mouthpiece. His abrupt tone was a marked contrast to that of Lasalle who she was used to conversing with.

Kelly thought about mentioning the EEG on Maurice Grant but, before she could speak, Joubert continued.

'I have nothing to tell you, Miss Hunt,' he said, his tone unequivocal.

'I'll have to tell Dr Vernon ...'

Joubert cut her short.

'Do as you wish, Miss Hunt.'

He hung up.

Kelly found herself gazing once again at the receiver. She slowly replaced it, her initial bewilderment at the Frenchman's unco-operative attitude subsiding into anger. Joubert had come close to being downright rude. Why, she wondered?

Was he hiding something?

If so, what reasons would he have?

She shook her head, annoyed both with Joubert and also with her own over-active imagination. Nevertheless, he had no right to sever contacts between the two Institutes. Perhaps she should speak to Lasalle, she had his home phone number.

Maybe *he* would contact her tomorrow.

She sighed and sat back in her chair, listening to the rain beating against the window behind her. On the desk before her lay the newest EEG read-out taken only an hour earlier from Maurice Grant. It looked normal, in marked contrast to the one taken when he'd been in the drug-induced state. She ran an appraising eye over the lines but could see nothing out of the ordinary. There was another polygraph scheduled for later, while Grant was asleep. Perhaps there would be discrepancies on that one, some kind of clue to the tricks his mind was playing.

She thought about his description of the nightmare. The ritualistic slaughter of his wife and child.

She wondered what it all meant.

7

Oxford

It was well past midnight when the powerful lights of the Audi cut through the gloom of the driveway which led up to Stephen Vernon's house. The rain which had been falling all day had stopped, to be replaced by an icy wind which battered at the windows of the car as if trying to gain access. Vernon brought the vehicle to a halt and switched off the engine, sitting for a moment in the darkness.

The moon was fighting in vain to escape from behind a bank of thick cloud and what little light it gave turned Vernon's house into some kind of dark cameo, silhouetted against the mottled sky. He sat there for a few more seconds then pushed open his door and clambered out. The wind dug freezing points into him, nipping at his face and hands. He ran towards the front door and fumbled for his key, his breath clouding around him as he exhaled. He finally found the key and opened the door, snapping on a light as he did so. The hall and porch were suddenly illuminated, driving back the shadows from the front of the house.

The building was surrounded by a high wooden fence which creaked menacingly in the high wind, so Vernon was effectively shut off from his closest neighbours. The house was tastefully decorated throughout, walls and carpets in soft pastel colours combining to form a welcoming warmth as he stepped inside and shut the door behind him, forcing out the wind.

There was a large envelope on the doormat. Vernon saw the postmark and hesitated a second before stooping to retrieve it. He carried it into the sitting room and dropped it on the antique writing bureau which nestled in one corner of the spacious room. Then he crossed to the walnut drinks cabinet, took out a tumbler and a bottle of Haig and poured himself a generous measure. As he drank he looked across at the letter on the bureau. When he put his glass down he found that his hand was shaking.

He passed into the kitchen, the fluorescents buzzing into life as he touched the switch. He hunted through the freezer and found a frozen chicken casserole. It took fifteen minutes according to the packet. Vernon decided that that was all he wanted to eat. He hadn't much of an appetite. He left the polythene-wrapped casserole in a pan of water and wandered back into the living room, ignoring the letter on the bureau which he still had not opened.

The stairs creaked mournfully as he made his way to the first floor. From the window on the landing he could see the two houses on either side. Both were in darkness, the occupants obviously having retired to bed. Vernon resolved to do the same thing as soon as he'd eaten.

Five doors led off from the landing: the door to his own bedroom, that of the spare room, then the bathroom and another bedroom which had once belonged to his son who had long since departed.

The fifth door remained firmly locked.

Vernon paused before it for a moment, swallowing hard.

He extended a hand towards the knob.

A window rattled loudly in its frame, startling him. He glanced at the door one last time then walked across the landing to his bedroom. Once inside he removed his suit, hung it up carefully and changed into a sweater and a pair of grey slacks. Without the restraint of a shirt, his stomach was even more prominent and it sagged sorrowfully over his waist-band. He tried to draw it in but lost the battle and allowed the fat to flow forward once more. Vernon glanced at the clock on the bedside table and decided that his supper would soon be ready so he flicked off the bedroom light and headed back across the landing once again.

As he approached the locked door he slowed his pace.

His breathing subsided into low, almost pained exhalations as he stood staring at the white partition. He felt his heart beating that little bit faster.

There was a loud crack and Vernon gasped aloud.

He spun round in the gloom, searching for the source of the noise.

The wind howled frenziedly for a second, its banshee wail drowning out his own laboured breathing.

The sound came again and he realized it came from inside the locked room. But it was muffled.

He took a step towards the door, freezing momentarily as he heard the sound once more — harsh scratching, like fingernails on glass.

On glass.

He realized that there was a tree directly beside the window of the locked room, it must be the wind blowing the branches against it. Nothing more.

Vernon felt angry with himself for having reacted the way he did. He glared at the door for a moment longer then turned and padded down the stairs. He walked through the sitting room, unable to avoid looking at the envelope which still lay on the bureau like an accusation. He would open it after supper he promised himself.

He sat in the kitchen and ate his supper, discovering that he wasn't as hungry as he thought. He prodded the food indifferently, left the plate on the table and went into the sitting room. There he poured himself another scotch and slumped in one of the high-backed armchairs near the fire. It was cold in the room and Vernon pulled his chair closer to the heat, watching as the mock flames danced before him. He downed most of the whisky, cradling the glass in his hand, gazing into its depths.

Above him, a floorboard creaked.

Merely the house settling down, he thought, smiling humourlessly.

He got to his feet and filled his glass once again, finally finding the courage to retrieve the letter. He slid his index finger beneath the flap of the envelope and started to open it.

The strident ringing of the phone pierced the silence and nearly caused him to drop the letter.

He picked up the receiver hurriedly.

'Stephen Vernon speaking,' he said.

'I tried to ring earlier but there was no answer.' The voice had a strong accent and Vernon recognized it immediately.

'What have you got for me, Joubert?' he said. The

Frenchman told him about Décard's prophecy.

'Does anyone else know?' Vernon asked.

'Only Lasalle,' the Frenchman told him.

'You haven't told Kelly?'

'No, you told me not to give her any information other than that which you authorised.'

'What about Lasalle?'

'He knows nothing of what is going on, he ...'

Vernon cut him short.

'I mean, what has he told Kelly?'

'She doesn't know anything about what happened today and from now on *I* will deal with her.'

Vernon nodded.

'Vernon? Vernon, are you there?'

He seemed to recover his senses.

'Yes, I'm sorry. Look, Joubert, when will you know for sure if the experiments have been successful?'

The Frenchman hesitated.

'That's difficult to say. I feel we *are* very close to a breakthrough though.'

'How long before you know?'

'You are asking for too much, Vernon. I cannot say for certain.'

'Then guess. I have waited too long for this.'

'You are not the only one.'

There was a long silence finally broken by Joubert.

'Two days, perhaps a little longer, but I can't promise.'

Vernon sighed.

'Remember, Kelly is to know nothing.'

'And if she becomes suspicious?'

'I'll take care of that.'

Joubert seemed satisfied by the answer. The two men exchanged cursory farewells then the Frenchman hung up. Vernon stood motionless for a moment then replaced the receiver, returning to his fireside chair. And his drink.

And the letter.

He opened it and pulled out the piece of paper inside. Vernon took another gulp from his glass before unfolding it.

Before he started reading he glanced, as he always did, at the heading on the paper:

FAIRHAM SANATORIUM

8

New York

Blake studied his reflection in the bathroom mirror. He shook his head. It was no use. The bloody bow-tie wasn't straight. As if he were grappling with some kind of angry moth, he pulled it from his throat and tried to fix it once again. He'd been trying for the best part of fifteen minutes but, so far, the bow-tie had resisted all attempts to remain in place and Blake was beginning to lose his temper. He looked at his watch and saw that it was 8.00 p.m., a fact confirmed by the announcer on the TV in his room who was in the process of introducing another re-run of *Magnum*.

Mathias had said he would pick the writer up at his hotel at 8.15. The drive to Toni Landers' house would take twenty or thirty minutes depending on New York's night time traffic.

Toni Landers was well known, by reputation anyway, to Blake. A stunningly beautiful woman who had, two nights ago, been presented with an Emmy for her performance in one of the year's biggest television spectaculars. At present, she was packing them in on Broadway in a production of Joe Orton's *Entertaining Mr Sloane*. Tonight she was giving a party to celebrate her triumph. Mathias had been invited and had cajoled Blake into joining him. The writer had been to showbusiness parties before and they usually bored him stiff, self-congratulatory affairs with clashes of ego which ranked alongside the collision of Mack trucks. In Los Angeles they were intolerable, the acting fraternity turning out in force to every one. Parties in L.A. were given for any reason, usually not good ones. Has-beens, no hopers, and would-be starlets thronged these almost masochistic gatherings where egos were flayed unmercifully. He had met writers who had yet to find a publisher but spoke as if they were the natural successor to Hemingway, encountered actors and actresses who spoke of the promised part they had in some forthcoming epic but who would more than likely end their days doing what they did between bit parts — either waitressing or cleaning cars.

New York parties were a little different. They had their share of bores, as did any party, but Blake found he could tolerate them slightly more easily because there didn't seem to be quite such a wealth of pretension in New York as there was on the West Coast. Nevertheless, he still did not relish the prospect of the party but Mathias had asked him, so what the hell?

He was still struggling with his bow-tie when his phone rang. Blake left the recalcitrant thing in its slightly lop-sided position and picked up the receiver.

'Yes.'

'There's someone for you in reception, Mr Blake,' the voice told him.

He looked at his watch. It was 8.15, on the nose.

'I'll be straight down,' he said and, flicking off the lights in his room, he closed the door behind him and made for the elevator.

Blake recognised Mathias' chauffeur standing by the reception desk. He was taking a few hurried puffs on a cigarette which he reluctantly extinguished when he saw the Englishman step out of the lift. Blake approached him, by-passing a red faced man who was complaining about the soap in his room being dirty. The chauffeur smiled.

'Mr Blake,' he said, 'Mr Mathias is waiting for you in the car.'

The two of them headed out of the hotel lobby with its uncreasing drone of Muzak, into the symphony of car hooters, shouts and roaring engines which was 59th Street. A police car, its sirens blaring, swept past adding its own noise to the cacophony which already filled the air.

The chauffeur motioned Blake towards a waiting black cadillac and, as he drew close, the door was pushed open for him. The writer felt like some kind of cheap gangster about to be taken for a ride. The grinning face of the chauffeur behind him and the inscrutable look of Mathias, who was seated in the back, added to that feeling.

The psychic was dressed completely in white. White suit. White shoes. White shirt. The only thing which broke up the pure expanse was a red tie. It looked as though Mathias was bleeding.

'Good evening, David,' Mathias said.

Blake returned the greeting. He wondered whether he should mention what had happened the previous afternoon. The voice in his room. The body floating in his bath. He eventually decided against it. He glanced across at Mathias, affording himself a swift appraising glance. The white suit seemed to make the psychic's feature's even darker, the areas around his eyes and neck almost invisible. His hands were clasped gently on his lap and Blake saw that he wore two rings, each one gold set with a large pearl.

'What sort of day have you had?' Mathias asked him.

'Considering I spent most of it in a library, not very inspiring,' the writer told him.

'More research?'

Blake nodded.

'Still trying to unlock the secrets of the mind?' the psychic chuckled.

Blake ignored the remark.

'Why did you ask me to come to this party with you tonight?' he enquired.

Mathias shrugged.

'You and I have become friends over the past six days and I thought you might enjoy it.' He smiled. 'You might, you know.'

'Are any of the guests clients of yours?' Blake wanted to know.

'Some of them have, from time to time, sought my help if that's what you mean.'

'In what ways?'

'Is it important?'

'I'm just curious.'

'You're curious about a lot of things, David,' the psychic said and looked out of the side window. Blake studied his profile for a moment then he too turned his attention to the busy street. On either side of them skyscrapers rose like concrete geysers spewed forth from the ground, black shapes surrounded by the dark sky. Many were invisible but for the odd lights which shone in some of their windows. It looked as if someone had taken hundreds of stars and hurled them at the gloomy monoliths. Multi-coloured neon signs burned above shops and cinemas, theatres and clubs, as if millions of glow worms had been sealed inside the glass prison of a bulb. The city that never slept was preparing for another night of insomnia.

'I asked you before why it was so important to you to discover the extent of my powers,' Mathias said, interrupting the relative silence which had descended.

'And I told you it was because I don't like mysteries,' Blake told him. 'I've never yet run into anything that's beaten me.' There was a firm, almost harsh, resolution in the writer's voice.

Even in the gloom of the cadillac's interior the psychic's icy blue eyes sparkled challengingly.

'There are some things ...'

Blake cut him short.

'... which it's better *not* to know.'

Both men laughed.

'Well, reeling off the world's worst clichés isn't going to stop me either,' the Englishman chuckled. A minute or two passed, then, his tone more sombre, Blake continued:

'This power, this manipulation of another person's Astral personality, if you do possess such abilities would you ever consider using them as a weapon?'

Mathias looked genuinely puzzled.

'I don't follow,' he said.

'If you can control someone else's mind and actions then there's no limit to what you can do. To what *you* can make others do.'

The cadillac was beginning to slow up. Ahead Toni Landers' house was a blaze of light.

'Do you think I haven't thought of that?' said Mathias, smiling.

The chauffeur brought the cadillac to a halt behind a bright red Porsche then clambered out and held open the door for Mathias. Blake didn't wait for the same treatment, he stepped out of the other side, tugging once again at his bow-tie as he did so.

The tarmac driveway which swung in a crescent before

44

Toni Landers' house looked more like a car showroom. Blake counted five cadillacs, a couple of Transams, the Porsche and a silver Plymouth Fury as he and the psychic walked towards the porch.

The house itself was a three storey affair, flanked on two sides by trees, beneath which were carefully tended flower beds. Strings of light bulbs had been hung from the house to the tree branches and it seemed as if a light glowed in every single window of the building. The house looked like a beacon amidst the darkness. It was set slightly on a hill, the nearest neighbour being about five hundred yards away. Even from outside Blake could hear music and, as the door was opened, it seemed to sweep over him like a wave, mingling with the sea of conversation.

A maid took Mathias and Blake through into a spacious sitting room which looked slightly smaller than a ballroom. A staircase rose in a spiral from the centre of the room, leading up to the first floor landing where Blake could see people standing in groups or in couples chatting amiably. Two huge chandeliers hung from the ceiling like clusters of diamonds. But, for all the apparent pomp and grandeur, the house had a homely feel to it. There was a piano in one corner of the room and five or six people were gathered around it. Blake noticed that one of them, a man about his own age, was playing softly, quite oblivious to the sound coming from the Hi-Fi. The writer recognized him as the lead singer with the band currently topping the American charts. He spotted three or four well-known actors and actresses, and a film director he'd seen once or twice on TV.

Toni Landers was standing by the large open fireplace, a glass of champagne cradled in her hand. She was talking to a distinguished looking grey-haired man in his fifties who was perpetually pulling at the end of his nose, doubtless in an effort to disguise the fact he was trying to see even further down the front of her dress than the plunging neckline allowed.

Blake had seen her before but never this close and she was even more beautiful than he had first thought. She was not a tall woman, barely five-six with the benefit of long stiletto heels. She wore a black dress slashed to the thigh which, each time she moved, allowed him a glimpse of her smoothly

45

curved legs. A shock of red hair cascaded over her shoulders, catching the light every so often to glisten like rust-coloured silk. She wore a black choker around her throat, a single diamond set in its centre.

'Our hostess,' said Mathias, nodding in her direction. He took a glass of champagne from the tray offered to him by a tubby waitress and Blake did likewise.

It was as he sipped his drink that Blake noticed eyes were beginning to turn in the direction of Mathias. In his white suit, the psychic was even more prominent, but Blake had the feeling that if he'd turned up in a worn-out sports jacket the effect would have been the same. A young woman approached him.

'You're Jonathan Mathias aren't you?' she said, the words sounding more like a statement than a question.

'Yes,' he answered, shaking her hand gently.

He introduced Blake who noticed that the girl seemed somewhat preoccupied. She smiled perfunctorily at the writer then turned back to Mathias, pausing to look at him as if he were a piece of precious metal before returning to the group from which she had emerged.

A man approached and shook hands with the psychic. Blake observed that same look of reverence on his face as had been on the girl's. He too smiled thinly at the writer then wandered away as if in some kind of daze. Blake looked on with mild amusement as this happened half a dozen times. With people constantly approaching Mathias, Blake felt rather like a dog waiting at its master's table for any scraps to fall. When a girl in a royal blue trouser suit spoke to him he was so surprised he hadn't time to answer before she walked away.

Blake took another glass of champagne when the tray came round. It wasn't that he particularly liked the bloody stuff, but at least it was better than standing there with his hands in his pockets looking like Mathias' bodyguard instead of a guest.

'They obviously know you,' he said to the psychic as the last of his admirers left them. Blake drained what was left in his glass and put the empty receptacle down on a nearby table. God, what he wouldn't give for a pint. Even a can of luke-warm lager would have been respite enough from the

46

endless flow of champagne.

'I've never met any of those people before, David,' said Mathias, sipping at his own drink.

'They know you by reputation then,' Blake insisted.

'People are fascinated by what they don't understand.' Those ice-blue eyes sparkled. 'And they can never hope to understand me.'

'Is that the way you want it?' Blake asked.

'That's *exactly* the way I want it.'

The two men regarded one another coolly for a second, eyes locked together like magnets.

'Jonathan.'

Both of them turned to see Toni Landers standing there. She was smiling broadly, displaying a set of teeth which testified to her dentist's expertise.

'I'm so glad you could come,' she said and kissed the psychic on the cheek.

'You look beautiful, Toni,' Mathias told her. 'It's a long time since we spoke.'

She turned to face Blake who returned her smile when he was introduced.

'Congratulations on winning the Emmy, Miss Landers,' he said, motioning to the statuette behind them on the mantelpiece.

'Thank you, please call me Toni,' she said. There was a soft lilt to her voice which made Blake feel immediately at ease. She was, indeed, a very beautiful woman combining a radiant innocence with that of uncultivated sexuality.

'What do you do, David?' she asked him.

'I'm a writer.'

'What sort of books?'

'Non-fiction, about the paranormal, the occult. That kind of thing.'

'No wonder Jonathan brought you along,' she said, slipping her arm through that of the psychic. 'Are you writing about him?'

'I'm trying.'

Toni chuckled and reached for her drink which was still on the mantelpiece. A ten by eight colour photo in a gilt frame perched there. It was of a young boy, no older than eight, Blake guessed. The lad was smiling, his blond hair brushed

47

back behind ears which were a little too large. Freckles dotted his nose and cheeks in an irregular pattern and, even beneath the glass of the frame, his eyes seemed to twinkle with some kind of untold mischief.

'That's my son, Rick,' she told him. 'He's staying with a friend for the night.'

Blake cast a quick glance at Toni's hands and saw no wedding ring. He wondered who the father of the child was.

'Do you have any family, David?' she wanted to know.

'I can hardly look after myself let alone anyone else,' Blake said, smiling.

'Rick means everything to me. If you had a child of your own you'd understand that,' Toni said, her tone changing slightly. She looked longingly at the picture. At her son. It had been an unwanted pregnancy and she had been through a difficult delivery. She still saw Rick's father now and again. He was one of the top publicity men at Twentieth Century Fox. He still lived in the house they had bought together those nine years earlier. It had been his idea that they live together. He was nearly ten years older than Toni so she listened to what he said. In those early days she would have done anything for him. She had worshipped him and he had adored her. The young, in-demand actress who had played two leading roles within six months of moving to L.A. from her home in Virginia. She was already commanding fees of half a million a picture and things seemed to be running smoothly until she became pregnant. At first he had accused her of sleeping with other men but, when he finally came to his senses, the decision he made had been swift and, she realized with the benefit of hindsight, almost inevitable.

Get an abortion or get out of the house.

A child, he had told her, would wreck her career. Besides, *he* wasn't ready to be a father. For the first time in their relationship, Toni had followed her own instincts. There would be no abortion and if it meant the end of the relationship then so be it. She had gone to stay with a friend, working for as long as she could, finally doing voice-overs for commercials when she was too far advanced.

The combination of the break-up and the difficult birth, (a Caesarean delivery after sixteen agonising hours of labour) had brought her close to a breakdown. For three months she languished in the throes of such deep post-natal depression that her close family sometimes feared for her sanity but slowly she began to drag herself out of it. She decided that she had to go on for her baby's sake. It had been a monumental effort but somehow she had managed it. She began work five months later, helping out an old friend who was with the script department of MGM. Another month and she had, after rigorous exercise and dieting, regained her shapely figure and, another two months after that, she was offered a leading role in a highly successful ABC series. It had been a small step from there back to films and now, to the stage.

'How is Rick?' Mathias asked her, also studying the photo.

'He's fine,' she beamed, the very mention of the boy's name causing her to perk up. 'Jonathan was a great help to me when I started work again after having Rick,' she explained to Blake.

The writer nodded.

'So, what are you working on next?' he asked her.

Her smile faded slightly.

'Well, I have a slight problem there.'

'I'm sorry,' Blake said.

'No, what I mean is, I have a decision to make and it's difficult.'

'What kind of decision?' Mathias asked.

She drained what was left in her glass and placed it alongside the Emmy on the mantelpiece.

'I've been offered a part in the next *Star Wars* movie but it means being away from home for three or four months. I don't think I want that. I don't want to be away from Rick that long.'

'But you've been on location before and left him,' said Mathias.

Toni shook her head.

'Only for days at a time, like I said, here we're talking about months.'

'So what are you going to do?' Blake asked.

'I guess I'll have to refuse the part.' She sighed. 'Shit, my agent won't be very pleased, he busted his ass to get it for me.'

'But your son won't be alone. He'll have people to look

after him won't he?' said the writer.

Toni turned to Mathias.

'Will he be OK, Jonathan? You can tell me. You can ... *see*.'

Mathias sighed.

'I hope you didn't invite me here tonight to perform some kind of fairground trick,' said the psychic.

'Please, Jonathan.' There was a note of pleading in her voice.

'What do you want to know?' he said, quietly.

A look of relief passed across her face.

'I want to know if Rick will be all right if I decide to leave him for a few months,' she said.

Mathias nodded. He sat down in one of the chairs beside the fireplace while Toni turned and scuttled off towards a door on the far side of the room. Blake watched with interest. He had an idea what Mathias was going to do, his suspicions confirmed when he saw Toni return moments later with a pack of cards. He could see immediately from their size that this wasn't an ordinary pack and, as she placed them on the coffee table before the psychic, he saw that they were Tarot cards.

An expectant hush seemed to fall over the room. The Hi-Fi was silent, only the steady click-click of the needle in the run-off grooves came from the speakers. Someone eventually removed it.

The group gathered around the piano stopped singing and turned towards Mathias who was gazing down at the cards, his brow knitted into deep furrows.

Blake took a step backward, his eyes straying alternately from Mathias to the cards and then across the table to Toni Landers. She, for her own part, settled in the chair opposite the psychic. He reached for the pack and shuffled it thoroughly.

'Now you,' he said to her, passing over the cards.

She followed his example and handed them back. Some of the other guests moved closer, anxious to see what was happening.

A large breasted girl with straw-coloured hair giggled.

Mathias shot her a withering glance, his eyes homing in on her like radar-guided rapiers. The colour drained from her

50

face and she clutched the arm of the man she was with, as if seeking protection from those piercing orbs.

Satisfied that he would not be forced to endure any further interruptions, Mathias proceeded to divide the cards into ten packs of seven. This done, he held the first pack, face down, before him.

'Pack one,' he said, his voice low and resonant in the silent room. 'That which is divine.' He laid it on the table.

'Pack two. Fatherhood.' That too he placed on the table, above and to the right of the first. 'Three. Motherhood.'

Blake and the others watched as he laid that one above the first pack, this time to the left.

'Four. Compassion. Five. Strength. Six. Sacrifice.'

Blake felt a slight tingle run up his spine and wondered if he were the only one.

'Seven. Love,' Mathias continued. 'Eight. The Arts. Nine. Health.'

Toni Landers shifted uncomfortably in her chair.

'Ten. Worldly matters.' Mathias sat back slightly. 'The Tree is complete,' he announced.

'Tree?' said someone behind him.

'The Tree of the Cabala,' Mathias answered without taking his eyes from the cards. He reached for the first pack and turned the card, repeating the process until all ten showed their faces.

Blake watched with interest; he had seen numerous Tarot readings over the years, all symbols usually carrying variant interpretations. He wondered how Mathias would read them? The psychic held one up.

'Number eight,' he said. 'A decision.'

Toni Landers kept her eyes on the cards, hands clasped on her knees.

The psychic reached for another card.

'Number seven. Travel.'

Blake noticed that Mathias' hand was shaking slightly as he reached for the next card. The older man swallowed hard and flipped it over for all to see.

'Sixteen. Change.'

'What kind of change?' Toni wanted to know.

Mathias fixed her in those powerful blue twin-points and shook his head almost imperceptibly.

51

'I don't know yet,' he said, turning over another card. It was a card of the Minor Arcana. The dagger.

There were eight cards lying away from the cabbalistic pattern made up by the remainder of the pack. Mathias chose one of these but he hesitated before he turned it over, his hand shaking more violently now.

'What's wrong?' Toni asked, her voice full of concern. 'What can you see? Tell me what you see.'

Blake, like most other people in the room was watching the psychic's quivering hand. He felt the chill begin to wrap itself around him more tightly, as if someone had clamped him in a freezing vice and was slowly turning the screw.

On the mantelpiece, the photograph of Rick Landers began to shudder, as if blown by some invisible breeze. 'Turn it over,' said Toni Landers, exasperatedly. Her breath was coming in short gasps now. 'I want to see the card. Tell me what *you* can see.'

The picture of Rick continued to vibrate, its movement unnoticed by all except the girl with the straw-coloured hair. She could not speak, all she could do was raise one finger in the direction of the photo.

'Jesus Christ,' said the man beside her, noticing the movement.

Mathias turned over the final card.

'Danger,' he said, breathlessly.

'What kind of danger?' Toni demanded, staring down at the card. 'Tell me.'

'Your son ...' Mathias began, falteringly.

There was a loud crash as the glass in the photo frame exploded outward as if there were a charge behind it. Slivers of crystal showered the guests nearby and Blake found himself stepping back to avoid the cascade.

A girl near him screamed.

The photo toppled from the mantelpiece and clattered to the ground. Toni Landers tore her gaze from the Tarot cards and saw the remains of the picture lying close by.

As she reached out to pick it up something red and shiny appeared on the photo, welling up from a cut in the paper.

It was blood.

Toni froze, watching as more of the crimson fluid dribbled over the slashed picture.

Blake looked on, mesmerised by the incident.

It was Mathias who finally snatched up the frame and its contents. He laid it gently on the table before him.

There was no more blood. The photo was unmarked.

Blake glanced at the psychic and then at the pieces of broken glass which littered the carpet beneath the mantelpiece.

'What happened?' Toni Landers wanted to know. 'What does this mean?'

Mathias hesitated.

'Is something going to happen to my son?' Toni asked. 'Jonathan, tell me, please.'

He nodded.

'Is he going to die?' she demanded.

'I saw danger, I didn't say he was going to die,' the psychic said in an effort at consolation but it didn't work.

Toni cradled the picture frame in her hands and stared down at the face of her son. Tears formed at her eye corners but she fought them back.

'I'm not leaving him,' she said. 'Not now.'

Mathias swallowed hard then looked up to see that Blake was watching him. The writer seemed relatively unmoved by what had happened. The other guests slowly began to disperse, their conversation now kept to a discreet whisper. The psychic got to his feet and put a hand on Toni Landers' shoulder.

'Perhaps it would have been better if I hadn't done the reading,' he said.

'No,' she whispered, shaking her head. 'I'm pleased you did. Thank you.'

'Will you be all right?' Blake asked her.

Another woman joined them, slightly older than Toni. She smelt of expensive perfume. The woman crouched beside her and gripped her hand. Blake and Mathias wandered across the room towards the open French windows, leading out into the garden. A cool breeze had sprung up and it washed over the two men as they walked out on to the patio.

'What *did* you see?' asked Blake, when they were out of earshot of the other guests.

'You know how to read Tarot cards, David,' said Mathias. 'You saw what I saw.'

53

'You know what I mean,' the Englishman challenged.

'Her son is going to die,' said Mathias, flatly. 'Is that what you wanted to hear?' He walked across the lawn towards a large ornamental fish pond which lay beneath the drooping arms of a willow. Leaves had fallen from the branches and were floating on the surface of the water. The liquid gleam caught the bright lights of the house in the background.

'You didn't read that in the cards did you?' said Blake, not sure whether it was intended as a question or a statement.

'No.'

'Then how did you know the boy was going to die?'

'You want to know all the secrets, David.'

'Yes I do.'

'I can't give you the answers.'

'You mean you *won't*.' Blake said, challengingly. 'What made the photo frame break? That glass looked as if it had been hit with a hammer.'

'The windows were open,' Mathias suggested. 'The breeze could have blown it off.'

'Come on, Jonathan,' said the writer, wearily. 'What the hell do you take me for?'

'What do *you* think made it break?' Mathias snarled, his brilliant blue eyes looking luminous in the darkness. 'This ... *power* of mine?' The psychic turned and headed back towards the house, leaving Blake alone beside the pond. The writer walked slowly around the pool, catching sight of a fish once in a while. He let out a tired breath. The broken frame. The prophecy. Were they more of Mathias' tricks? A mind-fuck — as he'd heard it put by an American psychologist? He was beginning to doubt if tricks was the right word. He had seen too much of the man over the past five or six days to dismiss him as a charlatan or fraud.

Blake shook his head and gazed into the pond, as if seeking his answers there. He caught sight of his own reflection.

Blake froze momentarily, gaping at the vision which stared back at him from the water.

It was his reflection but the features were contorted into a mask of sheer terror. The mouth open in a soundless scream, eyes bulging wide in the sockets.

He took a step back, eyes still riveted to the image, his feet

54

crunching on the hundreds of tiny stones which surrounded the pool. One of them bounced into the water, breaking the surface as it sent out endless ripples.

The reflection disappeared and, as the water slowly regained its stillness, Blake found that his image had also returned to normal. For long moments he looked down, as if expecting that terror-stricken visage to appear once more, but it didn't. A particularly cold breeze ruffled his hair and he shivered slightly, deciding that it was time he returned to the house.

Whistling through the branches of the nearby tree, the wind sounded like soft, malevolent laughter.

9

3.04 a.m.

Blake pushed back the covers and clambered out of bed. He had been tossing and turning for the past hour and still sleep eluded him.

Mathias' chauffeur had dropped him back at his hotel just after 1.30. By the time they had left Toni Landers' house only a handful of people remained and the atmosphere retained the air of solemnity which seemed to have descended after the incident with the cards.

Upon returning to the hotel, Blake had downed a couple of much-needed bottles of beer in the bar then retreated to his room but he had found the oblivion of sleep elusive. Now he stood at his window looking out on the dark mass that was Central Park. Trees bowed and shuddered silently in the wake of the wind and the writer thought how forbidding the place looked once the cloak of night had fallen over it.

He switched on the TV, flicking from channel to channel until he found an old black and white film. Audie Murphy was busy winning the war single-handed for the USA. Blake gazed at the screen for a while then changed channels once more. There was a programme about Chinese cookery so he left it on, turning the sound down. After five minutes he tired of that as well and switched the set off altogether, seeking comfort from the radio instead. He twisted the dial until he found the rock station, adjusting the volume as Y&T thundered out the opening chords of 'Mean Streak'.

Outside, the wind crept around the building as if seeking some means of entry, wailing mournfully every so often.

Blake padded into the bathroom and filled one of the tumblers with water which he gulped down thirstily. Then he returned to the bedroom, seating himself at the writing table where his notes were spread out. He had already filled three large pads with information, random jottings, hard facts and a lot of speculation. All that would have to be filtered and sifted through before he could begin preparing his next book. Blake disliked research at the best of times but, in this case, the dislike had intensified. The subject of Astral travel, Astral projection and its related phenomena, he had discovered, was even vaster than he had first thought. The paradox being that the more he learned the less he knew. He had the pieces but could not fit the jigsaw together.

As the author of five world-wide bestsellers he could afford to live comfortably, one of the few writers who ever succeeded in making a decent living from such a precarious profession. The money and the attention had been welcome if somewhat unexpected. Blake had never intended to earn his living from writing books about the paranormal, it had all come about rather suddenly.

He'd left home at twenty, hoping to make his mark as a journalist but working for the local paper covering events like school fetes, or interviewing people who were complaining because their sewers were bunged up, did not hold his interest for long. He began writing fiction in his spare time. Tucked away in his miniscule bed-sit above a laundrette in Bayswater he would return from the office and set to work at his own typewriter. He had left the paper for a job in a West End cinema but the financial rewards were small. He eked out his meagre earnings by supplying pornographic stories to a magazine called *Exclusive* who paid him fifty pounds for each 5000 word opus he delivered. He had a couple of articles published by *Cosmopolitan* then he decided to write a novel. It took him just three weeks and was subsequently rejected by eight publishers before finally gaining acceptance from a small, independent house. It went the way of most first novels, sinking into obscurity within a month. But, he had never been one to give up easily. He turned to non-fiction and, after six months of careful research and another two actually writing, he produced his first book about the paranormal.

After four rejections it finally found favour with a prominent hardback publisher.

A Light in the Black had been published two weeks before his twenty-second birthday.

Blake had used the advance to take a holiday. A luxury he had not been able to afford for three years. He returned to find that his book had not only been bought by Nova, a large paperback house, but the American rights had also been sold' for a substantial sum. Blake suddenly found that he could afford to leave his bed-sit and rent a flat in Holland Park.

Two years and two more books later he bought the place and now, with five world-wide successes behind him, he had, only five months earlier, bought a large house off Sloane Square.

He no longer needed to rush his work either. He now took up to eight or nine months on research and the rest of the time completing the mechanics of the book — the actual typing. Blake was at his happiest shut away in his study working. He was not a solitary man however, quite the contrary in fact. He was well liked by most people. An easy smile always at the ready, he was comfortable around people and yet at times still preferred his own company. Someone had once told him that the key to popularity was hypocrisy. If it was possible to be all things to all men at all times — do it. Blake had cultivated an easy-going image over the years which even those closest to him found hard to penetrate. He *was* all things to all men. Those he hated he spoke to with the same apparent warmth which he reserved for those who *were* allowed to pierce his facade.

Women were drawn to his practised charm, each one made to feel that *she* was the only girl in his life. The numerous encounters he had enjoyed since leaving home (that number increased once he became well-known) had only ever been superficial. To Blake at any rate. He smiled as he remembered something he'd read, attributed to Saul Bellow. He couldn't remember the words exactly but the gist of it was there.

'Telling a woman you're a writer is like an aphrodisiac. She can't wait to go to bed with you.'

He chuckled now as he flipped open his pad and reached for a pen.

Outside the hotel bedroom window the wind continued to blow strongly, hammering soundlessly at the panes as if threatening to break in. On the radio The Scorpions were roaring through 'Coming Home' and Blake decided he'd better turn the radio down.

That done he returned to his chair and scribbled a brief account of what had happened at Toni Landers' house that evening, including the incident with the picture frame and also of seeing his own twisted reflection in the pond.

As he wrote he found that his eyelids were growing heavy, as if someone had attached minute lead weights to them. He yawned and sat back for a moment, stretching. It was good that he felt tired, perhaps at last he'd be able to sleep. He scanned what he'd written and sat forward once more, allowing his eyes to close tightly.

The lamp flickered.

It was probably the wind disturbing the power lines, he thought but then remembered that he was in New York where cables ran underground, and not in the English countryside where they were suspended from pylons.

It flickered again, this time plunging the room into darkness for a second or two.

Blake muttered something to himself and peered at the bulb. The bloody thing was loose, no wonder it kept going on and off. He picked up his pen once more, now scarcely able to keep his eyes open. He turned to a fresh page but, before he could start writing, he had slumped forward in his seat and, within seconds, he was sound asleep.

The bathroom was full of steam,

Like a swirling white fog it curled and twisted in the air, condensation covering the mirror like a shroud so that when Blake looked into it, his reflection was smudged and unclear. He could still hear taps running, water splashing noisily into what was obviously an overfilled tub. Rivulets of water were running down the side of the bath which, for some reason, was hidden by the shower curtain which had been pulled around it. Blake shrugged, he didn't remember doing that.

He reached over and turned off the hot tap, cursing when he felt the heat in the metal. The condensation was on the shower curtain too, pouring down to puddle on the tiles beneath his feet.

Blake pulled back the flimsy plastic.

He shrieked aloud at the sight which met him.

Sitting up in the scalding water, skin covered by hideous welts from the blistering temperature, was a man.

The man was smiling broadly, his lips little more than ragged puffed up sores still leaking clear fluid. His head had obviously been immersed in the searing water because his face was red like a boiled lobster, the skin having risen to form innumerable liquescent blisters, some of which had burst and were spilling their contents down his cheeks. His entire body was scarlet and, such was the intensity of the water's heat, Blake noticed that three of the man's fingernails had been scalded free. They hung by thin tendrils of skin from the ends of the raw digits.

Blake stood rooted to the spot, his eyes gaping wide. But, it was not the appearance of the man which terrified him. It was his features.

Scalded and burnt though they were, they were unmistakably those of Blake himself.

He screamed again.

The scream woke him.

Blake sat bolt upright in his seat, perspiration beaded on his forehead. The lamp had stopped flickering, the room was bathed in a comforting yellowish glow. The sound of heavy rock music had been replaced by the sound of voices as the DJ interviewed his guest.

It took the writer a moment to realize that he'd been dreaming.

He swallowed hard and looked behind him to where the bathroom door was ajar. It was dark in there. No running water. No light. No steam.

Blake wiped his forehead with the back of his hand and released a sigh of relief.

'That's what you get for trying to work at this time in the

morning,' he told himself, reaching forward to close the notepad.

The page which had been blank before he dozed off had several sentences written on it.

The letters were large and untidy but the handwriting was unmistakably his.

Blake rubbed his eyes and turned back a page. He must have written the words before dozing off. But, as he re-read them, he realized that the words were new. He scanned the spidery writing:

The power does exist I have seen it I have seen the secrets

The writer swallowed hard as he scanned the words. His own words. Blake had heard of this kind of thing before, of so-called 'automatic writing' but it usually only occurred when the subject was in a trance. Was what he saw before him an example of automatic writing?

He sucked in a deep breath and held the paper before him. This time, he did *not* intend keeping things to himself. He would tell Mathias about what had happened and about the nightmare. Blake tore the piece of paper from the pad, wincing suddenly as he did so. He felt pain in his right hand and, as he turned it over he saw that his palm and wrist were bright red and swollen slightly.

As if they'd been scalded in very hot water.

10

Oxford

'How many days is it since you last slept?' Kelly asked Maurice Grant who was drumming agitatedly on the table at which they sat. Between them was a tape recorder, its twin spools turning slowly, the microphone pointed towards Grant.

'Two,' Grant snapped. 'Why the hell are you asking? You ought to know, you're the ones who keep pumping me full off fucking drugs.' He got to his feet and walked away from the table towards the large plate glass window in the far wall. Outside the sun was shining.

'Look out there,' said Grant. 'It's a beautiful day and I'm stuck in here with you two bastards asking me stupid questions.'

The man seated to Kelly's right leant closer.

'What are you giving him?' asked John Fraser, quietly.

'Thirty mg of Methadrine,' said Kelly. 'But without the Tubarine to put him out at nights.'

Fraser nodded and scribbled something down on the note pad before him.

The room they were in was light and airy, mainly due to the large window at the far end. Two or three bright paintings decorated the white walls, adding a touch of colour, but the room was dominated by the bulk of an EEG machine. The Eléma Schonander Mingograf was the most up to date of its kind and was one of four which the Institute owned. Readings had already been taken earlier that morning from Maurice Grant, over an hour ago according to the large wall clock which hung over the machine. But, at present, Kelly and her colleague were more concerned with Grant's verbal reactions than those culled from an electroencephalogrammatic scan of his brain. He had been deliberately deprived of sleep for the last two nights, unable to live out, subconsciously, the nightmare which he usually experienced.

Both investigators watched him as he paced agitatedly back and forth before the window.

'Why don't you come and sit down again?' said Fraser.

Kelly had worked with John Fraser on a number of occasions. He was ten years older than her but looked closer to fifty than thirty-five. His face had a mottled appearance to it as if he'd been out in the sun too long. His bulbous nose was shiny and reminded Kelly of a bald head. His eyes were rheumy and heavy-lidded like those of a man about to doze off. But he had a lean muscular body which looked as though it had somehow acquired the wrong head. The youthful frame and the haggard features seemed at odds.

61

'I said, why don't you ...'

Grant cut him short.

'Yeah, I heard you,' he rasped, hesitating a moment before stomping back to the table where he sat down heavily. 'Why the hell do you have to keep asking me so many questions? I just want to sleep.'

'Why do you want to sleep?' Fraser asked.

'Because I'm fucking shattered,' snapped Grant. 'Do I need a better reason?'

He glared at the two investigators with eyes full of rage. A razor hadn't touched his face for three or four days now and his cheeks and chin were carpeted by coarse bristles which rasped as he rubbed them.

'You knew that things might get a little uncomfortable when you first agreed to help us,' Kelly reminded him.

Maurice Grant didn't answer. He merely looked from Kelly to Fraser then back again.

'Are you ready to answer some questions?' she asked him.

'If I do, does that mean I can get some sleep?' he demanded.

She nodded.

'All right, ask your questions,' he said, picking at the skin around his fingernails, chewing it occasionally.

'When you can't dream, what do you think about?' she wanted to know, pushing the microphone closer to him.

'Things, I ...'

'What kind of things?' Fraser interrupted.

'Things,' Grant hissed. 'All kinds of things, thoughts.'

'Can you remember any of them?' Kelly enquired.

'No,' he said, flatly.

'Then try,' Fraser insisted.

Grant clenched his teeth, his malevolent gaze swinging round to focus on the investigator.

'I told you, I can't remember,' he said, the anger seething in his voice.

'Are any of the thoughts to do with your wife and son?' Kelly enquired.

Grant looked momentarily puzzled.

'Why should they be?'

'Look, if you keep answering a question with a question,' said Fraser, 'we're going to be here all day.'

Kelly shot her colleague an irritable glance while Grant rounded on him once more.

'What is this, some kind of fucking interrogation?' he snapped. 'You asked me to answer some questions, I'm trying to do that but you keep interrupting me.' His voice had risen in volume.

'Are any of the thoughts to do with your family?' Kelly asked him again.

Grant shook his head.

'Do you ever think about your wife and son when you can't sleep?' Kelly persisted.

'I just told you, no.'

'Come on, that's not natural. You mean to say you've wiped them from your memory?' said Fraser, a hint of sarcasm in his voice.

Grant brought his fist crashing down on the table top, his voice rising to a shout.

'I DON'T THINK ABOUT THEM.'

Fraser regarded the man warily. He was becoming a little nervous of Grant's aggression.

'Have you ever wanted to kill your wife and son?' Kelly asked.

'Kill them? Why?' Grant demanded.

'That's what we'd like to know,' said Fraser.

'Why should I want to kill them?'

'Because there may be a part of your mind which wants you to,' Kelly informed him. 'You've had a series of nightmares, in each one you kill your wife and son.'

'So what?' Grant snapped. 'What's so fucking important about a nightmare? Everyone has them.'

'You and your wife had experienced some problems hadn't you?' Kelly said. 'Marital problems.'

'What if we had? What's that got to do with this shit about nightmares?' demanded Grant, angrily.

'Would you like to kill your wife and son?' Fraser wanted to know.

Grant got to his feet.

'This is some kind of fucking game you're playing with me,' he growled, pointing an accusing finger at the investigators, both of whom moved back slightly from the table.

'Tell us the truth,' said Fraser. 'You want to kill them,

63

don't you?'

'No, you bastard.'

'You've told us.'

'No.'

'You want to murder them,' Fraser said, a little too forcefully.

'No. NO.' The shout became a scream of rage and Grant suddenly grabbed the heavy tape-recorder, lifting it from the desk, raising it above his head. The plug was torn from the wall, the spools falling uselessly from the machine. Kelly and Fraser jumped back hurriedly as Grant spun round and, with demonic strength, hurled the recorder at the large window. There was an ear-splitting crash as the glass exploded, huge thick shards flying out like crystal javelins.

'Get help, quick,' Fraser snapped as Grant turned on him.

As Kelly bolted for the door, Grant flung himself at Fraser. He hit the table on the way and the two men crashed to the ground amidst the shriek of snapping wood. Fraser tried to roll to one side but Grant fastened both hands around his neck and began throttling him. Fraser felt his assailant's finger-tips gouging into his flesh and he struck out with one hand, catching Grant a stinging blow across the temple. This only seemed to inflame him more for he straddled the investigator and began slamming his head against the floor.

Fraser looked up into the face of his attacker, the eyes blazing wildly, spittle dotted on his lips as he continued to bang his victim's head against the ground with gleeful force. Fraser gripped Grant's wrists and tried to prise open the vice-like grip but the relief was only momentary. He felt himself losing consciousness.

Then suddenly, the pressure on his throat eased and through pain-clouded eyes he saw two men grab Grant and pull him to his feet. Kelly was there too, so was Dr Vernon. He held a hypodermic needle in his hand.

Things seemed to swim before him as he rolled to one side, massaging his throat, the hot bile clawing its way up from his stomach.

'Strap him down,' Vernon urged, watching as the other two men dragged Grant towards the EEG. They forced him on to the trolley and swiftly fastened thick leather bonds around his wrists and ankles securing them. Grant had, however, begun to calm down somewhat and as the electrodes were attached to his head he seemed to stop thrashing about, content instead to eye his opponents with fury. His teeth were clenched, a thin, silvery trail of saliva dribbling from one corner of his mouth.

Kelly crossed to Fraser who was lying amongst the wreckage of the broken table, trying to clamber upright. She knelt beside him and offered a hand but he refused her help, struggling precariously to his feet, one hand still on his throat. He coughed and tasted blood. Vernon gave him a cursory glance then turned his attention back to Grant. The electrodes were in place on his forehead and temples, he was motionless but for the heaving of his chest.

One of the other investigators, a man with a button missing from one shirt cuff, stood beside the machine waiting. Kelly recognized him as Frank Anderson, a powerfully built man in his early forties.

Vernon nodded and Anderson flicked a switch which set the EEG in motion.

The five pencils swept back and forth across the paper as it left the machine, each one an indication of the brain waves picked up from Grant.

The fifth pencil, however, barely moved. Anderson noticed this and directed Vernon's attention to it. The older man looked puzzled.

'What the hell does that mean?' said Anderson but Vernon did not answer.

Kelly joined them, leaving Fraser to stagger over to the broken window where he gulped down lungfuls of air, still wincing in pain each time he swallowed.

'Could it be the area controlled by the subconscious?' Kelly said, directing her question towards Vernon but gazing at the virtually dormant line on the read-out.

Vernon didn't answer.

'Surely it must be,' she insisted. 'Theoretically, there should only be activity in that part of the brain when he's asleep. Put him out. This could be our chance to find out.'

Vernon did not hesitate. He rolled up Grant's sleeve, found a vein and ran the needle into it, keeping his thumb on the plunger until the last drop of Tubarine had left the slender receptacle.

Then, they waited.

They waited.

For ten minutes they waited. The only sounds in the room were the ticking of the wall clock and Grant's increasingly laboured breathing. Kelly stood over his immobile form and lifted one eye-lid, noticing how the pupil was dilated.

'He's asleep,' she said, softly, as if standing over a child she did not wish to wake.

Another five minutes and she noticed movement beneath the closed lids. The unmistakable motions of REM.

'He's dreaming,' she said, almost excitedly.

Vernon seemed not to hear, his eyes were riveted to the EEG read-out.

Four of the tracer lines were barely moving but the fifth was hurtling across the paper with frightening speed. He called Kelly to look at it.

'It certainly looks as if that fifth line denotes the area of the brain which controls the subconscious mind,' she said. 'It only registers activity when the subject is dreaming.'

All eyes turned to Grant.

'If only we knew *what* he was dreaming,' said Vernon. 'My God, this is incredible.' He was still watching the wildly swinging tracer. 'It looks as if the area is in the occipital lobe.' He lowered his voice slightly. 'The area of the brain concerned with vision.'

'Then he *is* seeing something,' said Frank Anderson.

Vernon nodded.

The knock on the lab door startled all of them.

At first no one moved but the knock came again, harder and more insistent.

Vernon muttered something under his breath and opened the door, surprised to find his secretary standing there.

'There's a phone call for you, Dr Vernon,' she said. 'It's ...'

He cut her short.

'Can't it wait? I'm very busy here.' he snapped.

'It's the police.'

Vernon nodded, aware of the interest now generated by his colleagues.

'I'll take it here,' he announced, indicating the wall phone. He crossed to it and lifted the receiver to his ear.

'Dr Vernon speaking. Yes, that's correct.'

Kelly watched him, noticing that his forehead was slowly beginning to crease into a frown.

'When did this happen?' he asked. There was a moment's silence. 'I see. Yes, I understand.'

'Look,' said Anderson, tugging on Kelly's sleeve.

She glanced down.

The fifth tracer had ceased its frenzied movement and was now drawing lazy parabolas on the read-out.

Kelly crossed to Grant and felt for his pulse, noticing how cold his flesh was to the touch.

Vernon, meanwhile, had replaced the receiver and rejoined his companions.

He sighed, scraping one thumb across his forehead.

'What's wrong?' Kelly asked.

'The police wanted to know if Maurice Grant had left the Institute during the last hour or so,' he told her.

Kelly looked puzzled.

'A neighbour called round to his house,' Vernon continued. 'She swears that she saw Grant there.'

'But that's impossible,' Anderson interjected.

'The neighbour was adamant.'

'I don't see why the police are so concerned about where Grant was or is,' Kelly said.

Vernon sucked in a deep breath.

'Less than twenty minutes ago his wife and child were attacked and killed in their house. Dismembered the police said.'

'Jesus,' murmured Anderson.

Kelly did not speak, her eyes were fixed on the restraining straps which secured Grant firmly to the table.

11

To Kelly, passing through the door of Dr Vernon's office was like crossing the threshold into a bygone age. The room, with its panelled walls and huge bookcases bearing endless leather bound volumes, was like something from a museum. It was a room to be looked at and appraised, one to be treated with reverence, much the same as an aged person. It did not seem like a room where anything constructive could be accomplished. It reminded her of the reading room in some gentleman's club, a place where cigars were smoked and glasses of port sipped. She even felt slightly out of place in it, dressed as she was in a khaki blouse, beige skirt and tan shoes. She felt as if she were intruding on the solemnity of the place, that she would have looked more at home in a crinoline.

Beside her, John Fraser was still massaging his neck, complaining about the pain despite having refused the attentions of a doctor. Vernon himself stood facing the window, looking out over the sun-drenched lawns, enjoying the heat on his face. Despite the warmth in the room he had not undone a single button of his jacket. He popped another cough sweet into his mouth and the smell of menthol seemed to intensify.

Fraser sipped at the cup of tea which Vernon's secretary had brought five minutes earlier and found that it was cold. He replaced the cup and returned to the more urgent task of rubbing his throat. His head was beginning to ache as well where Grant had slammed it against the floor. All in all he looked, and felt, fed up with the whole situation. Since he had joined the Institute five years earlier, Fraser had gained something of a reputation as a moaner but today he felt he was justified in his complaints.

His grumblings, however, were not reserved for his work. He'd been married for twelve years and, during that time, his wife had been forced to endure a continual barrage of bleating and criticism. Indeed, Fraser only seemed to be truly content when he had a drink in his hand.

He was a heavy drinker and had been since he was eighteen. Fraser was walking the tightrope between social drinking and alchoholism and, just lately, he seemed to be losing his footing.

'I don't see that you have any choice, Dr Vernon,' he said. 'Stop the research before any more accidents happen like the one today.'

Kelly looked at him angrily.

'We can't stop the research now,' she said. 'There's still too much we have to learn.'

'That man could have killed me. It would be madness to continue. He's dangerous.'

'For God's sake, John. He was in that state for a reason. He attacked you for a reason,' Vernon interjected. 'And Kelly's right, there's no question of stopping the research.'

'You didn't exactly help matters, John,' Kelly said. 'You provoked him to a certain extent.'

'Provoked him?' Fraser gaped, incredulously. 'Jesus Christ. I asked him some questions that was all.'

Vernon turned to face the investigators.

'If you don't like the risks, John, there is an alternative,' he said, his voice low but full of authority. 'If you don't wish to work on the project any longer you can be re-assigned.'

Fraser shook his head.

'No, I don't want that,' he said. 'I just think we should move away from the drugs if we can ...'

Vernon cut him short.

'It was agreed between the Investigators at the Metapsychic Centre and ourselves that *we* would use drugs, *they* would use hypnosis. It is important that we continue with our own methods. Today's incident was an isolated one.'

'How can you be so sure it won't happen again?'

Vernon fixed Fraser in an angry stare.

'It's a chance we will have to take,' he rasped. 'The work we are doing is very necessary. It will benefit a lot of people if we can find some of the answers we seek.'

'And it will benefit one person in particular won't it, Dr Vernon?' Fraser said.

The older man glared at him, his jaw set, the knot of muscles at the side pulsing angrily. His eyes looked like wet concrete.

Kelly looked puzzled.

'That's enough, Fraser,' the Institute Director said and Kelly heard the anger in his voice, well-disguised but nevertheless potent. 'The research will continue. If you don't wish to be a part of it then get out of my office now and stop wasting my time.'

Kelly was surprised at the vehemence in Vernon's tone, at the naked fury burning in his eyes. She saw Fraser visibly blench beneath the verbal onslaught. He slumped back in his chair, trying to hold the Director's stare but finding himself unable to do so. He lowered his head slightly and began picking at his nails.

Vernon sat down and folded his hands across his stomach, his eyes never leaving Fraser.

'It will benefit one person in particular.' Kelly looked at her fellow investigator, wondering what he had meant by the statement.

'I think it would be best if you left now, John,' Vernon said, quietly. 'There's nothing more to discuss.'

Fraser let out a deep breath and got to his feet. He glanced at Kelly then at Vernon before turning and heading for the door.

'And the next time?' said Fraser, challengingly. 'Will you take responsibility for what happens, Dr Vernon?'

The older man didn't look up.

'Get out, John,' he said, quietly.

As Fraser slammed the door behind him, Kelly, too, rose. She was anxious to speak with Fraser.

'Wait a moment, Kelly,' Vernon said.

She sat down again, brushing an imaginary speck of dust from her skirt.

'Do you want me to replace Fraser?' Vernon asked.

'I don't think it's up to me,' Kelly told him.

'You're the one who has to work with him.'

She opened her mouth to speak but the words remained locked inside and it was Vernon who broke the silence again.

'This project is too important to be jeopardised by one man.'

70

Kelly saw that the steel had returned to his eyes.

'I hope you agree with me?'

She nodded.

'Dr Vernon, don't you think that the murder of his wife and child might have some effect on Grant?'

'In what way?'

She shrugged, not sure whether or not what she was about to say would sound ridiculous.

'The catalyst, the object of his subconscious fantasies no longer exists,' she said. 'We assumed that his nightmares were unconscious manifestations of actual desires, but now his wife and son are dead he has nothing to direct that hostility towards.'

Vernon stroked his chin thoughtfully.

'You mean his wife was the object of his fury, the cause of the nightmares?' he suggested. 'So, theoretically, the nightmares should stop.'

Kelly nodded.

'It's strange though,' she said. 'She was murdered while Grant was under a drug-induced trance, in more or less the same manner as he had previously described. Almost as if the dreams had been warnings. Perhaps that's the key we're looking for. Maybe Grant's nightmares weren't unconscious desires, they were visions of the future.'

Vernon shifted the cough sweet around inside his cheek where it bulged like a gum boil.

'Possibly,' he murmured.

Kelly sat a moment longer then got to her feet.

'If there's nothing else, Dr Vernon.'

He shook his head.

Kelly walked to the door, watched by the Institute Director. He coughed and, as Kelly turned the handle, Vernon spoke once more.

'Remember what I said, Kelly. This project means too much. There's a lot at stake. If Fraser causes any trouble I want to know about it.'

She nodded and left him alone in the office.

Vernon dropped his pen, his fingers bunching into a fist.

Fraser.

The last thing they needed now was opposition.

Fraser.

Vernon's breath came in short, angry gasps. No, Fraser must not be allowed to disrupt the research programme.

No matter what it took to stop him.

Kelly checked in John Fraser's office, in the labs, in the library.

He was nowhere to be found.

As she made her way back across the polished wooden floor of the Institute's reception area she spotted him outside, clambering into his familiar red Datsun.

Kelly ran out on to the gravel drive-way and across to the other investigator who had already started his engine and was in the process of pulling out.

He saw Kelly but did not slow up until she had reached the side of the car and banged on the window. He rolled it down.

'What do you want?' he said, sharply.

'Where are you going?' she wanted to know.

'I'm taking the rest of the day off,' Fraser said, sarcastically. 'I'm going to find the nearest pub and have a few beers. Maybe some shorts to wash them down.' He jammed the car into first, the gearbox groaned in protest.

'What you said in Vernon's office,' said Kelly. 'What did you mean?'

The roar of the revving engine almost drowned out her words.

'I don't know what you're talking about,' said Fraser.

'About the research,' she said. 'You said it would benefit one person in particular. Who did you mean?'

Fraser stepped on the accelerator, the back wheels spiining madly. A flurry of pebbles from the driveway flew into the air.

'Did you mean Vernon?' she persisted.

'Ask him,' hissed Fraser and drove off.

Kelly watched as the Datsun disappeared from view along the tree-lined drive. She stood silently for a moment then made her way back towards the main building.

She was not the only one who saw Fraser drive away.

From the solitude of his office on the second floor, Vernon had watched the entire tableau.

He stepped back out of sight.

Dr Stephen Vernon poured himself another scotch and returned to his chair beside the fire-place. The gentle strains of the New World Symphony issued forth from the record player and Vernon closed his eyes for a moment, allowing the soothing sound to wash over him. It did little to relax him and he jerked his eyes open almost immediately, seeking comfort instead in the whisky which he downed almost in one gulp, allowing the amber liquid to burn its way to his stomach.

Outside, the wind stirred the branches of the trees and clouds gathered menacingly in the night sky, like dense formations of black clad soldiers.

Inside the house the fire was warm, the room bathed in the comforting glow from the flames and the two lamps which burned, one behind him and the other on the table nearby. But, despite the warmth, Vernon felt uncomfortable. As if the heat refused to penetrate his pores. He swallowed some more of the scotch, regarding warily the A4 size envelope which lay on the table nearby. Only when he had downed the last dregs of the fiery liquid did he find the courage to open the envelope.

Inside was a file, a ring binder, and there was a letter paper-clipped to it.

Vernon read it hastily then balled it up and tossed it into the waste-bin beside him. His grey eyes narrowed to steely slits as he opened the file. The first page, neatly typed, had the familiar notepaper headed:

FAIRHAM SANATORIUM

It also bore a photo. A ten by eight, glossy black and white of a woman in her middle forties, a warm smile etched across her face. Even given the monochrome of the photo there was a welcoming radiance about the eyes and Vernon found himself gazing deep into them. The photo had been taken six years earlier.

He turned the page and there was another picture, smaller this time, more recent.

If he hadn't known he would have sworn it was a different woman.

The welcoming glow in her eyes and the warm smile had been replaced by a vision from a mortuary. A gaze devoid of understanding stared back at him from sockets which looked as though they'd been hollowed out of the skull with a trowel. The mouth was thin-lipped, little more than a gash across the face. Hair which had once been lustrous and shiny now hung in unkept hunks, unbrushed and lifeless like kelp. Set side by side the most recent picture seemed to exist almost as a mockery to remind him of what once had been.

Vernon swallowed hard and read the report:

SUBJECT NAME: VERNON. JANET
KATHERINE. NEÉ HAMPTON.
AGE: 50
MARITAL STATUS: MARRIED.
DATE OF COMMITTAL: 14/5/78
TRUSTEE: VERNON. STEPHEN PHILLIP.
RELATIONSHIP TO SUBJECT: HUSBAND.
DIAGNOSIS: DEMENTIA, PARAESTHESIA,
CHRONIC PARANOID DEMENTIA, SERIOUS
IMPAIRMENT OF SENSORY-MOTOR
FUNCTION.
CAUSE:

Vernon closed the file and slammed it down onto the table, almost knocking over his glass. He snatched it up but found, to his annoyance, that it was empty. He looked across at the half-empty bottle of Haig and contemplated re-filling his glass once more but, eventually, decided against it. The file lay where he'd put it, a memory as painful as a needle in soft flesh.

Six years.

Dear God was it that long since he had been forced to commit his wife? That long since ...

The thought trailed away but he knew that he could never erase the memory of what had happened.

74

What had sent her to the verge of insanity.

Vernon got to his feet, turned off the fire and extinguished the lights, then, carrying the file, he trudged upstairs not bothering to put on the landing light. He moved slowly but easily through the darkness until he came to the locked door.

The wind had increased in strength and was howling now, like a dog in pain.

Vernon paused before the door, a cold chill enveloping him like some icy invisible glove which squeezed tighter the longer he stood there.

From the pocket of his cardigan he produced a key and, steadying his hand, inserted it in the lock.

There was a sharp crack from beyond the door, like bony fingers on glass, skeletal digits playing a symphony of torment in the gloom.

He turned the key.

The lock was well-oiled and opened without difficulty.

Vernon stepped into the room, shuddering as he did so. He felt like an intruder in this room. Like a thief in a church.

He heard the harsh clacking of the tree branch against the window and it startled him momentarily but, recovering his composure, he reached over and turned on the light.

The room smelt slightly of neglect, a faint odour of damp mingling with the more pungent smell of mothballs. There was a thin film of dust on everything. On the bedspread, the side-board, the chairs, even the photos. He crossed to the wardrobe and opened it. Her clothes still hung there, the smell of naptha more powerful now.

He had kept her in this room for three months before finally committing her. For three months after it happened he had brought her food and tried to feed her as a parent would feed a helpless child. For that was what she had become.

His Janet. His wife. The woman he had loved so much.

The woman who had been reduced to the mental status of a cabbage by what she had witnessed those six years ago.

He had tried to cope as best he could, he had tried to help her but she had withdrawn deeper inside herself until Vernon had felt as through he were nursing a corpse. Only the movement of her eyes, bulging wide constantly, gave any indication that she was even alive. He had used all his expertise to try and salvage what was left of her sanity but finally he had lost the battle and had her committed to Fairham. The doctors there had made no progress though perhaps it was not surprising when he considered the events which had sent her into this death-like state of catatonia. It would, he decided, have been enough to send anyone insane.

So far, he had been able to keep his secret.

In the beginning he had thought that he could handle the problem. But, word had spread around the neighbourhood — rumours, speculation and guess-work until finally, he had found that there was no other solution but to lock her up. No one knew why Janet Vernon was in a sanatorium and he knew that, for all their do-it-yourself detective work, none of the neighbours could ever imagine anything as horrific as that which had caused her to lose her mind.

Now he stood in the room, looking around, listening to the wind outside.

He had left the room just as it had always been. For six years, only he had been inside. It contained too many memories, too much pain.

Vernon flicked off the light and retreated back on to the landing, locking the door behind him. He stood looking at it for long seconds then turned and headed for his own bedroom.

Six years.

He had searched for answers for so long and now, he felt that he might be close. The research was furnishing him with what he'd always sought. A way to cure his wife. A way to unlock her thoughts. No one must be allowed to stand in his way.

But, as he undressed, a thought passed through his mind.

What effect would it have on her? The horror of what she had witnessed that day had festered in her thoughts for so long.

Dare he release those memories?

13

New York

'It sure beats the shit out of *E.T.*,' said Rick Landers, gleefully.

Beside him, Andy Wallace was similarly impressed.

'You bet,' he murmured, watching as *The Thing* devoured another victim, ripping off both his arms below the elbow before exploding from his stomach cavity. The two boys watched mesmerised as the alien head detached itself and then dragged itself across the floor using a tentacle.

'Rewind it,' said Andy. 'Let's see it again.'

Rick nodded and scuttled across to the video, his finger seeking out the appropriate button.

'Yeah, *E.T.* was OK for kids,' Andy continued.

'My mum met the guy who made this picture,' said Rick, smugly.

'John Carpenter? Wow, when was that?'

'At some party I think.'

He pressed the 'play' button on the video recorder and pictures once more began to fill the wide screen. The two boys settled down again.

They were both nine years old, Andy perhaps a month or two senior. Both attended the same school about three blocks away. Rick knew that his mother didn't like him watching too many horror movies. She'd turned the video off halfway through his fifth viewing of *The Evil Dead* but, today, she was out filming a commercial until six o'clock so that gave him and Andy another two hours.

Andy lived about three houses down from the Landers place. His father, Gordon, wrote scripts for one of ABC's most successful comedy series and his mother, Nina, was a theatrical agent, so Andy was no stranger to the crazy world of showbusiness.

The Thing had just sprouted spider's legs and was about to scuttle away when the picture on the TV broke up into a network of lines and dots.

The two boys groaned and Rick leapt towards the video.

From the kitchen, the sound of the vacuum mingled with that of the waste-disposal unit in the sink.

The noise stopped, at any rate the grinding of the disposal unit did, the vacuum seemed to roar even louder.

'Mrs Garcia,' yelled Rick.

No answer.

'Mrs Garcia,' he bellowed louder and the vacuum was switched off.

'What you want, Rick?' Elita Garcia asked, appearing from the kitchen like a blimp emerging from a hangar. She was a huge Mexican woman who always reminded Rick of an extra in a spaghetti western.

'The vacuum is screwing up the picture on the video,' Rick told her. 'Couldn't you do it later?'

'Your mother ask me to have this finish before she come home,' Mrs Garcia informed him.

'Yeah, but the video ...'

'I no help that. I do my job, Rick. Sorry.' And the vacuum started up again.

The two boys exchanged disconsolate glances and surrendered to Mrs Garcia and her cleaner. Rick switched off the video and the TV and suggested they go into the garden for a while.

'You no be long,' Mrs Garcia called above the roar of the vacuum. 'Your dinner ready soon.'

The two boys had been outside only minutes when Rick heard the approaching tones of an ice-cream van. He guessed it was less than a block away.

Lee Jacobs spun the wheel of the station-wagon, the tyres screaming as they tried to grip the road. The vehicle's back end skidded and slammed into a parked Ford.

'Jesus Christ, man,' snapped Tony Sollozzo, who was kneeling on the station-wagon's passenger seat. 'Look where you're fucking going will you.'

'You wanna drive, motherfucker?' shouted Jacobs, sweat pouring down his black face. It beaded in his short frizzy hair

78

like dew. 'Are the cops still behind us?'

The sound of a siren answered his question for him and he glanced in the rear-view mirror to see the black and white speeding along in pursuit, lights flashing.

'Step on it, will you,' Sollozzo urged. 'The bastards are gaining.'

'If you'd stolen a car with somethin' under the hood maybe we could outrun those lousy fucks,' Jacobs protested. 'Why the hell did you have to steal a fucking station-wagon?'

'Maybe I shoulda' walked around some showroom first, picked out somethin' you liked, huh?' Sollozzo countered.

'We shoulda' just turned ourselves in like I said,' Jacobs said, swerving to miss a bus.

'With nearly a kilo of smack in the glove compartment? Are you kiddin' me?'

'Stealing a station-wagon,' Jacobs grunted, trying to coax more speed from the vehicle. 'Dumb fuckin' wop.'

'Who're you callin' a wop you nigger son of a bitch. Now drive, man, they're gettin' closer.'

The blaring of horns greeted them as they sped through a red light.

The police car followed.

'What time does Mrs Garcia leave?' Andy Wallace asked, picking up the frisbee and throwing it back.

Rick Landers watched it carefully, jumping to catch it with one hand.

'She stays until my mum gets home,' he said.

'How come? She never used to did she?'

'Mum's been acting kind of weird for the last couple of days,' Rick disclosed. 'She says she doesn't like to leave me on my own too much.' He threw the frisbee back.

'*My* parents are as bad,' Andy confided. 'I mean, they must think we're kids.'

Rick nodded then he cocked his head on one side as he heard the chimes of the ice-cream van once more. It was closer now. Just turning into the street he guessed.

'You want to get an ice-cream?' he asked Andy, noticing the look of delight on his friend's face.

'You bet,' he said.

The frisbee was forgotten as they both hurried around to the front of the house.

.Lee Jacobs banged his hooter as the station-wagon narrowly missed a woman crossing the road. He yelled something and turned the vehicle into another street. Beside him, Tony Sollozzo slid a Smith and Wesson .38 from his jacket pocket. He flipped out the cylinder, checking that each chamber carried a round.

'What you doin', man?' asked Jacobs, glancing down at the gun.

'Just in case,' murmured Sollozzo, hefting the pistol before him.

'You crazy fuck, I didn't know you was packed,' Jacobs gaped. 'What you gonna' do?'

The police car drew closer, its bonnet little more than ten feet from the rear of the station wagon. Sollozzo could see the two uniformed men inside as he turned. He wound down his window, pulling back the hammer on the .38.

Up ahead, Jacobs caught sight of an ice-cream van parked in their way. It was blocking the route. To by-pass it he would have to drive up on to the wide pavement.

Sollozzo steadied himself, bringing the gun up to a firing position.

Rick Landers and Andy Wallace ran towards the ice-cream van, unaware of the two speeding cars hurtling down the road. Andy suddenly stopped as his money spilled out on to the ground. He had a hole in his trouser pocket. Rick chuckled and watched as Andy stooped in the driveway of the house to retrieve his coins. He, himself, reached the waiting white van and asked for a chocolate sundae with lots of nuts. He hoped Mrs Garcia wasn't watching.

As he turned to see where Andy had got to, Rick saw the two speeding cars.

Sollozzo took aim and fired twice, the pistol bucking in his fist. The first shot blasted off the wing mirror of the police car, the second punched a hole in its windscreen.

The station-wagon swerved violently as Jacobs momentarily took his eye off the road and glared at his companion.

'Stop it,' he shouted, reaching for the gun.

'Fuck you,' roared Sollozzo, firing again, a twisted grin across his face.

Jacobs looked ahead of him and screamed aloud as the white bulk of the ice-cream van loomed before him.

The station-wagon hit it doing about sixty, the impact catapulting Sollozzo through the windscreen. The steering column came back at Jacobs as if fired from a cannon, the wheel cracking, the column itself shattering his sternum and tearing through him as the two vehicles were pulped by the crash. Almost instantaneously, the petrol tank of the white van exploded with an ear-splitting shriek and both vehicles disappeared beneath a blinding ball of red and white flame.

Rick Landers, standing less than ten feet from the van, was lifted into the air as if by an invisible hand, his body catapulted a full twenty feet on to the pavement by the force of the explosion. His mangled body crashed to the ground, his clothes ablaze.

The patrolman driving the police car twisted the wheel to avoid the blazing inferno, the black and white mounting the sidewalk.

Too late the driver saw Rick's body lying ahead of him.

He slammed on his brakes but the car was travelling much too fast.

The front offside wheel ran across the boy's neck, crushing his spine and nearly severing his head. Blood burst from the shattered corpse, spreading out in a wide pool around it.

Watching from the driveway, Andy Wallace felt something warm and soft in the seat of his pants as he gazed at the carnage before him. A second later he fainted.

Tony Sollozzo lay on the grass nearby, his face and neck shredded by the glass of the windscreen. Flames from the wreckage licked hungrily at his outstretched hand. Above it all a black pall of smoke hung like a shroud.

The two policemen stumbled from their car, the first of them running towards the burning vehicles but unable to get close because of the blistering heat from the leaping flames. The driver knelt and saw the body of Rick Landers lying beneath the car.

'Oh Jesus God,' he murmured and straightened up, reaching inside the car for his radio.

He called for an ambulance and some back-up, trying to explain briefly what had happened.

As he walked away he saw that he left sticky footprints

behind him where he'd been standing in the pool of Rick's blood. He dropped to his knees on the grass verge and threw up.

14

David Blake dropped his pen and yawned. He blinked myopically and scanned the pages which lay before him.

He'd been working flat out since ten that morning, pausing briefly at one o'clock to devour half a cheeseburger and some fries. Most of that now lay neglected on the table behind him.

His stomach growled noisily and he patted it gently. It was time he ate something more substantial.

Blake got to his feet and walked to the bathroom, turning the television on as he passed. A glance at his watch told him it was 5.58 p.m. The news would be on in a minute or two. He smiled to himself. It was time to find out what had been going on in the 'real' world. He'd been so immersed in his work for the past eight hours that New York could have disappeared and he wouldn't have noticed. Once safely locked away, pen in hand, Blake was oblivious to all else.

He entered the bathroom, crossing to the wash basin where he splashed his face with cold water. As he wandered back into his room, a towel pressed to his face, the news was just beginning. Blake decided to hear the headlines then get something to eat. He dried his face off, the water mingling with the perspiration on his forehead.

'... has promised a crackdown on some of the city's illegal gambling establishments ...'

The voice of the newsreader droned on as Blake opened his wardrobe and took out a clean shirt.

'... and, as reported in our earlier bulletin, the son of Toni Landers, the actress who plays ...'

Blake spun round to face the set.

'... whose son, Rick, was tragically killed today when he

was involved in a car accident.'

'Jesus Christ,' muttered Blake as a photo of first Rick and then Toni Landers was flashed on to the screen. The writer sat down on the edge of the bed, eyes riveted to the set as the newsreader continued.

'Miss Landers, who was filming elsewhere in the city was unavailable for comment and it is believed that she is now at her home under sedation. Her son, Rick, is believed to have been killed at approximately 4.15 this afternoon after a stolen car crashed into an ice cream van outside his home. Both passengers in the car and also the van driver were killed but, as yet, the other three victims have not been named. Police ...'

Blake shook his head slowly, his eyes and ears focused on the TV but his mind back-tracking to the party at Toni Landers' house.

To Mathias.

To the prophecy.

'Her son is going to die.' The psychic's words echoed inside his mind.

'Her son is going to die.'

Blake sat for a moment longer, then pulled on his shirt and hastily buttoned it up, tucking it into his jeans. He pulled on a pair of boots and, leaving the television set on, he left the room and scuttled across to the elevator at the end of the corridor. He rode it to the ground floor and ran through reception, out of the main doors and past the doorman who was enjoying a sly drag on a Marlboro.

The writer turned to his left and headed for the newsstand on the corner of the street. He fumbled in his pocket for change with one hand as he retrieved a late edition with the other. Half-way down the page was a photo of Rick Landers and, above it:

SON OF ACTRESS DIES IN ACCIDENT

Blake handed the vendor some coins, not waiting for his change, then he turned and made his way back to the hotel.

Once inside his room, Blake read the full story. The details didn't matter. The child was dead. That was enough. The writer folded the paper and dropped it on to the bed. He suddenly didn't feel so hungry. For what seemed like an eternity he sat there, gazing at the TV screen and then at the photo of Rick Landers.

'Her son is going to die.' He spoke the words aloud.

Blake got to his feet and switched off the TV. He snatched up the leather jacket which was draped over the back of a nearby chair, pulling it on as he made for the door of his room.

Outside, the storm clouds which had been gathering for the past hour or so were split by the first soundless flash of lightning.

Blake paid the taxi driver, peered out through the rain splashed window then pushed open the door of the cab.

The deluge hit him like a palpable wave, the heavens continuing to dump their load without hint of a respite. The storm was raging, whiplash cracks of lightning punctuating the almost continual growl of thunder. It sounded as if somewhere, deep below the surface of the earth, a gigantic creature was clawing its way up. Rain hammered against the roads and buildings, bouncing off like tiny explosions. Even as Blake left the cab he felt the hair being plastered to the side of his face, the hot droplets penetrating the material of his shirt. He knew that the storm would not clear the air, it would merely make the humidity more acute. Beads of perspiration formed on the writer's forehead, only to be washed away instantly by the driving rain.

The house of Jonathan Mathias stood before him, a large forbidding three storey building fronted by well-kept lawn and ringed by a high stone wall. Blake noticed as he approached the wrought iron gates that there were closed-circuit television cameras mounted on each side of the gates. They watched him with their Cyclopean eyes as he walked up the short driveway towards the house itself.

The building was a curious mixture of the old and new. The main structure looked as if it had been built in mock Edwardian style whilst an extension made up of glass and concrete seemed to have been grafted on to the wrong house.

The windows were unlit and the glass reflected the lightning back at Blake, they lowered over him like some kind of malevolent spectre.

There were more closed-circuit cameras above the front door. He rang the bell, pressing it twice and, a moment later, the door was opened by a man who Blake immediately recognised as Mathias' chauffeur.

'Mr Blake isn't it?' said the man, eyeing the writer who looked a sorry state with his brown hair dripping and his clothes soaked.

'I'd like to see Mr Mathias if that's possible,' the writer said.

'He doesn't like to be disturbed when he's at home,' the chauffeur began. 'I'll ...'

'Let him in, Harvey.'

Blake recognised the voice immediately and, a moment later, Mathias himself stepped into view.

'Come in, David,' he said, smiling. 'You look as if you swam here.'

Blake stepped into the hallway.

'Come through into the study,' said the psychic.

Once inside the room, he poured himself a brandy and offered one to Blake who gratefully accepted, his eyes roving around the spacious room. He noted with bewilderment that there were no windows. The only light came from a desk lamp and two floor-standing spotlamps near the drink cabinet. On one wall there was a framed original sketch by Aleister Crowley depicting the Whore of Babylon. Blake looked closely at it.

'You knew Crowley?' he asked.

'We met once or twice,' said Mathias.

'The Great Beast himself eh?' murmured Blake, sipping his brandy. 'A self-confessed Black Magician.'

Mathias didn't answer.

Blake allowed his gaze to shift to a photograph. It showed Mathias and another man who looked familiar to him.

'Anton Le Vey,' said the psychic.

'Another friend?' asked Blake.

Mathias nodded.

'Another Black Magician,' the writer commented.

The psychic seated himself behind his desk and cradled his brandy glass in one hand, warming the dark fluid.

'What can I do for you, David?' he wanted to know. 'It must be important to bring you out in weather like this.' He downed most of his brandy in one swallow.

Blake seated himself on the closest chair.

'It is,' he informed Mathias. 'Have you seen a newspaper today, or watched television?'

'No, why?'

Mathias finished his brandy and got to his feet, walking past the writer who turned until he was gazing at the psychic's back.

'Toni Landers' son was killed earlier today,' he said.

Mathias filled his glass once again then turned round, the bottle still in his hand.

'He was killed in an accident,' the writer persisted.

'Do you want another drink?' Mathias asked, apparently uninterested in what Blake had to say.

'Did you hear what I said?' the writer asked, irritably. 'Toni Landers' son is dead. Haven't you got anything to say?'

Mathias regarded him indifferently then shrugged his shoulders.

'I'm very sorry,' he said, softly. 'He was only a young boy.'

'You knew he was going to die,' Blake said, flatly. 'You told me at the party the other night, after the Tarot reading. Only you didn't learn of his death through the cards did you?'

'The cards act as a guide,' said Mathias, sipping his drink. 'They point me toward the truth.'

'Come on, Jonathan,' Blake muttered, exasperatedly. 'You're not talking to one of your bloody "flock" now.'

The two men regarded one another coolly for a moment, a heavy silence descending upon them. It was broken by Mathias.

'I told you that the Astral body can be controlled,' he said. 'Well, it can also be projected forward in time. I "saw" that Toni Landers' son was going to die because I felt no Astral presence from him.' He sipped at his brandy once again. 'The Astral body is like the life-line on a hand, someone with the knowledge can "see" it.'

'Tell *my* future,' said Blake, reaching for a pack of Tarot cards which lay on the desk near to Mathias. 'Do it now.'

He had already begun shuffling the cards.

'No,' said Mathias.

Blake divided the cards into ten packs and laid them out in the correct pattern.

'Do it, Jonathan,' he urged.

86

'I told you, I'm not a fairground showman,' muttered the psychic, irritably. He regarded the cards without emotion, his gaze slowly rising until his brilliant blue eyes were fixed on Blake. 'I'd appreciate it if you would leave now, David,' he said, quietly.

The two men locked stares for a moment then Blake took a step backward, brushing one strand of hair from his face.

'Are you afraid of what you might see?' he asked.

Mathias didn't answer. His face was impassive, registering no emotion at all. Finally, he exhaled, his features softening slightly.

'You asked me about my power,' he said. 'This force inside me, it's the power of the shadow.'

Blake looked puzzled.

'Not the shadow cast by sunlight or reflected in a mirror,' Mathias continued. 'The shadow of the inner self. The alter ego if you like. The Ancients called it the shadow because it represented the darker side of man, the side which only appeared in times of anger or fear. The side which could drive a man to commit acts of which he was not normally capable. Acts which went against his nature. Human nature.'

'Like a split personality?' said Blake.

'No,' Mathias corrected him. 'In cases of split personality the victim retains *some* traces of good within himself. The shadow is wholly evil.'

'Then your power is evil,' Blake said.

'Who is to say what is good and what is evil, David?'

There was another long pause then Blake turned and headed towards the door.

'I've told you as much as I can,' Mathias said. 'What more do you need to know?'

'A lot more,' he said, opening the door. Then, he was gone.

The psychic sat alone in his study, the Tarot cards still laid out in their cabbalistic pattern before him. He paused for a moment then reached towards the seventh pack. To Love. He turned the card slowly.

Thirteen.

La Mort.

Death.

Mathias stared at the sythe-carrying skeleton depicted on the card for a moment then he reached for the top card on the ninth pack. To Health.

Fifteen.

Le Diable.

The Devil.

But he knew that the cards carried much more than their face value. The card marked XV also meant The Great Secret. Mathias smiled to himself. It seemed most appropriate in Blake's case.

He turned the card on the final pack, the breath catching in his throat as he did so.

Twelve.

Le Pendu.

The Hanged Man.

Mathias dropped the card as if it had been red hot; he swallowed hard and studied the image on the card.

The Hanged Man.

Catastrophe.

He wiped his brow, finding that he was perspiring slightly. It had another interpretation.

Saint or Sinner?

Outside the thunder rumbled loudly and Mathias sat still in his seat for a moment. He finally gathered up the cards, sorting them into some kind of uniformity.

As he reached for the one which bore The Hanged Man he wondered why his hand was shaking.

15

Oxford

As she approached the door which led into Maurice Grant's quarters, Kelly looked at her watch.

It was approaching 5.09 p.m.

She slowed her pace, conscious of the sound which her heels made in the solitude of the corridor. She felt strangely ill-at-ease, like a child who has performed, or is about to perform, an act for which it knows it will be punished. Kelly brushed one hand through her brown hair and attempted to control her accelerated breathing. This was ridiculous, she told herself. She had no reason to be nervous.

Over her skirt and blouse she wore a lab coat and in one of the pockets nestled a hypodermic syringe.

She had taken it, along with its contents, from the pharmacy on the first floor. Ordinarily, it was a place only frequented by the four doctors who worked for the Institute, although the other investigators were free to come and go as they wished amongst the rows and rows of bottles and medical equipment. Kelly had found what she sought without difficulty, then she had recovered a disposable syringe from the drawer which was so carefully marked. Everything in the pharmacy was maintained by a woman in her forties known to Kelly only as Mrs King. She was responsible for ensuring that everything was in its correct place and it was a job which she did very efficiently.

Kelly knew that Mrs King usually left for home at around 4.30 so she had waited until nearly 4.50 before venturing into the pharmacy.

To her relief it had been deserted but still she had felt the compulsion to hurry, wondering what explanation she was going to use if someone should discover her poring over the chemicals which were the domain of the physicians.

She had drawn off 10ml of atropine sulphate and then placed the syringe in her pocket.

Now, as she approached Maurice Grant's quarters thoughts began to tumble through her mind with increased rapidity. But one in particular seemed to flash like neon in her consciousness. The incident the day before last when Grant had finally persuaded her to undertake this new experiment without either the knowledge or authorization of Dr Vernon. Deprived of sleep for forty-eight hours, Grant had become violent and Kelly remembered how the subsequent tests on him had revealed activity in an area of the brain normally dormant. The question of what would happen to him if he were not allowed to sleep and dream for longer than two days had tortured her ever since. She had wondered what he'd be like after a week but Kelly didn't have a week.

She would not, could not, wait that long.

The injection of atropine would have more or less the same results.

She knew that, given in overdose, the drug caused stimulation of the brain and autonomic nervous system. The usual dosage was 2ml.

She planned to give Grant three times that amount.

Kelly knocked on the door and waited, casting one furtive glance up the corridor as she did so. The Institute was silent.

'Come in,' Grant called and Kelly did so.

He was sitting at a table finishing a plate of fish and chips which had been brought to him ten minutes earlier.

'Sorry if I'm interrupting your tea, Mr Grant,' Kelly said.

He smiled and shook his head.

'I was just finishing,' he told her. 'That's one good thing about this place, the food's terrific.' He belched loudly, excused himself and pushed the plate away.

Kelly thought how different he looked from the last time she'd seen him. In place of the demonic, violent and unkempt would-be killer there was a calm, clean-shaven even handsome man. Grant wore only a white shirt and grey trousers, both of which looked neat and fresh.

'What can I do for you now?' he asked.

'I'm afraid we need your help with something else,' Kelly told him.

'Which is your polite way of saying "Excuse me Mr Human Guinea Pig, we want you back on the slab," right?'

Kelly smiled thinly.

'Yes it is,' she said.

Grant chuckled.

'No need to sound so apologetic. After all, I was the bloody fool who volunteered for all this,' he remarked, good-humouredly.

Kelly had one hand dug deep in the pocket of her lab coat, fingers toying with the syringe.

'What exactly is it that you want me to do?' Grant enquired.

'Do you remember anything about the incident the day before last?' she wanted to know. 'When you attacked one of my colleagues?'

He shrugged.

'Not much. I remember trying to …' The words trailed off, almost as if he were ashamed of the recollection. 'I didn't hurt anyone badly did I?'

Kelly shook her head.

'You'd been kept awake for over forty-eight hours,' she told him. 'People become aggressive when they're forced to go without sleep for too long.'

'Why?' Grant wanted to know.

'If we knew that for sure, Mr Grant, you wouldn't still be here.' She thought about mentioning the dream theory then decided not to. There was a long silence broken eventually by Kelly. 'For the last two nights have you dreamed?'

'Yes,' he said.

'The dream about killing your wife and son?'

He nodded.

'But it wasn't as vivid. In fact, last night it was different. I woke up before I killed them.'

'That was probably because you weren't given any drugs,' Kelly told him. 'The amphetamines we'd been giving you had been intensifying the dreams up until that point.'

'So, what happens now?' he asked.

Kelly felt the hypodermic in her pocket.

'We try a different approach,' she said.

On the table beside Grant's bed was a new tape-recorder and Kelly checked that it was working properly. Satisfied, she asked Grant to lie down. There were restraining straps which could be fastened around his wrists and ankles but, as yet, Kelly did not touch them. She ensured that Grant was comfortable then asked him to roll up the sleeve of his shirt which he did. The vein bulged invitingly in the crook of his arm and Kelly carefully pushed the needle into it, one thumb on the plunger of the syringe.

She began to push, the atropine flooding into Grant's bloodstream.

She watched the markers on the syringe as she forced the liquid into his vein.

0.25ml.

0.75ml.

1ml.

Grant still had his eyes open, wincing slightly as Kelly pushed a little too hard on the syringe. She could see the

91

needle-point beneath his flesh as she pressed on the plunger again.

1.5ml.

2ml.

2.5ml.

She was trying to stop herself from shaking, worried that too much movement would tear the vein open. Grant sucked in a painful breath and Kelly apologised but kept the pressure on the plunger, watching as more of the liquid was transferred to the man's body.

3ml.

3.5ml.

4ml.

Grant closed his eyes, his chest beginning to heave as his respiration became more laboured. Kelly looked at his face then at the needle embedded in his arm and finally at the markers on the slim receptacle itself.

4.5ml.

5ml.

5.5ml.

Kelly knew that the atropine would not take long to work and, with the increased dosage she was administering, that time should be curtailed further.

6ml.

She hesitated. Grant had closed his eyes tightly now. His mouth also was clamped shut, his lips bloodless.

Kelly, the needle still clutched in her hand, the point buried in Grant's vein, looked at the man. He was visibly turning pale. Had she given him enough?

'Mr Grant,' she said.

He didn't answer.

'Mr Grant.'

A weary grunt was the only reply she received this time.

Kelly pushed harder on the plunger.

6.5ml.

7ml.

Perspiration formed in salty droplets on his face, some running together to trickle in rivulets across his flesh. On his arms too there was moisture, glistening like beads. The skin around the needle was beginning to turn a dark crimson, the blue veins pulsing more strongly.

7.5ml.

8ml.

Grant moaned, his mouth dropping open. Thick sputum oozed over his lips and onto the sheet beneath. His tongue lolled uselessly from one corner and he grunted again, coughed. Particles of spittle flew into the air and, as he moved slightly, the needle came free.

Cursing, Kelly pushed it back into the vein, ignoring the single tiny droplet of blood which had welled up through the first miniscule hole. She looked at his face which was now grey, streaked with perspiration. She knew she was taking a chance but this had to work.

9ml.

9.5ml.

10ml.

Kelly withdrew the needle and stepped back, dropping the syringe into her pocket once more. She switched on the tape recorder and moved the microphone as close as she dared to Grant. His body began to undergo almost imperceptible movements, tiny muscle contractions which made it look as if he were being pumped full of mild electrical current.

'Mr Grant,' she said. 'Can you hear me?'

He muttered something which she couldn't hear so she took a step closer, bringing the microphone nearer to his mouth.

'Mr Grant.'

His eyes were shut, the lids sealed as tightly as if they'd been stitched.

'Can you hear what I'm saying?'

Grant suddenly grabbed her wrist in a grip which threatened to snap the bones.

Simultaneously, his eyes shot open like shutters and she found herself looking down into two glazed, rheumy orbs which seemed to be staring right through her.

Kelly suppressed a scream and tried to pull away from the vice-like grip but it was useless.

'Help me,' murmured Grant, refusing to release Kelly. 'Oh God they're everywhere.'

He suddenly let her go, his hands clutching at his face.

'What can you see?' she demanded.

Grant suddenly sat up, his face contorted in a mask of rage

and hatred.

'Fucking bastard,' he snarled, his blank eyes turning to face her. 'You stinking cunt.' His lips slid back in a vulpine grin and more saliva dribbled down his chin. 'She betrayed me. She thought I didn't know. *She* thought she could fool *me*.'

Kelly edged away slightly.

'Who thought she could fool you?' asked the investigator, moving to the end of the bed.

'*Her*. My wife,' Grant rasped. 'Fucking whore. She made me think the child was mine when it was *his* all along.'

'Is that why you wanted to kill her?' asked Kelly, moving towards the restraining straps, waiting for her chance to slip them over Grant's ankles although she didn't give much for her chances.

And what if she failed ...?

'Yes, I wanted to kill her. Her and the child. *His* fucking child,' Grant raved.

But, his anger seemed to subside with alarming speed and he was cowering once more from some unseen menace. Shielding his face and eyes with shaking hands.

'Get them off me,' he shrieked.

'What can you see?' demanded Kelly, deciding that it was time to fasten the straps.

'Spiders,' he told her. 'Thousands of them. All over me. Oh God, no.'

Kelly managed to fasten the two ankle straps, securing Grant to the bed, at least for the time being. The leather looked thick and stout. She hoped that it would hold.

Maurice Grant wondered why she could not see the eight-legged horrors seething over the floor of the room and onto the bed. Over his body, inside his clothes. He could feel their hairy legs on his flesh as they crawled onto his stomach, up his trouser legs, across his chest, up his neck to his face. And there they tried to force their way into his mouth. He felt one on his tongue and he plunged two fingers into his mouth to pull the creature out. The probing digits touched the back of his throat and he heaved violently.

Above him, the spiders were coming through the ceiling. They were emerging from the stone-work itself and they were getting bigger. One the size of his fist dropped from the ceiling on to his face, its thick legs probing at his eyes and nose. One of the smaller creatures scuttled up his left nostril, trying to pull the swollen bulk of its abdomen inside the orifice.

From the wall beside him, a spider the size of a football emerged and clamped itself on his arm, pinning it to the bed. Another did the same with his right arm.

Kelly watched mesmerised as Grant wriggled beneath the imaginary host of arachnids but she was not too engrossed to by-pass the opportunity to secure his wrists to the bed.

'They're inside my head,' screamed Grant as he felt more and more of the spiders dragging themselves up his nostrils, into his ears.

'I know where they're coming from,' he screeched. '*She* sent them.'

'Your wife?' asked Kelly, watching as Grant continued to squirm.

'Fucking cunt. Fucking slut.'

His fear had been replaced once more by rage.

'I'm glad I killed her,' he roared. 'She deserved to die.'

The veins on his forehead bulged angrily as he strained against the straps. 'I don't care if anyone saw me. I had no choice. I saw them together', he said, his body jerking wildly. 'I saw her with him. He stuck it between her legs, in her mouth. AND SHE FUCKING WANTED IT. I don't want to see it anymore.'

'Can you see it now?' Kelly asked.

'Yes.'

'What can you see? Tell me exactly.'

Grant was using all his strength to tug himself free and Kelly noticed with horror that one of the wrist straps was beginning to creak under the pressure.

'I can see her on the floor of the bedroom. *Our* bedroom. She's naked and so is he,' Grant snarled.

'Who is *he*?' Kelly wanted to know.

'She's sucking his cock. He's using his tongue on her.'

The right hand strap creaked ominously as Grant continued to thrash around.

'I don't want to see it anymore. Never again.'

Kelly wondered if she should get help. Grant was hallucinating madly it appeared but he was largely coherent.

And, at last, she knew why he had wanted to kill his wife and son.

'She's rolled over on to her stomach and he's putting his cock into her. The filthy fucking whore. She wants him.'

'Who is he?' Kelly demanded.

'My brother,' roared Grant and, with that, made one last monumental effort to break free.

The right hand strap split first, then came free.

'I don't want to see it. I DON'T WANT TO SEE IT,' Grant bellowed, tugging himself out of the ankle restraints and the other wrist strap. He staggered to his feet, his chest expanding until it threatened to rip his shirt. 'I don't want to see it,' he said again and lurched towards the table in the middle of the room. There, his searching hands found the greasy fork.

'I NEVER WANT TO SEE IT AGAIN,' he shrieked and raised the pronged implement.

Kelly knew that she could never reach the door. Grant blocked her way but, as she looked at him anxiously, she saw that his anger was not directed at her.

'I won't watch,' he said, quietly, studying the fork which he held only inches from his face.

With quivering hand, he pushed the fork through his lower lid and into his eye. With infinite slowness he moved it in a digging action, the prongs gouging muscle and flesh as Grant shoved it further until the eye itself began to thrust forward. The prongs raked his skull as he prised the bursting orb from its socket. Blood gushed down his cheek, mingling with the vitreous liquid as the eye itself punctured. It did not come free but hung, suspended by the shredded remains of the optic nerve.

Mind numbing pain enveloped him but he managed to remain upright, guiding the fork towards his other eye.

Kelly gagged as she saw the prongs burrow through the upper lid this time, the curve of the fork enabling Grant to reach the retina itself. With a final despairing scream he managed to scoop the bloodied eye free of his skull.

There was a muffled, liquid plop as the orb left the socket, a vile sucking sound which was soon drowned out by Grant's agonised shriek.

The eye itself dropped to the floor and lay there intact

until Grant dropped to his knees, squashing it beneath him as if it had been an oversized grape.

Kelly found herself transfixed by those oozing sockets from which crimson was pumping in thick spurts, dribbling into the man's open mouth.

She finally tore her gaze away and bolted for the door, wrenching it open and dashing out into the corridor.

The room was soundproofed. Until Kelly opened the door, the building had remained quiet but now the agonised shrieks of the blinded Grant echoed along every inch of the building. So great was the dose of atropine he'd received, so powerful the boost to his nervous system, Grant was even denied the merciful oblivion of unconsciousness. He merely slumped to the floor of the room moaning, the remains of one eye still dangling uselessly by a strand of nerve.

Inside the room, the tape recorder obediently captured the sounds of agony. Preserving them forever.

16

'How much did you say you gave him?' Dr Vernon asked Kelly, reaching for the syringe.

'10ml, perhaps a little more,' she said, quietly.

Vernon nodded and held the hypodermic between his fingers for a moment before setting it down on the table again. He laid it beside the bloodstained fork, allowing his gaze to ponder on the implement for a few seconds. He exhaled and looked around the room. The floor was spattered with blood, droplets of it had splashed a wide area, puddling into bigger pools in one or two places. There was a purplish smudge close to his foot where the eye had been squashed and Vernon moved to one side.

The remains of the restraining straps lay on or near the bed and, he noticed that there were even a few speckles of crimson on the sheets.

Maurice Grant had been removed about fifteen minutes

earlier.

Now Vernon stood amidst the carnage, flanked by Kelly and John Fraser.

Fraser looked distinctly queasy and could not seem to tear his gaze from the blood-stained fork on the table. The mere thought of what it had been used for made him feel sick.

'Is he going to die?' asked Kelly, anxiously.

'The ambulancemen didn't seem to know one way or the other,' Vernon told her. 'Once the effects of the atropine wear off he'll go into shock. After that ...' He allowed the sentence to trail off.

'So, first he nearly kills me,' said Fraser. 'Now he more or less succeeds in killing himself. Surely this is enough for you, doctor?'

'What do you mean?' Vernon wanted to know.

'There will have to be a full-scale enquiry into what happened today. There's no way that you can continue with this research now.'

'As Director of the Institute *I* will decide if an enquiry is necessary or not,' Vernon told him.

'Do you seriously think that the outside authorities are going to let something like this drop without investigating it?'

'I couldn't give a damn about the outside authorities,' snapped Vernon. 'What goes on inside these walls is *my* concern.'

'And the fact that a man could have died today doesn't bother you?' Fraser said, challengingly.

'Grant knew that he might be taking risks when he agreed to participate in the experiments.'

'Acceptable risks, yes, but ...'

Vernon cut him short.

'Risks,' he said, forcefully.

Fraser now turned his attention to Kelly.

'With all due respect, Kelly, you are responsible for this,' he said.

'I realize that,' she said. Then, to Vernon:

'I'm prepared to resign.'

'No,' he said, without hesitation. 'That wouldn't solve anything.'

Kelly could not conceal the look of surprise which flickered across her face.

'She broke every rule of this bloody Institution,' growled Fraser. 'She nearly killed a man as well and you ...'

It was Kelly's turn to interrupt.

'Don't talk about me as if I'm not here,' she snarled. 'I know I was in the wrong. God knows I wish I could repair the damage I've done.'

'The research had to be taken to its logical conclusion,' Vernon said, supportively.

'That conclusion presumably being the death of the subject,' said Fraser, sarcastically.

'There was no way of knowing exactly how the atropine would affect Mr Grant,' said Vernon, as if he were defending himself instead of Kelly. She looked on dumbfounded as he came to her rescue.

'A dose of 5ml is considered dangerous. We all know the effects of the drugs we use. Kelly should have known that injecting Grant with twice that amount would have serious side-effects.'

'Did Grant actually say anything of use while he was drugged?' Vernon wanted to know.

'Is that important now?' Fraser said, angrily.

Vernon turned on him, his grey eyes blazing.

'Yes, it is important. The only thing that matters is that this project is successful. If certain sacrifices have to be made then that's unfortunate but unavoidable.'

'You're insane,' said Fraser, his tone a little more controlled now. 'This isn't research to you anymore, it's an obsession. How many more people are going to be injured or killed before you're satisfied? Before you have the answers you want?'

'That's enough, Fraser,' Vernon warned him.

'Do you honestly think that any of this is going to help *you*?' the investigator said, cryptically.

Kelly looked at him, wondering what he meant.

'Fraser.' There was more than a hint of anger in Vernon's voice.

'What *are* you looking for, doctor?' the investigator demanded. 'Or more importantly, why are you looking?'

'This isn't the time or the place to ...'

'Perhaps if we knew about whatever it is you've managed to hide for so long then ...'

Fraser's words were choked back as Vernon lunged forward and grabbed him by the lapels. The older man's face was flushed and there was a thin film of perspiration on his forehead. He fixed the investigator in his steely grey stare and held him there. Kelly looked on with concern and interest, wondering whether or not she should intervene.

'This time, Fraser, you've gone too far,' hissed the doctor. He pushed the investigator away, watching as he fell against the table. 'Now get out of here. Out of this room. Out of this Institute. You're finished here.'

Fraser dragged himself upright and steadied himself against the table.

'Perhaps the police might be interested in what happened here today,' he said, threateningly.

'The police will be informed, when I think it's necessary,' Vernon told him. 'Now, get out.'

Fraser looked at Vernon a moment longer, then at Kelly.

'I'm sorry, Kelly,' he said apologetically and made for the door. They both heard his footsteps echo away down the corridor.

Vernon pulled a handkerchief from his trouser pocket and wiped his face. He pulled a chair out from beneath the table and sat down, ignoring the bloodied fork which lay before him. Kelly watched as he popped a menthol sweet into his mouth and sucked it. His face was still tinged red with anger and he shuffled his fingers impatiently before him.

Kelly licked her lips, finding them dry, like her mouth. She wanted to ask Vernon what Fraser had meant, just as she had when he'd made the other cryptic remark two days before.

'... whatever it is you've managed to hide for so long.' Fraser's words stood out clearly in her mind. Why had Vernon reacted so angrily?

'Dr Vernon, Grant said that he'd killed his wife. It was like a confession,' she said. 'It's all on the tape, every word.'

Vernon didn't speak.

'What could he have meant?' she persisted.

'It must have been the effects of the drug, you said he was hallucinating.'

'Yes, but no one mentioned to him that a neighbour had identified a man like him the day his wife and son were butchered. Why should he say that?'

'Look, Kelly, I think we have enough to worry about with what happened today,' Vernon said, evasively. 'And it would be best if you left here. I'll call you in a fortnight or so, the research can't continue until after the enquiry anyway.'

'Can the authorities close the Institute?' she wanted to know.

Vernon shook his head.

'No. And don't worry, your job will still be here when you come back.'

'Why didn't you accept my resignation?' she asked.

'Because what you did was based on sound theory. It was a chance which had to be taken eventually.'

Kelly nodded although it was not an explanation which wholly satisfied her. Vernon appeared to have more than a scientific interest in the outcome of the research. The question was, why?

Finally, she slipped off her lab coat and decided it was time to leave. She and Vernon exchanged brief farewells and he repeated his promise to contact her in two weeks.

Vernon waited until she had left the room then he walked slowly around it, his eyes drawn occasionally to the spots and splashes of congealing blood, now slowly turning rusty as it solidified. There was a slight smell of copper in the air. He eventually reached the tape recorder. He pressed the re-wind button and watched as the twin spools spun in reverse. When the process was completed he took the full one and dropped it into his pocket, deciding to listen to it in the privacy of his office. As he made his way out of the room, two cleaners were entering armed with mops and dusters. They set about removing all traces of the horrors which had occurred in there.

Vernon crunched his cough sweet up and replaced it with another as he walked up the stairs towards his office. His secretary had gone home an hour earlier so he had the place to himself.

Nonetheless, he locked his office door before settling down to listen to the tape.

Twice he played it through, his face impassive, even when Maurice Grant's shrieks of agony began to erupt from the speaker. Half-way through the third play Vernon switched it off. He sat for what seemed like an eternity, his chair facing

101

the window, then he swung round and reached for the phone. He hurriedly dialled the number he wanted and tapped agitatedly on the desk top with his stubby fingers as he waited for the receiver to be picked up. He heard the click as it finally was.

'The Metapsychic Centre?' he asked. 'This is Dr Stephen Vernon. I want to speak to Alain Joubert. Tell him it's important.'

10.06 p.m.

Kelly folded the last of her clothes and laid the skirt gently on top of the other things. The only light in the bedroom came from a bedside lamp which cast a warm golden glow over the room. Kelly decided that she had packed enough clothes and lifted the case from the bed onto the floor. She felt stiff all over, her neck and shoulders in particular ached. She resolved to take a shower and have an early night.

She intended leaving early in the morning.

The day had been an exhausting one both mentally and physically and she felt the need to relax more than she usually did upon returning home in the evenings. She'd only half-eaten her dinner, washing it down with two or three Martinis. The effect of the drink was beginning to make her feel pleasantly drowsy. She unbuttoned her blouse, laying it over a chair before slipping out of her jeans and folding them carefully. Standing before the full length mirror on the wardrobe she unhooked her bra, her breasts remaining taut even when the garment was removed. Kelly skimmed off her panties and tossed them to one side, glancing at herself in the mirror. The reflection which stared back at her was a pleasing one.

Despite the fact that she was only five feet two inches tall, her slender frame gave her an appearance of striking elegance which was normally reserved for taller women. She had small but plump breasts, her lower body tapering in to form a tiny waist and smooth lean hips. Her legs were slim, usually appearing longer when she wore the high heels she favoured.

Kelly walked through into the bathroom and turned on the shower, stepping beneath its cleansing jets when it was at a suitable temperature. She stood motionless, allowing the water to run over her face, washing away what little make-up she used. She began soaping herself.

As she stood beneath the spray she allowed her mind to back-track to the events of earlier in the day. To Vernon.

Why was he protecting her? It didn't make sense. Unless, as Fraser had intimated, he *did* have something to hide. Vernon obviously saw Kelly as a useful tool.

As she closed her eyes, the vision of Maurice Grant, his eyes ripped from the sockets, flashed before her and she jerked her eyes open again.

She thought of his confession.

Had it been the drugs which had caused his outburst, she wondered? Instinct told her that there was more to it than that. And yet, how could he have killed his wife and son? She and three other people had seen him strapped down at the time the killings supposedly took place.

She stood beneath the shower a moment longer then flicked it off, dried herself and padded back into the bedroom. She sat on the edge of the bed and reached for the phone.

It was a recorded message, which suited her because she didn't feel much like talking. She scribbled down a few details as the metallic voice droned on then, finally, she replaced the receiver, glancing down at what she had written.

She would catch the 9.30 flight to Paris in the morning.

17

Paris

The restaurant in the Place de Wagram was crowded, more so than usual because many had sought shelter inside from the rain which was pelting down. Waiters threaded their way through the maze of tables balancing trays and plates precariously on their arms. A wine glass was dropped and shattered loudly on the wooden floor.

Lasalle spun round in his seat, startled by the sound. He

saw a waiter picking up the pieces of broken glass while a customer complained loudly.

'Did you hear me?'

The voice brought Lasalle back to his senses.

'What did you say?' he asked, blankly, turning back to face Joubert who was chewing hungrily on a piece of meat.

'I said, I don't like the idea of her working with us,' Joubert repeated.

'Come now, Alain, when these experiments first began it was agreed that there would be co-operation between the two Institutes. I don't understand your objections.'

'The experiments carried out in England have not been as successful as ours,' Joubert complained.

'How do you know that?' Lasalle asked, sipping at his wine.

His companion paused for a moment, swallowing the piece of food he'd been chewing.

'Because we'd have heard more,' he said, quickly.

Lasalle looked up and saw a familiar figure making her way back towards the table. He tapped Joubert's arm and motioned for him to be quiet but the other Frenchman merely muttered something under his breath.

Kelly sat down and smiled across the table at Lasalle. Joubert did not look up from his meal. She picked up her knife and fork and set about her salad once more.

She had arrived in Paris over three hours earlier and, after booking into a hotel, she had taken a taxi to the Metapsychic Centre. Once there she had introduced herself to the Director and asked if she could see Lasalle. The two investigators had been friends for some time and he was happy to allow her to work with him.

The reaction of Joubert could not have been more different. Upon hearing that Kelly was to assist them in their experiments he had barely been able to restrain his anger, managing only by a monumental effort of will to disguise his open dislike of her presence.

She had explained, briefly, what had happened with Maurice Grant and why she had been forced to come to France. Joubert had been unimpressed and, when she had asked to look at the notes which the two men had compiled, he had been openly hostile, guarding the files jealously. She wondered why he should have taken such a dislike to her.

'If you'd let me know you were coming,' said Lasalle, 'I could have made up the bed in my spare room. It would have saved you paying for a hotel.'

'I'm fine where I am thankyou,' Kelly assured him, smiling.

'When were you thinking of going back?' Joubert asked without looking up.

'Not for a while yet,' Kelly told him.

'What exactly do you think you can learn here?' Joubert continued, still not paying her the courtesy of a glance.

'It's not so much a case of learning,' Kelly began. 'I ...'

He cut her short, his dark eyes finally pinning her in a malevolent stare.

'Then what do you want here?' he hissed.

Kelly met his stare, her own anger now boiling up. Who the hell did Joubert think he was anyway? she thought.

'I told you why I came here,' she said. 'I couldn't carry on working at the Institute in England, not while the enquiry was being conducted. I thought I might be of some help to you.'

'Don't you think we're capable then?' he said, challengingly.

'Are you this rude to everyone or have *I* been singled out for that honour?' she said, angrily.

Joubert stopped eating and looked at her warily.

'Can't we all just finish our food in peace?' said Lasalle, looking at his two companions.

Joubert put down his knife and fork and wiped his mouth with a napkin.

'I've finished anyway,' he said. 'It's about time I went back to the Centre. There's a lot to do this afternoon.' He balled up his napkin and dropped it on to the table, getting to his feet. He looked down at Lasalle. 'I trust I'll see you later?'

Lasalle nodded.

'And no doubt you too, Miss Hunt,' Joubert added, scornfully. With that he pushed past some people who were waiting for a table and headed for the door. Lasalle watched him go.

'I must apologise for my colleague,' he said.

'I'm sorry if I've caused any trouble between the two of

105

you,' said Kelly.

'Joubert is a good man but, sometimes, he lets our work get to him.'

'I noticed,' Kelly told him, spearing a piece of tomato with her fork. 'Speaking of work, have you made much progress?'

'There is so much to discover,' said Lasalle. 'The unconscious mind is a vast area.' He took a sip of his wine. 'We did have some success three or four days ago. A subject named Décard. Whilst in a trance he was able to see the future.'

'Precognition?' she said, excitedly.

'But only while hypnotised. When he was brought out of the trance he could remember nothing of what he had seen.' The Frenchman paused. 'It was all rather unfortunate. He foretold the death of his own daughter.'

Kelly sat bolt upright, as if she had just been nudged with a cattle prod.

'I wasn't told about this,' she said.

Lasalle frowned.

'Joubert was supposed to have relayed the information to you.'

'I heard nothing,' Kelly assured him.

The Frenchman looked puzzled and a heavy silence descended momentarily.

Kelly wondered if she should mention the murder of Maurice Grant's family but she decided against it, content to let the thoughts and ideas tumble over inside her head.

'What I said about you staying with me,' Lasalle said. 'I hope you weren't offended by it.'

Kelly smiled.

'Of course not,' she said.

'I didn't mean anything by it but, since Madelaine died, the house has seemed ... bigger than it used to.' He smiled humourlessly.

'I understand,' Kelly told him. 'How are you managing on your own?'

'I get by,' he said, reaching inside his jacket for the bottle of tranquilizers. 'With a little help.' He held one of the capsules before him, swallowing it with some water.

Kelly studied his face, noticing how much he had changed since the last time she had seen him. His dark hair was streaked with patches of grey, particularly around his temples. Deep lines cut swathes across his forehead and around his eyes and his cheeks appeared bloodless. He had lost weight too she suspected. But, for all that his eyes retained a glint of passion and energy which seemed to have deserted the rest of his body.

'Probably if we had had children then it wouldn't have been so bad,' he said. 'As it is, there is no one else left for me.' He gazed at his wine glass for a moment longer then seemed to shake off the cloak of melancholy. A smile spread across his face. 'Enough of this,' he said. 'How are you, Kelly? Have you any plans to marry?'

She looked at him aghast.

'Definitely not,' she said.

'You mean there is no man waiting to sweep you off your feet?' He chuckled.

'If there is he's keeping himself well hidden,' Kelly replied.

Lasalle laughed, an infectious sound which cut through the babble in the restaurant and caused a couple of heads to turn.

Her tone changed slightly.

'Michel, about this man who had the precognitive vision. Décard you say his name was?'

Lasalle nodded.

'What exactly did he see?'

The Frenchman told her.

'And was Joubert present when this happened?' Kelly asked.

'Yes, he seemed quite excited by it all.'

Kelly brushed a hand through her hair, stroking the back of it with her palm. Why hadn't Joubert told her about the incident? Why the secrecy? When the two Institutes were supposed to be working together it seemed only natural that information as important as that should be available.

She wondered what else the Frenchman had neglected to tell her.

Lasalle looked at his watch.

'I suppose we should be getting back,' he said.

Kelly got to her feet and the two of them made their way towards the exit. Outside it was still raining, the banks of dark cloud overhead showing no promise of respite.

As they ran towards Lasalle's car, Kelly wondered if

Joubert's attitude might change as the afternoon wore on.

Somehow she doubted it.

18

Using a small wooden spatula Lasalle gently applied the sticky conductant to three places on Joubert's face. One at each temple and another just above the bridge of his nose.

Kelly attached the electrodes carefully and Joubert himself re-adjusted them, lifting his head slightly as Lasalle pressed the last two against the back of his head.

That done, Joubert lay back on the couch, hands clasped across his chest. The Frenchman lay motionless, his eyes peering at some point on the ceiling. Lasalle reached for his hand. He fumbled along the wrist and located the pulse which he took and noted on a clipboard. Then, like a doctor examining a patient, he took a penlight from his pocket and shone it in his companion's eyes, checking the pupillary reactions.

'Ready?' he asked.

Joubert nodded gently.

Lasalle turned to Kelly who flicked a switch on the EEG and, immediately, the five tracers began to move back and forth gently across the paper.

The Frenchman reached into his pocket and pulled out the pocket watch. He dangled it before Joubert, the golden time-piece twisting round slowly.

'Now, keep your eyes on the watch,' he said, seeing that his colleague's gaze had drifted to the spinning object. Lasalle began rolling the chain between his thumb and index finger.

'You can hear only my voice,' he said. Then, to Kelly:

'Turn off the lights will you?'

She left the EEG and scuttled across to the light switch, flicking it off. The room was immersed in darkness, lit only by a spot-lamp near the foot of the couch. The single beam

108

occasionally glinted on the watch making it look as if it were glowing.

'You can see nothing but the watch,' said Lasalle. 'You can hear nothing but my voice. Do you understand?'

'Yes,' said Joubert, throatily.

'I am going to count to five and, as I do, you will become increasingly more tired. Do you understand?'

'Yes.'

'By the time I reach five you will be asleep but you will still be able to hear me. Do you understand?'

'Yes.'

Kelly moved slowly and quietly back towards the EEG, glancing down at the read-out. The lines made by the tracers were still relatively level. None showed too much movement. Just a gentle sweep back and forth.

Lasalle began counting.

He saw his companion's eyelids begin to droop but he kept spinning the watch even after Joubert had finally closed his eyes.

Kelly looked on with interest.

'You are now in a deep sleep,' said Lasalle. 'But, you are able to hear everything I say. Do you understand?'

'Yes.'

'What is your name?'

'Alain Joubert.'

'How old are you?'

'Thirty-six.'

Kelly glanced at the EEG read-out once again, noticing that the five tracers had begun to slow their movements until they were practically running in straight lines, only the occasional movement interrupting their unerring course.

'What is *my* name?' Lasalle asked.

Joubert told him.

'Can you tell me if there is anyone else present in the room?'

'A woman. I can see her.'

Lasalle frowned and inspected his colleague's eyelids more closely. They were firmly shut. He reached back to the trolley behind him and picked up a stack of cards, each bearing a word.

'Tell me what this word is,' he said, running his eyes over

109

the card marked DOG.

Joubert told him.

'And this one?'

'Cat.'

'Again.'

'Pig.'

Kelly noticed some slight movement from the fifth of the tracers.

Lasalle went through another ten cards and each time Joubert was correct.

'I feel cold,' Joubert said, unasked. Indeed, his body was quivering slightly and, when Lasalle gripped his hand the flesh was ice cold.

The movement from the fifth tracer became more pronounced. The other four, however, did not deviate from their almost arrow-straight course. Kelly swallowed hard. There was something distinctly familiar about this type of read-out. The vision of Maurice Grant flashed into her mind as the fifth tracer began to trace a jerky, erratic path on the paper. Whilst in a drugged, subdued state, it had been the same area of Grant's brain which had shown activity. Now it was happening with Joubert.

'I can see ...' Joubert words trailed away.

'What can you see?' Lasalle asked him, urgently.

'A room. Like this one but there is a woman working in it. She's sitting at a typewriter with her back to me,' Joubert said. 'She doesn't know I'm behind her, she didn't hear me open the door.'

Kelly saw that the fifth tracer was now hurtling back and forth with such speed it threatened to carve a hole in the paper.

'Who is this woman?' Lasalle asked. 'Do you know her?'

'Yes, I've seen her many times before.'

'What is her name?'

'Danielle Bouchard.'

Lasalle swallowed hard.

'Describe her,' he snapped. 'Now.'

'She is in her thirties, long, curly hair. It's auburn, dyed I think. Her skin is dark, not negroid but coffee-coloured. She's wearing blue eye make-up, some lipstick.'

'Do you know her?' whispered Kelly to Lasalle.

The Frenchman nodded.

'She's part Algerian, a beautiful girl, she works in an office just down the corridor,' he said, quietly, one eye on Joubert who was now flexing his fingers spasmodically. In fact, his whole body was jerking involuntarily.

'What sort of response is showing on the EEG?' asked Lasalle.

'There's no activity in any part of the brain except for the area around the occipital lobe,' she told him. 'Exactly the same as the subject we had.' She paused, mesmerised by the rapid movements of the tracer.

Joubert spoke again.

'She is wearing jeans, a red top. There is a slight tear near the seam of the top, beneath her arm.'

'Is she still typing?' asked Lasalle.

'Yes, she hasn't noticed me yet.'

Lasalle chewed his bottom lip contemplatively.

'This doesn't prove anything,' he said to Kelly. 'Joubert could have seen this woman earlier today.'

Kelly looked once more at the EEG read-out. The fifth tracer continued its rapid movement.

'I'm walking towards her,' Joubert said. 'She has stopped typing now, she is taking the paper from the machine. She still has her back to me.' He was silent for a moment then the tone of his voice seemed to change, it became harsher, as if his mouth were full of phlegm. 'I want her.'

'Tell me what is happening,' Lasalle ordered.

'I grab her hair with one hand and put my other hand over her mouth to stop her screaming. She falls off the chair and I climb on top of her, I must hold her arms down. She is stunned by the fall, she has banged her head. I think she is dazed. I pull up her top to reach her breasts and I am squeezing them, making red marks on them.'

Kelly looked in awe at the fifth tracer which was moving so fast it was little more than a blur.

'I try to keep my hand over her mouth to stop her screaming but she seems to be recovering. I must stop her. I am putting my hands around her throat. It feels so good, my thumbs are on her windpipe, pressing harder. Her eyes are bulging. I am going to kill her. I want to kill her.'

Kelly looked at Lasalle then back at the EEG with its

wildly careering tracer.

'I WANT TO KILL HER,' bellowed Joubert.

There was a loud scream from outside the room, long and piercing. A moment's silence and it was followed by another.

'Bring him out of it,' snapped Kelly.

'Listen to me,' said Lasalle. 'When I count to one from five you will wake up. Do you understand?'

No answer.

From down the corridor there was the sound of a slamming door then another scream.

'Do you understand?' Lasalle said, loudly.

'Hurry,' Kelly urged.

Joubert did not respond.

'I can't bring him out of it,' Lasalle said, frantically.

He thought about shaking his colleague but he knew it would do no good. He swallowed hard and looked at Kelly who was already moving towards the door. 'See what's happening,' Lasalle told her.

Kelly hurried out into the corridor and saw that, about thirty yards further down, there were four or five people standing outside one of the doors. A tall man with blond hair was banging on it, twisting the handle impotently. He put his shoulder to it as he heard another scream from inside.

'Joubert, listen to me,' said Lasalle. 'I'm going to begin counting. Five ...'

'There's something happening,' Kelly told him.

'Four ...'

The tall blond man was taking a step back to gain more impetus as he tried to shoulder charge the door of the other room.

'Three ...'

Joubert stirred slightly.

'Two ...'

Down the corridor, the blond man gritted his teeth and prepared for one final assault on the locked door.

'One ...'

Joubert opened his eyes and blinked myopically.

He too looked round as he heard the shriek of splintering wood. The blond man crashed into the door, nearly ripping it from its hinges. It slammed back against the wall and he stumbled into the room, followed by the others who had

112

waited.

'What's happening?' asked Joubert, pulling the electrodes from his head.

Kelly walked back into the room, a look of concern on her face. She switched off the EEG and pulled the read-out clear.

'What's going on?' Joubert demanded, getting to his feet. He crossed to the door and looked out in time to see the blond man supporting a dusky skinned girl in jeans and a red top from a room further down the corridor. Even from where he stood, Joubert could see that her top was torn, part of one breast exposed. The girl was bleeding from a gash on her bottom lip and there were several angry red marks around her throat.

Lasalle and Kelly joined him in the corridor as the others approached them.

'What happened?' asked Lasalle.

'Danielle was attacked,' the blond man told him.

'Who by?' Lasalle wanted to know.

As he spoke, the dark-skinned girl lifted her head, brushing her auburn hair from her eyes. She looked at Joubert and screamed, one accusing finger pointing at him. With her other hand she touched her throat.

The girl babbled something in French which Kelly did not understand. She asked Lasalle to translate.

'She said that it was Joubert who attacked her,' the Frenchman said.

'That's impossible,' Joubert snorted, indignantly. 'Anyway, why would I do such a thing?' He looked at Danielle. 'She's hysterical.'

'Well,' said the blond man. 'Someone attacked her. She didn't make these marks herself.' He indicated the angry welts on the girl's neck. 'But I don't see how he got out. The door was locked from the inside.'

Lasalle and Kelly exchanged puzzled glances as the little procession moved past them, heading for the infirmary on the second floor. Danielle looked around, her eyes filled with fear as she gazed at Joubert.

'How could I have attached her?' he said, irritably, walking back into the room and sitting on the couch.

Kelly and Lasalle followed him.

'Can you remember anything of the last five or ten minutes?' Lasalle asked him.

Joubert shook his head, wiping his forehead with the back of his hand.

Kelly was the first to spot it.

'Joubert,' she said, quietly. 'Look at your nails.'

Beneath the finger nails of both hands were numerous tiny pieces of red cloth.

Exactly the same colour as the blouse worn by Danielle Bouchard. There were also several auburn hairs.

19

'Astral travel.'

Kelly's words echoed around the laboratory.

She looked at the pieces of cloth and hair which Joubert had scraped from beneath his fingernails and deposited in a Petri dish.

'You said you felt cold, just before it all began to happen,' she continued. 'That feeling of coldness is usually associated with Astral projection.'

'An Out of the Body Experience?' said Joubert, incredulously.

'Danielle Bouchard said she was attacked by you. I think she was right. You described her, you described how you tried to strangle her.' She held up the EEG read-out. 'There was a tremendous amount of activity in the occipital area of your brain at that time. That's exactly what happened with Maurice Grant.'

'But it isn't usual for the Astral body, once projected, to appear in tangible form,' Joubert countered. 'Danielle Bouchard doesn't just say she saw me, she says I touched her. Injured her.'

'Have you ever felt any feelings of anger or antagonism towards her?' Kelly asked.

'Not that I've been aware of,' Joubert told her.

'But, *subconsciously*, you may harbour some feelings such as those, for her. The hypnosis released those feelings, just as the drugs unlocked the violent side of Maurice Grant.'

'I don't understand what this has to do with the Astral body,' Lasalle interjected.

'The EEG read-outs seem to point to the fact that the area which controls the subconscious is housed in the occipital lobe,' Kelly said. 'The Astral body is controlled by the subconscious. It functions independently of the rest of the mind. That hidden area we've been looking for, this is it.' She jabbed the read-out with her index finger, indicating the fifth line.

'The subconscious mind controls the Astral body,' Joubert repeated, quietly.

'It looks that way,' Kelly said. 'You performed an act, while in the Astral state, which you could not have carried out while conscious.'

'Are you saying that the Astral body is the evil side of man?' said Lasalle. 'The violent, cruel part of us.'

'It's possible. And hypnosis or drugs can release that other identity,' she told him.

'The other identity knows nothing of right or wrong,' Joubert said. 'It's identical in appearance but not hampered by conscience, remorse or delusions of morality. A being which is completely free of the ethical restraints imposed upon it by society.'

Kelly caught the slight gleam in his eye.

'The Mr Hyde in all of us,' he said.

'What?' Lasalle asked, puzzled.

'Jekyll and Hyde. One side good, one side evil. The conscious mind is Jekyll, the unconscious is Hyde only it may be possible for that evil side to function independently of its host.'

'Think how this discovery will help the treatment of schizophrenia and other mental disorders,' Kelly said.

'But no one is to know of it yet,' Joubert snapped.

'Why?' Lasalle wanted to know. 'It is important, as Kelly says. People ...'

Joubert cut him short.

'It's too early to reveal our findings,' he rasped.

There was a long silence, finally broken by Lasalle.

'Kelly,' he began. 'How do we know that everyone, every man, woman and child, doesn't possess this inner force of evil?'

'I think it's safe to assume they do,' she said, cryptically. 'Only as far as we know, it can only be released by using drugs or hypnosis.'

'As far as we know,' he repeated, his words hanging ominously in the air.

Kelly looked at the dish full of hair and fabric and shuddered.

20

The clock on the wall above him struck one and Lasalle sat back, rubbing his eyes. He checked the time against his own watch and yawned.

He'd been hard at work since seven o'clock that evening, since returning from the Metapsychic Centre. Before him on the polished wood desk lay a 6000 word article which he had been slaving over for the past six hours. He'd stopped only once for a cup of coffee and a sandwich at about 9.30 but most of the sandwich lay uneaten on the plate beside the typewriter. He looked up and found himself caught in the gaze of a woman with flowing blonde hair whose crisp green eyes he seemed to drown in.

The photo of his wife stood in its familiar place on his desk at home. Each time he looked at it he felt the contradictory feelings which had plagued him ever since her death. To look at her brought back all the agony which he had suffered when she'd been taken from him so suddenly, but he also found comfort in those green eyes — as if a part of her lived on and remained with him. He reached for the photo and studied her finely-shaped features. He, himself had taken the picture three years earlier. It was all that remained of her. That and the memories.

He replaced the photo and shook his head, trying to dispel the drowsiness which was creeping over him like a blanket. He knew that he must go to bed soon but there was just one more thing left to do.

He picked up his pen, pulled the writing paper towards him and began writing:

To the Editor,

You will find enclosed an article which contains details of a discovery as important as it is fascinating. Having worked at the Metapsychic Centre in Paris for the past twelve years I have encountered many strange phenomena but nothing of this nature has ever presented itself to me until now.

I realize that the subject of Astral Travel/Projection etc. is one which has fascinated people for many years but never before have facts been so far reaching in their importance as in the case I have recounted in my article.

I hope that you will see fit to publish this article as I feel it has far-reaching implications for all of us.

Yours sincerely,

Lasalle signed it, re-read it then pushed it into the envelope with the article. He sealed it and left it on the desk, deciding to post it in the morning on his way to the centre.

He wandered into the kitchen and poured himself a glass of milk, standing at the sink while he drank it.

What they had discovered that afternoon was far too important to withhold. Besides, Lasalle felt unaccountably ill at ease. The incident with Danielle Bouchard had worried him. Even as he thought about it he felt the hairs on the back of his neck rise slightly.

Others had a right to know the truth.

Whether Joubert liked it or not.

117

New York

Blake picked up a copy of *Time* then decided to wander across to the paperbacks to see if there was anything to pass the time on the flight home. He ran his eyes swiftly over the magazine shelves once more before turning to the books.

He could have been forgiven for not noticing the slim volume.

The cover bore the title: *Journal of Parapsychology*.

Blake reached for it, one of the cover stories catching his eye: *Astral Projection: The Truth*. He flipped open the magazine, found the table of contents and traced the article he sought.

He read the first three paragraphs standing there then he paid for the magazine and left the airport newsstand.

The voice of the flight controller told him that he should go through to the departure gate. Blake hurried to the washroom.

He had flown many times before but he still felt the same twinge of nerves each time. Nerves? Who was he trying to kid? Flying scared him shitless, it was as simple as that. Already his stomach was beginning to turn gentle somersaults. He found that he was alone in the room. He crossed to a sink and filled it with cold water, laying his magazines on one side.

He splashed his face with water, wiping off the excess with his hands when he could find no towel. Blake straightened up and gazed at his reflection in the mirror. He looked pale, his eyes red-rimmed and as he glanced at his watch he saw that his hand was shaking slightly. He had ten minutes before his flight left. He scooped more water into his hands and onto his face, blinking as it stung his eyes. Blake peered into the mirror again.

The image of Mathias stared back at him.

Blake retreated a step, his eyes fixed on the vision in the mirror. The face of the psychic was immobile, only the eyes moved, those brilliant blue orbs pinning him in that hypnotic stare.

The writer tried to swallow but found that his throat was constricted. He raised both hands to cover his eyes.

He lowered them again slowly, peering into the mirror once more.

The image of Mathias was gone, only his own distraught face was reflected in the glass. Blake let out a relieved gasp and wiped the excess moisture from his face as he moved back to the sink. He peered down into the water.

This time it was his own reflection but the mouth was open in a silent scream, the eyes bulging wide in their sockets. The entire countenance was appallingly bloated and tinged blue.

'No,' rasped Blake and plunged his hands into the sink.

The apparition vanished and he stood there, immersed up to his elbows in water.

Indeed, the two men who walked into the washroom looked at him in bewilderment as he stood motionless, gazing into the sink, as if waiting for the screaming vision to re-appear.

'Hey, fella, are you OK?' one of the men asked, moving cautiously towards Blake.

He tapped the writer on the shoulder.

'I said ...'

Blake spun round suddenly, his expression blank. He looked like a man who had been woken from a nightmare.

'Are you feeling OK?' the man asked him again.

Blake closed his eyes tightly for a moment and nodded.

'Yes,' he said. 'I'm all right.' Then, fumbling for his dark glasses he put them on, snatched up his magazines and left the washroom.

'Probably freaked out,' said the first man.

'Yeah, he looks like a goddam pot-head.'

'And would you believe that?' the first man said, pointing at the mirror above the sink where Blake had been standing.

Five jagged cracks criss-crossed the glass.

22

Paris

It sounded as if someone were trying to pound a hole in the door.

Lasalle hurried from the kitchen, leaving his dinner on the table. The banging continued, loud and insistent. He turned the handle and opened it.

Joubert barged past him, his features set in an attitude of anger.

For a moment Lasalle was bewildered but he closed the door and followed his colleague through into the sitting room where he stood, splay-legged, in front of the open fire-place. He was gripping something in his right fist. A thin film of perspiration sheathed his face, the veins at his temples throbbing angrily.

'What's wrong?' asked Lasalle. 'It must be important for you to come barging into my house like this.'

'It *is* important,' rasped Joubert.

'Couldn't it have waited until tomorrow?' Lasalle said, a note of irritation in his own voice. He glanced at his watch. 'It is seven o'clock.'

'I know what time it is,' Joubert snapped.

'So what do you want?'

'I want to talk about *this*.' Joubert brandished the object in his right hand like a weapon for a moment before slamming it down on the coffee table nearby. 'What the hell do you mean by it?'

The copy of the *Journal of Parapsychology* lay before him on the table, bent open at the article written by Lasalle.

'What the hell did you hope to achieve by writing this ... garbage?' Joubert demanded.

'I felt that the discovery was too important to be hidden away,' Lasalle explained.

'It was my ...' He quickly qualified his words. 'It was *our* discovery. We agreed not to share it with anyone until the research was fully completed.'

'No we didn't. *You* decided that you wanted it kept secret,' Lasalle reminded him. 'I felt that other people had a right to know what happened.'

'So you took it upon yourself to write this article? And your ... friend. Does she know about it?'

'Kelly? No. She didn't know that I intended writing the article.' He paused for a moment. 'And even if she did, I don't see that any of this is your business. I am not answerable to you, Alain.'

'If news of this spreads we'll have the press swarming all over the Centre. Is that what you want?'

'Our discoveries on Astral projection are some of the most important ever made. Not just for our own profession but for others too. Many will benefit from our work. Hospitals, psychiatric institutions ...'

Joubert cut him short.

'And who will be credited with the discovery?' he asked, eyeing his colleague malevolently.

'Both of us of course. We ...'

Joubert interrupted again.

'No. Not both of us. *You*.' He pointed at Lasalle. 'You wrote the article.'

'But I mentioned your name, how we worked together.'

'That doesn't matter, it's you who will take the credit.' He picked up the magazine. 'What did they pay you for this?' he asked, scornfully.

'Ten thousand francs. Why?'

Joubert shook his head.

'They bought weeks of work for ten thousand francs!'

'The money isn't important,' said Lasalle.

'And the recognition?' Joubert wanted to know. 'Will you want that? Will you be able to cope with that?' His voice took on a sneering, superior tone. 'Still, you have your little tablets to help you.'

'Get out of here, Alain,' Lasalle snapped. 'Get out of my house.'

Joubert stuffed the magazine into his pocket and, with one last scornful glance at his colleague, he headed for the front door. Lasalle heard it slam behind him as he left.

Joubert brought the Fiat to a halt outside his house and switched off the engine. He closed his eyes for a moment, sitting in the shell-like confines of the vehicle, almost reluctant to leave it. He let out a long, almost painful breath and banged the steering wheel angrily. Damn Lasalle, he thought. He glanced down at the magazine which was on the passenger seat. It lay there as if taunting him and he snatched it up and pushed open the car door, locking it behind him.

As he reached the bottom of his path he heard the phone ringing inside his house. The Frenchman didn't hurry himself. He found his front door key and unlocked the door, glancing down at the phone on the hall table as he entered. It continued to ring but he hung up his jacket before finally lifting the receiver.

'Hello,' he said, wearily.

'Joubert? About time.'

He recognised the voice immediately.

'Dr Vernon, what do you want?' he asked.

'I want to know what's going on.'

'I don't know what you're talking about.'

'Let me read you something then.' There was a slight pause and Joubert heard the rustling of paper at the other end of the phone:

' "*The discovery of this form of Astral projection is the culmination of many weeks of work and many years of study*," ' Vernon quoted.

'Lasalle's article,' said Joubert.

'You were supposed to report any findings directly to me and now I read this plastered all over the magazine. What do you think you're playing at?'

'Don't lecture me, Vernon. That article was nothing to do with me. Perhaps you should ask the girl who works for you what she knows about it,' the Frenchman hissed.

'Who are you talking about?' Vernon wanted to know.

'Kelly Hunt. She's here. She's been with us for a week or more.'

There was a shocked silence, interrupted only by the occasional hiss of static.

'Vernon.'

'Yes.'

'I said she's been with us for more than a week,' Joubert hissed.

'I had no idea where she was,' Vernon said, irritably. 'I gave her some time off while the enquiry took place here. I didn't know she was going to work with you.'

'Well, she knows everything. You won't be able to hide anything from her any longer, Vernon.'

The Institute Director sighed.

'Anyway, that's your problem. I have my own with Lasalle,' Joubert continued.

'We cannot afford any more disclosures similar to the one in this magazine,' Vernon said, cryptically. 'As it is, this might alter our plans slightly.'

'You take care of the girl. I'll handle Lasalle. And I tell you this, Vernon, there will be no more disclosures. I will see to that.' He hung up and wiped his hands on his trousers. 'No more.'

There was a malevolent determination in his voice.

23

London

As the 747 touched down, Blake breathed his customary sigh of relief. The plane slowed down and he allowed himself a glance out of the window. Heathrow was covered by a film of drizzle which undulated and writhed like a living thing. The writer had tried to sleep on the flight back but had been constantly interrupted by the woman next to him who insisted that he should 'look at the wonderful view'. Blake had made the fatal error of telling her that he wrote books about the paranormal and had been regaled by her tales of tea-leaf reading and contacts with the spirit world. She had, she assured him, been blessed with this gift of second sight as compensation for the death of her smallest child five years earlier and the subsequent departure of her husband with another woman. Blake had nodded politely and smiled a lot during the verbal barrage, as was his habit. She had apologised for not having read any of his books but promised she would. Blake had smiled even more broadly at that point. He wondered if it was a general thing with writers, that anyone they spoke to immediately swore they would rush out and buy every book that writer had written.

Despite the distractions he had managed to snatch an hour or so of sleep but it had been troubled and he had woken, it seemed, every ten minutes.

At one point he had jerked bolt .upright in his seat, his body bathed in sweat, the last vestiges of a nightmare fading from his mind. The plane had crashed into the sea but he had survived the impact only to be drowned in the wreckage.

Now, as the plane came to a halt he got to his feet and stretched, trying to banish some of the stiffness from his joints. He checked his watch and noticed that he'd forgotten to adjust it according to the time difference. The clock on the plane showed 6.07 p.m.

After Blake had recovered his baggage he made his way through the terminal to the waiting taxis outside.

The drive took longer than he'd expected but, as the vehicle drew closer to his home he shook off some of his tiredness.

'Where do you want to get out?' the driver asked.

Blake directed him.

'Nice gaff,' said the driver, admiring Blake's house. 'Must have cost a fair old screw, eh?'

The man was obviously fishing for a tip and Blake didn't disappoint him. He gave him fifteen pounds and told him to keep the change.

'A reasonable screw,' he said as he walked away from the cab, suitcase in hand.

His house was set back from the road and was surrounded by a sufficient expanse of garden to protect him from the neighbours on either side. A privet hedge, which needed trimming, fronted the property and waist-high wooden fencing formed a perimeter elsewhere. There was also a garage built onto one side of the building. It housed a second-hand Jaguar XJS which he'd bought from a friend three years earlier.

As Blake made his way up the short path he fumbled for his front door key and inserted it in the lock. The door opened, and the familiar cloying scent of paint greeted him. He'd had the place redecorated prior to leaving for the States and the aroma hung thickly in the air. Blake flicked on the hall light and the porch light. He smiled to himself. When his porch light was on it always reminded him of running up the Standard at Buckingham Palace. It was his mark that *he* was now in residence.

He stepped over two weeks worth of mail which lay on the mat, closed the front door behind him then scooped it up. There were circulars, four or five letters (most of which he could identify by their postmarks) and a couple of bills. The writer dropped his suitcase in the hall deciding that he would unpack later. Right now all he wanted was to pour himself a drink and flop down in a chair.

He passed into the sitting room, pulling off his shirt as he did so. It was warm in the room despite the fact that it had been empty for a fortnight. He drew back the curtains and the dull twilight dragged itself into the room. Blake switched on the lamp which perched on top of the TV. He poured himself a large measure of brandy, topped it up with soda and took a hefty gulp, then he selected a record from his massive collection, dropped it on to the turntable and switched on the Hi-Fi. While Elton John warbled away in the background, Blake skimmed through his mail. The bills he noted and then stuck in a bulldog clip on the shelf near the fire-place, the circulars he balled up and tossed into the nearby bin. Then he opened his letters. There was one from his accountant, one from a group calling itself 'The Literary Co-operative' (a bunch of struggling local writers to whom Blake had spoken before) and what looked like a couple of fan letters. Blake was always happy to receive mail from the public and he read them both with delight.

He finished his drink, re-filled his glass and wandered into the kitchen. Peering out of the back window he saw several lumps of dark matter on his patio.

'Cat shit,' he muttered, irritably. 'I'll buy a cork for that bloody thing.' He was referring to the overfed Manx cat which belonged to the family next door. It had taken to using

125

his garden as a toilet whenever it could and, obviously, while he'd been away, had taken full advantage and dotted its calling cards about in abundance.

The writer opened his freezer and took out a pizza which he stuck under the grill. He didn't feel particularly hungry and, being basically lazy anyway, frozen food was heaven sent for his purposes. He left the pizza beneath the glow of the grill and returned to the sitting room.

It was large but comfortable and 'lived in' like the rest of the house. On the walls, framed carefully, were a number of film posters. *Taxi Driver* hung near the hall door whilst the wall nearest the kitchen bore an American print of *The Wild Bunch*. Beside it was *Halloween*.

But, pride of place went to a yellowed poster which hung over the fire-place. It was *Psycho*, and it bore Hitchcock's signature. Blake had been given it as a gift from a friend in the film business last time he had visited L.A.

The writer was not a man to overindulge in luxuries but, when he did, three things occupied him more than most. Films, books and music. His bookcase bulged, not with learned tomes and priceless first editions but with pulp creations. He read for entertainment, nothing more. Alongside the books, each one in its individual case, were video cassettes of his favourite films. Up to 300 in all.

His study, however, was a different matter.

Blake had been pleased, when he had bought the house, to discover that it not only possessed an attic but also a double cellar which ran beneath the entire building. He had converted the subterranean room into his study. Every day he retreated down the steps to work, free of the noises and distractions of everyday life.

Buried beneath the ground as it was, it reminded him of working in a giant coffin.

He kept the door locked at all times. The cellar was his private domain and his alone.

The smell of pizza began to waft from the kitchen. He ate it from the foil wrapper, saving himself any washing up. Then, still clutching his glass, he headed through the sitting room into the hall where he unlocked his case.

His notes were on top and Blake lifted them out carefully, hefting them before him. They had a satisfying heavy feel.

The fruits of so much research. The hard part was almost over. Another week or so of note-taking and preparation and he could get down to the serious business of writing.

As it was, there was one more thing he had to do.

Blake opened the cellar door, peering down into the blackness below. He smiled broadly to himself and flicked on the light.

'Welcome home,' he murmured and walked in.

Before he descended the steps he was careful to lock the cellar door behind him.

The silence greeted him like an old friend.

24

New York

Across the untarnished brilliance of the azure blue sky the only blemish was the thin vapour trail left by a solitary aircraft.

There wasn't a cloud in the sky. The sun, even so early in the morning, was a shimmering core of radiance throwing out its burning rays to blanket the city in a cocoon of heat.

The heavens did not weep for Rick Landers but there were others who did.

There were a handful of people at the graveside as the small coffin was lowered into the hole. Toni Landers herself stood immobile, eyes fixed on the wooden casket as it slowly disappeared from view. The only part of her which moved was her eyes and, from those red-rimmed, blood-shot orbs, tears pumped freely, coursing down her cheeks and occasionally dripping on to her black gloved hands. There was a photograph of Rick on the marble headstone but she could not bring herself to look at it. Every now and then, the rays of sunlight would glint on the marble and Toni would squeeze her eyes tightly together but, each time she did so, the vision of Rick flashed into her mind — memories of that day a week or more earlier when she had been forced to identify his remains. She had gazed on the mangled body of her child, stared at the face so badly pulped that the bottom jaw had been ground to splinters. The skull had been shattered in four or five places so that portions of the brain actually bulged through the rents. One eye had been almost forced from its socket. The head was almost severed.

It would have taken a magician not a mortician to restore some semblance of normality to a body so badly smashed.

Toni sucked in a breath, the memory still too painful for her. She shuffled uncomfortably where she stood and the two people on either side of her moved closer, fearing that she was going to faint. But the moment passed and she returned her attention to the gaping grave which had just swallowed up her dead child. The priest was speaking but Toni did not hear what he said. She had a handkerchief in her handbag yet she refused to wipe the tears away, allowing the salty droplets to soak her face and gloves.

Against the explosion of colours formed by countless wreaths and bouquets the dozen or so mourners looked curiously out of place in their sombre apparel.

Toni had deliberately kept the number of mourners to a minimum. She had phoned Rick's father in L.A. and told him but he had not condescended to put in an appearance. Amidst her grief, Toni had found room for a little hatred too. But now as she watched the ribbons which supported the coffin being pulled clear she felt a cold hand clutch her heart, as if the appalling finality of what she was witnessing had suddenly registered. Her son was gone forever and that thought brought fresh floods of tears from the seemingly inexhaustible reservoir of her pain.

This time her knees buckled slightly and her two companions moved to support her.

One of them, Maggie Straker, her co-star in her last film, slipped an arm around Toni's waist and held her upright. She could hear the other woman whimpering softly, repeating Rick's name over and over again as if it were a litany.

It was Maggie who first noticed that there was a newcomer amongst them.

The grave stood on a slight rise so his approach had been masked by the mourners on the far side of the grave.

Jonathan Mathias stood alone, a gigantic wreath of white roses held in his hand. He looked down at the final resting place of Rick Landers then across at Toni.

She saw him and abruptly stopped sobbing.

Mathias laid the floral tribute near the headstone, glancing at the photograph of Rick as he did so. He straightened up, listening as the priest finished what he was saying. He paused for a moment then asked those gathered to join him in reciting the Lord's Prayer.

Mathias stood by silently.

When the ritual was complete the mourners slowly moved away, back down the slight slope towards the black limousines which stood glinting in the sunlight like so many predatory insects. They too looked alien and intrusive amidst the green grass of the cemetery.

Mathias did not move, he stood at the head of the grave, gazing down into its depths at the small wooden casket. And it was towards him that Toni Landers now made her way, shaking loose of Maggie's supportive arm.

'I hope I'm not intruding,' the psychic said, softly.

'I'm glad you came,' Toni told him. She glanced down at the wreath he'd brought. 'Thank you.'

Maggie Straker approached cautiously.

'Toni, do you want me to wait I ...'

'It's OK, Maggie.'

The other woman nodded, smiled politely at Mathias then made her way down the slope behind the other mourners. Toni and the psychic stood alone by the grave.

'What will you do now?' he asked her. 'What are your plans?'

She sniffed.

'I'm going to spend some time in England with friends,' Toni informed him. 'I can't bear to be around here. Not now.' She wiped some of the moisture from her cheeks with a handkerchief which Mathias handed her. Toni turned the linen square over in her hands.

'You knew he was going to die didn't you?' she said, without looking at him.

'Yes,' Mathias told her.

'Why didn't you tell me?'

'It wouldn't have made any difference. There was nothing

you could have done about it.'

'Was there anything *you* could have done about it?'

'I wish there had been.'

He took her hand and, together, they made their way down the slope towards the waiting cars. But Toni hesitated momentarily, looking back over her shoulder towards the grave.

Towards her son.

It was over.

He was gone.

All that remained now were the memories.

She felt more tears streaming down her cheeks and Mathias put his arm around her shoulder, leading her away. She felt a strength and power in that arm and, as she looked up at him, a thought entered her mind. She looked back once more towards the grave of her son but this time there were no more tears.

A slight smile flickered briefly at the corners of her mouth.

Again she looked at Mathias.

25

Oxford

The smell of menthol was strong in the air.

Dr Vernon made loud sucking sounds as he devoured another of the cough sweets. The office smelt more like a pharmacy now.

Kelly crossed her legs, slipping one shoe off, dangling it by her toes as she waited for Vernon to finish reading the report.

It was her first day back at the Institute since she had returned from France barely thirty-six hours ago. In many ways she had been happy to return. The relationship between Joubert and Lasalle had deteriorated seriously since the appearance of the latter's article. The atmosphere had not been a pleasant one to work in and Kelly had decided that it was time to leave them to it. Armed with what she had learnt in France she was more confident about her own research, enjoying a newly-found enthusiasm which came only with a measure of success. However, she was worried about Lasalle. During the past week she had seen him wilt visibly beneath the open hostility displayed by Joubert. Loathe to intervene, Kelly had been a helpless spectator at their confrontations, each more vehement than before. She found it difficult to understand how so many years of friendship could, for Joubert, have been ruined so quickly and for what seemed a relatively minor aberration on Lasalle's part.

But, the question had plagued her for a while.

Kelly could still not understand why he had reacted so violently to Lasalle's article. People *did* have a right to know the facts, there was no disputing that. Joubert seemed not to agree. Despite her desire to return to England, Kelly had been somewhat reluctant about leaving Lasalle having seen his psychological deterioration over the past seven or eight days. The tranquilizers seemed to be of little help to him, despite the fact that he had upped the dosage from 45mg to 75mg a day. He was in a perpetual daze, a condition doubtless helped by the effect of the drugs. Kelly had felt something akin to pity for him. She hoped he wasn't becoming unbalanced again.

Nevertheless, she had decided to leave the Metapsychic Centre and had arrived home at around noon nearly two days ago.

Vernon's call had come within one hour of her return.

It was as if somehow he had been watching her, waiting for the right moment before calling.

She had not been surprised by the call itself, only by the urgency in the Institute Director's voice as he had asked her to return to work as soon as possible and to present him with a full report on what she had witnessed while working at the Metapsychic Centre.

Not until she had replaced the receiver did she begin to wonder how Vernon had known of her whereabouts.

She had certainly not mentioned her intentions when she left the Institute two weeks earlier.

131

Now, she sat impatiently, watching him as he leafed through her report. Kelly wondered if she should say something to him. Ask him how he knew where she had been? She bit her tongue for the time being.

There was probably a perfectly reasonable explanation, she told herself, although she wasn't altogether convinced.

She administered a swift mental rebuke. She was allowing her imagination to run away with her. She was becoming paranoid.

Wasn't she?

'Presumably you've noted everything which took place at the Metapsychic Centre during your time there?' Vernon asked, waving the report before him. 'There's nothing you could have left out or forgotten?'

'I wrote down everything which I felt was relevant to the investigation,' she told him, a slight trace of anger in her voice. She was becoming annoyed at his patronising tone.

Vernon shifted the menthol sweet to the other side of his mouth and tapped the report with his index finger. He was gazing into empty air.

'The area of the brain which controls the Astral body also controls emotions and desires,' he said, abstractedly.

'Yes,' Kelly said. 'But emotions and desires not present in the conscious mind. The Astral body appears to be the alter-ego and, from the material I collected on Grant and Joubert, it *can* become a tangible force.'

Vernon nodded.

'It sounded like a form of bi-location at first,' said Kelly. 'But I've never heard of a bi-locative presence becoming tangible before.'

'There was an American named Paul Twitchell,' Vernon explained. 'In the early sixties he began to teach what he called the Eckankar doctrine. A number of his pupils claimed to have seen him, in solid Astral form, while he was actually miles away.' Vernon sighed. 'But, Twitchell was one on his own. This ...' he picked up the report. 'This is more unusual.' He paused once again. 'It would explain many of the problems we have concerning the inner self, even some mental disorders.' He chewed his bottom lip contemplatively. 'Are you absolutely sure you've left nothing out?'

'I'm positive,' Kelly said in exasperation.

'Kelly, you don't need me to tell you how important this information is to our work, to …'

She cut him short, infuriated by his treatment of her.

'I'm not a fool, Doctor Vernon,' she said. 'Everything that I saw is noted down in my report, some of the conversations are verbatim.'

He nodded, placatingly, as if trying to calm her down.

'But there is one thing *I'd* like to know,' she told him.

Vernon eyed her warily.

'How did you know I was at the Metapsychic Centre?'

'I was in contact with them,' Vernon said. 'One of the investigators told me.'

Kelly wasn't altogether satisfied but she didn't press the matter. A heavy silence descended, finally broken by the woman.

'Have you seen anything of John Fraser since he left here?' she asked.

Vernon shrugged.

'He came back about a week ago to collect some things.' His tone abruptly changed, his eyes narrowing. 'Why do you ask?'

She detected the defensive note in his voice.

'I was just curious,' Kelly told him.

'Fraser has no more business here,' Vernon said, acidly.

Another long silence punctuated the conversation, the only sound being made by the Institute Director as he crunched up his cough sweet. Kelly eyed him suspiciously. Vernon was usually a calm, unflappable man but, in the last twenty minutes or so, he had revealed another side of his character — one which she had not seen before. His calmness had been replaced by a tetchy impatience, the unflappability giving away to an anxious and defensive demeanour. When he finally spoke again, however, some of the urgency had left his voice.

'Could what happened to Joubert be duplicated outside laboratory conditions?' he asked. 'I mean the Astral projection which he underwent.'

'I don't see why not,' Kelly told him. 'He was hypnotised, it was as simple as that. It should be perfectly possible to recreate the condition in another subject.'

Vernon nodded slowly, his grey eyes fixed on a point to

133

one side of Kelly. She did not move. He didn't speak.

Finally, she rose.

'If that's all, Doctor ...' She allowed the sentence to trail off.

'Yes,' he said. 'There's nothing else.'

'Could I have my report please?'

Vernon put his hand on the file.

'I'll keep it for now,' he said, his eyes fixing her in an uncompromising stare.

She hesitated a moment then nodded, turned and headed for the office door.

Vernon watched her leave.

He slumped back in his seat as she closed the door, his eyes falling to the report which lay before him. Long moments passed then he picked it up and dropped it into the black attaché case which stood beside his desk.

Before replacing it, he locked the case.

Kelly nodded politely to Dr Vernon's secretary as she walked out but she barely succeeded in masking her anger.

What the hell was Vernon playing at? she wondered. Since she'd returned he'd been like some kind of Grand Inquisitor, wanting to know every last detail of what happened in France. And why should he want to keep the report she'd made? He'd already perused it half a dozen times while she'd sat before him. That, apparently, was not sufficient for him.

She walked briskly down the corridor towards the stairs, her heels clicking loudly on the polished tile floor. Down one flight of steps to the first floor then along another corridor she walked until she came to Frank Anderson's office. Kelly tapped lightly on the door then walked in.

The room was empty.

She cursed silently and turned to leave but, before she did, she crossed to his desk and found a piece of paper and a pen. Kelly scrawled a quick note and left it where Anderson would see it.

A thought crossed her mind.

If Anderson could find it easily then so too could Vernon. The Institute Director had a habit of wandering, uninvited, into his investigators' offices and this was one note which she did not want him to read. She stood still for a moment, wondering what she should do.

'Need any help?'

The voice startled her but she spun round to see Anderson in the doorway. A smile of relief creased her lips.

'Frank. I was looking for you,' she said, balling up the note and stuffing it into the pocket of her shirt.

'I gathered that,' he said, pulling at one frayed shirt cuff. 'What can I do for you, Kelly?'

'You were a friend of John Fraser's weren't you?' she said, lowering her voice.

Anderson looked puzzled.

'Yes.'

'I need to speak to him.'

'I haven't seen him since he left here. He hasn't been in touch.'

Kelly frowned.

'But you know where he lives?' she asked.

Anderson nodded.

'And where he spends most of his time,' he said, smiling. 'The first is his home address, the second one is the pub he uses most often.'

Kelly turned to leave, scanning the piece of paper.

'Is something wrong?' Anderson called after her.

'That's what I want to find out,' Kelly told him and left him alone.

Anderson heard her footsteps echoing away and frowned. What did she want with John Fraser?

26

The hands of the dashboard clock glowed green in the gloom.

9.36 p.m.

Kelly parked the Mini in the gravelled area beside the pub and sat behind the wheel for a moment. High above her, rain clouds spat erratic droplets on to the land. It was warm inside the car — muggy and uncomfortable. Kelly felt her tee-shirt sticking to her back as she leant forward and she squirmed. It felt as if someone had wrapped her upper body in a damp towel. She clambered out of the car, relieved to find that there was a slight breeze. Rain spots momentarily stained her jeans as she walked towards the building, ignoring the dirty water from puddles which splashed her ankle boots.

'The Huntsman' was a large pub about a mile outside Oxford. It wasn't pretty and it wasn't quaint but it was functional. There was a cheap and, consequently, popular restaurant attached to it which did not, on this particular night, appear to be too busy, hence her ease of parking. Normally the area was jammed with vehicles. Not so tonight. Kelly tried to see Fraser's car but, in the darkness, identification was almost impossible.

She decided to try the lounge bar first.

It was crowded with people. In groups; in couples, on their own. One corner was occupied by seven or eight men who were playing cards around a large oblong table. Kelly scanned their faces, accidentally catching the eye of a ginger-haired youth in his late teens. He winked at her then directed his companion's attention to this slim newcomer. A chorus of subdued whistling and cheering rose from the men. Kelly turned away from them, searching the bustling bar for Fraser.

There was no sign of him.

She decided to try the Public bar.

If the noise inside the Lounge bar had been loud then in the Public bar it bordered on seismic proportions. A juke-box which was obviously set at full volume spewed forth an endless stream of the latest chart hits as if trying to drown out the clack of pool balls or the thud of darts as they hit the board. To add to the unholy cacophony, in one corner of the large room an electronic motor-racing game occasionally punctuated the din with the simulated explosion of a crashed car. Whilst, beside it, the ever hungry Pac-Man noisily devoured everything before it.

Kelly scanned the bar but could not see Fraser. She decided to sit and wait for him. There was a table near the door but it was occupied by a young couple who looked as though they were about to breach the Indecent Exposure act.

The youth had his hand buried beneath his girlfriend's miniscule skirt while she was rubbing his crotch with a speed which looked likely to cause friction burns.

The bar seemed to be populated almost exclusively by youngsters, most of whom were teenagers. She drew several admiring glances as she perched on a bar stool. When she'd finally managed to attract the barman's attention, she ordered a shandy and fumbled in her purse for some money. As he set her drink down she deliberately took her time counting out the change.

'Do you know John Fraser?' she asked him.

The barman nodded, wiping perspiration from his face.

'Yeah, why?'

'Has he been in here tonight?'

'Not yet, but he will.' The barman smiled.

'You sound very sure,' Kelly said.

'He hasn't missed a night since I've worked here and that's two years.' A call from the other end of the bar took the man away.

Kelly sipped at her drink and turned slightly on the stool so that she could see the door through which Fraser must enter.

'Hello, stranger.'

She spun round again to see that the voice came from a tall, black-haired youth who was leaning on the bar beside her. He was dressed in a grey sweater and maroon slacks. His companion, like himself, was in his early twenties, his hair cut short and shaped so that it appeared as if his head was flat. Spots and blackheads dotted his face liberally. He smiled, his gaze drawn to Kelly's breasts.

'Do I know you?' she said, trying to suppress a grin.

'No,' said the black-haired youth. 'But we can soon put that right, can't we?'

He introduced himself as Neville. His friend as Baz.

Kelly nodded politely, forced to sip at her drink again to prevent herself laughing. This was the last thing she needed.

'I haven't seen you in here before,' said Neville. 'I would have remembered if I had.'

Kelly smiled, aware that Baz was still gazing at her breasts as if he'd never seen a woman at close-quarters before. She had little trouble convincing herself that might well be the case.

'It's a bit noisy in here,' Neville said, as if telling her something she didn't know. 'Fancy a walk?'

'I'm waiting for someone,' she told him. 'Thanks all the same.'

'What's his name?' asked Neville, looking quite hurt.

'I'm waiting for a girlfriend actually,' Kelly lied.

Neville seemed to perk up. He nudged Baz in the ribs, momentarily interrupting his appraisal of Kelly's shapely body.

'That's even better. We can make it a foursome when she gets here.'

Kelly smiled again.

'You don't understand,' she said, flashing her green eyes at him. 'She's more than just a friend.'

Neville looked blank.

Baz looked even blanker.

'We're *very* close,' Kelly continued, barely able to keep a straight face.

It was Baz who spoke the revelatory words.

'She's a fucking lesbian,' he gaped, already pulling his colleague away as if Kelly had just announced she had bubonic plague. She chuckled as she saw them leave, casting anxious glances at her as if they thought she was going to follow them. Kelly took another sip of her drink and checked her watch.

9.58.

Where the hell was Fraser?

Another ten minutes, she decided, and she would drive to his house.

She finished her shandy and ordered an orange juice instead.

She had her back to the door when Fraser walked in.

He strode to the far end of the bar where he was engulfed by his usual drinking companions. Kelly turned her attention back to the door, occasionally checking the faces in the bar.

Almost by accident she spotted who she sought.

She slid down off the stool and walked across to him, tugging at his arm.

'Fraser.'

He turned and saw her, a mixture of surprise and distaste in his expression.

'Who's your friend, John?' one of the other men asked, admiringly.

Fraser ignored the remark, addressing himself to Kelly.

'How did you know where to find me?' he wanted to know.

Kelly told him.

'I need to talk to you,' she added. 'It's important.'

'I'm not sure I've got anything to say to you, Kelly. You or anyone else concerned with the bloody Institute.'

'I need your help.'

'How can *I* help you? Is Vernon looking for more human guinea pigs?'

'It's Vernon I want to talk to you about.'

Fraser relaxed slightly, more intrigued now than annoyed. He picked up his glass and motioned to an empty table close by. They sat down, watched by the group of men standing at the bar.

'So what's suddenly important about the good doctor?' he said, sarcastically.

'Listen,' said Kelly, leaning close to him to make herself heard over the blare of the juke-box. 'When Vernon dismissed you, it wasn't because you protested about the research was it?'

Fraser sipped at his drink.

'You tell me.'

'I'm not playing games, Fraser,' snapped Kelly, angrily. 'I came here tonight because I thought you could help me.'

He raised a hand in supplication.

'OK, what are you talking about?' he asked.

'You mentioned something to Vernon about the research, about it being of benefit to one person in particular.'

Fraser shook his head slowly.

'Did you mean Vernon himself?' she continued.

He didn't answer.

'And there was something else,' she persisted. 'About what Vernon was hiding that he'd been hiding for a time. What did you mean?'

Fraser downed what was left in his glass.

'Have you ever heard Vernon talk about his wife?' he asked.

'I didn't even know he was married.'

'It's not something he likes to broadcast, at least not any more.'

Kelly leaned closer as the juke-box launched another high decibel assault.

'For all I know, his wife could be dead now,' Fraser continued. 'Something happened to her about six years ago. No one knows what it was and, so far, no one's found out. Vernon's too clever for that. But, whatever it was his wife disappeared and nobody knows where she is now.'

'How do you know this?' Kelly demanded.

'Vernon's quite a respected figure in our little community. When the wife of a prominent man goes missing there's always the odd rumour floating about.'

'Could he have killed her?' asked Kelly, warily.

'I doubt it. Perhaps she left him. Upped and walked out. The intriguing thing is, what made her leave? Whatever happened to her he's certainly managed to keep it quiet.'

Kelly ran her index finger around the rim of her glass, gazing reflectively into the orange fluid.

'And you think he's using the research to help his wife. Indirectly?' she said, finally.

'It's a possibility.'

'But how is our work on the unconscious mind going to help his wife?' she mused aloud.

'You won't know that until you know what's wrong with *her*. Or what happened to her anyway.'

Kelly sipped at her drink, thoughts tumbling through her mind. The sounds of the juke-box, the pool table and the electronic games seemed to diminish as she considered what she had heard.

'What could have happened that was so bad Vernon would keep it secret for six years?' she pondered.

Fraser could only shrug his shoulders. He started to rise.

'Where are you going?' she wanted to know.

'To get another,' he said, indicating his empty glass. 'What about you?'

'No thanks. I'd better get going. Look, thanks for the help. I appreciate it.'

He nodded.

'You can contact me at home if you want to,' he began. 'My address ...'

She smiled.

'Anderson gave me that too,' she confessed.

'Frank always was thorough.'

They exchanged brief farewells and Kelly left.

As she emerged from the pub she found that the rain which had merely been spotting earlier had now been transformed into a fully-fledged downpour. She ran to her car, fumbling for her keys as the warm rain drenched her. She slid behind the wheel and sat there, gazing out through the rivulets of water which coursed down the windscreen. Kelly ran a hand through her hair and then wiped her palm on her jeans. Through the cascade of rain she could see Fraser's Datsun.

Fraser.

Could he be right about Vernon's wife? Kelly wondered.

She started her engine and guided the Mini out onto the road.

High above her, a soundless flash of lightning split the clouds, reaching earthward as it lit the heavens with cold white light.

Kelly felt an unexpected chill creeping around her.

It was almost 11.05 by the time John Fraser left the Public bar of 'The Huntsman'.

He had not consumed as much booze as he normally did and he felt almost abnormally clear-headed. Fraser rarely got drunk no matter how much he had and tonight, especially, he felt only a pleasing calmness. He climbed into his car and, at the third attempt, started the engine. He made a mental note to get his battery checked.

The rain continued to pelt down and the storm which had been building all night had finally broken. Thunder shook the sky while the lightning etched erratic lines across the tenebrous heavens.

As he pulled out of the pub car park, a lorry roared past and Fraser stepped on his brakes.

The pedal sank mournfully to the floor beneath the pressure of his foot.

The car continued to roll.

The lorry swerved slightly to avoid the Datsun and Fraser gripped the wheel in terror, as if awaiting the impact, but the larger vehicle swept on, disappearing around a bend in the road.

'Jesus,' murmured Fraser, stamping on the brake pedal. This time the car stopped dead.

He tried it once more.

No problems.

He shook his head and drove on. Bloody brakes. He'd only had them checked the day before.

27

She had not slept much the previous night. Her mind had been too active, all too ready to present her with snap answers to questions for which she so badly sought concrete solutions.

Kelly glanced down at the piece of paper on the parcel shelf and re-checked Fraser's address. A sign post at the corner of the street confirmed that she had found the right place. She turned the Mini into the street and slowed down, scanning the doors for the number she sought.

The storm of the night before had cleared the air and the sun shone brightly over the carefully maintained houses with their neat gardens. Kelly saw an old man mowing his front lawn. On the other side of the street a youth was busy washing his car.

'Number fifty-nine,' she murmured to herself, squinting at the houses. 'Number fifty-nine.'

She saw it and pulled the Mini into a convenient parking space, switching off the engine. Kelly sat behind the wheel for a moment gazing at the house. She was reasonably sure that Fraser had told her everything he knew about Vernon but she had spent half the night wondering if there might just be something else which he might have neglected to mention. Perhaps in his own home, away from the noisy distractions of the pub, he might be able to give her some more information. Exactly what she was going to do with it she wasn't yet sure.

Confront Vernon?

Why should she need to confront him?

Kelly shook her head, as if trying to force the thoughts to one side, then she pushed open the door and climbed out.

There was a pleasing smell of blossom in the air, as if someone had opened a gigantic air freshener. The sun, broken up by the branches of the trees which flanked the road, forced its way through the canopy of leaves and blossom to brush warming rays against her skin. The blossom itself, stirred by a gentle breeze, fell from the trees like pink tears.

Kelly walked up the path to the front door of number fifty-nine and rang the bell. As she stood there she noticed that the garage door was closed. There was no sign of Fraser's Datsun. She hoped that he was at home.

A minute passed and no one answered the door. Kelly rang again, this time keeping her finger on the bell button for a time.

At last she heard movement from inside.

The door swung open and she found herself confronted by a rotund, middle-aged woman in a dark blue dress. Her greying hair was swept back from her forehead, giving her round face a severity which it perhaps did not merit.

'Mrs Fraser?' Kelly asked.

'No. I'm her sister,' the woman said, eyeing Kelly up and down. 'Who are you?'

Kelly introduced herself.

'I used to work with John Fraser,' she explained. 'It was him that I wanted to see really.'

The woman didn't speak at first then, slowly, she lowered her gaze and her voice softened.

'My sister is upstairs sleeping,' she said, quietly.

Kelly didn't have to be a detective to realize that something was wrong.

'And Mr Fraser?' she asked.

'He was killed in an accident last night. His car hit a tree. He was dead before they got him to hospital.'

143

28

New York

There were two of them waiting outside the house.

One was smoking a cigarette and pacing agitatedly up and down while the other squatted on the pavement and adjusted his camera. Both of them would occasionally stop what they were doing and peer in the direction of the building.

Toni Landers replaced the curtain, wondering if the newsmen had seen her.

She had not seen these two before although, since her son's death, so many had thrust themselves at her with notepads and microphones that she doubted if she would remember faces. The actress walked across the room to the drinks cabinet and poured herself a large measure of J&B which she downed virtually in one swallow, coughing as the fiery liquid burned its way to her stomach.

The house was deathly silent. She had given Mrs Garcia some time off, promising to ring her when her services were required again. Exactly how long that would be even Toni herself was uncertain of. On the sofa before her the copy of *Variety* was folded open at an appointed spot and she glanced at it briefly before returning to her vigil at the window.

As she stood gazing out at the two newsmen, she thought how odd it had been that she should discover the story in such a journal. She had read with interest that Jonathan Mathias was to visit England to appear on a TV special. She had seen him as her last hope. The only one she knew who possessed the kind of abilities she had need of. Toni didn't intend to allow him to slip away.

She had need of his services.

There was a loud beeping sound and she looked out to see that the Ford Sedan had pulled up outside her house. The driver was banging the horn.

Toni drained what was left in her glass then scuttled for the front door, re-adjusting the dark glasses as she did so. She waited a second then walked out.

Immediately, the two newsmen approached her and she winced as the flash bulb momentarily hurt her eyes.

'I have nothing to say,' she told them.

'How soon will you be returning to the stage?' the first man asked, ignoring her declaration.

She swept on towards the waiting car.

'How will your son's death affect your career?'

The flash bulb exploded again, closer to her this time.

Toni struck out angrily, knocking the camera from the photographer's hands. It crashed to the ground, the lens splintering.

'Hey lady,' he shouted. 'That's an expensive fucking camera.'

She pulled open the rear door of the Ford and glanced at the driver.

'It ain't my fault your fucking kid is dead,' the photographer roared as the car pulled away.

'Where to, Miss Landers?' the driver asked.

She checked her watch. She had enough time.

'Kennedy,' she told him.

29

Paris

The occasional gusts of wind stirred the bells in the church tower, whistling through and around them to form a discordant, ghostly melody.

Michel Lasalle stood by the grave-side and read the inscription on the headstone.

Madelaine Lasalle; 1947-1982
Loved More Than Life Itself.

The wind stirred the flowers which adorned the grave, their

white petals standing out in dark contrast to the darkness of the night. Lasalle bent and removed them, laying them on one side.

He reached for the shovel.

Putting all his weight behind it he drove the pointed implement into the ground, pressing down on it with his foot, levering a huge clod of dark earth from the top of the grave. He tossed it to one side and continued digging. He could feel the perspiration soaking through his shirt as he toiled, gradually creating a mound of mud beside the grave. When he had excavated half of the plot he paused and pulled his shirt off, fastening it around his waist by the sleeves as if it were some kind of apron. Then he continued digging.

It took him nearly thirty minutes to reach the coffin.

He heard the sound of metal on wood and stood back triumphantly, jamming the shovel into the damp earth at the bottom of the hole. Lasalle dropped to his knees and began clawing the final covering of dirt from the casket. He split two finger nails as he did so, scrabbling there like a dog trying to find a bone. Blood oozed from the torn digits but Lasalle paid it no heed. Only when the last fragments of earth had been pulled free did he straighten up, reaching once more for the shovel. He slid the pointed end beneath one corner of the coffin and weighed down on it.

The screw which held it in place was rusted and he had little difficulty removing it. In fact, none of them presented too much of an obstacle and, with a grunt of satisfaction, he succeeded in prising the lid free. It came away with a shriek of splintering wood and he flung it aside.

A cloying stench of decay rose from the body of his dead wife.

Lasalle stared down at the corpse, his gaze travelling inquisitively up and down it. The skin on the face and neck was dry, drawn taught over the bones. The eye sockets were gaping, empty caverns filled only with a gelatinous substance which, from the left eye, had dribbled down the remains of the cheek. A thick yellowish fluid resembling pus was seeping from both nostrils. The mouth was open to reveal several missing teeth. The gums had dissolved and the tongue resembled little more than a strand of withered brown string. One hand lay across the chest, the skin having split and peeled back to reveal brittle bone beneath. The bottom of the coffin was stained with a rusty substance which looked black in the darkness.

Lasalle stepped into the coffin and knelt on the legs of his dead wife, wondering if the bones would snap beneath him. He was sweating profusely and his breath came in short gasps. As he wiped a hand across his forehead, blood from his torn fingers left a crimson smudge on his skin.

Madelaine had been buried in a black dress and Lasalle now bent forward and lifted it, pushing the fusty material up until it covered her putrescing features and exposed her festering pelvic region. Lasalle felt the erection bulging in his trousers and he tugged them down. He fell upon the body and spoke her name as he thrust, the stink of his own perspiration mingling with the vile stench which rose from her corpse.

A shadow fell across him.

Lasalle looked up and his grunts turned to screams.

Joubert stood at the grave-side, loking down at the obscenity before him, a smile etched on his face.

Lasalle screamed again and again.

Joubert continued to smile.

As he was catapulted from the nightmare, Lasalle gripped his head as if he were afraid it was about to explode. He could still hear screams and it was a second or two before he realized they were his own.

He sat up in bed, his body drenched and aching. As he swung himself round he discovered that he was shaking madly. His eyes bulged wildly in the sockets, the images from the dream still vivid in his mind.

He suddenly got to his feet and rushed to the bathroom, barely making it as the cascade of hot bile fought its way up from his stomach, gushing into his mouth. He bent double over the toilet and retched.

He staggered back, head spinning, and swilled out his mouth with water. Then, he staggered slowly back into the bedroom and sat down in the chair beside the window.

He did not sleep for the remainder of that night.

30

Oxford

It was a familiar drive for Blake. Although he hadn't visited the Institute of Psychical Study for over a year he had not needed to consult a map in order to find the place. He'd left London early, avoiding much of the worst traffic. The sun was shining with just enough power to make driving pleasant. Dressed in a pair of jeans and an open-necked white shirt, Blake felt comfortable and he whistled happily in accompaniment to the cassette as he swung the XJS into the driveway which led up to the Institute.

He found a parking space and turned off the engine, waiting until the track he'd been listening to had finished before getting out of the car. He slipped on a light jacket and made his way towards the main entrance of the building. There was a notepad stuffed into his pocket and the usual array of pens too. Blake chuckled to himself, remembering back to his days as a journalist when he'd dashed enthusiastically to each pissant little assignment armed with his trusty pad.

The entrance hall of the Institute was pleasantly cool and Blake paused, slowing his pace, trying to remember where he had to go.

He spotted someone emerging from a room ahead of him.

The writer was immediately struck by her shapely figure, the way her lab coat hugged her taut buttocks, the small slit at the back allowing him brief, tantalising glimpses of her slim calves. She walked easily and elegantly on her high heels and he realized that she hadn't noticed him.

'Excuse me,' he called, approaching her.

She turned and Blake found himself looking deep into her welcoming eyes. She smiled and the gesture seemed to light up her whole face. He chanced an approving glance at her upper body, her breasts pertly pressing against the material of her electric blue blouse.

'You're David Blake aren't you?' she said but it was more of a statement than a question.

He smiled broadly.

'Fame at last,' he beamed. 'How do you know me?'

'We have your books in our library, I recognize you from your photo on the jacket. It's the dark glasses,' she told him. 'They're quite distinctive.'

'Well, they hide the bags under my eyes,' he said, pleased when she chuckled. 'You seem to have me at a disadvantage, you know me but I don't know you.'

'Kelly Hunt,' she told him. 'I work here.'

Blake shook her small hand gently.

'You don't fit the image,' he said. 'I thought all investigators were crusty middle-aged men.'

'Not *all* of them,' Kelly said.

'So I see.'

They looked at each other for long moments, both liking what they saw.

'Is Dr Vernon in his office?' Blake said, finally breaking the silence.

Kelly frowned slightly.

'Are you here to see him then?' she asked.

Blake explained that he was. Kelly told him how to reach the Institute Director.

'Well, it's nice to have met you, Miss Hunt,' he said, heading for the stairs which led up to Vernon's office.

'You too,' Kelly said, watching as he disappeared out of sight.

She wondered exactly how friendly he was with Vernon.

Vernon was already on his feet, right hand extended, when Blake entered the office.

The men exchanged pleasant greetings and the writer sat down, accepting the drink he was offered.

'Sorry to call on you at such short notice,' he apologised. 'But I've written about two-thirds of the book and I need to check some details before I can finish it.'

Vernon produced Blake's letter from his desk drawer.

'I got it yesterday,' he said, smiling. 'So, how are things in the book business?'

Blake shrugged.

'It could be better I suppose but then again, it always could.'

'And how's your new book coming along?'

'Fine, as far as I can tell. But then who am I to judge?' He smiled.

Vernon's mood darkened slightly. He looked at Blake and then at the letter he'd received from the writer.

'You say your new book is about the unconscious mind?' he asked.

'The unconscious, dreams, Astral travel, that kind of thing. I've just got back from America, I spent some time with a man called Jonathan Mathias. You might have heard of him.'

Vernon nodded.

'He's a remarkable man,' Blake said. 'Powerful.' The writer's voice took on a reflective note.

'How do you mean, powerful?' Vernon wanted to know.

'It's difficult to explain. He performs acts of faith-healing and yet he's an atheist.' Blake paused. 'But, most important of all, he claims he can control the subconscious minds of other people. Their Astral bodies.'

'How?' Vernon demanded, sitting forward in his chair.

Blake regarded the older man over the top of his glass.

'It's some form of hypnosis,' he said. 'I'm sure of that.'

Vernon eyed the writer suspiciously.

'It's an extravagant claim,' he said.

Blake shrugged.

'Like I said, he's a remarkable man.'

The Institute Director reached forward and flicked a switch on his intercom.

'Could you send Miss Hunt up, please,' he said, then sat back in his chair once more.

'Do you believe what Mathias says about being able to control other people's subconscious minds?' he wanted to know.

Blake was about to answer when there was a knock on the door, and, a moment later, Kelly entered.

She looked at Blake but, this time, he was surprised to find that she didn't smile. He got to his feet.

150

'David Blake,' began Vernon. 'This is Kelly Hunt, one of our ...'

Kelly cut him short.

'We've met,' she said, curtly. 'Hello again, Mr Blake.'

The writer was puzzled by the coldness of her voice. All the earlier warmth seemed to have been drained from it.

'Mr Blake will be conducting some research here for his new book, I'd like you to help him with whatever he needs.'

'But my work ...' she protested.

'His work ties in with your own,' Vernon said, sharply.

'I hope I'm not causing anyone any inconvenience,' the writer said, aware of a newly found hostility in the air.

'It's no trouble,' Kelly said, sounding none too convincing.

He smiled thinly.

'Well, I suppose I'd better get started.' He thanked Vernon, then followed Kelly out of the office.

The Institute Director sat down at his desk and re-read the letter which Blake had posted two days earlier. He held it before him a moment longer then carefully, almost gleefully, tore it up.

'Did I do something to annoy you?' Blake asked Kelly as they headed down the stairs towards her office.

'What gives you that impression, Mr Blake?' she said.

'Your attitude,' he told her. 'And stop calling me *Mr* Blake will you? My name's David.'

'What sort of research are you interested in?' Kelly asked him, dutifully.

He repeated what he'd told Vernon.

'The old boy seemed very interested,' Blake said.

'How long have you been friends?' asked Kelly.

'Well, I wouldn't exactly call us friends. Acquaintances might be more to the point. I've been to the Institute a few times in the past while I've been working on other books.'

'How close are you?' she asked.

Blake stopped walking.

'What is this? Twenty questions?' he asked, irritably.

Kelly also stood where she was.

'Dr Vernon and I have met several times on what you might call a professional basis,' Blake told her. 'Although with all due respect, I don't really see that it's any of your

151

business, Miss Hunt.'

'No, you're right, it isn't,' Kelly confessed, some of the coldness having left her voice. 'I'm sorry, Mr Blake.'

He sighed.

'David,' he told her. 'Look, we have to work together for a day or two, we might as well make the time pass pleasantly.'

'David,' she agreed, smiling thinly.

They began walking again but more slowly this time.

'Why is it so important to you to know whether Vernon and I are friends?' he enquired.

'I was curious.'

'I'm *still* curious. When I arrived here, when we first spoke, everything was fine. Since I spoke to Vernon you don't want to know me.'

'It's difficult to explain,' she said, evasively.

'Then don't try,' Blake said, smiling.

Kelly looked at him, aware that she felt more than a passing attraction for this man.

Blake was not handsome but his finely chiselled features and sinewy frame, coupled with the easy-going personality he exuded, served their purpose well.

'Vernon said you'd been doing work on dreams,' he said.

'That's what I'm still working on,' Kelly explained as they reached her office. She ushered him inside and motioned for him to sit down but, instead, the writer wandered over to the window and looked out across the rolling lawns which surrounded the Institute. Kelly seated herself behind her desk, studying Blake's profile as he gazed out into the sunlit morning.

'The weather's too nice to work,' he said, quietly.

She smiled.

'Standing there isn't going to get your book written is it?' Blake turned and nodded.

'Quite right, Miss Hunt,' he said.

'Kelly,' she reminded him.

It was his turn to smile.

'How exactly *can* I help you?' she asked as he seated himself opposite her.

'I'd like to see the labs where you've been doing your research, ask you a few questions if that's all right but, otherwise, just give me free run of the library and I'll be happy. I'm not a difficult man to please.' He smiled that engaging smile once more and Kelly found herself drawn to him, to his eyes even though they were shielded behind his dark glasses. She felt a peculiar tingle run through her.

'Shall we start in the labs?' she said, getting to her feet again.

He nodded.

'Why not?'

Kelly led him out of her office.

The library at the Institute never failed to fascinate Blake. Built up, as it had been, over a hundred years, it had books which dated back as far as the sixteenth century. Before him on the table he had an original copy of Collin de Planncey's 'Dictionaire Infernale'. The pages creaked as he turned them, scanning the ancient tome, pleasantly surprised at how much of the French he could actually understand.

He'd been in the library for over four hours, ever since he'd left Kelly back in her office. Now, with the time approaching 5.15 p.m., he heard his stomach rumbling and realized that he hadn't eaten since early morning. The writer scanned what notes he'd written, realizing that he must check one or two discrepancies against his manuscript at the first opportunity. As it was, he replaced the old books in their correct position on the shelves, scooped up his pad and made for the stairs.

Kelly was on her way down.

'I was coming to see if you needed any help,' she said, the warmth having returned to her voice.

They had found it remarkably easy to talk to each other that morning. Their conversation had flowed unfalteringly and Kelly had felt her attraction for Blake growing stronger. She felt at ease in his company and she was sure the feeling was reciprocated.

'Did you find what you were looking for?' she asked him.

He smiled and ran appraising eyes over her.

'I think I found exactly what I was looking for,' he said.

She coloured slightly and waited on the stairs while he made his way up. They both walked out into the hall which was now much colder than when Blake had first arrived.

'Will you be back tomorrow?' she asked him.

'I got the information I needed,' he told her, 'with your help. But if I ever have a haunting you'll be the first one I get in touch with. You've really been very kind. Thanks.'

'Are you driving back to London now?'

'Not yet. I'm going to have something to eat first and then I thought I might take you out for a drink this evening if you're not doing anything else.'

Kelly chuckled, unable to speak for a moment, taken by surprise by the unexpectedness of his invitation.

'If I'm in a good mood, I might even let you buy a round,' Blake added.

'What if I am doing something else?' she asked.

'Then I'll have to wait for another evening won't I?'

She shook her head, still laughing.

'Can I pick you up about eight?' he asked.

'Eight will be fine,' she told him. 'But it might help if you knew where to pick me up *from*.' She scribbled her address and phone number on a piece of paper and gave it to him.

'Tell Dr Vernon I'll be in touch,' Blake said, and, for a moment, he saw a flicker of doubt cross Kelly's face. 'I'll phone him and thank him for letting me use the library.'

She nodded.

Blake turned and headed for the door.

'Eight o'clock,' he reminded her.

She watched him go, stood alone in the hallway listening as he revved up his engine. He turned the XJS full circle and guided it back down the driveway towards the road which led into Oxford itself.

Kelly smiled to herself and returned to her office.

From his office window, Dr Vernon watched as the writer drove away. He paused a moment then reached for the phone and dialled.

154

31

'Cheers,' said Blake, smiling. He raised his glass then took a hefty swallow from the foaming beer.

Across the table from him, Kelly did likewise, sipping her Martini and meeting the writer's gaze.

They were seated in the garden of 'The Jester', a small pub about a mile or so outside Oxford. There were three or four other people enjoying the evening air as well. It was still agreeably warm despite the fact that the sun was sinking, gushing crimson into the sky. When it got too chilly they could easily retire into the comfort of the lounge bar. Blake looked at his companion, pleased with what he saw. She was clad in a dress of pale lemon cheese-cloth, her breasts unfettered by the restraints of a bra. The writer noticed how invitingly her dark nipples pressed against the flimsy material. With the sinking sun casting a halo around her, drawing golden streaks in her brown hair she looked beautiful. He felt something akin to pride merely being seated there with her.

Kelly noticed how intently he was looking at her and smiled impishly.

'What are you looking at?' she asked him.

'A very beautiful young woman,' he told her. 'But, I was thinking too.'

'About what?'

He raised his eyebrows.

'No,' she said. 'Perhaps I'm better off not knowing.'

Blake laughed.

'I was wondering actually,' he began, 'how you came to be in the line of work you're in. It is unusual for a woman, especially of your age.'

'It was what I wanted to do when I left University,' she told him.

'How did your parents feel about it?' he wanted to know.

'They didn't say much one way or the other. I'd worked in a library for a few months before I joined the Institute. They'd probably have been just as happy if I'd stayed on there. Security is the be-all and end-all in our family I'm afraid.'

Blake nodded.

'What about you?' Kelly asked. 'Writing's a precarious business isn't it? What made you want to write?'

'Well, it wasn't because I needed to share my knowledge with others,' he said, tongue-in-cheek. 'Not in the beginning anyway. I wrote a couple of novels to start with.'

'Did you have any luck with them?'

He shook his head.

'Writing fiction successfully needs more luck than talent. You need the breaks. I didn't get them.'

'So you turned to non-fiction? The stuff you write now?'

'The ratio's different. It's fifty per cent talent and fifty per cent luck.'

'You sell yourself short, David.'

'No. I understand my own limitations that's all.'

'What about your parents. How do they feel about having a famous author for a son?'

'Both my parents are dead. My father died of a stroke five years ago, my mother had a heart attack six months after him.'

'Oh God, I'm sorry, David.'

He smiled thinly.

'You weren't to know,' he said. 'I just wish they could have lived to see my success that's all.'

A heavy silence descended, rapidly broken by Blake.

'Well, now we've got the morbid stuff out of the way,' he said, with a reasonable degree of cheerfulness. 'Perhaps we can carry on with this conversation.'

She sipped her drink and looked at him over the rim of the glass. Losing his parents within six months of each other must have been a crushing blow and obviously he didn't want to dwell on the memory.

'I suppose you must be reasonably secure as a writer now,' she said, attempting to guide the conversation in another direction.

'You can never be secure in my business,' he said. 'One flop and it's back to square one. It's like walking a tightrope in a pair of wellies.'

Kelly chuckled.

'Does it bother you living alone?' Blake asked.

'Not anymore,' she told him. 'It did to begin with but I'm used to it now.'

'And you've never felt like getting married?'

'No.' She dismissed the suggestion as if he'd just asked her to commit suicide. 'I'm not the settling down type, I don't think.'

'I know what you mean,' he confessed.

'You're not telling me *you* haven't been tempted. There must have been girls who you've been close too,' Kelly said.

'A couple. But none that I'd want to spend the rest of my life with.' He smiled. 'I'm a selfish devil. Sharing isn't one of my strong points.'

'Too much give and take, is that it?'

'You ask a lot of questions, Kelly,' he grinned.

'That's because I'm interested in you,' she told him.

'Now that *is* a compliment.'

They sat in silence for a time, looking at each other, enjoying the warmth of the dying sun, the smell of freshly cut grass and the gentle breeze. It stirred the trees which flanked the pub garden on one side. Birds nesting in the branches watched over the activity below them. Near to where Kelly and Blake sat, three sparrows were busily picking at a piece of bread thrown down by a young couple who were eating sandwiches. Somewhere in the distance Kelly could hear a cuckoo. She sat back in her seat feeling more relaxed than she had done for many months. The combination of the surroundings and Blake's company had a calming influence on her. She wondered if he felt the same way.

The writer downed what was left in his glass and looked at Kelly. She still had most of her Martini left.

'I'll have to bring you out more often,' he said, peering at the glass. 'If one drink lasts you this long you're going to save me pounds.'

They both laughed.

'You have another,' she said.

'Very generous,' Blake replied.

'Let me get it,' she offered, fumbling for her purse.

Blake looked indignant.

'Let a woman buy drink for me?' He winked at her. 'Good idea.'

She balled up a pound note and tossed it at him, watching as he retreated back into the bar to fetch another pint. It was a matter of moments before he returned, holding the glass in one hand and her change in the other. He sat down and supped a third of it immediately, wiping the froth from his lip with his thumb.

'Did Vernon say anything when you told him I'd left this afternoon?' the writer asked.

'No,' Kelly said, suspiciously. 'Should he have?'

Blake smiled, wryly.

'You know, Kelly,' he said. 'I could be forgiven for thinking you're a tiny bit paranoid about Dr Vernon.'

Kelly didn't answer.

'Every time I mention his name you go cold on me,' Blake continued. 'Why? Or is it my imagination?'

She took a sip of her drink.

'Perhaps it's *my* imagination,' she told him, wondering if that was the answer. Maybe she *was* becoming paranoid.

'What do you mean?'

She thought about mentioning what had been going on, her suspicions and suppositions but then decided against it.

'Forget it, David,' she asked. 'Please?'

He nodded.

Kelly finished her drink and pushed the glass away from her.

'Do you want another one?' the writer asked.

She smiled and shook her head.

'No thanks.'

There was another long silence between them then finally Kelly spoke.

'To tell you the truth, David,' she began, wearily, 'I'm a little bit concerned at the amount of interest Dr Vernon is showing in my research.'

Blake frowned.

'I don't understand,' he said. 'Surely he's got every right to be interested. He is Director of the Institute after all. It's only natural.'

'But he seems obsessed with my work.'

She told him about the incident with Maurice Grant, her trip to France and how Vernon had insisted on keeping her report.

Blake didn't speak, he merely finished the rest of his beer and put down the empty glass.

'Well,' she said, challengingly. 'Do you think I'm being paranoid now?'

'There's probably a perfectly reasonable explanation for it, Kelly,' he said.

'Don't try and humour me, David.' He was surprised at the vehemence in her words. 'There are other factors too. Things which don't make sense, which have no logical explanation.' She emphasised the last two words with scorn.

'Like what?' he wanted to know.

Kelly shivered as the slight breeze seemed to turn cold. She looked up and saw that the crimson of the setting sun had been replaced by a layered sky of purple. Kelly felt goose-pimples rise on her flesh and she rubbed her forearms.

'I don't feel comfortable talking about them here,' she told him, as if she feared some kind of surveillance in the peaceful garden.

'I'll take you home,' Blake said without hesitation.

They got to their feet and walked to the car park where the writer opened the passenger door of the XJS, allowing Kelly to slide in. He clambered in behind the wheel and started the engine, guiding the Jaguar out into the road.

'Are you all right?' he asked, glancing across at her, a little puzzled by her silence.

She nodded, feeling more at ease within the confines of the car. She even managed to smile at the writer who reached across and squeezed her hand gently. Kelly felt the coldness draining from her, as if Blake's touch had somehow restored her composure. She gripped his hand in return, reassured by his presence.

After a fifteen minute drive they reached her flat.

Kelly no longer felt the cold seeping through her and she looked at the writer almost gratefully.

'Home,' he said, smiling, and once more she found herself captivated by that smile of his. No, more than that. She was ensnared by it, drawn to him unlike any man before. He exuded a magnetism which she found irresistible, almost in spite of herself.

'How do you feel now?' he asked.

'I'm OK,' she told him. 'Thanks, David.'

'For what?' he wanted to know.

'Just thanks.' She reached across and touched his hand with her slender fingers. If any emotion registered in his eyes she couldn't see it because his dark glasses now hid them even more completely. 'Would you like to come in for a coffee?'

Blake needed no second bidding. He climbed out of the Jag and locked his door then walked around and let Kelly out, watching appreciatively as she walked ahead of him, searching through her bag for her key. The writer enjoyed the gentle sway of her hips as she walked, the muscles in her calves tensing slightly with each step she took, perched on her backless high heels.

He followed her.

Her flat was, as he'd expected it to be both spotlessly clean and impeccably neat. At her bidding he seated himself in one of the big armchairs which flanked the electric fire. Kelly passed through into the kitchen and Blake heard water running as she filled a kettle.

She returned a moment later, crossing to the window to close the curtains. Then she flicked on the record player, dropping a disc onto the turntable.

'Do you mind some music?' she asked.

'Not at all,' he said.

The sound of Simon and Garfunkel flowed softly from the speakers.

'Coffee won't be a minute,' she told him, seating herself in the armchair opposite and, as she did so, she found once again that her gaze was drawn to the writer.

'Is this your own place?' Blake asked.

'It will be eventually,' Kelly told him. 'In another twenty years time probably.' She shrugged. 'By the time I'm an old, withered spinster at least I'll own my own flat.'

Blake smiled.

'I don't think there's much chance of you becoming an old withered spinster, Kelly,' he said.

'My mother keeps asking me why I'm not married yet.

Why I'm not knee deep in wet nappies and babies.' Kelly smiled. 'Parents love the idea of grandchildren until they actually have them. Then they complain because it makes them feel old.' Kelly felt a warm thrill run through her as she relaxed in the chair, feeling quite happy to let Blake look at her, to examine her with his eyes. Every so often she would see them flicker behind the dark screen of his glasses.

'Are you sensitive to light, David?' she asked him. 'I mean, the dark glasses.' She pointed to them.

'Slightly,' he said. 'I suppose that's what comes of squinting over a typewriter for five years.'

The kettle began to whistle. Kelly got to her feet and walked back into the kitchen, returning a moment later with two steaming mugs of coffee, one of which she handed to Blake. Then, she kicked off her shoes and, this time, sat on the floor in front of him, legs drawn up to one side of her.

'Kelly, I don't want to pry,' Blake began. 'But you said there were things about Vernon which you didn't understand. What did you mean?'

She sucked in a weary breath and lowered her gaze momentarily.

'From what you told me at the pub, I can't see any reason to suspect that Dr Vernon's up to something, especially not anything as sinister as you seem to think,' said Blake. 'What reasons would he have?'

'David,' she said, trying to keep her voice calm. 'I was responsible for what happened to Maurice Grant. What I did was wrong. It broke the rules of the Institute. The authorities could have closed the place. That Institute is Vernon's pride and joy. He could have lost it because of me and yet he didn't so much as give me a warning or suspend me.' She decided to put down her mug. 'Instead, he protected me when he had every right to dismiss me on the spot. Then, when I got back from France, he wanted to know everything that happened and he kept my report.'

Blake sat forward in his chair.

'You make Vernon sound like a monster when all he tried to do was help you,' he said.

'He's hiding something, David,' she said, angrily. 'John Fraser knew what it was. That's why he was killed.'

'Who's Fraser?'

She explained as much as she knew about the events of the last two days.

'But if Fraser was killed in a car crash, how could Vernon be involved?' the writer wanted to know. 'It was an accident, surely?'

'He knew about Vernon's secret.'

Another heavy silence descended, finally broken by Blake.

'I don't see how you can suspect Vernon of being involved in Fraser's death,' he said.

'David, he won't let *anyone* come between him and this research.'

'Does that include you?' Blake asked, cryptically.

It was at that point that the phone rang.

32

For long moments neither of them moved as the strident ringing filled the room. Then, finally, Kelly got to her feet and walked across to the phone, lifting the receiver tentatively, wondering why she felt so apprehensive. Blake watched her, noticing the hesitancy in her movements.

'Hello,' she said.

No answer.

'Hello,' she repeated, looking across at Blake as if seeking reassurance.

Words suddenly came gushing forth from the caller at the other end, some of which she didn't understand. Not merely due to the speed with which they were uttered but because they were in French.

'Who is this?' she asked, holding the phone away from her for a second as a particularly loud crackle of static broke up the line. 'Hello. Can you hear me? Who's speaking?'

'Kelly. It's Michel Lasalle.'

She relaxed slightly.

'Listen to me, you must listen,' he blurted, and Kelly was

more than aware of the high-pitched desperation in his voice. His breathing was harsh and irregular, as if he'd been running for a long time. 'I saw Madelaine,' he told her, his voice cracking. 'I saw her.'

'You had a nightmare, Michel, it's understandable ...'

He interrupted.

'No, I touched her, felt her,' he insisted.

'It was a nightmare,' she repeated.

'No. Joubert saw her too.'

Kelly frowned.

'What do you mean? How was he involved?' she wanted to know. She felt the tension returning to her muscles.

'He was there, with me,' the Frenchman continued, panting loudly. He babbled something in French then laughed dryly. A sound which sent a shiver down Kelly's spine. 'He watched me making love to her. She felt cold in my arms but it didn't matter, she is still mine. I still want her.'

Kelly tried to speak but couldn't.

'Joubert has not forgiven me,' the Frenchman said, softly. 'I don't think he ever will.'

'Forgiven you for what?' Kelly wanted to know.

'Writing that article.'

'Did he speak to you?' she asked, wondering whether or not she should humour the distraught man.

'He is always there, Kelly. Always. Watching.'

An uneasy silence fell, broken only by the gentle hiss of static burbling in the lines.

'Michel, are you still there?' Kelly finally said.

Silence.

'Michel, answer me.'

She heard a click and realized that he'd hung up. For long seconds she stared at the receiver then slowly replaced it.

'What was it?' Blake asked, seeing the concern on her face.

She walked slowly back towards him and seated herself on the floor once again, reaching for her coffee. It was cold.

'Kelly, who *was* that?' the writer persisted.

'Lasalle. One of the men from the Metapsychic Centre,' she told him, then proceeded to relay what the Frenchman had said to her.

'He's convinced that it was real,' she said.

Blake shrugged.

'Nightmares are usually vivid,' he said.

Kelly shook her head.

'But Lasalle won't accept that he had a nightmare,' she protested. 'He's convinced that what he experienced actually happened.' She sighed. 'I hope to God he's not heading for another breakdown. He had one when his wife died.' She looked up at Blake. 'And Joubert, he mentioned that Joubert was present in the nightmare. He sounded frightened of him.' She lowered her gaze once more. 'First Fraser, now Lasalle. One man's dead, another is close to a nervous breakdown and all because of the research I'm engaged in.'

'You can't blame yourself, Kelly,' Blake said, reaching out and gently lifting her head with his right hand.

She gripped that hand, aware of the combination of gentleness and strength in it but more conscious of the warmth which seemed to flow from it, from his entire being. She looked up at him, trying to see his eyes, searching for a glimmer behind the tinted screens which masked them. Kelly kissed his hand and moved closer to him, resting her own right hand on his knee as he slowly stroked the back of her neck beneath her hair. She squirmed beneath his subtle caresses, moving nearer, anxious to touch him fully. His other hand began gently kneading the smooth flesh of her shoulder and she closed her eyes.

'What if Vernon *is* responsible for Fraser's death?' she said, quietly, enjoying the sensations which were coursing through her.

'Then he's a dangerous man,' Blake said. 'You should stay away from him.'

'And Joubert?'

'Kelly. If there is any possibility that either of them have some kind of psychic power then you'd do best not to let them know you suspect.'

'But I must know the truth, David,' she protested, turning to face him.

As she did so, Blake leant forward and kissed her. Their lips brushed gently for a moment then, unhesitatingly, Kelly pressed her mouth to his. Blake responded fiercely, matching her passion with his own desire.

164

Kelly snaked her hand up around his neck, as if reluctant to break the kiss. When she finally did, she was panting softly, her eyes riveted to Blake. Her body was burning, as if fire were pouring through her veins. She felt her nipples, now stiff and erect, straining almost painfully against her dress and between her slender legs she felt a glowing moistness. Blake sensed her excitement and she could see that he felt similarly aroused by the contact they had enjoyed. Her hand strayed to the beginnings of bulge in his trousers, massaging and rubbing until Blake himself grunted under his breath.

Kelly moved away from him slightly, lying back on the carpet before him, inviting his attentions. The writer was not slow to respond and he joined her, his hands moving over the thin material of her dress until they came to her breasts. He rubbed gently, feeling the hardened points beneath his palms as she arched her back. Kelly felt as if she were floating, the warm glow between her legs becoming an all-consuming desire which filled every part of her. She took Blake's left hand and guided it up inside her dress, moaning as his fingers stroked the smooth flesh of her inner thighs, pausing there for agonisingly exquisite seconds before moving higher. She felt his probing digits reach her panties, his forefinger hooked, pulling down the flimsy garment. She lifted her buttocks to allow him to remove them, watching as he first kissed the sodden material before laying it on one side.

She pulled him close to her, their mouths locking once more as she thrust her pelvis towards his searching hand, almost crying aloud as his finger touched the hardened bud of her clitoris and began rubbing gently. She fumbled for his zip and freed his bulging erection, encircling it with her slender fingers, working up a gentle rhythm as she teased his stiff shaft. For three or four minutes they remained like that and then she suggested they undress.

It took them mere moments then, naked, they were free to explore every inch of the other's body. Blake lowered his head to her breasts and took first one nipple then the other between his teeth, rolling it gently as he flicked it with his tongue. Kelly felt his other hand trace a pattern across her belly before gliding through her soft pubic hair once more to search for her most sensitive area and she rolled onto her side, allowing him to push his heavily muscled thigh against her. She ground hard against him, eventually manoeuvering herself so that he was beneath her. She straddled his stomach.

'Take these off,' she said, quietly, reaching for his dark glasses. 'I want to see your eyes.'

Blake himself removed them and then turned to look at her.

Kelly felt as if the breath had been torn from her, as if someone had punched her hard and winded her.

Blake's eyes were the colour of a June sky. A deep blue which she found overwhelming in their intensity. She felt as if she were a puppet, suspended by wires which came from those eyes, her movements and feelings controlled by them. A renewed and much more powerful surge of emotion shook her and she bent forward to kiss him. But, he gripped her waist and almost lifted her up on to his chest, smiling as she rubbed herself against him. He felt the wetness spilling from her, dampening his chest. She moved a little further so that he could reach her with his tongue.

Kelly gasped as she felt it flicking over her distended lips, reaming her swollen cleft before fastening on her clitoris. She spoke his name, her head thrown back as she surrendered to the feelings which were sweeping over her. Kelly felt a tightening around her thighs, the first unmistakable sign of approaching orgasm. His hands reached up and found her swollen nipples, adding to her overall pleasure which was now building up like an impending explosion.

She twisted around so that she could reach his penis, lying on him in order to allow it to reach her mouth. She studied the bulbous head for a moment then took it into her mouth, wrapping her tongue around it, her free hand working away at the root, fondling his testicles. She felt him stiffen, realized that his excitement was a great as hers. But she needed him more fully. Kelly rolled to one side, kissing him briefly as she did so then she knelt over his groin, cradling his throbbing member in one hand, lowering herself slowly until it nudged her aching vagina. They both gasped as the union was completed. She sank down onto him, his shaft swallowed by her liquescent cleft.

Kelly knew that she would not be able to hold back any

longer. She stared into Blake's eyes and began moving up and down. The sensations began almost at once. She was aware only of the throbbing pleasure between her legs and his welcoming blue eyes which seemed to fill her entire field of vision. She could not look away from him and, as she speeded up her movements, she felt as though she were being joined with him, melting into him to form one entity.

The power of the orgasm made her cry out loudly. She bounced up and down on him, each wave of pleasure more intense than the one before. She had never felt anything so overwhelmingly wonderful in her life and that pleasure, almost impossibly, suddenly re-doubled as she felt him writhe beneath her as his own climax washed over him. Kelly moaned loudly as she felt his hot liquid spurt into her and she ground herself hard against him, coaxing every last drop from him. Shaking and bathed in perspiration, she slumped forward, kissing him gently, unable to look anywhere else but at his eyes.

They lay still, coupled together as he softened within her.

It was a long time before either of them spoke. The record player was silent, the record having finished long ago. Only the sound of the wind outside was audible.

'You don't have to drive back to London tonight do you?' Kelly asked him.

'You try getting rid of me,' he said, smiling.

They both laughed.

Kelly ran a finger across his lips then kissed him softly.

Her gaze never left his deep blue eyes and, once more, she felt that glorious sensation of floating. As if she had no control over her own body.

Blake smiled broadly.

PART TWO

'All human beings, as we meet them, are
commingled out of good and evil ...'
— *Robert Louis Stevenson*

'He who shall teach the child to doubt,
Shall ne'er the rotting grave get out.'
— *William Blake*

33

London

The Waterloo Club, in the heart of London's Mayfair, was a magnificent anachronism.

Founded a year after the battle of Waterloo by a group of Wellington's infantry officers, the building was more like a museum. There was a subdued reverence about the place, much like that usually reserved for a church. It languished in cultivated peacefulness and had defied all but the most necessary architectural changes since its construction in 1816. But, for all that, it retained an archaic splendour which was fascinating.

David Blake sipped his drink and scanned the panelled walls. The room seemed dark, despite the lamps which burned in profusion, complimented by the huge crystal chandelier which hung from the ceiling. There were a number of paintings on view including excellent copies of Denis Dighton's 'Sergeant Ewart capturing the Eagle of the 45th', a picture which Blake remembered from a history book. Behind the bar was Sir William Allen's panoramic view of Waterloo, a full fifteen feet in length. It hung in a gilt frame, as imposing a piece of art as Blake had seen. On another wall were two polished cuirasses, the breast plates still carrying musket ball holes. Above them were the brass helmets of Carabiniers, the long swords of the Scots Greys and various original muskets and pistols.

Blake was suitably impressed with the surroundings despite being somewhat perplexed as to why the BBC should have chosen such a setting for the party to welcome Jonathan Mathias to England. Other guests chatted amiably, some, like himself, gazing at the paintings and other paraphernalia. He guessed that there must be about two dozen people there, most of whom he recognized from one or other branch of the entertainment industry.

He spotted Jim O'Neil sitting in one corner. He was on the British leg of a European tour which had, so far, taken him and his band to ten different countries encompassing over eighty gigs. He was a tall, wiry man in his late twenties, dressed completely in black leather. The rock star was nodding intently as two young women chatted animatedly to him.

The writer was aware of other well-known faces too. He caught sight of Sir George Howe, the new head of the BBC, speaking to a group of men which included Gerald Braddock.

Braddock was the present Government's Minister for the Arts, a plump, red-faced man whose shirt collar was much too tight for him, a condition not aided by his tie which appeared to have been fastened by a member of the thugee cult. Every time he swallowed he looked as though he was going to choke.

Next to him stood Roger Carr, host of the chat show on which Mathias was to appear.

Elsewhere, Blake spotted actors and actresses from TV, an agent or two but, as far as he could see, he was the only writer who had been invited.

He'd been a little surprised by the invitation although he had written for the BBC in the past, most notably, a six part series on the paranormal. When he learned that Mathias was to be the guest of honour he'd accepted the invitation readily.

At the moment, however, there was no sign of the American.

'Do you get invited to many dos like this?' Kelly asked him, looking around at the array of talent in the room.

Blake had been seeing her for just over a week now, driving back and forth to Oxford, staying at her flat most nights and returning to his home to work during the day. When he'd told her about the invitation, initially she'd been apprehensive but now, as she scanned the other guests, she did not regret her decision to accompany him.

'There *aren't* many dos like this,' he told her, looking around, wondering where Mathias had disappeared to.

The psychic arrived as if on cue, emerging from the club

cloakroom like something from a Bram Stoker novel. He wore a black three-piece suit and white shirt, a black bow-tie at his throat. Cufflinks bearing large diamonds sparkled in the light like millions of insect eyes. The psychic was introduced to Sir George Howe and his group. All eyes turned towards the little tableau and the previously subdued conversation seemed to drop to a hush. It was as if a powerful magnet had been brought into the room, drawing everything to it.

'He looks very imposing in the flesh,' said Kelly, almost in awe. 'I've only ever seen him in photographs.'

Blake didn't answer her. His eye had been caught by more belated movement from the direction of the cloakroom as a late-comer arrived.

'Christ,' murmured the writer, nudging Kelly. 'Look.'

He nodded in the appropriate direction and she managed to tear her gaze from Mathias.

The late-comer slipped into the room and over to the group surrounding the psychic. Kelly looked at him and then at Blake.

'What's *he* doing here?' she said, in bewilderment.

Dr Stephen Vernon ran a nervous hand through his hair and sidled up beside Sir George Howe.

Blake and Kelly watched as the Institute Director was introduced. Words were exchanged but, no matter how hard she tried, Kelly could not hear what was being said. Gradually, the babble of conversation began to fill the room again.

Kelly hesitated, watching Vernon as he stood listening to the psychic.

'Kelly,' Blake said, forcefully, gripping her arm. 'Come on. Let's get another drink.'

Almost reluctantly, she followed him to the bar where Jim O'Neil now sat, perched on one of the tall stools. He was still listening to one of the girls but his interest seemed to have waned. As Blake and Kelly approached he ran an appreciative eye over Kelly whose full breasts were prominent due to the plunging neck-line of her dress. A tiny gold crucifix hung invitingly between them. O'Neil smiled at her and Kelly returned the gesture.

'Hello,' said O'Neil, nodding at them both but keeping his

172

eyes on Kelly.

The writer turned and smiled, shaking the other man's outstretched hand.

Introductions were swiftly made. O'Neil took Kelly's hand and kissed it delicately.

'Would you like a drink?' asked Blake.

'Make it a pint of bitter will you,' the singer asked. 'I'm sick of these bleeding cocktails.' He pushed the glass away from him.

The barman gave him a disdainful look, watching as the other man downed half of the foaming pint.

'Christ, that's better,' he said.

Kelly caught the sound of a cockney accent in his voice.

'No gig tonight?' Blake asked.

O'Neil shook his head.

'The rest of the band have got the night off,' he said, scratching bristles on his chin which looked as if you could strike a match on them. 'My manager said I ought to come here. God knows why.' He supped some more of his pint. 'I'm surprised they invited me in the first place. I mean, they never play any of my fucking records on Radio One.' He chuckled.

Kelly pulled Blake's arm and nodded in the direction of a nearby table. The two of them said they'd speak to O'Neil again later then left him at the bar ordering another pint.

The writer was in the process of pulling out a chair for Kelly when he saw Mathias and his little entourage approaching. The psychic smiled broadly when he saw Blake. Kelly turned and found herself looking straight at Dr Vernon. They exchanged awkward glances then Kelly looked at Mathias who was already shaking hands with Blake.

'It's good to see you again, David,' said the American. 'How's the book coming along?'

'I'm getting there,' the writer said. 'You look well, Jonathan.'

'I see there are no need for introductions where you two are concerned,' said Sir George Howe, smiling.

'We're not exactly strangers,' Mathias told him. Then he looked at Kelly. 'But I don't know you. And I feel that I should.'

173

The psychic smiled and Kelly saw a glint in his eye.

She introduced herself then stepped back, one eye on Vernon, as Sir George completed the introductions.

Blake shook hands with Gerald Braddock, wincing slightly as he felt the pudgy clamminess of the politician's hand.

Then came Vernon.

'This is Dr Stephen Vernon, an old friend of mine, he ...'

'We've met,' Blake told Sir George. 'How are you, Dr Vernon?'

'I'm very well,' said the older man. He looked at Kelly. 'I didn't expect to see you here tonight, Kelly.'

She didn't answer.

'Well, it seems as if everyone knows everyone else,' said Sir George, aware of the iciness in the air. His stilted laugh died away rapidly.

'How long are you here for, Jonathan?' Blake asked the psychic.

'Three or four days. Long enough to do the show with Mr Carr, and a couple of newspaper interviews, radio pieces. You know the kind of thing,' Mathias told him.

'I saw in the paper that you were coming to England,' Blake said. 'When are you doing the TV show?'

'It's being broadcast the day after tomorrow,' Roger Carr said, stepping forward. 'You should watch it, Mr Blake, I mean you deal in the same kind of tricks don't you? Only you write about them instead.' The interviewer smiled.

Blake returned the smile.

'You know, Mr Carr, there's something I've never been able to figure out about you,' the writer said. 'You're either stupid, in which case I'm sorry for you, or you're pig-ignorant. But I haven't been able to figure out which it is yet.'

Carr shot him an angry glance and opened his mouth to speak but, before he could, all eyes turned in the direction of the cloakroom.

There was an unholy din coming from there, a cacophony of shouts through which the high-pitched voice of a woman could be heard.

Seconds later, a figure dressed in a grey coat, spattered with rain, burst into the peaceful confines of the Waterloo Club. Her hair was wind-blown, her make-up streaked by the rain. She stood panting in the doorway, her eyes fixed on Mathias.

'My God,' muttered Sir George. Then, to a green-coated doorman who had tried to stop the woman entering:

'Could you please eject this lady.'

'No,' Mathias said, raising a hand. 'Leave her.'

'David, who is she?' asked Kelly, noticing the look of recognition on Blake's face as he gazed at the woman.

'Toni Landers,' he said. 'She's an actress.' But the woman whom he had met in New York had been a radiant, sensuous creature. The woman who now stood in the doorway was pale and unkempt, her features haggard. She looked as though she'd aged ten years.

'Do you know this woman?' asked Sir George, looking first at Toni, then at Mathias who had not taken his eyes from her.

'Yes, I know her,' the psychic said.

'Could someone explain what the hell is going on?' Sir George demanded.

'Jonathan, I have to speak to you,' Toni said, her voice cracking. She leant against the bar for support.

Jim O'Neil was on his feet, ready to intervene. Toni looked ready to keel over. She sat down on a bar stool, her gaze still on the psychic.

'How did you find me?' he asked, moving towards her.

'I knew you were coming to England. I've been waiting for you. I found out which hotel you were staying in. They told me where you'd be tonight,' she admitted.

'She's bloody mad,' snapped Roger Carr, dismissively. 'Get her out of here.'

'Shut up,' Mathias rasped. 'Leave her.'

The doorman took a step away from Toni.

'Is this one of your theatrical tricks, Mathias?' Carr demanded.

Blake turned on him.

'Just for once, keep your bloody mouth shut,' he snapped. He motioned to the barman. 'Give her a brandy.'

The man hesitated, looking at Sir George.

'Come on, man, for Christ's sake,' Blake insisted.

'Give her the fucking drink. You heard him,' snarled Jim O'Neil, watching as the barman poured a large measure and handed it to Toni. She downed most of it, coughing as the fiery liquid burned its way to her stomach.

'Toni, what do you want?' Mathias asked her, quietly.

'I need your help, Jonathan,' she told him, tears glistening in her eyes. 'You're the only one who can help me now.'

'Why didn't you come to me before? What were you afraid of?'

She swallowed what was left in the glass.

'That you'd turn me away.'

He shook his head.

'Jonathan, I haven't been able to stop thinking about Rick. Every time I see a child I think about him.' The tears were coursing down her cheeks now. 'Please help me.' Her self-control finally dissolved in a paroxysm of sobs.

Mathias supported her and she clung to him, her body trembling violently.

'What do you want me to do?' he asked.

'Reach him,' she said, flatly. 'Now.'

Mathias didn't speak.

'Please, do I have to beg you?' Some of the despair in her voice had turned to anger. 'Contact my son.'

34

'This is a London club, not a fairground tent,' protested Sir George Ward as the massive oak table was dragged into the centre of the room by Blake, O'Neil and a third man.

'What I intend to do is no fairground trick,' Mathias told him, watching as a number of chairs were placed around the table.

The other guests looked on in stunned, anticipatory silence, Kelly amongst them. Every so often she cast a glance in Dr Vernon's direction, noticing that he was smiling thinly as he observed the proceedings.

Gerald Braddock plucked at the folds of fat beneath his jaw and shifted nervously from one foot to the other.

Toni Landers sat at the bar, the glass of brandy cradled in her shaking hand.

'What are you trying to prove by doing this, Mathias?' Roger Carr wanted to know.

'I don't have to prove anything, Mr Carr,' the psychic said, turning away from him. He held out a hand for Toni Landers to join him. She downed what was left in her glass and wandered across the room. 'Sit there,' the psychic told her, motioning to the chair on his right.

Blake watched with interest, aware that Kelly was gripping his arm tightly. He took her hand and held it, reassuringly.

'I cannot do this alone,' Mathias said, addressing the other guests. 'I must ask for the help of some of you. Not for my own sake but for this lady.' He motioned towards Toni. 'There's nothing to be afraid of. Nothing can hurt you.'

Jim O'Neil was the first to step forward.

'What the hell,' he said, sitting beside Toni then turning in his seat to look at the others.

Roger Carr joined him, sitting on the other side of the table.

Blake looked at Kelly and she nodded almost imperceptibly. They both stepped forward, the writer seating himself directly opposite where Mathias would be.

'Thank you, David,' said the psychic.

As if prompted by Kelly's action, Dr Vernon pulled up a chair and sat down next to her. She eyed him suspiciously for a moment then looked at Blake who had his eyes closed slightly.

'Sir George?' Mathias said, looking at the head of the BBC.

'No, I want no part of this,' said the bald man, defiantly.

Gerald Braddock, who had been rubbing his hands together nervously finally moved towards the table.

'What are you doing, Gerald?' Sir George asked him.

'It can't do any harm,' Braddock said, wiping his palms on his trousers. He looked at the others seated around the table and swallowed hard.

No one else in the room moved. Mathias walked to his seat between Toni Landers and Roger Carr. Opposite him was Blake. To *his* right, Kelly. At the writer's left hand sat Braddock then O'Neil.

'Could we have the lights turned off please?' Mathias asked. 'All but the one over the table.'

Sir George surveyed the group seated before him for a moment then with a sigh he nodded to the club's doorman who flicked off the lights one by one until the table was illuminated by a solitary lamp. Shadows were thick all around it, the other guests swallowed up by them.

'Could you all place your hands, palms down, on the table,' Mathias asked. 'So that your finger-tips are touching the hands of the person on either side of you.'

'I thought we were supposed to hold hands,' muttered Carr, sarcastically.

'Just do as I ask, please,' Mathias said.

Kelly looked up. In the half light, the psychic's face looked milk-white, his eyes standing out in stark contrast. She felt a strange tingle flow through her, a feeling not unlike a small electric shock. She glanced at Blake, who was looking at the psychic, then at Vernon, who had his head lowered.

'Empty your minds,' said Mathias. 'Think of nothing. Hear nothing but my voice. Be aware of nothing but the touch of the people beside you.' His voice had fallen to a low whisper.

The room was silent, only the low, guttural breathing of the psychic audible in the stillness.

Kelly shivered involuntarily and turned her head slightly looking at the others seated with her. All of them had their heads bowed as if in prayer. She too dropped her gaze, noticing as she did that Blake's fingers were shaking slightly. But then so were her own. Indeed, everyone around the table seemed to be undergoing minute, reflexive muscular contractions which jerked their bodies almost imperceptibly every few seconds.

Mathias grunted something inaudible then coughed. His eyes closed and his head began to tilt backward. His chest was heaving as if he were finding it difficult to breathe.

'Don't break the circle,' he muttered, throatily. 'Don't ... break ...'

He clenched his teeth together, as if in pain and a long, wheezing sound escaped him. It was as if someone had punctured a set of bellows. His body began to shake more violently, perspiration beading on his forehead, glistening in the dull light. His eyes suddenly shot open, bulging wide in the sockets, his head still tilted backward.

He groaned again, more loudly this time.

The light above the table flickered, went out then glowed with unnatural brilliance once more.

'The child,' croaked Mathias. 'The ... child ...'

His groans became shouts.

Kelly tried to raise her head but it was as if there was a heavy weight secured to her chin. Only by monumental effort did she manage to raise it an inch or so.

Somewhere behind her one of the swords fell from the wall with a loud clatter but none of those seated at the table could move to find the source of the noise. They were all held as if by some invisible hand, aware only of the increasing warmth in the room. A warmth which seemed to be radiating from the very centre of the table itself.

'The child,' Mathias gasped once more.

This time Kelly recoiled as a vile stench assaulted her nostrils. A sickly sweet odour which reminded her of bad meat. She coughed, her stomach churning.

The feeling of heat was growing stronger until it seemed that the table must be ablaze. But, at last, she found that she could raise her head.

If she had been able to, she would have screamed.

Toni Landers beat her to it.

Standing in the centre of the table was the image of her son.

His clothes, what remained of them, were blackened and scorched, hanging in places like burned tassles. Beneath the fabric his skin was red raw, mottled green in places. The left arm had been completely stripped of flesh and what musculature remained was wasted and scorched. Bone shone with dazzling whiteness through the charred mess. The chest and lower body was a mass of suppurating sores which were weeping sticky clear pus like so many diseased eyes. But it was the head and neck which bore the most horrific injury. The boy's head was twisted at an impossible angle, a portion of spinal column visible through the pulped mess at the base of the skull. The head itself seemed to have been cracked open like an egg shell and a lump of jellied brain matter bulged obscenely from one of the rents. The bottom lip had been torn off, taking most of the left cheek with it, to expose ligaments and tendons which still twitched spasmodically. Blood had soaked the boy's upper body, its coppery odour mingling with the overpowering stink of burned skin and hair.

Toni Landers tried to raise her hands to shield her eyes from this abomination which had once been her son but it was as if someone had nailed her fingers to the table. She could only sit helplessly and watch as the apparition turned full circle in the middle of the table, meeting the horrified gaze of all those present before bringing its milky orbs to bear on her. One of the eyes had been punctured by a piece of broken skull and it nestled uselessly in the bloodied socket like a burst balloon.

The apparition took a step towards her.

It was smiling.

Kelly looked across at Mathias and saw that there was perspiration pouring down his face as he gazed at the sight before him. She then turned slightly and looked at Blake. He was not looking at the child but at the psychic, the writer's own body trembling convulsively.

The figure of the boy moved closer to Toni Landers, one charred hand rising before it as it reached the edge of the table.

Finally, by a monumental effort of will, Toni managed to lift her hands from the table.

As she covered her face she let out a scream which threatened to shake the building.

'Look,' urged Jim O'Neil.

Like the image on a TV set, the apparition of Rick Landers began to fade. Not slowly but with almost breathtaking suddenness until the table was empty once more. Above them, the light dimmed again.

'My God,' burbled Gerald Braddock. 'What *was* that?'

Even if anyone heard him, no one seemed capable of furnishing him with an answer.

Sir George Howe strode to the panel of switches behind the bar and snapped on the lights himself.

Mathias sat unmoved at the table, his eyes locked with those of Blake. The writer was breathing heavily, as if he'd just run up a flight of long steps. The two men regarded one another a moment longer then Mathias turned to Toni Landers who was sobbing uncontrollably beside him.

'Fuck me,' was all Jim O'Neil could say. His voice a low whisper.

Dr Vernon stroked his chin thoughtfully, looking at the spot on the table top where the apparition had first materialized. It still shone as if newly polished. He inhaled. There was no smell of burned flesh any longer, no cloying odour of blood. Only the acrid smell of perspiration.

Beside him, Kelly touched Blake's hand, seeing that the writer looked a little pale.

'Are you all right, David?' she asked, aware that her own heart was beating wildly.

Blake nodded.

'And you?' he wanted to know.

She was shaking badly and Blake put one arm around her shoulder, drawing her close to him.

Roger Carr sat where he was for a moment, looking at the others around the table, then he got to his feet and stalked across to the bar where he downed a large scotch in two huge swallows. Only then did he begin to calm down. He looked back over his shoulder at Mathias.

Not only was this man very good at what he did, the bastard was convincing too. Carr ordered another scotch.

Jonathan Mathias finally managed to quieten Toni Landers, wiping away some of her tears with his handkerchief. He helped her to her feet and led her outside into the rain soaked night. He told his chauffeur to take her home and then return.

As the psychic stood alone on the pavement watching the car disappear from view he looked down at his hands.

Both palms were red raw, as if he'd been holding something very hot. His entire body was sheathed in sweat but he felt colder than he'd ever felt in his life.

35

Blake hit the last full stop, pulled the paper from the typewriter and laid it on top of the pile beside him.

Without the clacking of typewriter keys, the cellar was once more silent.

The writer picked up the pages next to him and skimmed through them. Another day or so and the book would be finished, he guessed. He had submitted the bulk of it to his publisher shortly after returning from the States. Now he was nearing the end. He sat back in his chair and yawned. It was almost 8 a.m. He'd been working for two hours. Blake always rose early, completing the greater part of his work during the morning. It was a routine which he'd followed for the last four years. Down in the cellar it was peaceful. He didn't even hear the comings and goings of his neighbours. But, on this particular morning, his mind had been elsewhere.

As hard as he tried, he could not shake the image of Toni Landers' dead child from his mind. In fact, the entire episode of the previous night still burned as clearly in his consciousness as if it had been branded there. He remembered the terror etched on the faces of those who had sat at the table with him, the horrified reactions of those who had looked on from the relative safety beyond the circle.

The gathering had begun to break up almost immediately after the seance. Blake himself, rather than drive back to Oxford, had persuaded Kelly to stay at his house for the night. She had readily agreed. She was upstairs dressing. He had woken her before he'd climbed out of bed, they had made love and she had decided to take a long hot bath before he drove her home.

He put the cover back on the typewriter and made his way up the stone steps from the subterranean work room, locking the door behind him as he emerged into the hall.

'What are you hiding down there? The Crown Jewels?'

The voice startled him momentarily and he spun round to see Kelly descending the stairs.

Blake smiled and pocketed the key to the cellar.

'Force of habit,' he said. 'I don't like to be disturbed.'

They walked through into the kitchen where she put the kettle on while he jammed some bread into the toaster. Kelly spooned coffee into a couple of mugs.

'Are you all right, Kelly?' he asked, noticing that she looked pale.

She nodded.

'I'm a little tired, I didn't sleep too well last night,' she told him.

'That's understandable.'

'Understandable, but not forgivable.'

He looked puzzled.

'David, I'm a psychic investigator. My reactions to the paranormal, anything out of the ordinary, should be ... well, scientific. But what I saw last night at that seance terrified me. I couldn't even think straight.'

'If it's any consolation,' he said. 'I don't think you were the only one.' He caught the toast as it popped up.

Kelly watched him as he buttered it, finally handing her a slice.

'I'd still like to know how Vernon managed to get an invitation,' she said.

'He's a friend of Sir George Howe, the old boy told us that.'

Kelly nodded slowly.

'I still don't trust him,' she said.

Blake leant forward and kissed her on the forehead.

'I don't trust anyone.'

The kettle began to boil.

It was 2.15 when Blake parked the XJS back in his driveway. The journey back from Oxford had taken longer than he'd expected due to a traffic hold up on the way back into the town. Now he clambered out of the Jag and headed for his front door, waving a greeting to one of his neighbours as she passed by with her two children.

Blake walked in and discovered that the postman had been

during his absence. There was a slim envelope which bore a familiar type-face. He tore it open and unfolded the letter, heading towards the sitting room as he did so. The writer perched on the edge of a chair and read aloud.

'Dear David, I'm sorry to have kept you waiting but I have only recently managed to read the manuscript of "From Within". I'm even sorrier to tell you that I do not feel that it matches the quality of your earlier work, which was based on solid facts and research. This latest effort seems comprised mostly of speculation and theorising, particularly on the subject of Astral travel and mind control. I realize that these subjects are open to question but the book does not convince me as to the validity of your statements. So how can we expect the public to believe it?

Despite the fact that you are well established and a proven top-seller, I feel that I cannot, as yet offer you a contract based on the manuscript in its present state.'

Blake got to his feet, still glaring angrily at the letter.

It was signed with the sweeping hand of Phillip Campbell, his publisher.

'I cannot offer you a contract ...' Blake muttered, angrily. He crossed to the phone and picked up the receiver, punching buttons irritably.

'Good morning ...'

He gave the receptionist no time to complete the formalities.

'Phillip Campbell, please,' he said, impatiently.

There was a click at the other line then another woman's voice.

'Phillip Campbell's office, good afternoon.'

'Is Phillip there?'

'Yes, who's calling?'

'David Blake.'

Another click. A hiss of static.

'Good afternoon, David.'

He recognized Campbell's Glaswegian accent immediately.

'Hello, Phil. I'd like a word if you can spare me the time.'

'Sure. What's on your mind?'

184

' "I cannot offer you a contract", that's what's on my mind,' Blake snapped. 'What the hell is going on, Phil? What's wrong with the bloody book?'

'I thought I told you that in the letter,' the Scot said.

' "Speculation and theorising" is that it?'

'Look, Dave, don't start getting uptight about it. If you can't stand a bit of criticism from a friend then maybe you're in the wrong game. What I wrote was meant to help.'

'You haven't seen the completed manuscript yet,' Blake reminded him.

'Fair enough. Maybe I'll change my mind once I have but, like I said, you need more concrete facts in it. Especially this business about someone being able to control another person's Astral Body. You're going to have trouble making the readers believe that.'

'Phil, I'm telling you, I know it can be done,' said Blake.

'Facts, Dave,' the publisher reminded him. 'Once I've seen the finished manuscript then maybe we can sort something out.'

There was a moment's pause then the Scot continued.

'David, I want this book in print as much as you do. We both stand to make a lot of money out of it but, in its present form, we'll be laughed out of court if we publish. You realize that.'

Blake sighed.

'Facts,' he said. 'All right, Phil, I'll get back to you.' He hung up. The writer stood there for a moment then he balled up the letter and threw it into a nearby waste-basket.

He headed back towards the cellar.

36

Oxford

The book fell from his hand and hit the bedroom carpet with a thud.

Dr Stephen Vernon sat up, disturbed from his light sleep. He yawned, retrieved the book and placed it on his bedside table. Then he reached across and flicked off the light. The hands of his watch glowed dully, showing him that it was almost 1.05 a.m. He pulled the sheet up to his neck and closed his eyes but the sleep which had come to him earlier now seemed to desert him. He rolled onto his side, then his back, then the other side but the more he moved the more he seemed to shed any desire to sleep.

He sat up again, reaching for the book.

He read three or four pages without remembering a single word and, with a sigh, replaced the thick tome. He decided that his best strategy was to get out of bed. He'd make himself a hot drink, that usually did the trick. Vernon clambered out of bed and pulled on his dressing gown. He left the bedside lamp burning and padded across the landing.

He was at the top of the stairs when he heard the faint knocking.

Almost instinctively he turned and looked at the door of the locked room but it took him but an instant to realize that the sound had originated downstairs.

He hesitated.

The knocking came again.

Vernon swallowed hard and moved cautiously down the first three or four steps.

Outside, in the darkness, he heard the sound of movement, the crunching of gravel beneath heavy feet.

Vernon peered over the bannister, down into the pit of blackness which was his hallway. The light switch was at the bottom, beside the large window which looked out onto the gravel drive and the front garden.

He glanced down, his heart quickening slightly.

He had neglected to draw the curtain across that window.

The movement seemed to have stopped so Vernon scuttled down the stairs, gripping the bannister with one hand in case he overbalanced in the gloom.

He was level with the window when he saw a dark shape three or four feet from the glass.

It moved rapidly back into the gloom and seemed to disappear.

Vernon felt himself perspiring as he reached the light switch, not sure whether to turn it on or not. If he did then *he* would be visible to anyone outside. His hand hovered over the switch but, eventually, he decided against it and moved cautiously into the sitting room, ears ever alert for the slightest sound.

From the brass bucket beside the fire-place he retrieved a poker then he turned and walked back into the hall, pausing at the front door, listening.

There was more movement outside.

Footsteps.

Should he call the police, he wondered? If it was burglars then there might be more than one of them. What if they should attack him?

What if he called the police but they didn't arrive in time?

What if ...

The sound was right outside the front door now.

Vernon, with excruciating care, slipped the bolt then the chain and fastened his hand around the door handle, raising the poker high above his head in readiness to strike. His heart was thudding madly against his ribs, his mouth as dry as parchment.

He pulled open the door.

Nothing.

Only the wind greeted him, a cool breeze which made him shiver. He exhaled almost gratefully and lowered the poker, squinting into the blackness in search of that elusive shape.

He saw nothing.

Vernon waited a moment longer then turned.

He almost screamed as the hand gripped his shoulder.

It appeared as if from nowhere and the older man tried to raise the poker once more but his co-ordination seemed to have deserted him. It fell from his grasp with a dull clang.

He turned to see the figure standing before him.

'You?' he gasped, one hand clutched to his chest. 'What do you think you're doing creeping about in the dark? I could have hit you with this.' He retrieved the poker. 'I wasn't expecting you so soon.'

Alain Joubert walked past Vernon into the house.

37

London

Toni Landers held the small bottle before her and read the label.

Mogadon.

She unscrewed the cap of the bottle and upended it, coaxing the contents into one hand. There were twelve of the white tablets, all that remained since she had begun taking them soon after Rick's death.

Rick.

The thought of his name brought a tear to her eye and she sat down on the side of the bath, still clutching the tablets, remembering the monstrous image which had appeared before her the night before, called by Mathias. That abomination, that disfigured, mutilated monstrosity had been her son.

She opened her hand and looked at the tablets again.

Would twelve be enough?

She had contemplated suicide only once since he'd been killed but, after what had happened the previous night, the prospect of ending her own life now seemed positively inviting. She wiped a tear from her eye and spread the tablets out on the ledge beside the sink.

It was after three in the morning but the house was not silent.

Across the landing she could hear the muted, muffled sounds of cautious lovemaking. An occasional stifled moan of pleasure, a whispered word. It only served to remind her of her own loneliness.

She had been staying with friends ever since Rick's death but she realized that she must go back to the States eventually. Back to her own home. The home she had shared with Rick.

She looked at the sleeping tablets once more and realized that there was no way she could return. Toni picked one up and held it between her fingers for a moment. It wouldn't be difficult. She'd take the tablets then wander back to bed and fall asleep. It was that simple. All she had to do was take the first tablet. Then the second. Then ...

She filled a beaker with water and got to her feet.

As she did so, she realized that the sounds of lovemaking had stopped. The house was silent again.

Toni heard footsteps, soft and light crossing the landing. She scooped up the Mogadon and pushed them back into the bottle, slipping it into the pocket of her housecoat. But, the footsteps receded momentarily and she guessed that whoever it was had gone into the nursery.

The baby was asleep in there, in the room close to her own.

The baby.

She felt tears welling up once more and, this time, they spilled down her cheeks. Her body was racked by a series of uncontrollable sobs which, no matter how hard she tried, she could not disguise. A second later there was a light tap on the bathroom door.

'Toni,' the voice asked. 'Are you all right?'

She choked back her sobs with a monumental effort and wiped her face with a flannel.

'Toni.' The voice was low but more insistent.

She crossed to the door and slid back the bolt, opening it slightly.

Vicki Barnes stood before her, her long, thick blonde hair uncombed, her eyes puffy from tiredness.

Even models could look ordinary at three in the morning.

'I was just checking on the baby,' Vicki whispered. 'I heard you crying.'

Toni shook her head.

'I'm OK now,' she lied, sniffing.

'Come on,' Vicki urged, taking her hand. 'Let's go downstairs. I'll make us both a cup of coffee. I can't sleep either.'

'I know,' Toni said, managing a slight smile. 'I heard you.'

Vicki raised her eyebrows and shrugged.

'Sorry,' she smiled. 'Paul says I should wear a gag when we have guests.'

The two women made their way across the landing, past the baby's room and down the stairs to the kitchen. Once there Vicki filled the electric kettle and plugged it in. In the cold white light of the fluorescents she could see how pale Toni looked, how dark her eyes were, the whites streaked with veins.

Vicki was two years younger than her friend. They'd met back in the mid-seventies when Vicki had been on a modelling assignment in New York. The bond between them had grown steadily since then and Toni had been Matron of Honour when Vicki had married a record producer three years earlier. The actress was also Godmother to their child, Dean, now almost fourteen months old.

'Vicki, do you ever think about dying?' asked Toni, staring straight ahead.

The model looked shocked.

'No,' she said, softly. 'Why do you ask?'

'I never used to, not until ...' The sentence trailed off as she bowed her head. Vicki got up and stood beside her friend, snaking an arm around her shoulder.

'Don't talk about it,' she said.

Toni reached for a tissue in her housecoat pocket and, as she did, the bottle of Mogadon fell to the floor. Vicki spotted it first and picked it up.

She understood immediately.

'Is this your answer, Toni?' she asked quietly, replacing the bottle on the table in front of the actress.

'I'm not sure I want to go on without Rick,' said the American, her voice cracking. She clenched her fists. 'He was all I had. He meant everything to me. Vicki, if you'd seen that ... thing the other night.'

'You mean at the seance?'

Toni nodded.

'He was there,' she paused for a moment, trying to compose herself. 'I know it was Rick. He looked the way he did when I had to identify him, just after it happened. After the accident. That was my son,' she said, tears running down her cheeks.

'No one's saying you haven't got a right to feel the way you do. But this isn't the answer.' Vicki held up the bottle of tablets. 'And before you beat me to it, I know it's easy for *me* to say.'

Toni didn't speak.

'Please Toni, for Rick's sake, think about it.'

The American nodded.

'I'm frightened, Vicki,' she admitted. 'When I get back to the States, I don't know how I'm going to be able to go inside that house again. There are too many memories there.'

'You'll do it. If I have to come with you, you'll do it.'

Toni smiled thinly. The other girl got to her feet and kissed her gently on the cheek. They held each other for long moments.

'Thank you,' Toni whispered.

'I wish there was more I could do,' Vicki said. She stepped back. 'Do you want to go back to bed now? If not I'll sit up with you.'

'You go, I'll be OK,' Toni assured her.

'And these?' Vicki held up the bottle of tablets.

'Take them with you.'

The model slipped them into her hand and made for the kitchen door.

'See you in the morning, Toni.'

The actress heard footfalls on the stairs as her friend made her way up the steps. For what seemed like an eternity, Toni sat in silence, sipping at her coffee then, finally, she got to her feet, rinsed the cup and wandered out of the kitchen, flicking the light off behind her.

As she reached the landing she trod more softly, not wanting to disturb her hosts. The house was silent. The only thing which she heard was her own low breathing.

Toni paused outside the nursery, looking at the door as if she expected to see through it. She reached for the handle, hesitated a second then turned it. She stepped inside and

191

closed it gently behind her.

The cot stood in the far corner of the room. On a table close to her was a small lamp which bathed the room in a warm golden glow. The walls were painted light blue, the lower half decorated with a kind of mural showing teddy bears riding bikes, flying aircraft and climbing trees. It had, she guessed, been painted by Vicki's husband.

A profusion of soft toys littered the floor near to the cot. A huge stuffed penguin in particular fixed her in the unblinking stare of its glass eyes and she saw her own distorted reflection in them as she approached the cot.

The child was awake but made no sound, he merely lay on his back gazing wonderingly up at her with eyes as big as saucers.

Toni smiled down at him, chuckling softly as he returned the gesture. She took one tiny hand in hers and shook it gently, feeling the little fingers clutching at her.

The baby gurgled happily and Toni reached down and ran her fingertips over the smooth skin of his chubby face, stroking the gossamer strands of his hair before moving her fingers to his mouth. She traced the outline of his lips with her nail, smiling at the little boy as he flailed playfully at the probing digit. His mouth opened wider and he gurgled.

Suddenly, with a combination of lightning speed and demonic force, Toni rammed two fingers into the child's mouth, pressing down hard as her nails raked the back of its throat.

The baby squirmed and tried to scream but the sound was lost, gurgling away into a liquid croak as blood began to fill the soft cavity.

With her free hand she clutched the child's head, holding it steady as she forced another finger into its mouth, hooking them inside its throat until it gagged on its own blood and the intruding fingers.

As Toni pushed a fourth finger into the blood-filled orifice, the soft skin at each side of the baby's mouth began to rip. Toni was pressing down so hard it seemed that she would push the child through the bottom of the cot.

Blood splashed her hand and flooded on to the sheet, staining it crimson and still she exerted yet more pressure, grunting loudly at the effort. The baby had long since ceased to move.

Toni lifted it from its cot, her fingers covered in blood, some of which ran up her arm to stain her housecoat. She held the child before her, gazing into its sightless eyes.

She was still holding the child when the door of the nursery was thrown open.

Toni turned slowly to face Vicki Barnes and her husband, both of whom stood transfixed by the sight before them.

Toni heard screams echoing in her ears but could not seem to comprehend that they were coming from Vicki who had dropped to her knees and was staring at the monstrous scene before her.

Then, as if someone had pulled a veil from her mind she was able to see herself just what she'd done. She held the bloodied bundle at arm's length, her expression a mixture of horror and bewilderment.

The next screams she heard were her own.

38

Oxford

The dining room table must have been fully eight feet long, perhaps half that in width and yet every single carefully polished inch of the surface seemed to be covered with pieces of paper. Some were still in the files they had originated in, others were scattered about like the pieces of some huge, unsolvable puzzle.

And to Dr Stephen Vernon, that was exactly what all these notes were. A puzzle. Yet somehow it had to be solved.

He looked across the table at Joubert who was making notes, scribbling down words and phrases, sifting through the mud in an effort to find those elusive nuggets of information. Since his arrival at Vernon's house the previous night, he had done little else. Now, as the clock ticked around to 6 p.m., he dropped his pen and sat back in the chair.

'There's something missing,' said the Frenchman, surveying the piles of paper, the type-written sheets, the crammed notepads, the EEG read-outs.

'But I thought you brought *all* your findings,' Vernon said.

'Lasalle must have some of the research material with him,' Joubert said, irritably.

'Then all of this is useless?' Vernon suggested.

'No, it isn't useless but there are other factors too,' the Frenchman said, getting to his feet and crossing to the phone.

Vernon watched him as he dialled, sucking enthusiastically on his cough sweet, enjoying the smell of menthol which filled the air around him.

Joubert drummed agitatedly on the side-board as he waited for the receiver to be picked up. Eventually it was and Vernon listened as the investigator rattled out some questions in French. In the middle of it all he caught the name Lasalle. Joubert muttered something and pressed the cradle down, dialling again. He waited for an answer.

'Lasalle,' he said, quickly, as the receiver was picked up. 'This is Joubert.'

'Alain, where are you? Why weren't you at the Centre, I ...'

'Listen to me, Lasalle,' he interrupted. 'Our notes on Astral projection, I need them. Do you have any?'

'That's what I wanted to tell you,' Lasalle said. 'All the files have gone from the Centre. Everything relating to that one project.'

'I know, I *have* them,' Joubert told him. 'But there are some missing.'

'You took them from the Centre?' he asked. 'But why?'

Joubert finally lost his temper.

'For God's sake. How many times do I have to say it? Shut up and listen to me,' he barked. 'Do you have any of the notes relating to that project?'

'Yes I have.'

'I'm going to give you an address, I want you to send everything you have to me. No matter how unimportant it may seem, I want the files. Do you understand?'

'Yes,' he answered, vaguely. His voice was almost subservient.

Joubert gave him the address of Vernon's house, his

irritation growing when he was forced to repeat it.

'Why are you in England?' Lasalle wanted to know.

'Send me those notes,' his companion snapped.

'Alain, you are needed here,' Lasalle said, weakly. 'There are newspaper and television people at the Centre every day. I can't cope with their questions. They want to know so much. I cannot work *and* answer them. I need help ... I feel overpowered ... trapped. Alain, please.'

'This fiasco is of your own making, Lasalle,' Joubert hissed. 'If you hadn't written that damned article none of this would be happening.'

'I need help here ...'

'And I need those notes,' he rasped and slammed down the phone. He stood motionless for a moment, the knot of muscles at the side of his jaw throbbing angrily. Vernon watched him in silence.

'He has what I need. I should have been more thorough,' the Frenchman said. He went on to tell Vernon what Lasalle has said about the press. As he did so, his face grew darker and finally, he slammed his fist down on the table top. '*I* should be the one being interviewed not him,' he snarled.

'Is the recognition *that* important to you?' Vernon asked.

Joubert sucked in a weary breath and nodded.

'Eight years ago I was working for the Metapsychic Centre investigating a series of hauntings in a hotel in the Hauts-de-Seine area of Paris.' He reached for a cigarette and lit it, drawing the smoke into his lungs. 'I was working with another man, named Moreau.' The Frenchman frowned, his eyes narrowing. 'We had been at the hotel for over two months, making recordings, taking statements from the people who stayed there. It seemed as if there *was* an entity of some kind present in the building. Eventually we managed to get a clear recording of its movements. The next night we even photographed it. A *true* haunting. As you know, most of those reported are either imagined or psychologically rooted but not this one. We had visual evidence.'

'What happened?' Vernon asked.

Joubert stubbed out what was left of his cigarette in the saucer and sat back in his chair.

'Moreau took the photographs and the tape recordings to the Director of the Metapsychic Centre. He claimed that *he* had discovered the entity. Despite my protestations, he was credited with it. Now he's one of the Directors of the Parapsychology Laboratory in Milan. One of the most respected men in his field in Italy. After that happened, I swore that I would never share any such finding with anyone. What I worked on, what I discovered would be mine. No one else's. But look what has happened. The single most important breakthrough in the study of the paranormal for twenty years and Lasalle is being credited with it. When this is over, who will remember Alain Joubert?' He glared at Vernon. 'No one. Well, this time it will be different. I had kept things quiet until the time was right to reveal the discoveries. The only reason I agreed to help you was because I knew that you offered no threat, you wanted the secret for your own reasons. You would not take away the recognition which was rightfully mine.' His tone turned reflective. 'I underestimated Lasalle.'

'I don't see that there's much you can do,' Vernon said. 'If the press have the story then ...' He shrugged, allowing the sentence to trail off. 'What *can* you do?'

Joubert did not answer, he merely gazed past Vernon to the overcast sky outside.

Clouds were gathering.

39

Paris

He awoke screaming.

Lasalle sat up, as if trying to shake the last vestiges of the nightmare from his mind. He gulped in huge lungfuls of air, one hand pressed to his chest as his heart thudded madly against his ribs.

He had seen her once more.

His wife.

His Madelaine.

Or what had once been her.

He had been bending over the grave laying fresh flowers on it when a hand had erupted from the earth and gripped his wrist, pulling him down as she hauled herself free of the dirt. She had sought his lips with hers, only hers were little more than liquescent pustules. She had embraced him with those rotting arms, pulling him close in an obscene attempt to push her decaying body against him, writhing at the contact. He had felt pieces of putrescent flesh peeling off in his hands like leprous growths as he fought to push her away.

Lasalle got to his feet, holding his stomach. He scurried to the kitchen and stood over the sink feeling his nausea building. He splashed his face with cold water and the feeling passed slowly. The Frenchman found that he was shaking uncontrollably so he gripped the edge of the sink in an effort to stop the quivering. Perspiration beaded on his forehead and ran in salty rivulets down his face.

He remembered falling asleep at the table in the sitting room. He'd been slumped across it when he'd woken. Lasalle closed his eyes, but the image of his dead wife came hurtling into his consciousness. He filled a glass with water then walked back into the sitting room, fumbling in the pocket of his jacket for the tranquilizers. He swallowed one. Two. Three. The Frenchman washed them down with the water and sat motionless at the table, his hands clenched into fists.

On the sideboard opposite, the photo of his wife smiled back at him and Lasalle, unaccountably, felt tears brimming in his eyes. He blinked and one trickled down his cheek.

'Madelaine,' he whispered, softly.

He closed his eyes once more, trying to remember how he had come to fall asleep so early in the evening. It was not yet 9 p.m.

It must have been after the phone call, he guessed.

The phone call.

He swallowed hard. He had spoken to Joubert. That much he *did* remember.

Lasalle raised both hands to his head as if he feared it might explode. He could not seem to think straight. Thoughts and images tumbled through his mind with dizzying speed.

The phone call. The nightmare. Madelaine.

197

He exhaled deeply, wiping more sweat from his face.

The nightmare still stood out with unwelcome clarity. That monstrous vision filled his mind again and he shook his head but, this time, there was something else. Something which he only now remembered.

As the decomposing corpse of his wife had embraced him, he had heard soft malevolent laughter and he knew what had propelled him, shrieking, from the nightmare.

The laughter had been coming from the graveside.

From Joubert.

40

London

The young make-up girl smiled as she applied the last few touches of foundation to the face of Mathias. She then took what looked like a small paint brush and flicked away the residue. The layer of make-up was sufficiently thick to protect his face from the bright studio lights he would soon be facing.

Mathias returned her smile, watching as she gathered her brushes, powder pots and small bottles and slipped them back into a leather bag she carried. He thanked her then got to his feet and opened the door for her. She smiled and left.

As the psychic was about to close the door again he saw a tubby man approaching along the corridor. The man was dressed in jeans and a grey sweatshirt and he had a set of earphones around his neck.

'Are you ready, Mr Mathias?' he asked. 'There's two minutes before you go on.'

The psychic nodded and stepped back inside the dressing room for a moment to inspect his reflection in the large mirror, then he followed the tubby man along the corridor towards a door marked: STUDIO ONE.

As they drew closer he could hear the muted sounds of many voices coming from inside. An occasional laugh which signalled that the audience were settling down. There was a red light above the door and a sign which read: ON AIR.

The tubby man opened the door carefully and ushered Mathias through.

The sound of the audience was very loud now but Mathias paid it little heed as he was led to a chair behind the main set.

From where he sat he could see numerous spotlights suspended over the set but, other than that, he could see only crew members dashing furtively about, obeying the orders of the floor manager whose instructions they received via their headphones. High up above the studio was the room where the director and his assistants sat, watching everything on banks of screens, relaying information to the floor.

Mathias could hear Roger Carr's voice. He was speaking about the supernatural, dropping in the odd joke where he felt it necessary. The audience laughed happily. Mathias sipped at the glass of water on the table before him and shook his head.

The tubby man turned to him and held up one finger.

The psychic got to his feet.

Roger Carr turned towards the camera on his right hand side, noticing that a red light had just blinked into life on top of it. He smiled thinly at it, getting himself more comfortable in his leather chair.

'My last guest tonight,' he began. 'Many of you may already have heard of. Certainly in America, he's what you might call an institution. Some might even say he should be *in* an institution.'

The audience laughed.

'He's revered by millions as a healer, an expert on the supernatural. Someone even dubbed him "The Messiah in the Tuxedo".'

Another ripple of laughter.

'Whether his powers are genuine or not remains to be seen but there are countless Americans who claim that he is truly a miracle worker. Perhaps after this interview, you can form your own opinions. Saviour or charlatan? Messiah or magician? Judge for yourselves.' Carr got to his feet. 'Please welcome Jonathan Mathias.'

There was a sustained round of applause as the American walked onto the set. He glanced at the audience and smiled as he made his way towards Carr. The host shook hands with him and motioned for him to sit. The applause gradually died away.

' "The Messiah in a Tuxedo" ' said Carr, smiling. 'How do you react to comments like that?'

'I don't take much notice of criticism,' Mathias began. 'I ...'

Carr cut him short.

'But surely, some of the things you claim to have done do leave you open to it?'

'If I could finish what I was saying,' Mathias continued, quietly. 'Yes, I do receive criticism but mostly from people who don't understand what I do. Didn't someone once say that any fool can criticise and most do.'

There was a chorus of chuckles from the audience.

'You mentioned what you do,' Carr continued. 'You claim to be a faith-healer and ...'

'I've never claimed to be a *faith*-healer,' Mathias corrected him.

'But you do perform acts of healing? Non-medical acts.'

'Yes.'

'If that isn't faith-healing then what is it?'

'People come to me because they know I will help them. I have never claimed ...'

'You charge money for this "healing"?' Carr said.

'A small fee. Usually people donate money. I don't ask for much from them. They give because they want to. As a token of appreciation.'

Carr nodded.

'You also appear on American television, do you not?' he said. 'Presumably you are well paid for that?'

'I don't have a pay cheque on me right now,' Mathias said, smiling. 'But, yes, the pay is good. As no doubt yours is, Mr Carr.'

'You wouldn't deny then that your basic interests are commercial.'

'I have a talent, a gift. I use it to help others.'

'But you wouldn't perform for nothing?'

'Would *you*?'

There was a ripple of laughter from the audience.

'No,' Carr told him. 'I wouldn't. But then I don't exploit the fears and gullibility of sick people.'

'I wasn't aware that *I* did, Mr Carr.'

The interviewer shifted uncomfortably in his seat, angry that Mathias was taking his verbal assault so calmly.

'Then what do you class yourself as?' he asked. 'Surely not an ordinary psychic? The fact that you're a multi-millionaire seems to lift you out of the category of ordinary.'

'My powers are greater than an ordinary psychic ...'

Carr interrupted.

'Can you give me an example of your *power*?' he said. 'Read my mind.' He smiled.

'Would it be worth it?' Mathias japed.

The audience joined him in his amusement. Carr did not appreciate the joke. The veins at his temple throbbed angrily.

'If we wheel in a couple of cripples could you make them walk?' the interviewer hissed.

'I don't perform to order, Mr Carr,' the psychic told him.

'Only if the price is right, yes?'

The floor manager looked anxiously at the two men, as if expecting them to leap at one another. Mathias remained calm.

'How would you answer the charge of charlatan?' Carr said.

'It's for each individual to decide whether or not they believe in my powers,' the American said. 'You may believe as you wish.'

The two men regarded one another for long seconds, the interviewer seeking some flicker of emotion in the piercing blue eyes of his guest. Haw saw none. Not even anger. Carr eventually turned away and looked directly into the camera.

'Well, as you have heard, Mr Mathias invites us to make up our own minds as to his ... *powers*. Although, having seen and heard his answers tonight I, for one, will draw just one conclusion. And I think you know what that is. Goodnight.'

As the studio lights dimmed, Carr got to his feet and glared down at Mathias.

'Clever bastard aren't you?' he snarled. 'Trying to make me look like a prick in front of millions of viewers.'

'I don't think you needed my help on that score,' Mathias said. 'You were the one looking for the fight, not me.'

'Well, you can take your fucking powers and shove them up your arse,' he snapped.

As he stormed off the set, the floor manager shouted something about the director wanting to see him.

'Fuck him,' Carr retorted and disappeared through the exit door.

Mathias was getting to his feet when the floor manager approached him.

'The director told me to apologise to you for Mr Carr's remarks during the interview,' said the man.

Mathias smiled.

'No harm done,' he said.

The floor manager nodded and walked away.

Only then did the psychic's smile fade.

41

The bedroom window was open and the cool breeze caused the curtains to billow gently.

Roger Carr lay naked on his back, arms folded behind his head. He was gazing up at the ceiling, his eyes fixed on a fly which was crawling across the emulsioned surface. It eventually made its exit through the open window and Carr was left gazing at nothing but white paint. He lay there for a moment longer then rolled on to his side and reached for the bottle of beer which was propped on the bedside table. He tipped it up, discovering to his annoyance that it was empty. Carr tossed it away and it landed with a thud on the carpet, close to a pair of discarded knickers. The owner of the garment was out of the room at present. Carr thought about shouting to her to fetch him another bottle of beer. Instead he rolled over once more and returned to gazing at the ceiling.

With his hands behind his head, the ticking of his watch

sounded thunderous in the silence. The hands had crawled round to 12.18 a.m.

He wondered what Mathias was doing.

Bastard.

Flash Yank bastard.

Carr had been surprised by the American's composure during the interview earlier in the evening. Most people usually crumbled beneath such a concerted verbal onslaught, but Mathias had managed to remain calm throughout.

Fucking bastard.

Carr realized that the psychic had bettered him during the argument. It could scarcely be called a discussion after all. In front of millions of viewers and the studio audience, Carr had met his match and that hurt him deeply. The image of Mathias flashed into his mind and he sat up, his breath coming in short, angry grunts. He swung himself off the bed and walked across to the window where he inhaled the cool night air and looked out into the darkness.

The street was quiet, but for the barking of a dog. The house was less than five minutes drive from the BBC and Carr had chosen it for its peaceful surroundings. He didn't like noise, he didn't like interference. He was a solitary person once he left the studio. He liked to pick and choose whose company he kept, therefore few people ever got close to him. Or wanted to for that matter.

Since his wife had walked out on him over three years earlier, Carr had become even more embittered and antagonistic in his dealings with others. At the time she had tried to force him into a reconciliation but Carr was not a man to be forced into anything. He'd even packed one suitcase for her before hurling her car keys at her and showing her the door. She had told him she would give him another chance if he could try to change his ways. Four affairs in as many years had been too much for her.

Carr hadn't wanted another chance.

He smiled as he remembered that night she left but the smile faded as he found himself thinking again about Mathias.

Once offended, Carr would stop at nothing to make things even. He bore grudges almost gleefully.

'Yank bastard,' he said, aloud.

'First sign of madness.'

The voice startled him, he hadn't heard her footfalls on the stairs. Carr spun round to see Suzanne Peters perched on the edge of the bed with a glass of milk in her hand.

'What did you say?' he asked, irritably.

'I said it's the first sign of madness,' she told him. 'Talking to yourself.'

Carr didn't answer her, he merely turned around and walked back to the bed, flopping on it lazily.

Suzanne muttered something to him as she almost spilt her milk. She placed it on the table beside the bed and stretched out beside him pushing her naked body against his, allowing her ample breasts to press into his side while her left hand snaked across his chest.

At twenty-two, Suzanne was almost half his age. She worked as a receptionist at Broadcasting House and had done for the past ten months. During that time, she and Roger Carr had become lovers although it was a term Carr disliked because, to him, it implied that there was some emotion involved in the relationship. In his eyes that was certainly not the case.

She nuzzled his chest, kissing it as she allowed her hand to reach lower towards his penis. She took his organ between her fingers and began to rub gently. He stiffened slightly but then she felt his own hand close around her tiny wrist, pulling her away from him. Suzanne sat up, sweeping her thick blonde hair back and looking at her companion with bewilderment.

'What's wrong with you tonight?' she wanted to know.

Carr didn't even look at her.

'I've got something on my mind,' he said.

'That's obvious. Is it anything *I* can help with?'

Carr eyed her almost contemptuously.

'*You*, help me? Give it a rest.'

He returned to staring at the ceiling.

'I only asked,' she said, lying down beside him once more. She ran one finger through the thick hair on his chest, curling it into spirals.

'That bastard Mathias made me look like an idiot,' Carr said, angrily. 'He's a bloody con-man.' The interviewer's voice took on a reflective tone. 'I'll have him for what

204

happened tonight. One way or another I'll fix that shitbag.'

Once more Suzanne allowed her hand to reach lower towards his groin. She enveloped his penis in her smooth grip and, this time she felt him respond. He stiffened in her hand and she kissed his chest, nipping the flesh of his stomach as she moved down onto his growing erection. Suzanne flicked at the bulbous head with her tongue, watching as a drop of clear liquid oozed from it. Her lips closed around his throbbing shaft and she felt him thrusting his hips upwards trying to force himself further into the velvet warmth of her mouth. Her hand continued to move expertly on his root and she sensed an even greater swelling as his penis grew to full stiffness.

Carr gripped her by the back of the neck and pulled her off, dragging her across him, kissing her hard. His hands found her breasts and she almost cried out as he kneaded the soft mounds with furious vigour, but the discomfort was tempered by an overriding pleasure and her nipples grew into hard buds as he rubbed them with his thumbs.

She felt his knee rise to push against her pubic mound as he rolled her over first onto her back and then her stomach. She felt him grip her hips and she arched her back to allow him easier access. He thrust into her violently, a deep angry grunt accompanying his almost frenzied penetration of her. Suzanne gasped, both at the pleasure and the power of his movements. She knelt, feeling his heavy testicles against her buttocks as he moved inside her. Suzanne ground herself back to meet his every thrust and, as they formed a rhythm, she felt her own excitement growing.

Carr gripped her hips, clinging onto her soft flesh so hard that he left red welts where his fingers had been. He pulled her onto his throbbing shaft, grunting more loudly now.

She could not suppress a whimper of pain as he grabbed a large hunk of her hair and pulled, tugging her head back with a force which threatened to snap her neck. He held her like that, still spearing her unmercifully, only now her pleasure had given way to pain. Carr made a guttural sound, deep in his throat and pulled harder on her long hair. Some of it came away in his hand.

'No,' she managed to squeal, breathlessly.

He ignored her complaint, his own climax now drawing

closer. The speed of his thrusts increased.

She could no longer bear his weight so she lowered herself until she was lying face down on the bed, her legs still splayed wide as Carr drove into her relentlessly.

Suzanne felt a sudden, unaccountable flicker of fear as he fastened first one, then two hands around her throat.

He began to squeeze.

She let out a wheezing gasp and tried to claw at his hands to release the increasing pressure but the more she tugged at those twin vices, the harder he pressed. She felt his nails digging into her flesh as he crushed her windpipe and, all the time, he continued his violent movements which threatened to split her in two.

White light danced before her eyes and she flailed helplessly behind her, trying to scratch Carr. Anything to relieve the unbearable pressure on her throat. It felt as if her head were going to explode.

Roger Carr grinned crookedly, his face a mask of rage and triumph as he held her beneath him.

Suzanne felt herself growing weaker. It seemed only a matter of moments now before she blacked out.

With one last vigorous thrust he felt the pleasure build to a peak then, gasping loudly, he pumped his fluid into her. Carr shuddered as the sensations gradually subsided. He withdrew from her and lay on one side.

He wondered why she wasn't moving.

Suzanne coughed, horrified to see spots of blood mingling with the sputum which stained the pillow. Still lying on her stomach she raised one quivering hand to her throat and tentatively felt the deep indentations there. She felt Carr's hands on her shoulders, turning her over and, despite her pain she found the strength to push him away. He looked down at her ravaged neck and raised both hands to his head. In the semi-darkness his eyes looked sunken, only the whites standing out with any clarity.

She coughed again and tried to sit up, her head spinning. Carr reached out to touch the welts on her flesh, his gaze straying to those on her hips too. She slapped his hand away and staggered to her feet.

'You stay away from me,' she croaked, pointing at him with a shaking finger. 'I mean it.'

Carr got to his feet and moved towards her.

'Suzanne, I ...'

'Get away you ...' She coughed and more blood-flecked spittle dribbled over her lips. 'You're mad. You could have killed me.'

He hesitated, listening as she crossed the landing to the bathroom.

Carr sat down heavily on the edge of the bed, head bowed. He was drenched in perspiration but he felt almost unbearably cold. He found his dressing gown and pulled it on. His fingers, he noticed, had some blood on them so he hurriedly wiped it off with the corner of a sheet. His initial bewilderment by now had turned to fear. Carr rubbed his face with both hands, aware that his chest was heaving from the effort of trying to slow his rapid breathing. He looked at his hands as if they were not his own, as if they had been guided by a will other than his.

Suzanne returned from the bathroom and gathered up her clothes.

'Look, I don't know what to say ...' he began.

She interrupted.

'Don't say anything,' she told him.

'I don't know what came over me, I ...'

'Just leave me alone,' she demanded, picking up the last of her clothes. He watched as she hurried from the room, listening as she made her way down to the ground floor.

Carr shuddered once more as a chill ran through him.

He found her pulling on her jeans, tears trickling down her cheeks to smudge her make-up.

'Suzanne,' he said, almost apologetically. 'Honest to God, I don't know what happened.'

'I do,' she snapped, fastening the button at the waist. 'You tried to kill me.'

'I didn't know what I was doing.'

She pointed to the angry red marks on her neck.

'How am I supposed to explain these away?' Suzanne asked.

She pulled on her coat and turned towards the door which led through to the kitchen. 'I'll go out the back way, I don't even want anyone to know I've been with you.'

He followed her, slapping on the light.

'Stay away from me, Roger,' she said, a note of concern in her voice. 'I mean it.'

'You have to believe me,' he said. 'I didn't know what I was doing.' Again he felt that cold chill sweeping through him.

He caught her by the arm, spinning her round.

'Let go,' she shrieked and struck out at him, raking his cheek with her nails, drawing blood.

Carr's nostrils flared and his face darkened. With a roar he hurled Suzanne across the kitchen.

She slammed into the cooker and lay motionless for a moment but, as she saw Carr advancing on her, she managed to claw her way upright. He overturned the table in his haste to reach her.

Suzanne made a lunge for the door but Carr grabbed her by the collar. The material of her blouse ripped, the buttons flying off. Her large breasts were exposed but she cared little for that. Her only thought was to get out of the house.

But Carr moved too quickly. He shot out a grasping hand and tugged her back by her hair, slamming her head against the fridge as he did so. A cut opened just above her hairline, crimson fluid running down her face and staining the white door of the fridge as she lay against it.

As he lunged for her once more she flung open the fridge door and rammed it against his legs, struggling to get to her feet.

Carr snarled angrily and almost fell but he recovered in time to see her pull a long serrated blade from the knife rack on the wall nearby. She turned on him, the vicious blade glinting wickedly. He did not hesitate, he grabbed for her, his hands aimed at her throat but Suzanne struck out with the knife.

The combined force of his momentum and her own upward thrust was devastating.

The blade punctured the palm of Carr's right hand and erupted from the back, sawing through several small bones as it did so. Blood burst from the wound and Suzanne tore the knife free, nearly severing his thumb as she did so. He roared in pain and held up the mutilated limb almost as an accusation, watching the tendons and muscles beneath the skin moving frantically. It felt as if his arm were on fire but, despite the severity of the wound, Carr did not hold back. He reached for a chair and lifted it above his head, bringing it down with bone-crushing force across Suzanne's outstretched arm.

The knife was knocked from her grasp and she fell backwards, blood now flowing more freely from the rent in her scalp.

Carr grinned maniacally and struck again.

So violent was the impact this time that the chair broke as he brought it down across her face and upper body. Her bottom lip exploded, her nose merely collapsed as the bones in it were obliterated. In one fleeting second, Suzanne's face was a bloody ruin.

Carr dropped to his knees, one hand groping for the discarded knife. He gripped it in his gashed hand, ignoring his own pain as he took hold of a hunk of Suzanne's hair and lifted her head.

She tried to scream but her bottom jaw had been splintered and the only sound she could make was a liquid gurgle.

Carr pressed the knife to her forehead, just below the hairline, using all his strength as he moved the serrated blade quickly back and forth, shearing through the flesh of her scalp. He slid it in expertly towards her ear, slicing off the top of the fleshy protruberance as he did so and, all the time, her body jerked violently as waves of pain tore through her.

The knife grated against bone as he sawed madly at her head, tugging on her hair as he did so until finally, with a loud grunt, he tore most of it free.

Like some bloodied wig, the hair came away in his hand, most of the scalp still attached.

Suzanne lay still.

Carr staggered upright, the grisly trophy held before him.

There was loud banging from the direction of the front door, growing louder by the second.

Carr closed his eyes tightly, suddenly aware of an unbearable pain in his right hand. The entire limb was going numb, he could hardly lift it. He staggered back, seeking support against the sink and, gradually, a vision plucked raw and bloody from a nightmare swam before him. Only he wasn't dreaming.

He looked down in horrified disbelief at the scalped body of Suzanne Peters, almost shouting aloud as he recognized the matted mass of hair and flesh which he held. He dropped it hurriedly.

'No,' he murmured, quietly. 'Oh God, no.' His voice began to crack and he edged away from the girl as if she were somehow going to disappear. He continued to shake his head, not able to comprehend what had happened. Or how.

The banging on the front door intensified but all Roger Carr was aware of was the agonising pain in his hand, the stench of blood which hung in the air like an invisible pall.

And the icy chill which had wrapped itself around him like a frozen shroud.

42

The restaurant was small, what the owners liked to refer to as intimate. But, due to the number of people crowded into it, the place looked more like a gigantic rugby scrum. Not at all intimate, thought David Blake as the waiter led him through the melee towards the appropriate table.

Amidst the sea of lunch-time faces, the writer spotted Phillip Campbell immediately.

The Scot was sitting near to the window, sipping a glass of red wine and poring over a thick pile of A4 sheets, scribbling pencilled notes on the pages every so often. He was dressed in a light grey suit which seemed to match the colour of his hair. A red rose adorned his button-hole as it did on every occasion that Blake saw him. He wondered, at times, if Campbell was propagating the flowers in the breast pocket of his jacket. As each new one came up. Snip. Into the button hole.

He looked up as Blake reached the table, rising to shake hands with the writer.

They exchanged pleasantries and the younger man sat

down, loosening his tie as he did so. The waiter scuttled over and placed a large glass before him.

'Thank you,' said Blake, looking rather surprised.

'Vodka and lemonade,' Campbell told him, smiling. 'You haven't started drinking something else have you?'

The writer chuckled, shook his head and took a sip from the glass.

'I make a point of knowing all my author's requirements,' the Scot said, raising his glass. 'Cheers.'

Both men drank. The waiter arrived with the menus and left them to decide.

'What do you think of the completed manuscript now that you've read it?' Blake asked, indicating the A4 sheets.

'You're no closer, David,' Campbell told him. 'I'm still not convinced about half the things you claim in here.' He tapped the pile of typewritten pages.

The writer was about to speak when the waiter returned. The two men ordered and he hurried off through the throng to fetch their first course.

'It's too muddled,' Campbell continued. 'You don't name any sources for some of the theories you've put forward, especially the ones to do with Astral projection. *Control* of the Astral body.'

'I met a girl at the Institute of Psychical Study,' Blake said. 'She's conducted laboratory tests into this kind of thing.'

'Then why isn't she named as a source?'

'Her superior is keeping a pretty tight rein on the research they're doing. I don't think he'd be too pleased if her findings turned up in my book.'

'How well do you know this girl?'

'We're pretty close,' Blake told him.

Campbell nodded.

'The Astral body can be activated by artificial stimulus like drugs or hypnosis, she told me.'

'Then use her name for Christ's sake,' snapped Campbell. 'Can't you speak to her superior about this information? Maybe he'll release some details.'

The waiter returned with the first course and the two men began eating.

'I can't use her name or her findings and that's final,' Blake told him.

'Then you've still got nothing concrete and until you have, this manuscript is no good,' said Campbell, pushing a forkful of food into his mouth.

'I take it that means you're not ready to negotiate a contract?' Blake said.

Campbell nodded.

Blake smiled humourlessly.

'You could do with a demonstration, Phil,' he said.

The Scot took a sip of his wine.

'That I could,' he smiled. 'See if you can arrange it, eh?'

Blake chuckled. Behind the tinted screens of his dark glasses his eyes twinkled.

43

Gerald Braddock reached forward and wound up the window of the Granada. It was warm inside the car but he decided that the heat was preferable to the noxious fumes belching from so many exhaust pipes. The streets of London seemed even more clogged with traffic than usual. High above, in the cloudless sky, the sun blazed away mercilessly.

The politician fumbled for the handkerchief in his top pocket and fastidiously dabbed the perspiration from his face. He thought about removing his jacket but decided against it, realizing that they were close to their destination. The driver threaded the car skilfully through the traffic, hitting the horn every so often to clear offending vehicles out of the way.

Braddock sat back and closed his eyes but he found it difficult to relax. The events of two nights before were still uncomfortably fresh in his mind.

He had told no one of what he had witnessed at the seance, least of all his wife. For one thing she would probably never have believed him and, if she had, Braddock realized that mention of it may well have disturbed her. For his own part, the image of that maimed and burned child had surfaced, unwanted, in his mind on a number of occasions since. Albeit fleetingly. He wondered how long it would take to fully erase the image and the memory. He was thankful that nothing about the incident had appeared in any of the papers. Even the gutter press had so far remained blissfully ignorant of what would, for them, have been front page fodder. Braddock was grateful for that because he knew that the Prime Minister would not have looked kindly on his participation in such a fiasco.

He had held the post of Minister of the Arts in the last two Conservative administrations. Prior to that he had served as a spokesman on Finance in a career in the House of Commons which spanned over twenty years. Some had seen his appointment as Arts Minister as something of a demotion but Braddock was happy with his present position as it removed some of the pressure from him which had been prevalent when he'd been with the Exchequer.

As traffic began to thin he decided to roll down the window slightly. A cooling breeze wafted in, drying the perspiration on him. He glanced to his right and saw a sign which read: BRIXTON ½ MILE.

Another five minutes and the Granada began to slow up.

As Braddock looked out he saw that there was already a sizeable crowd gathered in the paved area which fronted the new Activity Centre. The building had been converted from four derelict shops, with the help of a two million pound Government grant. The minister scanned the rows of black faces and felt a twinge of distaste.

As the driver brought the car to a halt he saw two coloured men approaching. Both were dressed in suits, one looking all the more incongruous because, perched on his head, was a multi-coloured woollen bonnet. His dreadlocks had been carefully pushed inside. Braddock smiled his practised smile and waited for the driver to open the car door.

He stepped out, extending his hand to the first of the black men.

Braddock cringed inwardly as he felt his flesh make contact with the other man and he hastily shook hands with the Rastafarian, allowing himself to be led across the concrete piazza towards a make-shift platform which had been erected in front of the entrance to the Activity Centre.

As he made his way up the three steps the crowd broke into a chorus of applause.

Braddock scanned the faces before him, some white but mostly black. He continued to smile although it was becoming more of an effort. The first of the organisers, who had introduced himself as Julian Hayes, stepped forward towards a microphone and tapped it twice. There was a whine from the PA system and Hayes tapped it again. This time there was no interference.

'It's been more than two years since building first started on this Centre,' Hayes began. 'And I'm sure we're all happy to see that it's finally finished.'

There was some more clapping and the odd whistle.

Hayes smiled broadly.

'As from today,' he continued. 'We shall all be able to use the facilities. I would like to call on Mr Gerald Braddock to officially open the Centre.' He beckoned the politician forward. 'Mr Braddock.'

There was more applause as the minister reached the microphone. Beside it he noticed there was a small table and on it lay a pair of shears with which he was meant to cut the gaily coloured ribbon strung across the doors of the centre.

He paused before the microphone still smiling, scanning the rows of dark faces. Braddock felt the disgust rising within him. He coughed, suddenly aware of a slight shiver which ran down his spine. The sun continued to beat down relentlessly but, despite the heat, the politician felt inexplicably cold.

'Firstly,' he began, 'I would like to thank Mr Hayes for asking me to declare this new centre open. He must take credit for so much of the organisation which went into ensuring that the project was completed.'

There was more vigorous clapping.

Braddock smiled thinly and gripped the microphone stand.

'The cutting of the ribbon is symbolic,' he said, 'in as much as it marks the cutting of ties between you people and my Government. We have pumped over two million pounds into the development of this Centre. I hope that it will be put to good use.'

Hayes looked at his Rastafarian companion who merely shrugged.

'In the past we have tried to help this area but, up until

now, that effort has been largely wasted,' Braddock continued. 'Our good faith has not been repaid. I sincerely hope that it will not be the case this time.' The politician's voice had taken on a dictatorial tone, one not unnoticed by the crowd.

There were one or two disapproving comments from the assembled throng. A babble of unrest which grew slowly as Braddock pressed on regardless.

'There are many deserving causes to which we could have given a grant such as the one received to convert these old shops into this fine new Centre,' he said, 'most of which would normally come higher on our list of priorities. Nevertheless, partly through pressure from leaders of your community, we decided to furnish your committee with the appropriate funds.'

Julian Hayes looked angrily at Braddock's broad back then at the crowd who were muttering amongst themselves, angered by the politician's remarks.

'You seem to think that you qualify as a special case,' Braddock said, vehemently, 'because you're black.'

'Steady, man,' the Rastafarian rumbled behind him.

Hayes raised a hand for him to be silent although his own temper was becoming somewhat frayed as the minister ploughed on.

'It will be interesting to see how long this Centre remains intact. How long before some of you decide to wreck it. As it is, one of the few advantages that I can see is that it will give some of you a place to go, instead of hanging idly around on street corners.'

The crowd, by this time, were now gesturing menacingly at Braddock. Someone shouted something from the rear of the crowd but the minister either didn't hear it or ignored it. His own face was flushed, perspiration running in rivulets over the puffy flesh, yet still he felt himself encased in that invisible grip which seemed to squeeze tighter, growing colder all the time.

'Perhaps now,' he hissed, 'with your own Centre, you will stop bothering the decent white people who are unfortunate enough to have to live in this filthy "ghetto" you have created in Brixton.' He was breathing heavily, rapidly. His eyes were bulging wide and, when he spoke it was through

215

clenched teeth.

'That's it,' snapped the Rastafarian, stepping forward. 'Who the hell do you think you are, man?'

Braddock spun around, his eyes blazing.

'Get away from me you stinking nigger,' he roared, his voice amplified by the microphone.

The crowd raged back at him.

'Mr Braddock ...' Julian Hayes began, moving in front of his colleague to face the politician. 'We've heard enough.'

'You black scum,' rasped the minister.

In one lightning movement, he snatched the shears from the table and drove them forward.

The twin blades punctured Hayes' stomach just below the navel and Braddock tore them upwards until they cracked noisily against the black man's sternum. Blood burst from the hideous rent and Hayes dropped to his knees as a tangled mess of purplish-blue intestines spilled from the gaping hole. Hayes clawed at them, feeling the blood and bile spilling on to his hands and splattering down the front of his trousers. He whimpered quietly as he attempted to retain his entrails, pushing at them with slippery hands.

In the crowd someone screamed. Two or three women fainted. Others seemed rooted to the spot, not sure whether to run or try to confront Braddock who stood on the platform facing the Rastafarian, the dripping shears now held in both hands.

'Motherfucker,' rasped the black man and lunged forward.

Braddock sidestepped and brought the razor sharp blades together once more.

They closed with ease around his opponent's neck and, with a movement combining demonic force and seething anger, the politician snapped the blades together.

Two spurting crimson parabolas erupted from the Rastafarian's neck as the shears bit through his carotid arteries, slicing through the thick muscles of his neck until they crushed his larynx and met against his spine.

Braddock roared triumphantly, exerting more force on the handles until the black man's spinal column began to splinter and break. He was suspended in mid-air by the shears, held there by Braddock who seemed to have found reserves of strength he hadn't formerly been aware of. Blood gushed madly forth, much of it covering the politician himself, but he ignored the crimson cascade, grunting loudly as he finally succeeded in severing his opponent's head. It rose on a thick gout of blood as the body fell to the ground, twitching slightly.

The head rolled across the platform, sightless eyes gazing at the sky as torrents of red fluid poured from the stump of the neck.

Some of the crowd, by now, had scattered, others had surrounded the platform but, understandably, seemed reluctant to approach Braddock.

The politician had lowered the shears and his breathing seemed to have slowed. He stood motionless, like a child lost in a supermarket. Those watching saw him raise one bloodied hand to his forehead and squeeze his eyes tightly shut. When he opened them again his expression had changed from one of anger to utter horror. He looked at the headless corpse at his feet, then at Julian Hayes who was rocking gently back and forth clutching at his torn belly.

Finally, Braddock lifted the shears before him, staring at the sticky red fluid which covered them. And him.

He dropped the weapon and staggered backward, his face pale and drained.

Somewhere in the distance he heard a police siren.

As the sun burned brightly in the sky, he shivered, his entire body enveloped by an icy chill, the like of which he had never experienced before.

Gerald Braddock took one more look at the carnage before him then vomited.

44

The dashboard clock showed 6.05 p.m. as Kelly pulled the Mini into Blake's driveway. She tapped the wheel agitatedly, wondering, when she didn't see his XJS, if he was out. She decided that he might have put it in the garage, hauled herself out of her own car and ran to his front door, clutching the two newspapers which she'd gathered from the back seat.

The sun was slowly sinking and the air was still warm from the daytime heatwave. Kelly felt her blouse sticking to her. The drive had been a long and tortuous one, especially once she'd reached inner London. Now she banged hard on Blake's front door, almost relieved that she'd completed the trip.

She waited a moment but there was no answer.

Kelly banged again, this time hearing sounds of movement from inside. The door swung open and she saw Blake standing there.

'Kelly,' he beamed. 'What a great surprise. Come in.' He ushered her inside, puzzled by her flustered appearance and look of anxiety.

'Is something wrong?' he asked. She had still not smiled.

'Have you seen the news today?' she asked. 'Or watched TV at all?'

Blake shook his head in bewilderment.

'No. I had lunch with my publisher. I've been working since I got back. I haven't had time to look at the papers. Why?'

She held two newspapers out before him, both were folded open to reveal headlines. He looked at one, then the other:
ACTRESS KILLS BABY
Blake read it then looked at Kelly.

'Read the other one,' she told him.
TELEVISION PERSONALITY CHARGED WITH MURDER

Below it was a photograph of Roger Carr.

The writer looked at the first article once more and noticed the name Toni Landers.

'Jesus Christ,' he murmured, sitting down on the edge of a chair. 'When did this happen?'

'Last night they found Roger Carr in his house with the body of a girl,' said Kelly. 'The night before, Toni Landers killed the baby. The article said it belonged to her friend.'

Blake frowned and skimmed the articles quickly.

'That's not all,' Kelly told him. 'When I was driving home from the Institute today, I had the radio on. Do you remember Gerald Braddock?'

Blake nodded.

'According to the radio he went crazy this afternoon and killed two people,' Kelly told him.

The writer hurriedly got to his feet and switched on the television.

'There might be something on here about it,' he said, punching buttons until he found the appropriate channel.

'... Mr Braddock today. The Arts Minister is now in the Westminster Hospital, under police guard, where he was treated for shock prior to being charged.' The newsreader droned on but Blake seemed not to hear the rest.

'Treated for shock?' said Kelly. 'That's a little unusual isn't it? Do murderers usually go into a state of shock after committing the crime?' She exhaled deeply.

'I wish I knew,' said Blake. 'I know less than you do.' He scanned the papers once more. 'As far as I can make out Toni Landers and Roger Carr can remember nothing about the murders they committed. Yet they were both found *with* their victims.'

'So was Gerald Braddock,' Kelly added. 'Only there were witnesses in his case.'

'Three respected people suddenly commit murder for no apparent reason,' Blake muttered. 'They can't remember doing it and nothing links them.'

'There *is* a link, David,' Kelly assured him. 'They were all at the seance the other night.'

The two of them regarded each other warily for a moment then Blake got to his feet once more and picked up the phone. He jabbed the buttons and got a dial tone.

'Can I speak to Phillip Campbell, please?' he asked when the phone was finally answered. He waited impatiently while the receptionist connected him.

'Hello, David,' the Scot said. 'You were lucky to catch me, I was just about to leave.'

'Phil, listen to me, this is important. Do the names Toni Landers, Roger Carr and Gerald Braddock mean anything to you?'

'Of course. Toni Landers is an actress, Carr's an interviewer and Braddock's a politician. Do I get a prize for getting them all right?'

'In the past two days, each one of them has committed a murder.'

There was silence from Campbell's end.

'Phil, are you still there?' Blake asked.

'Yes, look, what the hell are you talking about, David?'

'It's all over the papers, on the TV as well.'

'But I know Braddock,' Campbell said in surprise. 'He couldn't fart without help, let alone murder anyone.'

'Well, all that changed today,' Blake said. He went on to explain what had happened to Toni Landers and Roger Carr. 'None of them could remember what they'd done. It's almost as if they were in some kind of trance. In my book I've discussed the possibility of some kind of unconscious reaction to an external stimulus ...'

Campbell interrupted.

'If you're trying to use three random killings to justify what *you've* written, David. Forget it,' snapped the Scot.

'But you'll admit it's a possibility?'

'No. Christ, that's even more bloody conjecture than you had before. Ring me when you've gathered some *real* evidence.'

Blake exhaled wearily and dropped the receiver back into place.

'What did he say?' Kelly asked, tentatively.

The writer didn't answer. He was staring past her, his eyes fixed on the twin headlines:

ACTRESS KILLS BABY
TELEVISION PERSONALITY CHARGED WITH MURDER

Outside, the dying sun had coloured the sky crimson.

Like cloth soaked in blood.

45

The smell of roast meat wafted invitingly through the air as Phillip Campbell stepped into the sitting room of his house.

The television was on and, through the open kitchen door, he could hear sounds of movement. As he drew closer, the smell grew stronger, tempting him toward the kitchen like a bee to nectar. He paused in the doorway and smiled. His daughter had her back to him, busily inspecting the dials on the cooker. Her black hair was long, spilling half-way down her back, almost to the waist band of her jeans. She looked a little too large for the pair she wore, possessing what were euphemistically known as 'child-bearing hips'. But her legs were long and relatively slender. She wore a baggy sweater, cut off at the elbows, which she'd knitted herself during her last break from University. She always came home during the holidays, only this time she had felt it as much out of duty as a desire to be with her parents.

Campbell's wife was in Scotland and had been for the past two weeks. Her mother was terminally ill with colonic cancer and was being nursed through her final few weeks by her family. Campbell himself had been up to see her twice but, after the second visit, he had been unable to bear the sight of the old girl wasting away. His wife phoned every other night and the presence of his daughter in some way compensated for her absence.

'Whatever it is it smells good,' the publisher said, smiling.

Melissa spun around, a look of surprise on her face.

'I didn't hear you come in, Dad,' she told him. 'You must be getting sneaky in your old age.' She grinned.

'You cheeky little tyke,' he chuckled. 'Less of the old age.' Her mood changed slightly.

'Mum phoned earlier,' Melissa told him.

Campbell sat down at the carefully set table.

'What did she say?' he wanted to know.

'Not much. She sounded upset, she said something about being home next week.'

'Oh Christ,' Campbell said, wearily. 'Well, perhaps it's a kindness if her mother does pass on. At least it'll be the end of her suffering.'

There was a moment's silence between them then Campbell got to his feet.

'I'm going to get changed before dinner,' he said.

'You've got about five minutes,' Melissa told him. 'I don't want this to spoil.'

'You cooks are really temperamental aren't you?' he said, smiling.

The cuckoo clock on the wall of the kitchen burst into life as the hands reached 9 p.m.

Campbell set down the plates on the draining board and picked up a tea-towel as Melissa filled the sink with hot water.

'I'll do the washing up, Dad,' she told him. 'You go and sit down.'

He insisted on drying.

'Are we going to be seeing any more of this young fellow Andy or whatever his name was, next term?' Campbell asked, wiping the first saucepan.

'I don't know. He's gone grape-picking in France for the summer,' she chuckled.

'You were keen on him though?'

'You sound as if you're trying to get me hitched.'

'Am I the match-making type?' he said with mock indignation.

'Yes,' she told him, handing him a plate. 'Now, can we change the subject, please?'

Her father grinned.

'What sort of day have *you* had?' Melissa asked him.

They talked and joked while they cleared away the crockery, pots and pans and cutlery then Melissa decided to make coffee.

'I've got a few things to read before tomorrow,' he told her.

'I thought you didn't usually bring work home with you?'

222

'Sometimes it's unavoidable.'

'I'll bring your coffee in when it's ready,' she said.

He thanked her then wandered through into the sitting room, searching through his attaché case for the relevant material. Seated in front of the television, Campbell began scanning the synopses and odd chapters which he had not found time to get through at the office. There was work from established authors, as well as unsolicited efforts from those all too anxious to break into the world of publishing. The mystique which seemed to surround the publishing world never ceased to amaze the Scot.

Melissa joined him in the sitting room and reached for the book which she had been reading. They sat opposite one another, undisturbed by the television. Neither thought to get up and turn it off.

It was approaching 11.30 when Melissa finally put down her book and stretched. She rubbed her eyes and glanced at the clock on the mantlepiece.

'I think I'll go to bed, Dad,' she said, sleepily.

Campbell looked up at her and smiled.

'OK,' he said. 'I'll see you in the morning.'

He heard the door close behind her as she made her way upstairs. The Scot paused for a moment, his attention taken by a photograph of Gerald Braddock which had been flashed up on the TV screen. He quickly moved forward and turned up the volume, listening as the newscaster relayed information about the horrific incident in Brixton that afternoon. Campbell watched with interest, remembering his phone conversation with Blake. He shook his head. How could there possibly be any link between Blake's theories and Braddock's demented act? He dismissed the thought as quickly as it had come, returning to the work before him. Campbell yawned and rubbed his eyes, weariness creeping up on him unannounced. He decided to make himself a cup of coffee in an effort to stay awake. There wasn't much more to read and he wanted everything out of the way before he eventually retired to bed. He wandered into the kitchen and filled the kettle, returning to his chair in the sitting room. He slumped wearily into it and decided to watch the rest of the late news before continuing.

He yawned again.

Phillip Campbell made his way quietly up the stairs, pausing when he reached the landing. He heard no sounds from Melissa's room and was certain that he hadn't disturbed her. The Scot slowly turned the handle of her door and edged into the room. He smiled as he looked at her, sleeping soundly, her long black hair spread across the pillow like a silken smudge. She moved slightly but did not awake.

Campbell paused for a moment running his eyes over the numerous pen and ink, watercolour and pencil drawings which were displayed proudly in the room. Beside the bed was a plastic tumbler crammed with pieces of charcoal, pens and pencils and, propped against the bedside table was an open sketch-pad which bore the beginnings of a new drawing.

Campbell moved closer to the bed, his eyes fixed on his sleeping daughter. Even when he stood over her she did not stir.

He bent forward and, with infinite care, pulled down the sheets, exposing her body. She wore only a thin nightdress, the dark outline of her nipples and pubic mound visible through the diaphanous material. Campbell felt his erection growing, bulging urgently against his trousers. Without taking his eyes from Melissa, he unzipped his flies and pulled out his rampant organ.

It was then that she rolled on to her back, her eyes opening slightly.

Before she could react, the Scot was upon her, tearing frenziedly at the nightdress, ripping it from her, exposing her breasts. He grabbed one roughly, using his other hand to part her legs. She clawed at his face then attempted to push him off, using all her strength to keep her legs together but he knelt over her and struck her hard across the face. Still dazed from sleep, she was stunned by the blow and her body went momentarily limp. Campbell took his chance and pulled her legs apart, forcing his penis into her.

Melissa screamed in pain and fear and bit at the hand which he clamped over her mouth but he seemed undeterred by her feeble assaults and he struck her once more, harder this time. A vicious red mark appeared below her right eye.

With a grunt of triumph he began to thrust within her, using one forearm to hold her down, weighing heavily across her throat until she began to gasp for air. She flailed at him weakly and he slapped her hands away contemptuously as he speeded up his movements, thrusting harder into her.

With his free hand, Campbell reached for the bedside table and pulled a pencil from the pastic container. The point had been sharpened repeatedly to a needle-like lead tip and he gripped it in one powerful hand.

Melissa, who was already on the point of blacking out now seemed to find renewed strength as she saw him bringing the pencil closer, but the weight on top of her prevented her from squirming away from her father.

He guided the pencil inexorably towards her ear.

She tried to twist her head back and forth but he struck her again and she felt the pressure on her throat ease as he held her head steady.

With fastidious precision, Campbell began to push the needle sharp pencil into her ear, putting more weight behind it as the wooden shaft penetrated deeper.

He felt his daughter's body buck madly beneath him and her eyes bulged wide as he pushed the pencil further, driving it into the soft grey tissue of her brain, forcing it as far as it would go. Almost a full half of the length had disappeared before she stopped moving but still Campbell forced the object deeper, as if he wished to push it right through her skull, to see the bloodied point emerge from the other side.

The Scot grunted in satisfaction and continued to pound away at her corpse, a crooked smile of pleasure on his face.

Phillip Campbell awoke with a start, his body bathed in perspiration. He was panting like a carthorse, his heart thudding heavily against his ribs. He looked across at the empty chair opposite him.

'Melissa,' he breathed, a note of panic in his voice.

He hauled himself out of his chair and bolted for the stairs, taking them two at a time, stumbling as he reached the landing. He threw open the door of his daughter's room and looked in.

She was sleeping soundly but, as he stood there, breathless, she murmured something and opened her eyes, blinking myopically at the figure silhouetted in her doorway.

'Dad?' she said, puzzlement in her voice. 'What's wrong?'

He sucked in a deep, almost painful breath.

'Nothing,' he told her.

'Are you all right?'

The Scot wiped his forehead with the back of his hand.

'I must have dozed off in the chair,' he said, softly. 'I had a nightmare.' He dare not tell her about it. 'Are *you* OK?' he added, his voice full of concern.

She nodded.

'Yes, of course I am.'

Campbell exhaled.

'I'm sorry I woke you,' he croaked, and pulled the door shut behind him.

He walked slowly back across the landing, pausing as he reached the top step.

There was a sticky substance on his underpants, a dark stain on his trousers. For a moment he thought he'd wet himself.

It took but a second for him to realize that the substance was semen.

46

How long the phone had been ringing he wasn't sure but the discordant tone finally woke him and he thrust out a hand to grab the receiver.

'Hello,' Blake croaked, rubbing a hand through his hair. He glanced at the alarm clock as he did so.

It was 12.55 a.m.

'David, it's me.'

Blake shook his head, trying to dispel some of the dullness from his mind.

'Sorry, who is it?' he asked.

Beside him, Kelly stirred and moved closer to him, her body warm and soft.

'Phillip Campbell,' the voice said and finally Blake recognised the Scot's drawl.

'What do you want, Phil?' he said, with surprising calm.

'I had a dream ... a nightmare. It was so vivid.'

'What about?'

Campbell told him.

'So now you believe what I've been telling you about the subconscious?' Blake said, almost mockingly.

'Look, we'll sort out the contract in a day or two. All right?'

'That's fine.'

Blake hung up.

Kelly, by now, was partially awake.

'What was that, David?' she purred. Her voice thick with sleep.

He told her of Campbell's insistence on going ahead with the book.

'I'm glad he's decided to publish the book, I wonder why he changed his mind?' she said.

Blake didn't speak. He merely kissed her gently on the forehead then lay down again.

Kelly snuggled up against him and he pulled her close.

In no time they had both drifted off to sleep again.

47

Paris

The full moon was like a huge flare in the cloudy sky, casting a cold white light over the land. The breeze which was developing rapidly into a strong wind, sent the dark banks scudding across the mottled heavens.

Michel Lasalle stopped the car and switched off the engine, sitting motionless behind the wheel. Despite the chill in the air he was sweating profusely and wiped his palms on his trousers before reaching over onto the back seat where the shovel lay. He pushed open his door and clambered out.

The gates of the cemetery, as he'd expected, were locked but Lasalle was undeterred by this minor inconvenience. He tossed the shovel over the wrought iron framework where it landed with a dull clang. He stood still, looking furtively around him in the darkness then, satisfied that no one was around, he jumped and managed to get a grip on one of the gates, hauling himself painfully upward until he was in a position to swing over the top.

The impact jarred him as he hit the ground but the Frenchman merely rubbed his calves, picked up the shovel and headed across the darkened cemetery towards the place he knew so well. Trees, stirred by the wind, shook their branches at him, as if warding him off, but Lasalle walked on purposefully, a glazed look in his eye.

The gendarme had heard the strange noise and decided that his imagination was playing tricks on him. But, as he rounded a corner of the high wall which guarded the cemetery, he saw Lasalle's car parked outside the main gates. The uniformed man quickened his pace, squinting at the vehicle through the gloom in an attempt to catch sight of anyone who might be inside. He moved slowly around the car, tapping on two of the windows, but received no response.

As the moon emerged from behind the clouds he peered through the gates of the graveyard.

Illuminated in the chilly white glow was a figure.

A man.

The gendarme could see that he was busy digging up the earth of a grave.

The uniformed man looked up and saw that the walls were covered by barbed wire, his only way in was over the metal gates. He leapt at them, gained a grip, and began to climb.

Lasalle had dug his way at least three feet down into the earth of his wife's grave when he looked up and saw the gendarme approaching. Lasalle murmured something to himself and froze for precious seconds, not sure what to do.

He bolted, still clutching the spade.

'Arrêtez!'

He heard the shout and looked over his shoulder to see that the gendarme was pursuing him.

Lasalle didn't know where he was going to run. The

228

uniformed man had blocked his only way out of the cemetery. He had no chance of scaling the wall at the far side and, more to the point, the other man was gaining on him. Weakened by the exertions of his digging, Lasalle stumbled, peering round a second time to see that his pursuer was less than ten yards behind. The uniformed man shouted once more and Lasalle actually slowed his pace.

He spun round, the shovel aimed at the gendarme's head.

A blow which would have split his skull open missed by inches and cracked into a tree.

The uniformed man hurled himself at Lasalle and succeeded in bringing him down. They crashed to the ground, rolling over in the damp grass. The gendarme tried to grip his opponent's arms but, despite Lasalle's weakness, he found a reserve of strength born of desperation and, bringing his foot up, he flipped the other man over. The gendarme landed with a thud, the wind knocked from him as he hit a marble cross which stood over one of the graves.

Lasalle snatched up the shovel again and brought it crashing down.

There was a sickening clang as it caught the other man on the back, felling him as he tried to rise.

Lasalle hesitated a moment then sprinted back the way he had come, towards the grave of his wife.

The gendarme hauled himself to his feet and spat blood, trying to focus on his fleeing quarry. He tensed the muscles in his back, wincing from the pain where he'd been struck but there was a determined look on his face as he set off after Lasalle once more.

It only took him a moment to catch up with the running man.

Again, Lasalle swung the shovel, his blow shattering a marble angel, the head disintegrating to leave a jagged point of stone between the wings.

The swing set him off balance and the gendarme took full advantage, hitting the other man with a rugby tackle just above the knees.

Lasalle grunted. The sound turning to a scream as he toppled towards the broken angel.

The moon shone brightly on the jagged stone.

The point pierced Lasalle's chest below the heart, snapping ribs and tearing one lung. Wind hissed coldly in the gaping wound as he tried to suck in an agonised breath. Impaled on the marble angel, he tried to pull himself free but blood made the stone slippery. He tasted it in his mouth, felt it running from his nose as his struggles became weaker.

The gendarme rolled free and attempted to pull the other man clear, the odour of blood filling the air around them.

Lasalle finally freed himself and toppled backward, blood pumping madly from the gaping hole in his chest. His body shook once or twice but, even as the uniformed man knelt beside him, he heard a soft discharge which signalled that Lasalle's sphincter muscle had given out. A rancid stench of excrement made him recoil.

The moon shone briefly on the dead man's open eyes.

The gendarme shuddered as the wind hissed through the branches of a nearby tree.

It sounded like a disembodied voice.

A cold, invisible oration spoken for the man who lay before him.

The last rites.

48

Oxford

The sun shone brightly, pouring through the windows of her office and reflecting back off the white paper before her. She told herself that was the reason she found it so hard to concentrate. She had read the same two pages half-a-dozen times but still not a word had penetrated. It was the heat. It had to be the heat that was putting her off.

Kelly sat back in her chair and dropped the wad of notes.

She sighed, knowing full well that her lack of concentration had nothing to do with present climatic conditions.

Since arriving at the Instiute that morning she had been able to think of nothing but Blake. Even now, as the vision of him drifted into her mind she smiled. For a moment she rebuked herself, almost angry that she had become so strongly attached to him. She felt almost guilty, like a schoolgirl with a crush on a teacher but, the more she thought about it, the more she realized how close to love her feelings for Blake were becoming. Was it possible to fall in love with someone in such a short time? Kelly decided that it was. She was certain that he felt the same way about her. She felt it in his touch, in the way he spoke to her.

Kelly shook her head and chuckled to herself. She could hardly wait for the evening to see him again.

Once more she began reading the notes before her.

There was a light tap on the door and, before she could tell the visitor to enter, Dr Vernon walked in.

Kelly's eyes widened in unconcealed surprise.

Standing with the Institute Director was Alain Joubert.

He and Kelly locked stares as Vernon moved into the room.

'I believe you already know Alain Joubert,' he said, motioning to the Frenchman.

'Of course,' Kelly told him, shaking hands with Joubert curtly.

'How are you, Miss Hunt?' Joubert asked, his face impassive.

'I'm fine, I didn't expect to see you again so soon. Is Lasalle here too?'

Joubert opened his mouth to speak but V rnon stepped forward. His face was suddenly somehow softer and Kelly noticed the difference in his features.

'Kelly, you were a friend of Lasalle's weren't you?' he said, quietly.

'What do you mean "you were"? Why the past tense?' she asked.

'He was killed in an accident last night.'

'What kind of accident?' she demanded, her voice a mixture of shock and helplessness.

'We don't know all the details,' Vernon explained. 'The Director of the Metapsychic Centre informed me this morning. I thought you had a right to know.'

She nodded and brushed a hand through her hair wearily.

'He was dying anyway,' Joubert said.

'What do you mean?' Kelly snapped, looking at the

231

Frenchman.

'He was cracking up. Taking more of those pills of his. He was dying and he didn't even realize it.'

Kelly detected something close to contempt in Joubert's voice and it angered her.

'Doesn't his death mean anything to you?' she snapped. 'The two of you *had* worked together for a long time.'

The Frenchman seemed unconcerned.

'It's a regrettable incident,' Vernon interjected. 'But, unfortunately, there's nothing we can do.' He smiled condescendingly at Kelly, the tone of his voice changing. 'That wasn't the real reason I came to speak to you, Kelly.'

She looked at him expectantly.

'You're probably wondering why Joubert is here?' he began.

'It had occurred to me,' Kelly said.

'I want you to work with him on the dream project.'

Kelly shot a wary glance at the Frenchman.

'Why?' she demanded. 'I can handle the work alone. I've been doing it since John Fraser ... left,' she emphasised the last word with contempt.

'Joubert is more experienced than you are. I'm sure you appreciate that,' Vernon said. 'In fact, I felt it only fair to put him in charge of the project.'

'I've been involved with the work from the beginning. Why should Joubert be given seniority?'

'I explained that. He's more experienced.'

'Then you don't leave me much choice, Dr Vernon. If you put Joubert over me, I'll resign.'

Vernon studied Kelly's determined features for a moment.

'Very well,' he said, flatly. 'You may leave.'

Kelly tried to disguise her surprise but couldn't manage it.

'If that's the way you feel, then I won't try to stop you,' Vernon continued, unwrapping a fresh menthol sweet. He popped it into his mouth.

She got to her feet and, without speaking, picked up her leather attaché case and fumbled for the notes on the desk.

'Leave the notes,' said Vernon, forcefully.

She dropped them back on to the desk.

'I'm sorry you couldn't have accepted this situation,' Vernon told her. 'But, as you know, the work of the Institute

232

comes first.'

'Yes, I understand,' she said, acidly. 'I hope you find what you're looking for.' She glanced at Joubert. 'Both of you.'

Kelly felt like slamming the door behind her as she left but she resisted the temptation. As she made her way up the corridor towards the entrance hall she felt the anger seething within her.

She stalked out into the bright sunshine but paused for a moment, narrowing her eyes against the blazing onslaught. She found that the palms of her hands were sweating, her breath coming in short, sharp gasps. She marched across to her waiting car and slid behind the wheel, sitting there in the cloying heat, not allowing herself to calm down. She thumped the steering wheel in frustration, looking to one side, towards the Institute.

How could Vernon let her walk out just like that? She inhaled and held the breath for a moment.

And Joubert.

The arrogant bastard. She wondered if his research was the only reason for being in England.

The reality of the situation suddenly seemed to hit her like a steam train and she felt tears welling in her eyes.

Tears of sadness for Lasalle.

Tears of frustration for herself. Of anger.

Her body shook as she felt the hot, salty droplets cascading down her cheeks and she reached for a tissue, hurriedly wiping them away.

She wondered if Joubert and Vernon were watching her.

The seed of doubt inside her mind had grown steadily over the past few weeks until now, it had become a spreading bloom of unquenchable conviction.

There was, she was sure, a conspiracy taking place between the Frenchman and the Institute Director. Nothing would dissuade her from that conclusion now.

First John Fraser, then Michel Lasalle. Both had been involved with the projects on Astral projection and both were now dead.

Coincidence?

She thought about what had happened over the past couple of days as she started the engine and drove off.

The seance.

Toni Landers. Roger Carr. Gerald Braddock.

She glanced over her shoulder at the gaunt edifice of the Institute.

Even in the warm sunshine it looked peculiarly menacing.

She rang Blake as soon as she got in. She told him what had happened that morning. He listened patiently, speaking softly to her every now and then, calming her down. She felt like crying once more, such was her feeling of helplessness and rage.

He asked her if she was OK to drive and, puzzled, she said that she was.

'Will you come and stay with me?' he wanted to know.

Kelly smiled.

'You mean move in?'

'Stay as long as you like. Until this is sorted out or, you never know, you might even decide that you can put up with me for a few more weeks.'

There was a long silence between them finally broken by Blake.

'Best food in town,' he said, chuckling.

'I'll start packing,' she told him.

They said their goodbyes and Kelly replaced the receiver, suddenly anxious to be with him. She hurried through into the bedroom, hauled her suitcase down from the top of the wardrobe and began rummaging through her drawers for the items she would need.

She felt a slight chill but disregarded it and continued packing.

49

London

The crushed lager can landed with a scarcely audible thud on the stage in front of the drum riser. A roadie, clad in jeans and a white sweatshirt, scuttled to pick up the debris and remove it. On the far side of the stage two of his companions were dragging one of the huge Marshall amps into position alongside three others of the same size. Each was the height of a man.

Jim O'Neil picked up another can of drink and downed half in one huge swallow. He wiped his mouth with the back of his hand and wandered back and forth behind the curtain. From the other side he could hear the sound of almost 2,000 voices muttering, chatting expectantly. Whistles punctuated the gathering sea of sound.

He guessed that the theatre was full to capacity and the crowd were growing restless as the minutes ticked away until the curtain rose. The place smelled of sweat and leather.

O'Neil himself looked like something from a gladiatorial arena clad as he was in a pair of knee boots, leather trousers and a waist-coat decorated with hundreds of studs. On both arms he wore leather wrist-bands which covered his muscular forearms, the nickel-plated points glinting in the half-light.

There was a burst of sound from his left and he turned to see his lead guitarist, Kevin Taylor, adjusting his amps.

A loud cheer from the other side of the curtain greeted this involuntary action and when the drummer thundered out a brief roll there was even more frenzied shouting from the waiting crowd.

O'Neil wandered over towards Kevin Taylor and tapped the guitarist on the shoulder. He turned and smiled at the singer. At twenty-four, Taylor was almost five years younger than O'Neil but his long hair and craggy face gave him the appearance of a man much older. He wore a white tee-shirt and striped trousers.

'Go easy on the solos tonight,' O'Neil said to him, taking another swig from his can of lager. 'There are four of us in the band you know.'

'I don't know what you mean,' said the guitarist, a slight Irish lilt to his accent.

'At the last gig you nearly wore your fucking fingers out you played so many solos.'

'The audience seems to enjoy it,' Taylor protested.

'I don't give a fuck about the audience. I'm telling you, don't overdo it and keep it simple. Nothing fresh. Right?'

'You're the boss.'

'Yeah,' O'Neil grunted. 'I am.' He finished the lager, crushed the can in one powerful hand and dropped it at the Irishman's feet.

O'Neil walked away, wondering if he was the only one who felt cold.

'Two minutes,' someone shouted.

The singer moved towards the front of the stage and tapped the microphone then, satisfied, he retreated out of view and waited for the curtain to rise. The lights were lowered until the theatre was in darkness and, as the gloom descended, the shouts and whistles grew in intensity finally erupting into a shattering crescendo as the curtain began to rise and the coloured lights above the stage flashed on and off. As the band opened up with a series of power chords which would have registered on the Richter scale, even the swelling roar of the audience was eclipsed. The explosion of musical ferocity swept through the hall like a series of sonic blasts, the scream of guitars and the searing hammerstrokes forged by the drummer merged into a force which threatened to put cracks in the walls.

O'Neil took the stage, his powerful voice soaring like an air raid siren over the driving sound of his musicians.

As he sang he ran from one side of the stage to the other, grinning at the hordes of fans who clamoured to get closer to the stage, occasionally pausing to touch their upraised hands. Like some leather clad demi-God he strode the platform, his disciples before him, fists raised in salute and admiration.

The heat from the spotlights was almost unbearable but still O'Neil felt an icy chill nipping at his neck, spreading slowly through his entire body until it seemed to fill him. He gazed out at the crowd, their faces becoming momentary blurs to him as he spun round and moved towards Kevin Taylor.

O'Neil raised the microphone stand above his head, twirling it like a drum-major's baton, much to the delight of the crowd.

Even Taylor smiled at him.

He was still smiling when O'Neil drove the stand forward like a spear, putting all his weight behind it, forcing the metal tube into Taylor's stomach. The aluminium shaft tore through his midsection and, propelled by O'Neil, erupted from the guitarist's back just above the kidneys. Blood burst from both wounds and Taylor croaked in agony as he was forced back towards the stack of amps behind him. O'Neil let go of the mike stand as Taylor crashed into the speakers.

There was a bright flash as they shorted out and, the guitarist, still transfixed, began to jerk uncontrollably as thousands of volts of electricity ripped through him.

There was a blinding white explosion as the first amp went up.

The PA system began to crackle insanely as a combination of feed-back and static accompanied the short circuit.

Another amp exploded.

Then another.

Rigged to the same system, it was like dropping a lighted match into a full box.

Flames began to lick from the first amp, devouring Taylor's twitching body hungrily, writhing in his long hair like yellow snakes. He looked like a fiery Gorgon. On the far side of the stage the other banks of speakers began to blow up, some showering the audience with pieces of blazing wood.

Those in the front few rows clambered back over their seats, anxious to be away from the terrifying destruction before them but those behind could not move fast enough and many were crushed in the mad stampede to escape. Anyone who fell was immediately trodden underfoot as fear overcame even the strongest and panic rapidly became blind terror. On the balcony, some stared mesmerised at the stage which was rapidly becoming an inferno.

Flames rose high, destroying everything they touched. The other musicians had already fled the stage and a roadie who dashed on to help was crushed beneath a falling amp, pinned helplessly as he burned alive, his shrieks drowned out by the deafening crackle coming from the PA and the horrified shouts of the crowd.

The curtain was lowered but flames caught it and it became little more than a canopy of fire, suspended over the stage like some kind of super-nova. Dozens of lights, unable to stand up to the heat, shattered, spraying glass on to those below. A large frame holding eight football-sized spotlights came free of its rigging and plummeted into the audience where it exploded. Dozens were crushed, others were burned or sliced open by flying glass which hurtled around like jagged crystal grapeshots.

Motionless on the stage, framed by fire, stood Jim O'Neil, his face pale and blank as he gazed uncomprehendingly around him at the destruction. He saw people in the audience screaming as they ran, he saw others lying on the floor, across seats. Bloodied, burned or crushed.

A roadie ran shrieking across the stage, his clothes and hair ablaze. The acrid stench of burned flesh filled O'Neil's nostrils and he swayed as though he were going to faint.

Behind him, still impaled on the microphone stand, the body of Kevin Taylor was being reduced to charred pulp by the searing flames which leapt and danced all around the stage.

O'Neil could only stand alone and shake his head. Like some lost soul newly introduced to hell.

Sweat was pouring from him but, despite the blistering temperatures, he felt as if he were freezing to death.

50

As darkness crept across the sky, Blake got to his feet and crossed the room to draw the curtains. Kelly watched as he shut out the gloom, feeling somehow more secure, as if the night were comprised of millions of tiny eyes — each one watching her.

The writer paused by the drinks cabinet and re-filled his own glass. Kelly declined the offer of a top-up. She felt that she had already consumed a little too much liquor since arriving at Blake's house earlier in the day.

Throughout the journey to London she had felt an unexplained chill, an inexplicable sense of foreboding which only seemed to disappear once she saw Blake. She felt safe with him. But, more than that, she was now even more convinced that she was falling in love with him.

He returned to his chair and sat down, glancing across at Kelly.

Barefoot, clad only in a pair of skin tight faded jeans and a tee-shirt, she looked more vulnerable than he had ever seen her before. And also, perhaps because she was unaware of it, more alluring. Yet he knew, beneath that apparently anxious exterior, she still retained the courage and determination which had first drawn him to her.

'Are you feeling all right?' he asked, noticing how intently she stared into the bottom of her glass.

'I was just thinking,' she told him, finally gracing him with her attention. 'I know we've been over this dozens of times but I can't seem to get it out of my mind. I'm convinced that someone at that seance is responsible for what's been going on, for these murders.'

'Go on,' he prompted her.

'The only one who knew all five victims ...'

Blake interrupted.

'How can you call Braddock and the other two, *victims*

when they were the ones who committed the murders?'

'They did them against their will. They were used.' She looked intently at him. 'And I'm sure that the same person who influenced them was also responsible for the deaths of Fraser and Lasalle. It has to be Dr Vernon.'

Blake shook his head.

'Fraser was killed in a car crash, right? You've already told me that Lasalle was starting to crack up again. What proof is there that Vernon had anything to do with *their* deaths?' he said. 'Who's to say that both men didn't die in bona fide accidents?'

'Whose side are you on?' she snapped.

'It's nothing to do with sides, Kelly,' he said, angrily. 'It's a matter of practicality. You can't go accusing someone like Vernon without proof. Besides, if it were true, how the hell are you going to prove it? There isn't a policeman in the country who'd believe you. The whole idea of controlling someone else's Astral personality is difficult enough to understand, even for people like you and I, let alone for someone with no knowledge of the subject.'

'Are you saying we're beaten?' she muttered.

'No, I'm just trying to be practical,' Blake explained.

'Three of the people involved in that seance have already commited murder. What about the rest of us? How long before something happens to us?'

Blake picked up the phone.

'I'm going to call Mathias and Jim O'Neil,' he said. 'I want to know if they're aware of what's been happening. They could be in danger too.'

'And so could we,' Kelly added, cryptically.

Blake didn't answer.

'Grosvenor House Hotel. Can I help you?' said a female voice.

':I'd like to speak to Mr Jonathan Mathias,' said Blake. 'He has a suite at the hotel. My name is David Blake.'

There was a moment's silence and, from the other end of the line, Blake heard the sound of paper rustling.

Kelly kept her eyes on him as he stood waiting.

'I'm afraid Mr Mathias checked out this morning,' the voice told him.

'Damn,' muttered the writer; then to the receptionist,

'Have you any idea where he is? Where he went? It is important.'

'I'm sorry, I can't help you there, sir,' she said.

Blake thanked her and pressed his fingers down on the cradle.

'No luck?' Kelly asked.

'He's probably back in the States by now,' the writer said, reaching for a black notebook which lay close to the phone. He flipped through it, running his finger down the list of names and numbers. He found what he was looking for and tapped out the correct number, listening as the purring tones began.

'Come on,' he whispered, impatiently.

'Are you calling O'Neil?' Kelly wanted to know.

Blake nodded.

'He's probably on stage at the moment but perhaps if I can talk to one of his crew I can get him to ring me back.' The purring went on. Blake jabbed the cradle and pressed the numbers again.

Still no answer.

'What the hell are they playing at?' he muttered.

He flicked the cradle and tried yet again.

A minute passed and he was about to replace the receiver when he heard a familiar click from the other end.

'Hello, is that the Odeon?' he blurted.

The voice at the other end of the line sounded almost unsure.

'Yes. What do you want?'

Blake detected a note of unease in the voice. Fear perhaps?

'Is Jim O'Neil still on stage? If …'

The man at the other end cut him short.

'Are you from a newspaper?' he asked.

'No,' Blake told him, puzzled. 'Why?'

'I thought you might have heard about the accident. No press allowed. The police won't let any of them through.'

'What's happened there?' the writer demanded. 'I'm a friend of O'Neil's.'

'There was an accident, a fire. God knows how many people are dead.' The man's voice began to crack. 'O'Neil killed one of his band. It happened on the stage. I …'

241

'Where's O'Neil now?'

Kelly got up and walked across to the table. Blake picked up a pencil and scribbled a note on a piece of paper. She read it as he continued speaking: O'NEIL HAS KILLED. FIRE ON STAGE. PEOPLE IN AUDIENCE KILLED.

'Oh my God,' murmured Kelly.

'Where is O'Neil at the moment?' the writer repeated.

'The police took him away,' the other man said. 'I've never seen anything like it. He looked as if he didn't know what was going on, he ...'

The phone went dead.

Blake flicked the cradle but could get no response. He gently replaced the receiver.

For long moments neither he nor Kelly spoke, the silence gathering round them like an ominous cloud.

'Toni Landers. Gerald Braddock. Roger Carr and now O'Neil,' Kelly said, finally. 'Who's going to be next?'

Her words hung, unanswered, in the air.

51

New York

Jonathan Mathias raised both arms above his head and stood for a moment, surveying the sea of faces before him. All ages. All nationalities. But with a single purpose.

To see him.

The hall in the Bronx was the largest that he used and as he ran an appraising eye over the throng he guessed that somewhere in the region of 2,000 people had packed into the converted warehouse. They stood in expectant silence, waiting for a sign from him.

'Come forward,' Mathias said, his powerful voice reverberating around the crowded meeting place.

Men working for the psychic, dressed in dark suits, cleared an aisle through the middle of the horde, allowing the procession of pain to begin. First came the wheelchairs, some of their occupants looking expectantly towards the stage where Mathias stood. He saw a young woman being brought forward by two men who had laid her on a stretcher. She lay motionless, sightless eyes gazing at the ceiling, her tongue lolling from one corner of her mouth.

Dozens hobbled towards the psychic on crutches, many struggling with the weight of the callipers which weighed them down. Others were supported by friends or relatives.

Mathias counted perhaps twenty or more figures moving slowly behind those on crutches. Most carried the white sticks which marked them out as blind, others were led forward by members of the crowd or by the dark-suited stewards. One of them, a man in his forties, stumbled and had to be helped up, but he continued on his way, anxious to reach the figure whom he could not see but who he knew would help him.

As the last of the sick passed through the midst of the crowd, the gap which had opened now closed. The people drifting back to their places. From where Mathias stood, it looked like one single amoebic entity repairing a self-inflicted rent in itself. The sea of faces waited as the lights in the hall dimmed slightly, one particularly bright spotlight focusing on the psychic, framing him in a brilliant white glow.

The psychic had still not lowered his arms. He closed his eyes for a moment and stood like some finely attired scarecrow, his head slightly bowed. In the almost palpable silence, even the odd involuntary cough or whimper seemed intrusive.

Without looking up, Mathias nodded imperceptibly.

From the right of the stage, a woman put her strength into pushing a wheelchair up the ramp which had been erected to facilitate the countless invalid chairs. A steward moved forward to help her but Mathias waved him back, watching as the woman strained against the weight contained in the chair. Eventually, she made it and, after a swift pause to catch her breath, she moved towards the psychic who fixed both her and the boy in the wheelchair in his piercing gaze.

The occupant of the chair was in his early twenties, his ruddy features and lustrous black hair somehow belying the fact that his body was relatively useless. The boy had large, alert eyes which glistened in the powerful light and he met Mathias' stare with something akin to pleading. He still wore a metal neck-brace which was fastened to his shattered spine by a succession of pins. Paralysed from the neck down the only thing which moved were his eyes.

'What is your name?' Mathias asked him.

'James Morrow,' the youngster told him.

'You're his mother?' the psychic asked, looking at the woman fleetingly.

She nodded vigorously.

'Please help him,' she babbled. 'He's been like this for a year and ...'

Mathias looked at her again and, this time, his gaze seemed to bore through her. She stopped talking instantly and took a step back, watching as the psychic gently gripped her son's head, circling it with his long fingers, their tips almost meeting at the back of the boy's skull. He raised his head and looked upward, momentarily staring at the powerful spotlight which held him like a moth in a flame. His breathing began to degenerate into a series of low grunts and the first minute droplets of perspiration started to form on his forehead. The psychic gripped the boy's head and pressed his thumbs gently against his scalp for a moment or two, passing to his temples, then his cheeks.

James Morrow closed his eyes, a feeling of welcome serenity filling him. He even smiled slightly as he felt the psychic's thumbs brush his eyelids and rest there.

Mathias was quivering violently, his entire body shaking madly. He lowered his head and looked down at Morrow, his own teeth now clenched. A thin ribbon of saliva oozed from his mouth and dripped on to the blanket which covered the boy's lower body.

The psychic gasped, a sound which he might have made had all the wind suddenly been knocked from him. He felt his hands beginning to tingle but it wasn't the customary heat which he experienced. It was a searing cold, as if someone had plunged his hands into snow.

James Morrow tried to open his eyes but was unable to do so due to the fact that Mathias' thumbs held his lids closed. The boy felt a slight increase of pressure on the back of his head as the psychic gripped harder.

Mathias felt the muscles in his arms and shoulders throbbing as he exerted more force, pushing his thumbs against Morrow's closed eyes. He was aware of the youngster trying to pull his head back and, as if from a thousand miles away, Mathias heard him groan slightly as the fingers and thumbs dug into him.

The psychic looked down at him and smiled thinly, his face appearing horribly distorted by the blinding power of the spotlight.

Even if Morrow had been aware of what was happening, there was nothing he could have done to prevent it. All he felt was the steadily growing pain as Mathias gripped his head with even more force, a vice-like strength which threatened to crack the bones of his skull. But, as it was, all he could do was remain helpless in the wheelchair, unable to sqirm away from those powerful hands which felt as if they were intent on crushing his head.

The pressure on his eyes became unbearable as Mathias' thumbs drove forward.

Mathias felt some slight resistance at first but then he grunted triumphantly as he felt Morrow's eyes begin to retreat backward beneath the force he was exerting. Blood burst from the corner of the left one and cascaded down the younger man's cheek. Mathias felt the glistening orb move to one side, his thumb slipping into the crimson wetness which was the socket. His nail tore the lid of Morrow's right eye, scraping across the cornea before puncturing the entire structure. The psychic felt his other thumb tearing muscle and ligaments as he began to shake his paralysed victim.

With both thumbs embedded in Morrow's eyes, Mathias forced him backwards, aided by the motion of the wheelchair.

The watching crowd were stunned, not quite sure what was going on. They saw the blood, they saw Morrow's mother running forward but still they looked on in dumb-struck horror.

It was Morrow's keening wail of agony which seemed to galvanise them into action.

In the watching throng, a number of other people screamed. Shouts rose. Shouts of fear and revulsion.

One of the screams came from James Morrow's mother

who ran at the psyshic, anxious to drag him away from her son, who sat motionless in his wheelchair as the psychic continued to gouge his thumbs ever deeper into the riven cavities of his eye sockets. Blood was running freely down the boy's face now, staining his shirt and the blanket around him.

Mathias finally released his hold, turning swiftly to strike the approaching woman with one bloodied hand. The blow shattered her nose and sent her sprawling.

The body of James Morrow, sitting upright in the chair, rolled towards one side of the stage where it tipped precariously for a second before toppling over. The lifeless form fell out and the psychic watched as Mrs Morrow, her face a crimson ruin, crawled helplessly towards it, burbling incoherently.

Mathias blinked hard, aware that people were moving away from the stage. Away from *him*. He glanced down at the struggling form of Mrs Morrow, draped over her dead son like some kind of bloodied shroud. He took a step towards the carnage then faltered, his head spinning, his eyes drawn to the twin gore-filled holes which had once been James Morrow's eyes.

The psychic looked down at his own hands and saw that they were soaked with blood. A fragment of red muscle still clung to one thumb nail. The crimson fluid had run up his arms, staining the cuffs of his shirt.

He shook violently, struggling to breathe as he surveyed the grisly scene before him.

The spotlight pinned him in its unremitting glare but, despite the heat which it gave off, Mathias found that he was shivering.

52

London

Kelly slipped off her jeans and shivered momentarily before climbing into the large bed in Blake's room. She heard the sound of footfalls approaching across the landing.

Blake entered the room and pulled the door closed behind him. He began unbuttoning his shirt.

'I'll drive to the Institute tomorrow,' he said. 'Confront Vernon. I'll mention his wife. Anything I have to in order to get him to respond.'

He walked to the bedside cabinet and knelt down. The bottom drawer was locked but a quick turn of the ornate gold key and the writer opened it. He reached inside and lifted something out, hefting it before him.

It was a .357 Magnum. A snub-nose model. Blake flipped out the cylinder and carefully thumbed one of the heavy grain bullets into each chamber then he snapped it back into position. He laid the revolver on top of the cabinet.

Kelly regarded the gun warily.

'If Vernon does respond,' said Blake slipping into bed beside her, 'then, at least you'll know you were right. If he doesn't, then you can start looking for another suspect.'

'That narrows the field down quite a bit,' Kelly said, cryptically. She moved close to him, nuzzling against his body, kissing first his chest then his lips. 'Please be careful,' she whispered.

Blake nodded, glanced one last time at the Magnum then reached over and flicked off the lamp.

She was blind.

Kelly thrashed her head frantically back and forth, the terror growing within her.

She could see nothing.

She tried to scream but no sound would come forth.

It took her a second or two to realize that she had been gagged. A piece of cloth had been stuffed into her mouth, secured by a length of thick hemp which chafed against the soft flesh of her cheeks. Her eyes had been covered by more, tightly fastened, strands of knotted material, sealed shut as surely as if the lids had been sewn together.

She felt someone moving beside her, felt a hand gently stroking her flat stomach before first moving upwards to her breasts and then down to her pubic mound.

Kelly attempted to move but, as she did, red hot pain lanced through her wrists and ankles as the rope which held her to the bed rasped against her skin. She made a whimpering sound deep in her throat, aware that her legs had been forced apart. She lay spreadeagled, her body exposed to whatever prying eyes chose to inspect it. Her legs had been pulled apart to such an extent that the muscles at the backs of her thighs felt as if they were about to tear. Pain gnawed at the small of her back, intensifying as she struggled in vain to free herself. The rope which was wound so tightly around her wrists and ankles bit hungrily into her flesh until she felt a warm dribble of blood from her left ankle.

Kelly was aware of movement, of a heavy form positioning itself between her legs.

She felt fingers trickling up the inside of her thighs, seeking her exposed vagina.

In the darkness she felt even more helpless, unable to see her assailant because of the blindfold.

Something nudged against her cleft and she stiffened.

Whatever it was, it was excruciatingly cold on that most sensitive area. She lay still as the freezing object probed deeper and, again, she tried to scream.

Kelly heard soft chuckling then a guttural grunt of pleasure.

It was followed by a rapid, rhythmic slopping sound which seemed to keep time with the low grunts.

She realized that her invisible assailant was masturbating.

The cold object between her legs pushed deeper, now adding pain to the other sensation she was feeling.

Another second and Kelly felt warm fluid spilling onto her belly in an erratic fountain. The grunts of her captor grew louder as he coaxed the last droplets of thick liquid from his penis.

Light flashed into her eyes as the blindfold was torn free and, in that split second, she saw the face of her attacker.

His penis still gripped in one fist, the other hand holding the gun against her vagina, he grinned down at her.

She heard a noise which she knew to be the pulling back of the revolver's hammer but her senses were already reeling as she stared with bulging eyes at the man who hovered above her.

David Blake smiled down at her, his face twisted into an unearthly grimace.

Kelly awoke from the nightmare bathed in perspiration. She let out a moan of terror and sat up, looking around her, trying to convince herself that what she had experienced had been the work of her imagination.

The room was silent.

Blake slept soundly beside her, his chest rising and falling slowly.

She let out a long, almost painful breath and ran her hands through her sweat-soaked hair.

As she did so she became aware of a slight tingling in her hands and feet so she pulled the sheet back and glanced down.

Kelly stifled a scream.

On both her wrists and ankles, the flesh was puffy and swollen. Ugly, vivid red welts disfigured the skin.

They were very much like rope burns.

249

53

The sound of the alarm shattered the silence and shocked Blake from his slumber. He shot out a hand and silenced the insistent buzzing before lying back for a moment to rub his eyes. He took two or three deep breaths and blinked at the ceiling before easing himself slowly out of bed.

Beside him, Kelly did not stir.

The writer gathered up some clothes and crept out of the room in an effort not to wake her. He paused once more when he reached the bedroom door, satisfied that Kelly had not been disturbed.

He showered and dressed, returning to the bedroom once more to retrieve the Magnum. He then made his way downstairs where he slipped the revolver into his attaché case and clipped it shut.

Blake ate a light breakfast then he got to his feet and, case in hand, headed out to the waiting XJS.

The drive to Oxford should take him a couple of hours.

Kelly watched from the bedroom window as Blake climbed into the Jag and started the engine.

She remained hidden in case he looked round but she need not have worried. The sleek vehicle burst into life and the writer guided it out onto the road.

Kelly had heard the alarm clock earlier but had lain awake, eyes still closed, while he had slipped away. She had feigned sleep, aware of his presence in the room. She had heard him moving about downstairs and then, finally, she'd listened as he had walked out to the car. Only at that point had she clambered, naked, out of bed and crossed to the window to watch him leave. Now she returned to the bed and sat down on the edge.

First she inspected her ankles, then her wrists.

They were unmarked.

She told herself that she should have woken Blake immediately after she'd had the nightmare but it had frightened her so much that she had decided to remain silent. Even now, in the light of day, she could not find the courage to speak to him about it. That was why she had chosen to give him the impression she was still sleeping when he left.

The dream had been so vivid. Too vivid. Parts of it still burned brightly in her mind like a brand. Ugly and unwanted.

Kelly dressed and made her way downstairs where she found a note propped up on the kitchen table.

SEE YOU LATER, SLEEPYHEAD.

It was signed with Blake's sweeping signature.

She smiled, folded up the note and slipped it into the pocket of her jeans. As she waited for the kettle to boil she put two pieces of bread in the toaster and propped herself against the draining board, waiting.

Should she tell Blake about the dream when he returned? She ran a hand through her hair and decided that she shouldn't. After all, it had been only a dream, hadn't it?

She looked at her wrists and remembered the rope burns which she'd seen the previous night.

Kelly sighed. She wasn't even sure she *had* seen them.

The toast popped up and she buttered the slices, chewing thoughtfully.

She heard a noise from the front of the house and wandered through the sitting room in time to see the postman retreating back up the path. Kelly walked through into the hall and picked up the mail he'd pushed through. As she straightened up she glanced across at the door which led to Blake's underground workroom.

The key was in the lock.

Kelly placed the mail on a nearby table and wandered across to the cellar door. She turned the handle and found that the door was unlocked anyway. She pushed it, reaching for the light switches inside. Kelly slapped them on and the cellar was bathed in the cold glow of fluorescents.

Apart from the steps which led down to the work area itself, the floor had been carpeted. She scurried down the stairs, the coldness of the concrete on her bare feet giving her added speed. Finally she stood at the bottom, glad of the warmth from the carpet. The cellar was large, stretching away from her in all four directions. A huge wooden desk occupied central position and she noticed that there was a typewriter on it. A small waste bin, overflowing with scraps of balled up paper stood nearby. There was a telephone too. The entire cellar had been decorated in white; it positively gleamed and, as she moved around, Kelly detected the scent of an air freshener. Bookcases lined two walls, huge, dark wood creations creaking with hundreds of volumes but, unlike those which Blake displayed on his shelves upstairs in the sitting room, these books were more in the manner of research material. A great many were bound in leather and, as Kelly drew closer, she realized that most were very old.

She reached up and took one.

The gold leaf title was cracked and barely readable so she opened the book and scanned the title page: *Inside the Mind*. She checked the publication date and saw that it was 1921. Replacing it she found another, this one even older: *Psychiatry and the Unknown*. It was dated 1906.

No wonder Blake kept these books hidden away, Kelly thought, scanning more titles. They must be worth a fortune. She ran her index finger along the shelf, mouthing each title silently as she went.

She came to a shelf which consisted entirely of ring binders, each one labelled on the spine. She recognised Blake's writing on the labels.

'*Dreams*,' she read on the first and took it down, flipping through quickly.

Some of the pages were typed, others hand-written. Here and there she spotted a photograph. There was one of Blake's house and, beside it, a rough drawing of the same building. It was almost childlike in its simplicity, drawn, as it was, with a thick pencil. However, the similarity was unmistakable. Kelly replaced the file and reached for another.

'*Hypnosis*,' she murmured.

There was a photo of Mathias inside.

Kelly turned the page and found one of Blake himself but apparently he was sleeping. It must, she reasoned, have been taken with an automatic timer. She was puzzled as to why he should have taken such a shot though. Kelly scanned what was written beneath the photo but saw only a date. The photo, it seemed, had been taken over a year ago. She wondered if Blake had, perhaps, asked someone else to take it but she still couldn't understand why he would need such a photograph.

She reached for another file marked 'Astral Projection' and skimmed through that.

There were more photos.

Of Mathias. Of Blake himself.

Of Toni Landers.

She turned a page.

There was a newspaper clipping which featured Roger Carr.

Kelly swallowed hard and perched on the edge of the desk as she read one of the typewritten sheets in the file.

'*December 6th*,' she read, keeping her voice low, as if she were in a library.

'*The Astral body is a separate entity. I am sure of that now. From what I have observed and read, but, more importantly, from experimentation upon myself, I know that it can be summoned in tangible form. By a long and tortuous process I have actually managed to separate my Astral body from my physical body at will. To unlock the part of the mind previously unexplored by scientists and psychologists. I now feel confident enough to use this process on others.*'

Kelly swallowed hard and read on:

'*In order to confirm that tangible Astral projection is possible, I conducted the following test. While in a self-induced trance, I inflicted injury upon my own Astral body and discovered that this injury was subsequently manifested on my physical body.*'

There were two photographs beneath. One showed Blake looking at the camera, the other, identical in appearance, highlighted a small scar on his left shoulder. The photos were marked with dates and times. The unblemished one bore the legend: *December 4th 7.30 p.m.* The second: *December 5th 8.01 a.m.*

'*This proved two important things, firstly that it is possible to possess two centres of consciousness simultaneously and also that any injury sustained in the Astral state will manifest itself on the host body. The proof is irrefutable. Tangible*

Astral projection is possible, so too is the manipulation of another person's subconscious mind.'

Kelly closed the file, got to her feet and replaced it. For long seconds she stood motionless in the silent cellar then she scurried back up the steps, aware of the icy chill which seemed to have enveloped her.

She closed the cellar door behind her, noticing that her hand was shaking.

54

It was almost 3.15 p.m. when the XJS came to a halt outside the house.

Kelly, watching from the sitting room, peered out and saw Blake lock the vehicle before gathering up his attaché case. He headed for the front door and, a moment later, she heard the key turn. As it did she moved across to the sofa and sat down, her eyes on the hall door.

Blake smiled at her as he entered.

She watched as he laid the attaché case on the coffee table and flipped it open, removing the Magnum which he placed beside it.

'Vernon didn't try anything?' she said, looking at the gun.

The writer shook his head.

'If he has acquired some kind of power then he knows how to control it,' he said, crossing to the drinks cabinet and pouring himself a large measure of Haig. He offered Kelly a drink and she accepted a Campari.

'Did he say anything at all?' she wanted to know.

'Nothing that I found incriminating if that's what you mean,' Blake told her. 'I mentioned his wife. You were right, he does get touchy about *that*. He wanted to know how I knew about her, what I knew about her. When I mentioned John Fraser he threatened to have me thrown out or arrested.' The writer downed a sizeable measure of the fiery liquid.

'You didn't accuse him of killing Fraser did you?'

'Not in so many words. I just told him what *you'd* told *me*. He didn't react very favourably.'

There was a long silence, finally broken by Blake.

'I don't know where we go from here,' he said.

Kelly didn't speak for a moment then she sucked in a long breath and looked at Blake.

'David, how much do *you* know about Astral projection?' she asked.

He sipped at his drink, his eyes glinting behind the dark screen of his glasses.

'Why do you ask?' he said, his voice low.

'I was just curious,' she told him. She opened her mouth to speak again but couldn't seem to find the words.

Blake sat beside her on the sofa and placed one arm around her, drawing her to him. He smiled reassuringly. She moved closer to him, aware of an icy chill which surrounded her.

He held her firmly and only when her head was resting on his shoulder did his smile disappear.

He looked across at the Magnum.

55

Oxford

The strains of 'God Save the Queen' died away gradually to be replaced by a rasping hiss of static, so loud that it jolted Dr Stephen Vernon from his uneasy dozing. He moved to get up, almost spilling the mug of cocoa which he held in one hand. He switched off the television and stood silently in the sitting room for a moment. He was alone in his house. Joubert was at the Institute and would be for the remainder of the night, going through reams of notes so far untouched.

Vernon gazed down into his mug of cold cocoa and winced as he saw the film of skin which had covered the surface. He put it down and headed for the sitting room door, turning off lights as he went.

He had reached the bottom of the staircase when he heard the noise.

Vernon froze, trying to pinpoint the direction from which it had come. He felt his heart begin to beat a little faster as he heard it once more.

A dull thud followed by what sounded like soft whispering.

He turned, realizing that it came from the study, behind him to the left. The white door was firmly shut however, hiding its secret securely.

Vernon hesitated, waiting for the sound to come again.

He heard nothing and prepared to climb the stairs once more. He'd left the window in the room open. A breeze might well have dislodged something in there, knocked it to the floor, caused ...

He heard the sound like whispering again and, this time, turned and approached the door.

Vernon paused outside, his ear close to the wood in an effort to detect any sounds from within. His hand hovered nervously over the knob, finally closing on it, turning it gently.

He tried to control his rapid breathing, afraid that whoever was inside the study would hear his approach. Also, as he stood there waiting for the right moment to strike, he felt suddenly vulnerable. He released the door knob and looked around the darkened hallway for a weapon of some kind.

There was a thick wood walking stick propped up in the umbrella stand nearby; Vernon took it and, for the second time, prepared to enter the study.

Beyond the closed door all was silent once again, not the slightest sound of movement disturbed the solitude. A thought occurred to Vernon.

What if the intruder was aware of his presence and, at this moment, was waiting for *him*?

He swallowed hard and tried to force the thought from his mind.

He gripped the knob and twisted it, hurling open the door, his free hand slapping for the light switches just inside.

As the study was illuminated, Vernon scanned the area before him, the walking stick brandished like a club.

His mouth dropped open in surprise as he caught sight of

the intruder.

Hunkered over the large table, one of the files open before him, was David Blake.

'You,' gasped Vernon, lowering his guard.

That lapse of concentration was all that Blake needed. He flung himself across the table, catapulted as if from some gigantic rubber band. He crashed into Vernon, knocking the walking stick from his hand, rolling to one side as the older man lashed out at him. Vernon managed to scramble to his feet, bolting from the room but Blake was younger and quicker and he rugby-tackled the doctor, bringing him down in the hallway. They grappled in the gloom and Vernon found that his fear gave him added strength. He gripped Blake's wrists and succeeded in throwing him to one side. The younger man crashed against a nearby wall but the impact seemed only to slow him up for a moment. He scrambled to his feet and set off after the older man again, following him into the kitchen this time.

Vernon tugged open a drawer, the contents spilling across the tiled floor. Knives, forks, spoons, a ladle — all rained down around his feet with a series of high pitched clangs. He snatched up a long carving knife and brandished it before him.

Blake hesitated as he saw the vicious blade winking at him and, for what seemed like an eternity, the two men faced one another, eyes locked. Like two gladiators, they both waited for the other to move first.

'What do you want?' asked Vernon, the knife quivering in his grip.

The younger man didn't answer, he merely edged forward slightly.

'I'll kill you, Blake, I swear to God I will,' Vernon assured him, making a sharp stabbing movement with the blade.

Blake was undeterred. He took another step forward, something on the worktop to his right catching his eye.

It was a sugar bowl.

With lightning speed, he picked it up and hurled the contents into Vernon's face. The tiny grains showered him, some finding their way into his eyes, and he yelped in pain, momentarily blinded by the stinging shower of particles. Blake took his chance. Dropping to one knee, he grabbed a corkscrew and hurled himself at Vernon who somehow managed one last despairing lunge before Blake reached him.

The blade sliced through the younger man's jacket and laid open his left forearm just above the wrist. Blood spurted from the cut and plashed on to the tiles. But Blake slammed into Vernon with the force of a pile-driver, knocking him back against the sink. He snaked one arm around the older man's neck and held him firmly, bringing the corkscrew forward with devastating power.

The sharp point pierced Vernon's skull at the crown and he screamed in agony as Blake twisted it, driving the curling metal prong deeper until it began to churn into the older man's brain. White hot pain seared through him and he felt himself blacking out but, just before he did, Blake tore the corkscrew free, ripping a sizeable lump of bone with it. Greyish red brain matter welled up through the hole and Vernon fell forward on to the tiles as Blake struck again. This time driving the corkscrew into the hollow at the base of his skull, ramming hard until it erupted from Vernon's throat. There was an explosion of crimson as blood spouted from both wounds and his body began to quiver uncontrollably as Blake tore the twisted weapon free once more

He stood there for a moment, gazing down at the lifeless body before him, now surrounded by a spreading pool of red liquid. Then, almost contemptuously, he tossed the corkscrew to one side, stepped over the body and headed back towards the study.

Kelly let out a strangled cry as she sat up, the last vestiges of the nightmare still clinging to her consciousness like graveyard mist.

She closed her eyes tightly for a moment, aware that her heart was thundering against her ribs. But, gradually, she slowed her breathing, aware that the dream was fading.

Blake was sleeping peacefully beside her. Apparently he had not heard her frightened outburst. She thought about waking him, telling him what she had dreamt but she thought better of it. Kelly could hear his gentle, rhythmic breathing beside her and she looked down at his still form.

The breath caught in her throat.

There was a small dark stain on the sheet.

She prodded it with her finger and found that it was still damp. Kelly noticed that whatever the substance was, it also coloured her finger. In the darkness of the bedroom it looked black but, as she sniffed it, she caught the unmistakable odour of blood.

Blake moved slightly, turning on to his side.

Kelly pulled the sheet back further and ran her gaze over his body.

On his left forearm, just above the wrist, there was a cut.

She stood in the bedroom doorway for a full five minutes, her eyes riveted to Blake's sleeping form then, certain that she had not disturbed him, she crept downstairs to the sitting room.

Kelly did not turn on the light, not even one of the table lamps. She found the phone and selected the appropriate number, waiting for the receiver to be picked up, hoping that she had remembered Dr Vernon's number correctly.

She didn't have to wait long for an answer.

'Yes.' The voice sounded harsh and she realized that it wasn't the doctor.

'Can I speak to Dr Vernon, please?' she whispered, casting a furtive glance towards the door behind her.

'Who is this?' the voice asked.

'I'm a friend of his,' she persisted. 'Could I speak to him please?'

'That isn't possible. Dr Vernon was murdered earlier tonight.'

Kelly hung up, banging the phone down with a little too much force. She wondered if Blake had heard her but the thought swiftly vanished. There was no sound of movement from upstairs. She stood alone in the dark sitting room, perspiration forming droplets on her face and forehead.

Vernon murdered.

She sat down on the edge of the sofa, her head cradled in her hands, still not fully comprehending what she had heard.

She thought of the blood on the sheet. Of her nightmare. The cut on Blake's wrist.

And of what she had read earlier in the day;

'An injury sustained in the Astral state will manifest itself on the host body.'

Kelly suddenly felt more frightened than she could ever remember.

56

Kelly brought the Mini to a halt and sat behind the wheel for a moment, scanning the area in front of Dr Vernon's house. In addition to the doctor's Audi, there was a dark brown Sierra in the driveway and, by the kerbside itself, a Granada. She could see two men seated in that particular car. One was eating a sandwich while the other, the driver, was busy cleaning his ears out with one index finger. Both men wore suits despite the warmth of the early morning sunshine.

She wound down the window a little further, allowing what little breeze there was to circulate inside the car. She was perspiring, but not all of it was due to the heat of the day.

The drive from London had taken over two hours. She'd told Blake that she wanted to pick up some more clothes from her flat. He'd seen her off like the dutiful lover he'd become, then retired to his workroom for the day. She had not mentioned anything to him about either her nightmare or the phone call to Vernon's house. She had not slept much the previous night, not after returning to bed. What was more, she'd been mildly disturbed to find that the bloodstains on the sheet had all but disappeared and, that morning, Blake's wrist appeared to be uninjured but for a minute red mark which looked like little more than a cat-scratch.

Now Kelly sat in the car staring across the road at the Granada and the house beyond it, realizing that, sooner or later she was going to be forced to make her move. Her palms felt sticky as she reached for the door handle and eased herself out of the Mini. She sucked in a deep breath then headed across the road towards the driveway.

She was a foot or two beyond the Granada when a voice called her back and she turned to see one of the men getting out, his cheeks bulging, hamster-like, with the last remnants of his sandwich.

'Excuse me, Miss,' he said, trying hurriedly to swallow what he was chewing.

Kelly turned to face him, noticing as she did that he was reaching inside his jacket. He produced a slim leather wallet and flipped it open to reveal an ID card which bore his picture. It was a bad likeness, making his thick brown hair appear ginger.

'I'm Detective-Sergeant Ross,' the man told her. 'May I ask what you're doing here?'

'Police?' she said, feigning surprise.

He nodded and succeeded in forcing down the last of his food.

'What are you doing here?'

Ross smiled thinly.

'*I* asked first, Miss,' he said.

The lie was ready on her tongue.

'I've come to see my father,' she told him.

Ross's smile faded suddenly and he almost took a step back.

'We weren't aware that Dr Vernon had any close family,' he told her.

Kelly felt her heart beating a little faster.

'Is something wrong?' she wanted to know, hoping that her little act was working.

'Could you come with me please, Miss?' the DS said and led her up the driveway towards the house. As they drew nearer, Kelly tried frantically to slow her rapid breathing. She had suddenly begun to doubt the success of her little venture. The front door opened and a man dressed in a grey suit, carrying a black briefcase, emerged.

He exchanged brief words with Ross then climbed into the Sierra, reversed out of the driveway and sped off.

'You still haven't told me what's going on?' Kelly insisted, not trying to disguise the mock concern in her voice.

They were inside the house by now and Ross ushered her into a sitting room where she sat down on one of the chairs.

'I'll be back in a minute,' he told her and disappeared.

Kelly looked around the room, hands clasped on her knees. She swallowed hard and attempted to stop her body quivering. Her roving eyes scanned the shelves and tables for photos. If there was one of Vernon's daughter then she was finished. Although Ross had told her that the police were unaware he'd had a family, it did little to comfort her. She was still in the process of composing herself when Ross returned, accompanied by a taller, older man with a long face and chin which jutted forward with almost abnormal prominence. He introduced himself as Detective Inspector Allen.

'You're Dr Vernon's daughter?' he asked, eyeing her up and down.

'Yes,' she lied.

Allen looked at his companion then at Kelly. He cleared his throat self-consciously and proceeded to tell her what had happened the previous night. Kelly reacted with all the rehearsed shock and grief she could muster.

'As far as we know, nothing was stolen,' Allen continued. 'There was still money in one of the drawers upstairs and your father's wallet was in his jacket which is hanging in the hallway.'

'So why was he killed?' Kelly asked, reaching for a handkerchief which she clutched between her hands in mock despair, tugging at it most convincingly.

'We were hoping you might be able to shed some light on that,' Allen said. 'Did he have any enemies that you know of?'

Kelly shook her head.

'He kept himself to himself,' she said, lowering her eyes slightly.

'Did you know that there was someone living in the house with him?' the DI wanted to know. 'One of the guest rooms is occupied.'

'I didn't know that,' she said, with genuine surprise.

Allen frowned.

'How often did you see your father, Miss Vernon?'

Kelly licked her lips self-consciously. She was going to have to tread carefully.

'Not regularly. I live in London at the moment. But that's not my permanent address.'

'Alone?'

'What?'

'Do you live alone?'

262

She paused a second or two longer than she should have and, what was more, she was aware of that fact. Kelly realized that she was on the verge of blowing the entire facade wide open.

'You'll have to excuse me,' she said, pressing the handkerchief to her eyes. 'I can't seem to think straight. After what you've told me about my father I ...' She allowed the sentence to trail off.

Allen nodded comfortingly.

'I realize it must be difficult,' he said, softly. 'Take your time.'

How many more questions, she wondered?

She was spared the trouble of answering by Ross who popped his head around the corner and called to his superior. Allen excused himself and left the room for a moment. Kelly let out an audible sigh of relief, grateful for the momentary respite. She heard voices in the hallway, one of which she was sure she recognised.

A moment later, Alain Joubert entered the sitting room, followed by Allen.

The Frenchman stopped in his tracks when he saw Kelly, who shot an anxious glance in the policeman's direction, thankful that he hadn't noticed her reaction. He did, however, glimpse the surprised expression of Joubert.

'Do you two know each other?' Allen asked.

'We ...'

Kelly cut him short.

'My father introduced us about a month ago,' she said, stepping forward. 'How are you, Mr Joubert?'

The Frenchman managed to conceal his bewilderment and Kelly prayed that he wouldn't give the game away.

'I'm sorry to hear what happened,' Joubert said, flatly.

Kelly nodded.

'Were you aware that Mr Joubert had been staying at your father's house for the past two weeks?' asked the policeman.

'No,' Kelly said. 'But I knew that he was working on a new project with someone. I wasn't aware it was Mr Joubert though. My father likes to keep his work to himself.

'You claim that you've been at the Research Institute all night?' Allen said to the Frenchman.

'Yes I have,' Joubert told him. 'The night-watchman will

263

verify that if you ask him.'

'As far as we can see, nothing of Dr Vernon's was taken, but you might like to check your own belongings,' the DI suggested.

Joubert nodded.

'It would be more convenient for all of us if you could leave the house for a day or two, sir,' Allen said. 'While the lads from forensic go over the place.'

Joubert nodded.

'I'll book into a hotel,' he said. 'I'll get some things from upstairs.' The Frenchman glanced once more at Kelly then left the room.

'How *was* my father killed?' Kelly asked.

'He was stabbed,' said Allen, hastily.

'Knifed?'

The policeman swallowed hard.

'No. He was stabbed with a corkscrew. I'm sorry.'

Kelly closed her eyes for a moment, the details of her dream suddenly flashing with neon brilliance in her mind. She felt a twinge of nausea but fought it back. Allen moved towards her as if he feared she would faint but she waved him away.

'I'm all right,' she assured him, smiling thinly.

Joubert returned a moment later carrying what looked like an overnight bag.

'There is one more thing I'd like to check on before I leave,' he said, entering the study.

Kelly and DI Allen followed him.

The Frenchman muttered something in his own tongue as he surveyed the empty table in the study.

'The files,' he said, wearily. 'They've been taken.'

'What files?' Allen demanded.

'The project that Dr Vernon and I were working on,' Joubert snapped. 'All the information was compiled in half a dozen files. They're gone.'

'What kind of information?' the policeman persisted.

'Just research notes, of no importance to anyone but us.' He cast a sly glance at Kelly.

'Are you sure they've been taken?' said Allen.

'They were here,' Joubert snapped, tapping the table top.

'Can you describe them?' asked Allen.

264

The Frenchman shrugged.

'Six plain manilla files, what more can I tell you?'

'Whoever took them knew what they were looking for,' Kelly interjected.

Joubert nodded and looked at her once more.

'Damn,' he said, under his breath.

'Well,' Allen told him. 'It's not much to go on but, we'll do our best to trace them.' He paused for a moment. 'I'd like the name of the hotel you're staying in, Mr Joubert, if you could phone me at the station as soon as you've booked in.' He handed the Frenchman a piece of paper with a phone number on it. 'And you, Miss Vernon, I'd appreciate an address where I can reach you.'

She gave him that of her flat in Oxford.

'I don't think we need keep you any longer,' the DI told them. 'But we'll be in touch.'

Joubert was the first to turn and head for the front door.

Kelly followed, catching up with him as he reached his car. She glanced round, making sure they were out of earshot.

'Did Lasalle know what was in those files?' she asked.

'What the hell has *he* got to do with all this?' Joubert barked. 'And you are taking a chance posing as Vernon's daughter aren't you?'

'Joubert, I have to speak to you. But not here.'

His expression softened somewhat.

'It's important,' she persisted.

'Very well. Perhaps you could recommend a hotel.' He smiled humourlessly.

'I've got my car,' she told him. 'Follow me into the town centre. We must talk. There's a lot that needs explanation.'

He regarded her impassively for a moment then nodded, climbed into his Fiat and started the engine. Kelly scuttled across the road to her own car and twisted the key in the ignition. She waited until Joubert had reversed out into the street, then she set off. He followed close behind. Kelly could see the trailing Fiat in her rear view mirror as she drove.

She wondered if finally she would learn the answers to the questions which had plagued her for so long.

57

There were only a handful of people in the bar of 'The Bull' hotel. It was not yet noon and the lunchtime drinkers had still to appear.

Kelly sat over her orange juice, waiting for Joubert to join her. When he finally sat down opposite her she noticed how dark and sunken his eyes looked, a testament to the fact that he had been working all night. He sipped his own drink and watched as Kelly did the same.

'You said you wanted to talk,' the Frenchman said. 'What had you in mind?'

'For one thing, I'd like to know what the hell you and Vernon had been up to for the past month or so,' she said, challengingly. 'Ever since the two institutes began work on Astral projection and dream interpretation it's been more like working for MI5 than a psychic research unit. What were you and Vernon working on?'

'What happened to the famous English quality of tact?' he said, smiling. 'What do you want to know?'

'If I asked all the questions that are on my mind we'd be here until this time next year. Right now I'll settle for knowing why you and Vernon were so secretive about the research findings.'

Joubert sipped his drink once more, gazing into the glass as if seeking inspiration.

'How much did you know about Vernon?' he asked.

'Personally, not a great deal. Professionally he seemed obsessed with the work on Astral projection and mind control,' Kelly said.

'He was. But with good cause, as I was. We both had reasons for wanting the findings kept quiet until a suitable time.'

'Reasons worth killing for?' she asked.

Joubert looked aghast.

'Certainly not,' he said, indignantly. 'Why do you say that?'

'The death of Lasalle didn't seem to make much of an impression on you.'

'You thought I was responsible for Lasalle's death?' he said, although it sounded more like a statement than a question.

She nodded.

'He was cracking up, close to insanity when he died,' said Joubert. 'No one could have helped him, least of all me. He was afraid of me.'

'You gave him cause to be. I noticed the hostility between you.'

'It was nothing personal. I was angry with him for revealing our findings so early. That was all.' The Frenchman lowered his voice slightly. 'Lasalle was a good friend of mine,' he said, reflectively. 'But he did a lot of damage to our research with that article he wrote. It brought too much media attention to a project which should have been fully completed before being put up for scrutiny. And, he ruined my chances of making a name for myself in our field.' He went on to recount the story he had told Vernon, about how the limelight had been snatched from him once before. 'So, perhaps you can understand *my* reasons for secrecy. That was why I was unco-operative with you. I didn't want anybody or anything to interfere with my chances of making the breakthrough. *I* wanted to be the one who was remembered for making one of parapsychology's greatest finds.'

Kelly exhaled.

'And Vernon?' she said. 'Why was he so fascinated by mind control?'

'His reasons were even more genuine than mine,' said the Frenchman.

'One of my colleagues said that he was hiding something about his wife. He ...'

Joubert interrupted.

'Vernon's wife has been irretrievably and irreversibly insane for the past six years. When you masqueraded as his daughter this morning you took a bigger risk than you could have imagined. Vernon *has* a daughter. Admittedly, he

267

hadn't seen her for six years and, as far as she is concerned, he had no place in her life but she exists nevertheless.'

Kelly raised her glass to her lips but she lowered it again, her full attention on Joubert as he continued.

'He had a Grandson too. As he explained it to me, the child, who was less than a year old at the time, was being cared for by Mrs Vernon. She doted on the boy, worshipped him as if he were hers. Vernon himself has always been a nervous man, afraid of burglars and intruders. He and his wife owned two Dobermans. They were kept in a small compound during the day and released at night.' He sighed. 'This particular day, they escaped. The baby boy was crawling on the lawn. There was nothing Mrs Vernon could do. The dogs tore the child to pieces before her eyes.'

'Oh God,' murmured Kelly.

'She went into a state of shock and then slipped into a catatonic trance. Vernon thought that if he discovered a way to unlock the subconscious mind, he could use it to cure his wife. That was his *secret*. Nothing sinister.'

Kelly shook her head almost imperceptibly.

'If only he'd said something,' she whispered.

'He never intended the truth to be revealed,' Joubert said. 'But now it doesn't matter.'

'Who would want to kill him?' she asked, as if expecting the Frenchman to furnish her with an answer.

'The same person who would want to steal those files,' he said. 'I can't think what possible use they would be to anyone not acquainted with the paranormal. Besides, who else but Vernon and myself even knew they were at the house?' He shook his head.

'I saw Vernon murdered,' Kelly said, flatly.

Joubert looked at her aghast.

'In a dream,' she continued.

'Have you had precognitive dreams before?' he asked, somewhat excitedly.

'Never.'

'Did you see who killed him?'

Kelly took a long swig from her glass, wishing that it contained something stronger. She nodded.

'His name is David Blake,' she said. 'The man I'm living with.'

Joubert watched her across the table, aware that she was quivering slightly.

'Could there have been some mistake?' he asked.

She shrugged.

'I don't know what to believe any more.'

'Kelly, if it's true then you could be in a great deal of danger.'

'He doesn't know I suspect him,' she said, her voice cracking. 'Besides,' Kelly wiped a tear from her eye corner, 'I love him.' Her eyes filled with moisture which, a second later, began to spill down her cheeks. 'Oh God it can't be Him. It can't.'

Joubert moved closer and curled one comforting arm around her shoulder.

'He wouldn't hurt me though, I know he wouldn't,' she murmured.

'How can you be sure?'

She had no answer.

58

London

It was late afternoon by the time Kelly drew into the driveway outside Blake's house. There was no sign of his XJS. He was either out for a while or the car was in the garage. She left her Mini where it was, locked it, then headed for the front door.

As she stepped inside the hall, the silence seemed to envelop her like an invisible blanket and she stood motionless for a moment as if reluctant to disturb the solitude. She glanced across at the cellar door.

It was open slightly.

Kelly approached it silently, listening for the noise of a clacking typewriter from below but there was none.

'David,' she called and her voice sounded hollow in the stillness.

No answer.

She walked back to the sitting room door; opened it slightly and peered in, calling his name as she did so.

Nothing.

Kelly wandered to the bottom of the staircase and looked up.

'David, are you up there?'

The silence reigned supreme.

She opened the cellar door wider and gazed down into the subterranean chamber.

Kelly began to descend.

Half way down the stairs she called his name once again, now satisfied that the house was empty. The extractor fan was on, a slight whirring sound filling the calmness. Kelly felt that all too familiar ripple of fear caress her neck and spine. The cellar looked vast, stretching out all around her, making her feel vulnerable and exposed. She moved towards his desk, her pace slowing, her jaw dropping open.

Perched on top of the typewriter were the six manilla files.

Kelly froze for a second then reached forward and picked one up, flipping it open. She recognised Lasalle's handwriting on the first page.

'Found what you're looking for?'

The voice sounded thunderous in the silence.

Kelly spun round, almost dropping the file, her eyes fixed on the figure at the top of the stairs.

Blake stood there motionless for a moment then slowly descended the steps.

His face was expressionless as he approached her, one hand extended. He motioned for her to give him the file which she did, not shifting her gaze from his eyes, trying to look through those twin dark screens which covered them.

'Why did you kill Dr Vernon?' she asked, falteringly.

'Kelly,' he said, softly. 'You shouldn't have come down here. What goes on in this room is my business.'

'You did kill him didn't you, David?' she persisted.

'Yes,' he said, unhesitatingly. 'I needed the files.'

'I've been to his house today. I've spoken to Joubert.'

Blake chuckled.

'Not so long ago you were convinced that Vernon and Joubert were responsible for these events,' he said.

'Tell me why you did it,' she said. 'Why you caused all those deaths.'

He didn't answer.

'Why?' she roared at him, her voice a mixture of fear and desperation.

He saw a single tear trickle from her eye corner. She wiped it away angrily.

'Ever since I can remember, even before I began writing about the paranormal, the idea of Astral projection has fascinated me,' he began, his tone measured and calm. 'Not just travelling through space on an ethereal level, but actual *physical* movement of the Astral body through time. The tangible realization of that movement which meant I could literally be in two places at once. In control of *two* centres of consciousness. I made it work. It took years to master but I learned how to do it and the more I learned, the more I realized that it was possible to manipulate the subconscious personalities of others as well. To use them.' He regarded her with no hint of emotion on his face.

'Like Toni Landers and the rest?' she said.

'I learned to control the Shadow inside them.'

'The Shadow?' Kelly said, looking vague.

'The alter-ego. What you know as the subconscious. That part of the mind which controls our darker side, that's the Shadow. I found a way to release it.'

'How?' she wanted to know. 'Is it by a form of hypnosis?'

'Yes, combined with my own ability to absorb the energy which the Shadow radiates. It's like an infra-red beacon to me. I can tap into it. Feed on it. It increases my own power. Everyone, no matter who they are, has this darker side to their nature. Most people are able to control it, and it's kept in check by their code of morals or by the law. But when the force is released, they act out thoughts and desires which had previously been hidden.'

Kelly shook her head.

'Why did you do it, David?' she asked, tears brimming in her eyes once again. 'What did you hope to achieve by having Toni Landers kill that baby, or Roger Carr murder that girl. Or Braddock or O'Neil. Why did they have to kill?'

'I had to be sure of my own abilities. Now I am,' he said, impassively. 'The seance gave me a perfect opportunity to

271

use that power, to prove once and for all that I could influence other people's alter-egos. Use them. Can't you appreciate what this means?' His voice had taken on a note of excitement. 'Politicians could be manipulated. Leaders of the Church, Heads of State.'

'You're mad,' she said, taking a step back.

'No, Kelly, I'm not mad,' he said. 'This power is too great to be wasted. Think about it. There need be no more wars, no more civil unrest, because those who provoke such incidents could be found and destroyed before they were able to create trouble. Any trace of evil inside their minds would be visible to someone like me who knew how to use the power of the Shadow.'

'And if you did discover some evil inside them?'

'I told you, they would be destroyed. Executed. This knowledge gives me the power of life and death over anyone I choose. It's a weapon too.'

'For selling?' she asked, cryptically.

'If necessary,' he told her. 'There's no weapons system on earth to match it.'

'But why use it to kill?'

'Every discovery has its sacrifices,' he said, smiling. 'You should know that.'

'No one will believe it.'

Blake smiled and crossed to his desk. He pulled open one of the drawers and took out a letter. Kelly watched him, warily.

'If you'd searched my office more thoroughly,' he said. 'You'd have found this.' He unfolded the letter. 'It arrived two days ago, from Thames TV. I've been invited onto a discussion programme. Myself and two other "experts" are supposed to discuss whether or not the supernatural is real or imaginary. Nice of them to include me don't you think?'

'What are you going to do?'

His smile faded.

'I'm going to prove, once and for all, exactly how powerful the Shadow is,' Blake told her.

Kelly took another step back.

'I loved you, David,' she said, softly, tears rolling down her cheeks.

'Then stay with me,' he said, moving towards her.

'You're a murderer. I saw you kill Vernon.'

'Ah, your dream,' he said, that chilling grin returning. 'I had already been probing your mind for a week or two prior to that little incident. Can't you see, Kelly, you and I are one. We belong together. You can share this power with me. Learn how to use it.'

'Learn how to kill, you mean?' she said, vehemently.

'All right then, leave. Go to the police. Tell them I killed Dr Vernon but who the hell is going to believe you? How could I have killed him?' he added, mockingly. 'I was in bed with you last night.'

She swallowed hard, realizing he was right.

'Go. Get out,' Blake roared. 'I offered you the chance and you refused. Leave here.'

He watched as she turned and hurriedly climbed the stairs, disappearing into the hall. A moment later he heard the front door slam behind her. His expression darkened as he gripped the file. He clutched it a second longer then, with a grunt, hurled it across the room.

Kelly knew Blake was right.

As she started the engine of the Mini she realized she would never convince the police of his guilt. She was helpless, something which made her feel angry as well as afraid.

She guided the car out into traffic, wiping more tears away with the back of her hand. Combined with that feeling of helplessness was also one of loss, for somewhere inside her, despite what she knew, she retained her affection for Blake. Kelly felt as if the world were collapsing around her.

She knew that she must tell Joubert what she had learned. There was a phone box on the corner of the street. Kelly slowed down and prepared to swing the car over. She checked her rear view mirror.

She could not supress a scream.

Reflected in the mirror, glaring at her from the back seat, was the face of Blake.

Kelly twisted the wheel, her eyes riveted to the visage in the mirror.

All she heard was the loud blast of the air horns as the lorry thundered towards her.

It was enough to shake her from her terror and now she looked through the windscreen to see the huge Scania bearing down on her. The driver was waving madly for her to get out of his way.

She pushed her foot down on the accelerator and the Mini shot forward, swerving violently, missing the nearest huge wheel by inches. Kelly yelped as the car hit the kerb with a bone jarring bump before skidding across the pavement and coming to rest against the hedge of the garden opposite.

A car behind her also came to a grinding halt and the lorry pulled up a few yards further on, the driver leaping from the cab.

Kelly shook herself and twisted in her seat.

The back seat was empty.

There was no sign of Blake.

She felt sick, the realization of what had just happened slowly dawning on her. She heard footsteps approaching the car then her door was wrenched open.

The lorry driver stood there, his face flushed.

'Are you all right?' he asked, anxiously.

She nodded.

'What the hell were you doing? You pulled straight in front of me. I could have killed you.'

Kelly closed her eyes tightly for a moment.

'I'm sorry,' she whispered.

The driver of the other car had arrived by now and he reached in to undo Kelly's seatbelt. The two men helped her from the car, standing beside her as she sucked in deep lungfuls of air.

'I'll phone for an ambulance,' said the truck driver.

'No.' Kelly caught his arm. 'I'll be OK. I wasn't hurt.'

'You look pretty shaken up,' he told her.

'Please. No ambulance.'

She wasn't sure what had disturbed her the most. Nearly being hit by the lorry or the sight of Blake's leering face.

'I'm fine, really,' she assured them both.

Other vehicles slowed down as they drove by, glancing at the roadside tableau.

Kelly eventually clambered back into the Mini and strapped herself in. The two men watched as she guided her car off the pavement back on to the road.

'Thanks for your help,' she said and drove off, leaving the two men shaking their heads as she disappeared into traffic.

After another mile or so and Kelly came to a second phone box. Glancing somewhat nervously into her rear-view mirror she signalled then pulled in, clambering out of the car and reaching the box moments before two young girls, who began muttering to each other and pacing up and down outside.

Kelly fumbled for some change and dialled the number of Joubert's hotel. She tapped agitatedly on one glass panel of the phone box as she waited to be connected. Finally she heard the Frenchman's voice.

Scarcely had he identified himself than she began babbling her story to him. About Blake. About Vernon's death. The murders committed by Toni Landers and the others. Blake's TV appearance.

The power of the Shadow.

The Frenchman listened in stunned silence, only his low breathing signalling his presence on the other end of the line.

The rapid pips sounded and she pushed in another coin.

'Kelly, you must get away from there,' Joubert said, finally.

'I can't leave now,' she told him.

'For God's sake, he could kill you too.'

'He must be stopped.'

'But Kelly ...'

She hung up, paused a moment then walked back to her car. As she opened her hand she glanced at the bunch of keys resting on her palm.

One of them unlocked the front door of Blake's house.

The thought hit her like a thunderbolt. She scrambled behind the steering wheel and started the engine.

It was 5.56 p.m.

She had time but it was running out fast.

PART THREE

'We'll know for the first time,
If we're evil or divine ...'
— *Ronnie James Dio*

'The evil that men do lives after them ...'
— *Julius Caesar, Act III, Scene II*

59

At 6.35 David Blake walked from his house, climbed into the waiting XJS and started the engine. Despite the relative warmth of the evening, the sky was a patchwork of mottled grey and blue. Away to the north clouds were gathering in unyielding dark formations and Blake wondered how long it would be before the impending storm arrived. As if to reinforce his supicions, a distant rumble of thunder rolled across the sky.

He guided the Jag out into the street and swung it right.

He didn't see Kelly.

She had been standing about twenty yards further down the street for almost an hour, watching and waiting, the key to Blake's front door clutched in her hand.

Now she watched as the XJS pulled away, disappearing around the corner.

As if fearing that he might return, she paused for another five minutes then began walking briskly towards the house, not hesitating as she made her way up the path, attempting to hide the anxiousness in her stride. She reached the front door and pushed in the key.

'He's just gone out.'

She gasped aloud as she heard the voice, turning to discover its source.

Kelly saw the middle-aged man who lived next door to Blake. He was struggling to hold his Alsatian under control, the large dog pulling on its leash as if threatening to tug the man off his feet. He stood there, watching as Kelly turned the key in the lock.

'I don't know where he's gone,' the man persisted.

She smiled as politely as she could manage.

'It's all right, I'll wait,' she told him and stepped inside.

Through the bevelled glass of the front door, Kelly could see the distorted image of the man next door. He appeared to be standing staring at the house but, after a moment or two, he moved on. She sighed and moved quickly across the hall to the staircase, scuttling up the steps towards Blake's bedroom.

She paused outside the door, aware of a slight chill in the air but she ignored it and walked in. The silence swallowed her up and she was aware only of the sound of her own heart beating.

Kelly moved around the bed to the cabinet, her eyes fixed on the ornate gold key in the lock of the bottom drawer. She dropped to her knees and turned it.

It was almost seven o'clock by the time she left the house. As she clambered into the Mini she guessed that the drive across London would take her forty-five minutes if she was lucky. She prayed that the traffic wouldn't be too heavy. Her heart was still thumping hard against her ribs and she took a tissue from her handbag to wipe the moisture from the palms of her hands.

As she dropped the bag on to the passenger seat she noticed how heavy it was.

The .357 Magnum nestled safely inside.

Blake turned up the volume on the casette and drummed on the steering wheel as he waited for the lights to turn green. Traffic in the centre of London was beginning to clog the roads but the writer seemed unperturbed by the temporary hold-up. The show he was due to appear on was going out live but he looked at his watch and realized he'd make it in time. He smiled as he saw the traffic lights change colour.

Another fifteen minutes and he would be at the studio.

Another ominous rumble of thunder shook the heavens. The storm was getting closer.

Kelly looked first as the dashboard clock and then at her own watch. She drove as fast as she was able in the streams of traffic, slowing down slightly when she saw a police car cruise past in the lane next to her. Almost without thinking, she reached over and secured the clasp on her handbag, ensuring that the revolver didn't fall out. Kelly could feel the perspiration on her back and forehead, clinging to her like dew to the grass.

She guessed that Blake must have reached his destination by now.

Another glance at her watch and she estimated it would be over ten minutes before she caught up with him.

The first spots of rain began to spatter her windscreen.

60

By the time Kelly reached the Thames Television studios in Euston Road the rain was falling in torrents. Large droplets of it bounced off the car and she squinted to see through the drenched windscreen. Her wipers seemed quite inadequate for the task of sweeping away the water which poured down the glass.

She found a parking space then jumped out of the car, picking up her handbag. She sprinted towards the main entrance, slowing her pace as she saw a uniformed doorman barring the way. A thought crossed her mind.

What if he wanted to search her bag?

She held it close to her and looked at him warily but his only gesture was to smile happily at her. Kelly smiled back, as much in relief as anything else. The man opened the door for her and she walked inside the vast entry-way.

'Could you tell me which studio David Blake is in?' she asked.

'Who?' he said.

'David Blake,' she repeated. 'He's a writer. He's taking part in a discussion programme tonight at eight. I hope I'm not too late.'

'Oh yes, that's Studio One, they started about ten minutes ago. It's that way.' He hooked a thumb in the general direction.

Kelly walked past him.

'Just a minute, Miss,' he called.

She froze.

'Have you got a ticket?' he wanted to know.

She opened her mouth to speak but he continued.

'There's a few seats left. If you see that young lady behind the desk, I'm sure she'll be able to help you.' He smiled and indicated a woman who was sitting beneath a large framed photo of a well-known comedian.

Kelly asked for a ticket.

'I'm afraid that the programme in Studio One is being transmitted live,' said the other woman, apologetically. 'It's not normal policy to allow members of the audience in while the show is on.'

'Damn, my editor will kill me,' said Kelly, with mock exasperation. 'I'm supposed to cover this show for the paper, talk to the guests afterwards. We're doing a feature on one of them this week.'

'Do you have your press card with you?' asked the receptionist.

'No, I don't, I was in such a rush to get here I ...' She shrugged, wondering if the ruse would work.

The woman ran an appraising eye over her.

'Which paper?' she asked.

'*The Standard*,' Kelly lied. 'It is very important.' She played her trump card. 'You can call my editor if you like.'

The woman thought for a moment then shook her head.

'No, that won't be necessary. I think we can get you in.' She called the doorman over. 'George, can you show this lady into Studio One. But they are on the air at the moment.'

The doorman nodded, smiled politely at Kelly and asked her to follow him. She swallowed hard, trying to control her breathing as they made their way up a long corridor. The walls on either side bore framed photographs of celebrities past and present. Kelly felt as if she were being watched, scrutinised by each pair of monochrome eyes, all of whom knew her secret. The .357 suddenly felt gigantic inside her handbag and she hugged it closer to her, watching as the doorman paused beneath a red light and a sign which proclaimed: STUDIO ONE. He opened the door a fraction and peered inside.

'Keep as quiet as you can,' he whispered and led Kelly into the studio.

Apart from the area which made up the studio floor, the

entire cavervous room was in darkness. Kelly saw rows and rows of people before her, their attention directed towards the four men who sat in front of them.

She caught sight of Blake.

The doorman ushered her towards an empty seat near the back of the studio where she settled herself, mouthing a silent 'Thankyou' to him as he slipped away. A man seated in front of her turned and looked at her briefly before returning his attention to the discussion being conducted by the four men.

Kelly glanced around the studio.

Cameras moved silently back and forth. She saw a man with headphones hunched close to the interviewer, a clipboard clutched in his hand. He was counting off seconds with his fingers, motioning a camera forward as one of the four men seated amidst the modest set spoke.

Blake was seated between the interviewer and an elderly priest who was having trouble with a long strand of grey hair which kept falling over his forehead. He brushed it back each time he spoke but, within seconds, the gossamer tentacle had crept back to its original position.

Arc lights burned brightly, pinpointing the men in their powerful beams while sausage-shaped booms were lowered carefully by the sound engineers, all of whom were intent on staying out of camera shot. The sound was coming through loud and clear but Kelly seemed not to hear it. Her gaze was riveted to Blake who was in the process of pouring himself some water from the jug on top of the smoked-glass table before him. He smiled cordially at a remark made by the old priest and sipped his drink.

Kelly watched him, unable to take her eyes from the writer's slim frame. She heard his name spoken then his voice filled the studio.

'In the course of my work I've come across all manner of religions, each one as valid as the next,' he said.

'But you mentioned voodoo earlier,' the old priest reminded him. 'Surely you can't class that as a religion?'

'It's the worship of a God or a set of Gods. As far as I'm concerned that makes it a religion.'

'Then you could say the same about witchcraft?' the priest countered.

'Why not?' Blake said. 'The deities worshipped by witches were thought to be powerful in their own right. A God doesn't have to be benevolent to be worshipped.'

'Do you have any religious beliefs yourself, Mr Blake?' asked the interviewer.

'Not in God and the Devil as we know them, no,' the writer told him.

Kelly sat motionless, watching him, her eyes filling with tears once more. She touched the Magnum inside her handbag but, somewhere deep inside her, she knew that she could not use the weapon. What she should be feeling for Blake was hatred but, in fact, she felt feelings of love as strong for him now as she had ever known. Could this man really be evil? This man she felt so much for?

'What do you believe in then?' the interviewer asked Blake.

'I believe that there is a force which controls everyone's lives but I don't believe that it comes from a God of any description,' the writer said. 'It comes from here.' He prodded his own chest.

'Don't you, in fact, use this theory in your forthcoming book?' the interviewer said. 'This idea of each of us having two distinct sides to our nature. One good, one evil.'

'That's hardly an original concept,' said the psychiatrist, haughtily. 'Surely every religion in the world, in history, has revolved around the struggle between good and evil.'

'I agree,' said Blake. 'But never before has it been possible to isolate the evil side of man and make it a tangible force independent from the rest of the mind.'

Kelly shuddered, her mind suddenly clearing as if a veil had been drawn from it.

She slid one hand inside her handbag, her fist closing around the butt of the .357. She slowly eased back the hammer, glancing around furtively to see if anyone else had noticed the metallic click.

There was a man standing directly behind her.

He wore a short sleeved white shirt and dark trousers and, Kelly caught a quick glimpse of the badge pinned to his chest: SECURITY.

She took her hand off the Magnum and hurriedly turned to

283

face the studio floor once again, her heart beating madly against her ribs. She glanced at Blake.

A camera was moving closer towards him.

She realized the time had come.

'What exactly are you suggesting?' the interviewer asked, smiling.

Blake looked into the camera.

'Everyone can be *made* to commit acts normally abhorrent to them,' he said.

The camera zoomed in on him.

Kelly allowed her hand to slip back inside the handbag, and, once more, she gripped the revolver. She could hear the low breathing of the security guard behind her but she realized that she had no choice.

She began to ease the gun slowly from its place of concealment.

Behind her, the security man moved and Kelly swallowed hard as she heard his footsteps gradually receding. The next time she saw him he was a good fifty feet away, to the left of the studio's set. Kelly watched him for a moment longer then turned her attention back to Blake.

He was staring into the camera, motionless in his chair.

The other three men looked at him in bewilderment and, after a minute or so of silence, some impatient mutterings began to ripple through the audience but Blake merely sat as he was, his eyes fixed on the camera as if it were a snake about to strike him.

The cameraman was not the only one in the studio to feel as if iced water had been pumped through his veins. He shivered.

Kelly too felt that freezing hand grip her tightly but the tears which ran down her cheeks were warm.

She could not take her eyes from Blake and now the cold seemed to be intensifying, growing within her until it was almost unbearable.

She slid the Magnum from her handbag and stood up, holding the gun at arm's length, fixing Blake hurriedly in the sights.

The man in front of her turned and opened his mouth to shout a warning.

From the studio floor, the security guard spotted her.

He raced towards her, his eyes fixed on the gleaming Magnum.

The noise was thunderous.

As Kelly squeezed the trigger, the .357 roared loudly. The savage recoil nearly knocked her over and she winced as the butt smashed against the heel of her hand. The Magnum bucked violently in her grip as it spat out the heavy grain bullet. The barrel flamed brilliant white for precious seconds and, in that blinding illumination, members of the audience dived for cover, most of them unaware of what had made the deafening blast.

The bullet hit the floor and drilled a hole the size of a fifty pence piece in the hard surface.

Kelly fired again.

The second shot shattered the smoked glass table in front of Blake who turned and looked up into the audience, the muzzle flash catching his eye. Shards of glass sprayed in all directions and the old priest yelped in pain as one laid open his cheek. He felt himself being pulled to one side by the psychiatrist.

Blake rose, his arms outstretched.

The writer presented a much bigger target and, this time, Kelly didn't miss.

Moving at a speed of over 1,430 feet a second, the heavy grain slug hit him squarely in the chest. It shattered his sternum and tore through his lung before erupting from his back, blasting an exit hole the size of a fist. Lumps of grey and red viscera splattered the flimsy set behind him and Blake was lifted off his feet by the impact. He crashed to the floor and rolled over once, trying to drag himself away, but Kelly fired once more.

The next bullet hit him in the side, splintering his pelvis, decimating the liver as it ripped through him.

He clapped one hand to the gaping wound as if trying to hold the blood in. His chest felt as if it were on fire and, when he coughed, blood spilled over his lips and ran down his chin, mingling with that which was already forming a pool around him.

Nevertheless, fighting back the waves of agony which tore

through him, he managed to claw his way across the set and he was on his knees when the third bullet hit him. It smashed his left shoulder and spun him round, fragments of bone spraying from the exit wound, propelled by the eruption of blood which accompanied the blast.

He sagged forward across the chair, hardly feeling any pain as another round practically took his head off. It caught him at the base of the throat, the massive force throwing him onto his back where he lay motionless, a crimson fountain spurting from the large hole.

Kelly stood at the back of the studio, the gun hot in her hand, her palms stinging from the constant recoil. The smell of cordite stung her nostrils but she seemed not to notice it and, as the security man approached her, one eye on that yawning barrel, she merely dropped the Magnum and looked blankly at him.

He slowed his pace as he drew closer and she saw his lips moving as he spoke but she heard nothing. Only gradually did the sounds begin to filter back into her consciousness.

The screams. The shouts.

She shook her head then looked in bewilderment at the security man, her eyes wide and uncomprehending. She looked down at the gun which lay at her feet then back at the set.

Kelly saw two or three people gathered around a body and it took her a moment or two to realize it was the body of Blake.

She saw the blood. Smelled the cordite. Her ears were still ringing from the explosive sound of the gunshots.

First aid men scurried on to the set to tend to Blake but she saw one of them shake his head as he felt for a pulse and heartbeat. Another man removed his jacket and laid it over Blake's face.

She realized that David Blake was dead.

The security guard took her by the arm and she looked at him, her eyes wide and questing. She shook her head, glancing down once more at the gun.

In that instant, as she was being led away, Kelly felt as if her entire body had been wrapped in freezing rags.

61

The room inside Albany Street police station was small. Despite the dearth of furniture it still appeared miniscule. Less than twelve feet square, it contained two chairs, one on each side of a wooden table. A cracked wash-basin was jammed into one corner near the door and there was a plastic bucket beneath it to catch the drips which dribbled through the chipped porcelain. The room smelt of perspiration and cigarette smoke, but the windows remained firmly closed. Powerful banks of fluorescents, quite disproportionately bright for the size of the room, blazed in the ceiling.

Inspector Malcolm Barton lit up another cigarette and tossed the empty packet onto the table in front of Kelly.

'How well did you know David Blake?' he asked.

'I've already told you,' Kelly protested.

'So tell me again.'

'We were lovers. I was living at his house. I had been for about a fortnight.'

'Then why did you kill him?'

'I've told you that too.'

Barton blew out a stream of smoke and shook his head.

'You can do better than that, Miss Hunt,' he said. 'First you told me you intended to kill Blake then you said you didn't remember pulling the trigger. Now, I'm just a thick copper. I like things plain and simple. Tell me why you shot him.'

Kelly cradled her head in her hands and tried to keep her voice calm. She had been at the police station for over an hour, taken directly there from the Euston Road studios.

'He was dangerous,' she said.

'He never seemed like a nut-case to me the odd times I saw him on the box. What gave you this special insight?' The policeman's voice was heavy with scorn.

'He told me about his powers,' said Kelly, wearily.

'Of course, his *powers*. I'd forgotten about them.'

'If you won't believe me then at least let someone else back up what I've told you. Blake had the ability to control people's minds, to make them act out their worst desires. That was his power.'

'And you know of someone who'll verify that do you?' Barton chided. 'I'd be interested to meet him.'

'Then let me make a bloody phone call,' Kelly snapped. 'Like you should have done when you first brought me here.'

Barton pointed an accusatory finger at her.

'Don't start giving me orders, Miss Hunt, you're not in a bargaining position,' he hissed. 'Jesus Christ you were seen by dozens of people. You told me yourself that you had to kill Blake.'

'Have I ever denied I shot him?' she said, challengingly.

'You said you didn't remember pulling the trigger.'

'I didn't. I wasn't even sure what had happened until I saw him lying there.'

There was a moment's silence then Barton crossed to the glass panelled door behind him.

'Tony, bring the phone in here will you,' he called, then turned back to face Kelly. 'All right, you make your phone call.'

A tall, slim man in a sergeant's uniform entered the room carrying a trimphone which he plugged into a socket in the wall near Kelly. He hesitated a moment then walked out.

'Go on,' urged the Inspector, nodding towards the phone.

Kelly picked up the receiver and dialled the number of the hotel where Joubert was staying. She wiped perspiration from her face with her free hand, looking up occasionally at Barton who was rummaging through his pockets in search of another packet of cigarettes. He found one and lit up.

On the other end of the line, Kelly heard the sound of Joubert's voice.

'Blake made the broadcast,' she told him. 'I couldn't stop him in time.'

He asked where she was.

'I killed Blake. The police are holding me here now. Please Joubert, you must come to London. It might already be too late.' She gave him instructions on how to reach the police station then hung up.

'Too late for what?' Barton wanted to know.

'Everyone who watched that programme,' she said.

'He might have been bluffing,' said Barton, disinterestedly.

'I wish to God he had been,' Kelly said, quietly.

There was a knock on the door and the tall, slim sergeant entered, carrying a piece of paper. He passed it to Barton. The Inspector read it, glancing occasionally at Kelly as he did so. He sucked hard on his cigarette.

'What do you make of it, guv?' said the sergeant.

'When did these reports come in?' Barton wanted to know.

'These were the first three, they came in less than an hour ago.'

Barton looked puzzled.

'What do you mean, the first three?' he asked.

'We've had five more reports since,' the sergeant told him.

'I suppose you'd take this as proof of your little story would you, Miss Hunt?' the Inspector said, tapping the piece of paper.

'What is it?' she asked.

'At 8.07 a pet shop owner in Kilburn slaughtered every single animal in his shop with a knife. One of our constables found him in the street outside the shop. He'd just gutted a couple of kittens. At 8.16 a woman in Bermondsey held her eight-week-old child against the bars of an electric fire until it died. At 8.29 a man in Hammersmith killed his wife and daughter with a chisel.'

Kelly closed her eyes.

'Oh God,' she murmured.

'Go on then, tell me it was your friend Blake who caused these killings.'

'It doesn't matter any more,' said Kelly, wearily. 'It's already begun and there's no way to stop it.'

This time Barton did not add a sarcastic remark.

He felt inexplicably afraid as he lit up another cigarette.

And he wondered if he was the only one who felt the peculiar chill in the room.

62

Manchester

8.36 p.m.

The scissors fell to the carpet with a dull ring as Laura Foster knocked them off the arm of the chair. She reached down and retrieved them, replacing them next to her. Her husband, Paul, got to his feet as she handed him the trousers she'd finished turning up. He pulled them on and strutted around the sitting room happily.

'They're OK aren't they?' he asked.

'They are now,' Laura told him. 'You'd have worn them without me turning them up. They looked like concertinas on your shoes.'

Paul slipped them off again and walked across to her chair, bending down to kiss her. She giggled as he slipped one hand inside her blouse and squeezed her unfettered breasts.

'Shall I bother putting my others back on?' he asked.

Laura chuckled again, pointing out how comical he looked in just his socks and underpants.

He moved closer, kissing her fiercely and she responded with equal fervour, one hand straying to the growing bulge in his pants. She slipped her hand beneath his testicles and fondled them, feeling his erection throbbing against her fingers.

Paul closed his eyes as she pulled his pants down, freeing his stiff organ.

The next thing he felt was an unbearable coldness as the scissor blades brushed his testicles. His eyes jerked open and, for interminable seconds he found himself gaping at Laura. Her own eyes were glazed, almost unseeing. Her face was expressionless.

The blades snapped together.

Laura sat impassively as he dropped to his knees, hands clutching his scrotum. Blood sprayed from the neatly severed veins and Paul found that his agony was mixed with nausea as he saw one egg-shaped purple object glistening on the carpet before him.

As he fell backward he heard laughter and, just before he blacked out, he realized that it was coming from the television.

Liverpool

8.52.

The child was small and it had been common sense to keep him in plain view at all times since his premature birth two weeks earlier. Now he gurgled happily in his carry-cot, his large brown eyes open and staring at the multi-coloured TV screen nearby.

Terry Pearson looked down at the child and smiled.

'Is he all right, love?' asked his wife, Denise, who was glancing through the paper to see what other delights the networks were offering for the remainder of the evening. She and Terry had been watching the screen since six that evening. Though Denise doubted if there'd be anything else to match the excitement of what had happened on the chat show they'd been watching.

'I suppose there'll be something on *News at Ten* about that fella getting shot,' she said, putting down the paper and crossing to the carry-cot.

Terry nodded, not taking his eyes from his son. Denise also gazed down at the baby, both of them mesmerised by it.

It looked so helpless. So tiny.

Terry reached into the cot and, with contemptuous ease, fastened the fingers of one powerful hand around the baby's neck, squeezing tighter until the child's face began to turn the colour of dark grapes. He held it before him for a moment longer, watched by Denise, then, with a grunt, he hurled the child across the room as if it had been a rag doll.

The baby hit the mirror which hung on the far wall, the impact bringing down the glass which promptly shattered, spraying the carpet with needle-sharp shards of crystal.

Terry crossed the room and prodded the tiny body. There was blood on the wall and a sickly grey substance on the

291

carpet.

He reached for a particularly long piece of mirror, ignoring the pain in his hand as it cut into his palm. Blood dribbled down his arm, the flow increasing as he put his weight behind the rapier-like implement.

Denise chuckled as she watched her husband tear her child's flesh and raise it to his lips.

Then she held the tiny body still as Terry set about hacking the other leg off.

Norwich

9.03.

The book fell from her grasp and she awoke with a start, picking the paperback up, muttering to herself when she saw that she'd lost her page. Maureen Horton found her place and folded down the corner of the page, checking that Arthur wasn't looking. He hated to see books being mistreated and, as far as he was concerned, folding down the corner of a page was a particularly heinous crime. He'd reminded her time and again what bookmarks were for. Well, she didn't care. This was one of *her* books. A good old romance. Not that pompous Jeffrey Archer stuff that Arthur always had his nose in.

Arthur.

She looked across to his chair but he was gone.

Probably out making a cup of tea, she reasoned. He'd left the TV on as usual. She was always nagging him about wasting electricity. What was the point of having the television on if they were both reading she insisted? Arthur always tried to tell her he preferred what he called 'background sound'.

She smiled to herself and leant forward to turn up the volume. The news had just started.

She heard a slight whoosh then felt a numbing impact across the back of her head as her husband struck her with the petrol can.

Arthur Horton grabbed his semi-conscious wife by the hair and dragged her back into her seat.

She lay there, twitching slightly, watching him through

pain-racked eyes. Maureen could feel something warm and wet running down her back, pouring freely from the cut on her skull.

He moved to one side of her and she heard the noisy squeaking of the cap as he unscrewed it. Arthur gazed down at her with glassy eyes, the aroma of petrol stinging his nostrils. He upended the can, emptying the golden fluid all over his wife and the chair, watching as she tried to move. Maureen opened her mouth to scream but some of the petrol gushed down her throat and she gagged violently.

He struck the match and dropped it on her.

Maureen Horton disappeared beneath a searing ball of flame which hungrily devoured her skin, hair and clothes. She tried to rise but, within seconds, the searing agony had caused her to black out. Her skin rose in blisters which burst, only to be replaced by fresh sores. Her skin seemed to be bubbling as the flames stripped it away, leaving only calcified bone.

Arthur Horton stood motionless as his wife burned to death, the leaping flames reflected in his blank eyes.

63

London

9.11 p.m.

Kelly coughed as Inspector Barton stubbed out his half-smoked cigarette, the plume of grey smoke rising into the air. The entire room seemed to be full of fumes, so much so that she felt as if she were looking at the policeman through a fine gauze.

'Is there anything in this statement you want to amend?' he said, tapping the piece of paper before him with the end of his pen.

'What's the point?' she wanted to know.

'The point *is*, that you're looking at a twenty year stretch for murder, that's what the point is.'

'Perhaps I should plead insanity,' she said, cryptically.

'Looking at some of the things that are in this statement you'd probably get away with it too,' snorted Barton.

'Why can't you understand?' Kelly rasped. 'Blake had the ability to reach people on a massive scale. For him, this TV show provided the ultimate opportunity to display his ability to control the minds of those watching, to summon their evil sides. From the amount of reports you've been getting, it looks as if he succeeded.'

'It's coincidence,' said Barton, although he sounded none too convinced.

'No, Inspector,' Kelly sighed. 'It isn't coincidence and, so far, the reports have been restricted to a small area of London. That show was networked, nationwide.'

'So you're telling me there are people carving each other up from one end of Britain to the other?'

'Anyone who saw that programme is at risk,' Kelly said.

'That's bollocks,' snapped Barton, getting to his feet. He left the statement lying on the table in front of her. 'You read that over again, I'll be back in a while, perhaps you'll have some more convincing answers for me then.' He closed the door behind him. Kelly heard the key turn in the lock.

She slumped back in her chair, eyes closed. Where the hell was Joubert? It had been over an hour since she'd phoned him. She opened her eyes and looked down at her hands. The hands which had held the gun. Kelly found that she was quivering.

She remembered reaching into her handbag for the pistol but, after that, her mind was a blank. Nothing remaining with any clarity until the point when she was grabbed by the security guard. She wondered if Toni Landers, Roger Carr, Gerald Braddock and Jim O'Neil had felt the same way after committing *their* crimes.

She glanced at her statement, aware of how ridiculous the whole affair must appear to someone like Barton.

Alone in that small room she felt a crushing sense of desolation.

Blake had released a wave of insanity which was now unstoppable.

64

Glasgow

9.23 p.m.

The shrill whistling of the kettle sounded like a siren inside the small flat.

Young Gordon Mackay got slowly to his feet and wandered through from the sitting room, glancing back at the television as he did so.

'Turn it off, Gordon,' shouted his younger sister, Claire. 'It'll wake the baby up.'

He nodded wearily and switched off the screaming kettle.

'Why couldn't you do it?' he asked Claire who was sitting at the kitchen table with three or four books spread out in front of her.

'Because I'm doing my homework,' she told him. 'Anyway, all you've been doing all night is sitting in front of the television.'

'Fuck you,' grunted Gordon, pouring hot water on to the tea bag in his mug. He stirred it around then scooped the bag out and dropped it into the waste-disposal unit of the sink. As he flicked it on it rumbled into life, the vicious blades churning noisily as they swallowed the solitary tea-bag. That was one of the perks of baby-sitting, Gordon thought. Normally his mother wouldn't let him near this lethal device but, when she and his father left him to mind the other three kids, it was like a new toy to him. He took some withered flowers from a vase on the window sill and watched as they were gobbled up by the hungry mouth of the machine.

'Mum said you weren't to use that,' Claire bleated.

Gordon ignored her, feeding more refuse into the gaping hole.

Claire got to her feet and crossed to the sink.

'Turn it off, Gordon,' she said, angrily.

He ignored her.

Claire reached across him for the button which controlled the machine.

Gordon grabbed her arm tightly.

'Let go,' she shouted, striking him with her free hand, trying to pull away.

As he turned to look at her, his eyes were glazed, as if he didn't see her at all. Claire was suddenly afraid.

With a strength that belied his size, Gordon wrenched her towards the sink, guiding her hand towards the churning blades of the waste-disposal unit.

Claire began to scream as her finger tips actually brushed the cold steel of the sink bottom. She clenched her hand into a fist but it only served to prolong the moment for precious seconds.

Gordon thrust her hand into the machine, forcing her arm in as far as the wrist.

Blood spurted up from the razor sharp blades, spewing up crimson fountains as the limb was first lacerated then crushed. He heard the noise of splintering bone as her arm was dragged deeper into the yawning hole, the skin being ripped away as far as the elbow. The stainless steel sink flooded with thick red fluid and, as Claire's shrieks of agony grew shrill, the noise of the machine seemed to be deafening. Her hand was torn off and she fell back, blood spurting from the shredded stump that was her arm. Gordon looked down at her, at the pulped flesh and muscle and the spreading puddle of crimson which formed around the mutilated appendage.

He didn't realize that bone was so white. It gleamed amidst the crimson mess, fragments of it floating on the red puddle.

The sound of the waste-disposal unit filled his ears.

Southampton

9.46.

The garage door opened with a distressing creak and Doug Jenkins peered from beneath the bonnet of his car to see who had come in. He saw the door close and the sound of footsteps echoed throughout the garage as Bruce Murray approached the old Ford Anglia.

'Sorry, Doug,' Murray said. 'That all night spares place doesn't carry the parts for a car as old as this. I rang them before I came over.'

Jenkins cursed under his breath.

'Why the hell don't you buy a new car?' Murray wanted to know. 'This one's twenty years old at least.'

'I've had this since I was eighteen,' Jenkins protested. 'I've got a soft spot for it.'

'The best spot for it would be the bloody junk yard,' Murray chuckled as he stepped forward to inspect the engine. 'Have you been working on it all night?'

'No, only for the past hour or so, I've been watching TV.'

Jenkins stepped back, wiping his hands on an oil-covered rag. He shuddered, despite the warmth inside the garage.

'Pass me that wrench will you, Doug?' said Murray, holding out a hand.

His companion selected one from the dozens which hung on the wall and passed it to Murray. The wall was like something from a hardware store. Hammers, spanners, saws, wrenches, hatchets and even a small chainsaw were hung neatly from nails, all of them in the correct order. Doug Jenkins was nothing if not methodical. He rubbed his eyes with a dirty hand, leaving a dark smudge on his face. The cold seemed to be intensifying.

'I heard there was some trouble on TV earlier,' said Murray, his back to his friend. 'Somebody got shot in full view of the camera or something. Did you see it?'

Silence.

'Doug, I said did you see it?' he repeated.

Murray straightened up and turned to face his companion.

'Are you going deaf, I ...'

The sentence trailed away as Murray's jaw dropped open, his eyes bulging wide in terror. A sound like a revving motorbike filled the garage.

'Oh Jesus,' Murray gasped.

Jenkins advanced on him with the chainsaw, holding the lethal blade at arm's length, its wicked barbs rotating at a speed of over 2,000 rpm.

'What are you doing?' shrieked Murray, gazing first at his friend's blank eyes and then at the murderous implement levelled at him.

Jenkins drove it forward.

Murray tried to knock the blade to one side with the wrench but fear affected his aim. The chainsaw sliced effortlessly through his arm just below the elbow. He shrieked as blood spouted from the stump and he held it up, showering both himself and Jenkins with the sticky red fluid.

Jenkins brought the spinning saw blade down in a carving action which caught Murray at the point of the shoulder. There was a high pitched scream as the chainsaw cut through his ribs, hacking its way deeper to rupture his lungs which burst like fleshy balloons, expelling a choking flux of blood and bile. The churning blade chewed easily through muscle and sinew, finally severing Murray's bulging intestines. Like the glutinous tentacles of some bloodied octopus, his entrails burst from the gaping rent in his stomach, spilling forth in a reeking mass.

As he fell forward into a pool of blood and viscera, his body jerked uncontrollably as the final muscular spasms racked it.

Jenkins switched off the chainsaw and, in the silence, looked down at the corpse of Murray.

He looked on disinterestedly as blood washed over his shoes.

London

9.58.

The diesel was picking up speed.

As the train hurtled through Finsbury Park station, people on the platforms appeared only as rapid blurs to Derek West. He had only been driving for about five or ten minutes, since picking up the diesel at the Bounds Green Depot earlier on. Up until then he and five or six of the other drivers and guards had been sitting idly around reading the papers or watching TV. Derek had consumed yet another mug of strong tea then clambered into the cab and started the powerful engine. The diesel was pulling eight tankers behind it. Each one containing almost 71,000 litres of liquid oxygen.

Now, Derek felt the massive engine throbbing around him

as he glanced down at the speedometer.

As the train roared through the last tunnel it was travelling at well over ninety miles an hour.

Up ahead of him, Derek could see the massive edifice which was King's Cross, lights gleaming in the darkness.

He smiled thinly.

Out of his eye corner he caught sight of a red warning light but he paid it no heed.

The needle on the speedo touched ninety-five.

The diesel thundered on, travelling as if it had been fired from some gigantic cannon. It swept into the station, the air horn sounding one last defiant death-knell which echoed around the cavernous interior of the station.

It struck the buffers doing ninety-eight.

Concrete and metal seemed to dissolve under the crushing impact of the hundred ton train. The huge machine ploughed through the platform, sending lumps of stone and steel scything in all directions like shrapnel. Such was the power with which it hit, the engine buckled and split open, the top half of it somersaulting, blasting massive holes in the gigantic timetable a full fifty feet from the buffers. Screams of terror were drowned as the engine exploded, followed, a second later, by a series of devastating detonations as the liquid oxygen tanks first skewed off the track and then blew up.

An eruption of seismic proportions ripped through the station as a screaming ball of fire filled the giant building, melting the glass in the roof and roaring upward into the night sky like a searing, monstrous flare which scorched everything around it. Concrete archways were simply brushed aside by the incredible blast and part of the great canopy above fell inward with a deafening crash. It was impossible to hear anything over the high-pitched shriek of the flames which shot up in a white wall. People not instantly incinerated by the fireball were crushed by falling rubble or flattened by the shock wave which ripped the station apart as if it had been made of paper. The searing temperatures ignited fuel in the engines of other trains and more explosions began to punctuate the persistent roar of the main fire. Wheels, buffers, sleepers and even lengths of rail flew through the air, those that hadn't already been transformed to molten metal by the fury of the temperatures.

The glass front of the station exploded outward, blown by the incredible shock wave, and the street beyond was showered with debris. Taxis waiting in the forecourt were overturned by the blast.

It was as if the station had been trodden on by some huge invisible foot. Huge tongues of flame still rose, snatching at the darkness, melting everything near them with the blistering heat. Platforms had been levelled, people inside the once proud building had been blasted to atoms, pulverised by the ferocity of the explosion. The entire building had become one massive ball of fire.

It looked as if a portion of Hell had forced its way up through the earth.

65

Mere seconds after she heard the loud bang, Kelly felt the floor move. She gripped the table and looked anxiously around her as if fearing that the roof were going to fall in on her. She heard the unmistakable sound of shattering glass and was thankful that the room had no windows. There were shouts and curses from the rooms beyond hers.

She guessed that the violent vibrations continued for a full fifteen seconds then the room seemed to settle once again. A couple of pieces of plaster fell onto the table and she cast an anxious glance at the ceiling once more.

Kelly was aware that there had been a massive explosion somewhere close but she could not have imagined it was as close as King's Cross.

Phones began to ring. It sounded like pandemonium beyond the locked door.

She closed her eyes, wondering what could have caused the blast, her mind tortured by the fact that the perpetrator was more than likely acting out some maniac scheme previously hidden deep within his subconscious.

Until tonight.

Until Blake had ...

She got to her feet and paced up and down for a moment, still partially stunned by the bang and its subsequent tremor.

Even she had not fully believed that anyone could possess such an awesome power as Blake had claimed. Now, she had been given ample proof. Kelly wondered what would have happened if she had arrived at the studios earlier. If she had not walked out on him. If she had joined him.

If she had killed him earlier.

The questions were immaterial now. The final act had been completed. The horror unleashed.

She glanced up at the clock, then at her own watch.

Where was Joubert?

Had he been butchered by some demented victim of Blake's master plan? she wondered, but then hurriedly pushed the thought to the back of her mind. He would come. She knew he would come. How foolish she had been to doubt him. Those suspicions stung even more now as she remembered how she had confided in Blake, never suspecting the man she had trusted, lived with. Loved.

She sat down once more, her head cradled in her hands, eyes fixed on the statement before her — her admission of guilt, although she still did not remember pulling the trigger and blasting the writer into oblivion. All she remembered was the feeling of cold, a sensation she had experienced many years earlier whilst in a haunted house. The coldness which comes with absolute evil.

Kelly slumped forward on the desk, tears trickling down her face.

She didn't raise her head when she heard the footsteps from the direction of the door.

'What happened?' she asked. 'I heard an explosion.'

Silence greeted her enquiry.

'I asked you what happened,' Kelly said, wondering why her companion was silent. She looked up.

Had she been able to, Kelly would probably have screamed. As it was, she felt as if someone had fastened a cord around her throat and was slowly twisting it, tighter and tighter, preventing her from making any sound. She shook her head slowly from side to side.

Standing before her was David Blake.

66

For long seconds, Kelly could not speak. Her eyes bulged madly in their sockets as she gazed at Blake.

Or was it Blake? Was she too losing her grip on sanity?

He reached forward and touched her hand and she felt a shiver run through her. It seemed to penetrate her soul.

'How?' was all she could gasp, her voice a horrified whisper. 'I saw you die.' She screwed up her eyes until they hurt then looked again.

Blake remained opposite her.

'Tell me how,' she hissed.

'The power of the Shadow,' he told her, quietly. 'It enabled my Astral body to live on after death. Only total destruction of my physical form can cause my Astral body to disappear.'

She ran both hands through her hair.

'How will it end?' she asked him.

Blake didn't answer.

'Did you use hypnosis?' she said.

'A form of hypnosis, but the word is inadequate.'

'Stop it now, please,' she begged. 'Let it end.'

'It's only just beginning,' he whispered.

Kelly finally did manage a scream, a long wild ululation of despair. Tears were squeezed from her eyes as she closed the lids tightly. She slumped forward on the table, sobbing.

'Make it stop,' she whimpered. 'Please, make it stop.'

She raised her head.

Blake was gone. She was alone once more.

The door to the room was flung open and Barton dashed in.

'What's wrong?' he asked, seeing how distraught she looked. 'We heard you scream.'

Kelly could not answer him. Tears dripped from her face

and stained the statement sheet below. She saw Barton motion to someone behind him and, a second later, Joubert entered the room.

'They told me what happened,' said the Frenchman, watching as she wiped the tears from her face. She looked at Barton.

'Where was Blake's body taken after he was shot?' she asked.

Barton looked bewildered.

'Great Portland Street Hospital,' he said. 'What the hell does that matter?'

'It has to be destroyed,' Kelly told him. 'Burned. Dismembered. Anything. But please, Inspector, you must destroy Blake's body.'

'You *are* off your head,' the policeman said.

She turned to Joubert.

'Blake was here. In this room. Not two minutes ago,' she babbled. 'He's found a way for his Astral body to survive beyond death. These atrocities will continue unless the physical form can be destroyed.'

'Hold up,' Barton interrupted. 'Are you trying to say that Blake isn't dead, because if he's not, who's the geezer laid out at Great Portland Street ...'

'*I* understand what she means, Inspector,' Joubert interrupted.

'Well I fucking well don't,' snapped the policeman. 'Now one of you had better start making some sense, and fast, because I'm not known for my patience.'

'Just destroy the body,' Kelly said, imploringly.

'Forget it,' said Barton. 'Who the hell do you think I am? The body's at the hospital and it stays there until it's buried.'

He turned and left the room, slamming the door behind him.

Kelly and Joubert looked at each other and, if defeat had a physical face, then it was mirrored in their expressions.

67

The light flickered once then died.

'Sod it,' muttered Bill Howard getting to his feet. He put down his copy of *Weekend* and fumbled his way across to the cupboard set in the far wall. He banged his shin on one of the slabs and cursed again, rubbing the injured area.

There was some light flooding into the basement area but it was largely dissipated by the thick glass and wire mesh which covered the ground level window, the only window in the morgue of Great Portland Street Hospital.

Bill had worked there for the past thirty-eight years, ever since he'd been de-mobbed. He'd tried a spell as ward orderly but his real niche had been down below in the morgue. He felt curiously secure within its antiseptic confines. He knew it was a place where he would not be disturbed by the day-to-day running of the hospital. As long as he did his job then things went along fine. Clean up the stiffs, make sure they were ready for the post-mortems which were carried out in the room next door. Not once, in all his years at the hospital, had the task bothered him. Hardly surprisingly really, he reasoned, after having spent six years in the army medical corps treating all manner of wounds, gangrene, dysentery and other illnesses from Dunkirk to Burma. He'd seen sights which made his present job positively tame.

His wife had died three years earlier after a long battle with cancer but now Bill lived quite happily with his dog in a nice little flat not far from the hospital. Another half an hour and he'd be able to go home.

Bill found his way to the cupboard and opened it, peering through the gloom in search of the strip-light he required. In the dark confines of the morgue he had but one companion.

Bill had been informed that the body would be removed the following day by the police. It had been brought in at about 8.30 that evening, the man had been shot, so Bill had been told. He'd waited until the police and hospital officials had left then he'd lifted the plastic sheet which covered the body and glanced at it. They had left it clothed and the name tag pinned to the lapel of the man's bloodied jacket read 'David Blake'.

Now Bill took the light tube from its cardboard casing and went in search of a chair to stand on.

As he passed the body he shuddered involuntarily. The morgue was usually cold but tonight it seemed positively wintry. Bill saw his breath form gossamer clouds in the air as he exhaled. He wouldn't be sorry to get home in the warm. He would not have to return until nine the following morning.

Bill clambered up onto the chair and removed the old light and slotted in the replacement.

He heard a faint rustling sound.

Bill froze, trying to detect where the noise was coming from. He realized that it was coming from the direction of his desk. He paused a moment, ears alert.

Silence.

He stepped down off the chair.

The rustling came again.

Bill hurried across to the light switch, his hand poised over it but, as he was about to press it, he saw what was making the noise. A slight breeze coming from the half open door was turning the pages of his magazine. He smiled.

Getting jumpy in your old age, he told himself.

Bill almost gasped aloud as he felt a particularly numbing sensation on the back of his neck. It felt as if someone had placed a block of ice against his back. He felt his skin pucker into goose-pimples.

Bill switched on the light and turned.

He suddenly wished he hadn't.

68

The night was alive with the sound of sirens as dozens of accident and emergency vehicles raced towards the blazing inferno which was King's Cross. For miles around flames could still be seen leaping through the fractured roof, turning the clouds orange. A dense pall of smoke hung over the ruins raining cinders down on all those nearby.

Inside Albany Street Police station Sergeant Tony Dean was hurriedly, but efficiently, answering phone calls and barking instructions into the two-way radio on his desk. The tall sergeant was sweating profusely due to his exertions.

'How's it going?' asked Inspector Barton.

'I've called in the blokes who were off duty tonight,' Dean told him. 'And we've got every available man at the scene.'

'Don't spread us too thin, Tony,' Barton reminded him. 'With so many coppers in one place, the villains could have a field day.'

'Scotland Yard have been on the blower, they've sent an Anti-Terrorist squad to the station to check it out.'

'It must have been a bloody big bomb then,' said Barton, sceptically, remembering the devastating explosion. He looked warily at the sergeant. 'Have there been any more reports in like the ones we had earlier? You know, the murders.'

Dean nodded.

'Another six since nine o'clock,' he said. 'I checked with a couple of other stations as well. It's happening all over the city, guv.'

Barton didn't answer, he merely looked towards the door which hid Kelly and Joubert from his view. He decided he'd better check on them. As he turned he heard Dean's voice, loud in his ear:

'You took your bleeding time, didn't you?'

The Inspector saw PC Roy Fenner hurrying through the

door towards the desk where he stood.

'Sorry, Sarge, I got held up, there was loads of traffic,' he babbled. 'Evening, Inspector,' he added.

'Get your uniform on and get back out here,' Dean told him.

'What's been going on anyway?' Fenner wanted to know. 'I've been watching telly all night. First this bloke got shot. In full view of the camera, I thought it was a gimmick but ...'

'Move yourself,' bellowed Dean and the PC disappeared into the locker room to change.

Barton stroked his chin thoughtfully, a flicker of uncertainty passing across his eyes.

'Something wrong, guv?' the sergeant asked him.

He shook his head slowly.

'No,' he murmured then passed through the door which led him to Kelly and Joubert.

Dean snatched up the phone as it rang again and jammed it between his shoulder and ear as he scribbled down the information.

'Christ,' he muttered, as he wrote. 'What was that again? Some bloke's killed his wife by pressing a red hot iron into her face. Yes, I got it. Where was this?' He scrawled down the location. 'Gloucester Place. Right. Have you called an ambulance? OK.' He hung up. Dean stared down at what he'd written and shook his head, then he turned towards the door of the locker room.

'What are you doing, Fenner? Making the bloody uniform?'

The door remained closed.

'Fenner.'

There was still no answer.

Dean opened the door and poked his head in.

'For Christ's sake, what ...'

His sentence was cut short as Fenner leapt forward, bringing his hard-wood truncheon up with bone-crushing force.

The impact lifted the sergeant off his feet and the strudent sound of breaking bone filled his ears as he heard his lower jaw snap. White hot agony lanced through him and he felt consciousness slipping away from him. But, through a haze of pain, he saw the constable advancing. Dean tried to speak but as he did, blood from his smashed jaw ran down his face and neck and the sound came out as a throaty croak. He could see Fenner looking at him, but the constable's eyes did not seem to register his presence. He looked drunk.

Dean managed to scramble to his feet as Fenner brought the truncheon down again.

The sergeant succeeded in bringing his arm up and the solid truncheon cracked against his forearm but he managed to drive one fist into Fenner's face, knocking him backward. He fell with a crash, the truncheon still gripped in his fist.

All three of them heard the sounds from beyond the door but Kelly was the first to speak.

'What's happening out there?' she asked.

Barton hesitated a moment, looking first at Kelly, then at Joubert. They stood motionless for a moment then there was another loud crash, like breaking wood. Barton turned and scuttled through the door.

'We have to get out of here,' said Kelly.

'But how?' Joubert wanted to know.

'There has to be a way. We must find Blake's body and destroy it.' She was already moving towards the door which she found, to her relief, was unlocked.

'No,' said Joubert, stepping ahead of her. 'Let me go first.' He pulled the door open and both of them saw that a narrow corridor separated them from another, glass panelled door about twenty feet further away. Through the bevelled partition they could see the dark outlines of moving figures. Shouts and curses came from the room beyond and Kelly swallowed hard as they drew closer.

They could have been only a yard away when they heard a demonic shout.

A dark shape hurtled towards the glass-panelled door.

Inspector Barton crashed through the thick glass, his upper body slumping over the door which swung under the impact. Shards of glass flew towards Kelly and Joubert, one of them slicing open the Frenchman's left ear; he clapped a hand to the bleeding appendage, using his body to shield Kelly from the worst of the flying crystal. Barton lay across the broken shards, one particularly long piece having pierced his chest. The point had burst from his back and now held him there, blood running down it.

Joubert pulled the door open a fraction more, edging through.

Kelly followed.

She was almost through when she felt a bloodied hand close around her wrist.

Joubert spun round as she screamed and he saw that the dying Barton had grabbed her as she passed. Impaled on the broken glass, the policeman raised his head as if soliciting help. Crimson liquid spilled over his lips and he tried to lift himself off the jagged points but, with one final despairing moan, he fell forward again.

Kelly shook free of his hand and followed Joubert through the door.

Albany Street Police station resembled a bomb-site.

Filing cabinets had been overturned, their contents spilled across the floor. Furniture was smashed and lay in pieces everywhere. The windows were broken. Kelly saw blood splashed across the floor and on the far wall.

Close by lay the body of Sergeant Dean, his face pulped by repeated blows from the truncheon. A foot or so from him, the leg of a chair broken across his head, lay PC Fenner.

'Come on, let's get out of here,' said Joubert and the two of them bolted. They dashed out into the rainy night, pausing momentarily to gaze at the mushroom cloud of dark smoke and orange flame which still ballooned upward from the blazing wreckage of King's Cross. Then, Joubert pulled her arm, leading her towards his car.

They scrambled in and he started the engine.

'How far is Great Portland Street Hospital from here?' the Frenchman asked, guiding the Fiat into traffic.

'Not far,' she told him.

Joubert glanced at her but Kelly was looking out of the side window.

If they could get to Blake's body, perhaps they still had a chance to stop the horror he had released.

Perhaps.

69

'There,' Kelly shouted, pointing to the dimly lit sign over the hospital entrance.

Joubert waited for a break in the stream of traffic then swung the Fiat across the street and parked it outside the large building. Apart from the dozen or so lights which burned in the big windows, the hospital appeared to be in darkness. Kelly scrambled out of the car and hurried up the stone steps to the main entrance, Joubert following closely behind.

The entry-way was bright but the light was not welcoming. It reflected off the polished floors as if they were mirrors, causing Kelly to wince. There was a desk directly opposite, a steaming mug of coffee perched on it. Whoever it belonged to was nowhere in evidence. For fleeting seconds a terrifying thought crossed Kelly's mind.

What if one or more of the patients had seen the programme earlier in the evening? Even now, the wards could be full of butchered, helpless invalids. She shuddered and tried to push the thought to the back of her mind but it refused to budge.

'Kelly, here,' said Joubert, pointing to a blue sign which proclaimed: MORTUARY. A white arrow pointed down a flight of stone steps and, moving as quickly and quietly as they could, the two of them made their way towards the morgue.

As they descended, the darkness seemed to grow thicker until it swirled around them like a cloud, hardly broken by the low wattage lights set in the walls. As they reached the bottom of the stairs a long corridor faced them and, almost unconsciously, both slowed their pace, suddenly not so eager to reach their destination. The lights in the corridor flickered ominously for a second then glowed with their customary brilliance once more. Kelly swallowed hard as she advanced towards the door of the morgue, her heels clicking noisily in the cloying silence.

They drew closer.

It was Kelly who noticed that the door was ajar.

There were some spots of dark liquid on the polished floor which Joubert knelt and touched with his finger. He sniffed it.

'Blood,' he told Kelly, softly.

Inside the morgue itself, apart from the half-light coming through the street-level window, everything was in darkness.

The door opened soundlessly and the two of them stepped inside, glancing to left and right for any sounds or movements.

There was a faint humming in the background which Kelly took to be the hospital generator. Other than that, the morgue was unbearably silent. She heard the blood singing in her ears, her heart thumping noisily as she tip-toed towards the one slab which bore a body.

Covered by a sheet, it looked shapeless in the gloom.

They both approached it slowly, their eyes not leaving the motionless body.

There was more blood on the floor beside the slab.

A dark shape suddenly passed over them and Kelly spun round in panic.

It was a second or two before she realized that it had merely been the shadow of a person walking by outside.

Joubert looked at her and she nodded slowly in answer to his unspoken question.

The Frenchman gripped one corner of the sheet which covered the body.

Kelly moved closer.

There was a soft click behind them and, this time, Joubert felt his heart skip a beat. He squinted through the gloom to see that a slight breeze had pushed the morgue door shut. The Frenchman used his free hand to wipe a bead of perspiration from his forehead.

He took hold of the sheet more firmly, aware of the biting chill which seemed to have filled the room.

Kelly nodded and, gritting his teeth, he whipped the sheet away.

Lying on the slab, glazed eyes bulging wide in terror, was

the body of Bill Howard.

Kelly and Joubert exchanged anxious glances, the Frenchman touching the face of the dead man with the back of his hand.

'He hasn't been dead long,' he told Kelly, keeping his voice low.

She took a step back, allowing an almost painful breath to escape her lungs.

Bill Howard had obviously died in agony and it showed in his contorted features. A long metal probe had been rammed into his mouth, puncturing his tongue before being driven through the base of his skull above the hollow at the back of his neck.

A question burned brightly in her mind.

Where was Blake's body?

As the two of them emerged from the stairway into the hospital entry-way, they were surprised to find it still deserted. Once more Kelly wondered if the patients had been butchered in their beds, maybe the staff as well. She slowed her pace slightly, her eyes shifting to the solitary mug of tea which still stood on the desk. It was no longer steaming. Whoever had put it there had not returned to claim it.

'Kelly, come on,' Joubert urged, making for the main door. She hesitated a moment longer then followed him out to the car.

'Where to now?' he asked.

She gazed ahead of her, her voice soft but determined.

'There's only one place left where the body could be.'

Joubert understood.

70

The traffic was surprisingly light in the city centre. The drive to Blake's house took less than thirty minutes. Joubert brought the Fiat to a halt and switched off the engine, peering through the side window at the large building.

Rain coursed lazily down the windows of the car and, overhead, a loud rumble of thunder was instantly answered by a vivid but soundless flash of lightning.

Kelly brushed fingers through her hair, noticing that her hand was shaking. She clenched her fists together for a moment, drawing in a deep breath.

'What if the body *isn't* in the house?' asked Joubert, cryptically.

'It has to be there,' she said. 'Blake would feel safe hiding it there.'

They both clambered out of the Fiat, ignoring the rain as they stood facing the house. A single light burned in the porch. Far from looking forbidding, Blake's house seemed positively inviting. It beckoned to them and they responded, moving quickly but cautiously towards the dwelling, never taking their eyes from it. Once more Kelly felt a shiver run up her spine.

They paused at the end of the short driveway.

'It'd be better if we split up,' Kelly said. 'That way we'll have a better chance of finding the body. And it won't take so long.'

Joubert regarded her warily for a moment.

'I'll check inside the house,' she said, producing her key ring and showing him the key to Blake's front door which she still possessed. 'You search the garden and garage.'

The Frenchman nodded.

A particularly brilliant flash of lightning lashed across the rain-soaked heavens, bathing the two investigators in cold white light. For fleeting seconds they resembled ghosts, their faces distorted and white in the flash.

Kelly hesitated a moment longer then, with a final look at Joubert, she headed towards the front door.

He waited until she was inside then he moved cautiously forward, his sights set on a door at the side of the garage.

Kelly stepped into the hall and quickly looked around her, searching the darkness with uncertain eyes. She raised her hand, wondering whether or not she should put on the light, but she felt simultaneously exposed *and* safe in the glow. She eventually decided to switch it on.

Nothing moved in the hallway.

To her right, the sitting room door was slightly ajar.

Ahead of her, the stairs disappeared upward into the impenetrable darkness of the first floor.

On the left, the door of the cellar was closed and, this time, there was no key in it. She decided to leave it until last and moved towards the sitting room, pushing the door wide open. Light from the hall offered her sufficient illumination to find the nearest table lamp. This she also switched on.

Standing in the sitting room, Kelly could feel the silence closing in around her as if it were a living thing.

Outside, the storm was reaching its height.

Joubert found that the door which led into the garage was unlocked but the catch was rusty and he needed to put all his weight behind it to shift the recalcitrant partition.

It swung open with a despairing shriek and the Frenchman practically fell into the dark abyss beyond. He stumbled but managed to keep his feet, looking round for a light switch. He found one close to the door and flicked it on. The fluorescents in the ceiling sputtered into life and Joubert scanned the inside of the garage. The floor was spotted with congealed patches of oil and slicks of petrol but, apart from a small toolbox shoved into one corner, the place was empty. There was certainly nowhere to hide a body.

He took one last look then retraced his steps, flicking off the light as he did so.

Outside in the rain again he wiped some of it from his face and decided which direction to follow next.

There was a narrow passageway beside the garage and the

314

side of the house which, he suspected, led to the back garden. Joubert moved cautiously towards it, attempting to see through the short, but darkness-shrouded, passageway. It was less than four feet wide, perhaps three times that in length and it was as black as the grave in there. He put out one hand and fumbled his way along the stone wall, unable to see a hand in front of him.

There was a loud clap of thunder and Joubert prayed for a flash of lightning which would at least give him a few seconds of light. Enough to reach the end of the passage or perhaps alert him if he were not alone in the gloom.

He tried to force that particular thought to the back of his mind but it would not budge.

Inch by inch he edged onward, deeper into the blackness.

Something touched his leg.

Something solid.

Joubert jumped back, not knowing what he was going to do, fear overwhelming him.

In that split second there was an ear-shredding whiplash of lightning which lit up the entire passage.

A foot or so from the end of it, there was a wooden gate. He had walked into it in the blackness, unable to see the object.

Joubert closed his eyes for a second and smiled thinly, moving forward once again. He succeeded in slipping the catch on the gate and passed through and out of the passage. The Frenchman found himself in the back garden. The rain continued to pelt down, plastering his hair to his face, streaming into his eyes. Another crack of lightning lit the heavens and Joubert saw that, ten or twelve yards further on, nestling in some trees at the bottom of the garden, was what looked like a wooden shed. He trod quickly over the sodden grass towards the small hut and tugged on the handle.

It was locked.

He pulled on it again, finally using his foot to dislodge the timber door. It swung open, a pungent smell of damp and decay billowing out to greet him. He coughed and stepped inside.

There was no light in the hut.

The bulb was still in place but it was broken. He narrowed his eyes in an effort to see around the confines of the small structure, which seemed, to all intents and purposes, like a garden shed. He saw a lawn-mower, a roller and sundry other garden implements.

Joubert even spotted a large, double-handed axe. Blake had obviously intended chopping down some of the overhanging branches which grew around the shed, Joubert assumed. He moved forward and picked up the axe, glad of a weapon though he wondered if it would be of any help if the need arose.

The rain was pounding the shed so violently now that it reminded the Frenchman of waves breaking continually on rocks. He shivered in his wet clothes and took one last look around the tiny hut.

Hidden behind a pile of boxes and encrusted with grime as it was, he almost failed to see the freezer.

It was long, perhaps six feet and at least half that in depth. Quite large enough ...

Gripping the axe tighter, he moved towards it, pulling the boxes aside in his wake until he could reach the old freezer without any trouble. He hooked his fingers beneath the rim and prepared to fling it open.

There was a harsh crack as the wind blew the shed door shut, plunging Joubert into darkness.

He muttered something in French and hurried across to the door, pushing it open once again, allowing the rain to lash his face for a second, then he returned to the freezer. He dug his fingers under the filthy lid and lifted.

It was empty.

Only a large spider and some woodlice scuttled about inside.

Joubert slammed the lid down again, his heart still beating fast. He wiped his face with the back of his hand and leant back against the empty freezer to catch his breath.

The lights inside the house dimmed for a moment then glowed once more as thunder continued to roll across the heavens. Kelly stood quite still in the darkness, her eyes darting back and forth, ears alert for the slightest sound. But all she heard was the driving rain and the fury of the storm outside.

As the lamp in the sitting room came on she moved slowly

towards the kitchen.

The door was open.

Kelly stopped for a second and glanced over her shoulder before entering the next room. She flicked on the lights and looked around. There were a couple of dirty mugs in the sink but, apart from that, everything seemed to be in its place.

The lights went out again.

She waited for the brightness to return, her heart thudding more rapidly in her chest.

She waited.

Outside the thunder roared loudly.

Waited.

'Come on, come on,' she whispered, trying to steady her breathing.

Waited.

The house remained in darkness.

From inside the garden shed, Joubert had seen Kelly turn on the kitchen lights and now, as he stood looking at the house, he too wondered how long it would be before the power supply was restored. The Frenchman decided that he would be better employed aiding Kelly in her search of the house. Carrying the axe with him, he headed for the door.

A gust of wind slammed it in his face.

He gripped the rusty knob irritably and tugged it open.

Joubert found himself face to face with David Blake.

Before the Frenchman could move, he felt powerful hands grabbing for his throat, hands which felt like blocks of ice as they squeezed. He struck out vainly at Blake who finally hurled the intruder to one side where he crashed into a pile of boxes. As he tried to rise he felt an incredible pressure on his skull as Blake gripped him in a vice-like grip, his fingers resembling talons as they threatened to plunge through the Frenchman's skull.

Joubert felt the cold filling his head, his torso. His entire body.

He screamed but the sound was lost as thunder tore open the dark clouds and the rain lashed the hut unmercifully.

He felt himself being hurled to the floor where he landed with a jarring impact. When he opened his eyes there was no sign of Blake. Joubert didn't know how long he'd been

317

unconscious. A minute? An hour?

The Frenchman got to his feet, picking up the axe as he did so. He held it before him, studying the heavy, wickedly sharp blade. He looked towards the house and thought of Kelly. The axe felt as if it were a part of him, an extension of his arms.

He kicked open the door and trudged across the lawn towards the darkened house, the large, razor-sharp weapon held before him.

A smile creased his lips.

71

When the power inside the house went off, Kelly could hear nothing but the rumbling of thunder. The electric wall clock stopped ticking and she was deprived of even that welcome sound.

Now she stood alone in the darkness, praying for the light to return. The thought that the fuse box might have blown began to creep into her mind.

Or had someone in the house turned the power off?

She spun round, her imagination beginning to play tricks on her. Had she seen movement in the sitting room behind her?

The lights came back on so suddenly she almost shouted aloud in surprise and relief.

Kelly licked her lips but found that her tongue felt like old newspaper. She quickly checked in the pantry then turned, intent on heading back through the house to look upstairs.

In the light flooding from the kitchen windows, she saw Joubert approaching across the small lawn.

She breathed an audible sigh of relief and knelt to undo the bolt on the back door, preparing to turn the key in the lock to let him in. He obviously hadn't found anything, she reasoned, except for the axe which he carried. He had almost reached the back door.

She turned the key in the lock, her hand resting on the knob.

As he saw the door opening, Joubert uttered a high-pitched yell of fury and swung the axe with all his strength. It scythed through the wooden door, ripping it free of one hinge. Kelly's own scream mingled with the shriek of splintering wood. She turned and ran for the sitting room as Joubert stove in the remainder of the door and crashed into the kitchen.

Kelly slipped and fell as she reached the hall, looking over her shoulder in time to see him emerge from the kitchen.

He looked like something from a nightmare with his hair plastered down, his face scratched and bruised and his mouth spread in a kind of rictus. He hurdled a coffee table and hurried after her.

Kelly leapt to her feet, slamming the hall door behind her, darting towards the stairs.

She took them two at a time, stumbling once again at the top.

Below her, Joubert flung open the door and hurried across the hall, pausing on the bottom step before ascending slowly.

Kelly was faced by four doors.

She raced towards the first, hearing his heavy footfalls on the stairs as he climbed higher.

The door was locked.

Kelly hurried to the second one, praying that it was open.

She pulled open the door and ran inside, flinging herself beneath the bed.

Through the half-open door, she could see when Joubert reached the landing. He stood at the top of the stairs for what seemed like an eternity, only his feet visible to Kelly but she realized that he must be deciding which door to try first.

He moved towards the room on her left.

The locked one. She heard him twisting the handle then she heard the sound of shattering wood as he smashed off the knob and kicked the door open.

Kelly closed her eyes, wondering if this was all a nightmare. If she would wake up in a second. She tried to swallow but her throat was constricted.

She heard his footsteps, saw his feet as he stood in the doorway of the room in which she hid.

319

He took a step inside.

Kelly bit her fist to stifle a cry.

He moved closer towards the bed.

If only she could roll out on the other side, run for the door ...

But what if she slipped? What if he reached the door before her?

What if ...?

He was standing beside her now, his feet together.

She imagined that axe poised over the bed.

With a strength born of terror, Kelly snaked her arms out, fastened them around Joubert's ankles and tugged. She succeeded in pulling his legs away from him and he went down with a heavy thump, the axe falling from his grip.

She rolled over, scrambling clear of the bed, jumped to her feet and ran for the door.

Joubert was up in a second. He flung out a hand and managed to grab a handful of her hair. Kelly yelped as some of it came out at the roots and she felt herself overbalancing. She grabbed for the door frame and managed to retain her stance but he had slowed her up and, as she reached the landing, the Frenchman hurled himself at her, bringing her down in a pile-up which knocked the wind from them both.

Kelly struck out with her nails, raking his face. Joubert bellowed in pain and tried to pull her down again but Kelly got to her feet and kicked him hard in the side, bringing the heel of her shoe down on his outstretched hand so hard that it penetrated. Blood welled from the puncture and Joubert rolled to one side. But, he was still between Kelly and the stairs.

As the Frenchman struggled to his knees, Kelly ran at him and lashed out again with a kick which caught him firmly in the solar plexus. He fell backward, clutching at empty air for a second before tumbling down the stairs, thudding to a halt at the bottom with his head at an unnatural angle.

She gazed down at his motionless form realizing that his neck must be broken. Kelly ran into the bedroom and picked up the double-handed axe, moving quickly from bedroom to bedroom in search of Blake's body.

The rooms were empty.

Kelly began descending the stairs, the axe held firmly in

her hands. She paused beside the body of Joubert, holding the razor sharp blade above his head as she felt for a pulse.

Nothing. As she'd thought, his neck had been broken in the fall.

She suddenly felt overwhelmed by sadness, not just for his death but for all the other people who had died that night and who would die if she did not complete her task. Her grief slowly became anger as she realized that all of the carnage, all of the suffering had been caused by Blake.

There were two more rooms in the house to be searched.

She went through the dining room quickly. That left the cellar.

The door was locked but that did not deter Kelly. She brought the axe down twice, shattering the lock, knocking the door wide open. She slapped on the lights and slowly descended into the subterranean room.

The silence crowded around her, an almost physical force. She stood still at the bottom of the steps, her eyes searching.

Next to one of the large bookcases, almost invisible on first glimpse, was a small door, no bigger than three feet square, its handle also painted white to make it even more inconspicuous. Kelly bent and tugged on the handle.

It opened effortlessly and she recoiled as a rancid smell of rotten wood and damp earth rose from the tiny compartment. But, if the door was small then what lay beyond it was not. The space behind the door looked as though it had been made many years earlier. It stretched back into darkness, she wasn't sure how far. The walls were soft and slimy and she had to duck low to avoid scraping her hair on the dripping ceiling. The stench was almost overpowering.

Lying undisturbed, covered by a blanket, amidst the muck and filth, was the body of Blake.

Kelly grabbed both ankles and, using all her strength, pulled. Inch by inch, the corpse came clear of its resting place until it lay in full view in the cellar. Kelly noticed that the eyes were still open. They seemed to fix her in a reproachful stare and, for a moment, she was rooted to the spot.

There was another deafening clap of thunder, audible even in the depths of the cellar.

The room was plunged into darkness as the lights flickered then died.

A second later they came back on again and Kelly finally managed to tear her gaze from the body of Blake.

She reached for the axe and raised it above her head, knowing what she must do, praying for the strength to perform this final act of destruction. Tears welled up in her eyes then trickled down her cheeks and the axe wavered in the air. Kelly squeezed her eyes tightly shut for a moment, anxious to avoid the reproachful stare of Blake's dead eyes.

The lights began to flash on and off, blinking wildly as the thunder now seemed to become one continual salvo of sound.

Kelly screamed as she brought the axe down.

The blade buried itself in the right shoulder of the corpse and she heard a loud cracking of bone as the scapula was shattered. Kelly wrenched it free and struck again, her aim slightly off but the weight of the weapon was enough. It severed the right arm. She lifted it again and, after two more powerful strokes, succeeded in hacking off the other arm. Tears were now pouring freely down her cheeks and the storm offered a macabre accompaniment to her own sobs and the thick, hollow sound the axe made as it sheared through dead flesh.

She changed position to attack the right leg, the axe skidding off the pelvic bone and shaving away a portion of thigh. Kelly recovered her balance and struck again, forced to stand on the torso to pull the blade free. Her next blow exposed the femur and, with a despairing grunt, she smashed the thick bone and managed to hack the leg off. The remains of the body shuddered beneath each fresh impact but Kelly continued with her grisly task, perspiration soaking through her clothes. It took five attempts to sever the left leg.

Panting like a carthorse, she took a step back, realizing that she had still not completed the monstrous task.

With a blow which combined horrified determination and angry despair, she struck off the head. It rolled for two or three feet across the floor, coming to rest on the stump. She noticed with relief that the sightless eyes were facing away from her.

Kelly stood amidst the pieces of dismembered corpse and dropped the axe, shaking her head gently. Her breath came in great choking gasps which seared her throat and lungs. She

322

leant back against the nearest wall for support, closing her eyes for a moment.

The cellar door slammed shut and Kelly shot an anxious glance towards it.

At the top of the stairs stood David Blake.

Kelly shuddered as the room seemed to fill with icy air, as if someone were sucking all the warmth from the cellar and replacing it with the bone-chilling numbness she now felt.

Blake began to descend, his eyes fixed, not on her, but on the hewn corpse.

'It's over, Blake,' she said, her voice a harsh croak.

He didn't answer. He merely continued his purposeful stride, his face impassive until he reached the bottom of the stairs. Then, his nostrils flared. With a roar of rage he ran at her.

Tired from her exertions, Kelly could not move fast enough to avoid his fearsome lunge. He grabbed her by the throat, lifting her bodily from the ground.

Kelly found herself looking deep into his eyes — into bulging orbs which were pools of sheer hatred. But there was something else there too.

Fear?

She felt the cold seeping through her like gangrene through a rotting limb but Blake's powerful grip was beginning to weaken. With a grunt he lowered her to the floor where she sprawled before him, gazing up at his contorted features. He took a step back, almost tripping over the mutilated remains of the corpse. *His* corpse.

The Astral body of David Blake, the tangible embodiment of his evil, staggered drunkenly for a second, one hand held towards Kelly in a last act of defiance.

With a despairing groan, he dropped to his knees, his eyes still fixed on the girl who was cowering a few feet from him. Kelly saw him open his mouth to scream but the sound, when it came forth, was like nothing human. The thunderous utulation rattled around the cellar, causing Kelly to cover her ears for fear that they would be damaged. The lights in the room went out for a moment then came back on with an increased brilliance.

Blake's scream died away as his face began to split open. Huge, jagged fissures opened in his flesh, as if his mirror image had been broken. An evil-smelling, yellowish-white substance bubbled up from the rents which were now spreading all over his body. He clawed at his chest, pulling his shirt open, a large lump of skin coming with it, exposing the bloodied internal organs beneath. His fingers seemed to shrivel like dying flowers and Kelly saw more of the pus-like fluid oozing from the deep cuts which were spreading along his arms and legs like rips in fabric.

He fell forward, his head disintegrating as he hit the ground. It split open, pus and blood bursting from the ruptured skull. A tangle of intestines snaked upward, as if propelled by some inner force as his stomach burst.

Kelly looked away, feeling her stomach somersault. The odour of corruption, that rank and fetid stench which floated in the air like an invisible cloud, surrounded her. She coughed and thought she was going to be sick. But the feeling passed.

The room was plunged into darkness again as the lights dimmed for fleeting seconds and a massive thunderclap shook the house.

Kelly managed to look back at the decaying form of Blake. The last moments lit by the faintly glimmering lights which seemed to act like strobes as they flickered.

As the electrical power was restored, the cellar was bathed in the cold white light of the fluorescents.

Blake had vanished.

Nothing remained.

No blood. No pus.

Nothing.

Only the dismembered corpse lay before her.

Kelly got slowly to her feet, swaying uncertainly for a moment. She was soaked with sweat. Every single muscle in her body ached and it took a monumental effort for her to even walk. She was completely drained. As close to collapse as she could ever remember but, somewhere amidst that exhaustion, there was a feeling of triumph. She had succeeded in stopping Blake. Now she prayed that she had been able to end the reign of terror he'd unleashed. There was no way of knowing yet.

All she could do was wait.

And hope.

She knew that there was one more thing which had to be done.

Crossing to the phone on the nearby desk, she lifted the receiver and pressed out three nines. She had no choice but to tell the police. Kelly heard the purring at the other end of the line.

The lights flickered once more and she muttered under her breath as she heard the phone go dead.

She was about to try again when the hand closed on her shoulder.

She spun round, the scream catching in her throat.

The figure which faced her was identical in every respect. A mirror image of herself.

And it held the axe.

Her alter-ego smiled as it brought the vicious weapon down with incredible force. The blade aimed at Kelly's head.

It was the last thing she saw.

She knew that the phones are more than what had to be said.

Carrie, in the phone or the nearly deserted. I told the weatherman I had last three times. He had to hang up to put the phone. Kelly hung the phone in the other end of the line.

The lights is sharp and more and she matter-of-factly then because round up of our garage.

Maybe, she turns to you yet when she told us for her brother.

She spun hand and spread out into in her shoulder. Trailers a while and she saw was the matters after to get.

A minor image of herself.
And it held me and.

She smiled at myself as if to smile the flowing work them and candle in front. She turns up and say "It's a if we find out thing she saw.

MIRROR

Graham Masterton

On the other side of the mirror lies a world beyond your darkest nightmares . . .

Screen writer Martin Williams is a man possessed. His obsession – 'Boofuls', the darling boy-angel of 30s Hollywood, whose horrific death was more spectacular than anything Hollywood ever dreamed up . . .

Now fifty years later all Martin wants is to make the movie that will bring Boofuls back to life. He can't believe his luck when he manages to buy a mirror from his idol's house. But that mirror was there when Boofuls died, and it has seen many things, more than the human eye can imagine . . .

Strange things happen in the mirror. Stranger things happen to the people who try to probe its secrets. And Martin is about to enter the gateway through which all hell will break loose . . .

Also by Graham Masterton in Sphere Books:

REVENGE OF THE MANITOU   THE WELLS OF HELL
THE DEVILS OF D-DAY   THE HEIRLOOM
CHARNEL HOUSE   TENGU
NIGHT WARRIORS   DEATH TRANCE

HORROR
0 7474 0191 8